PÆNVICTA: DEATH'S

by

Nigel Stuart Byram

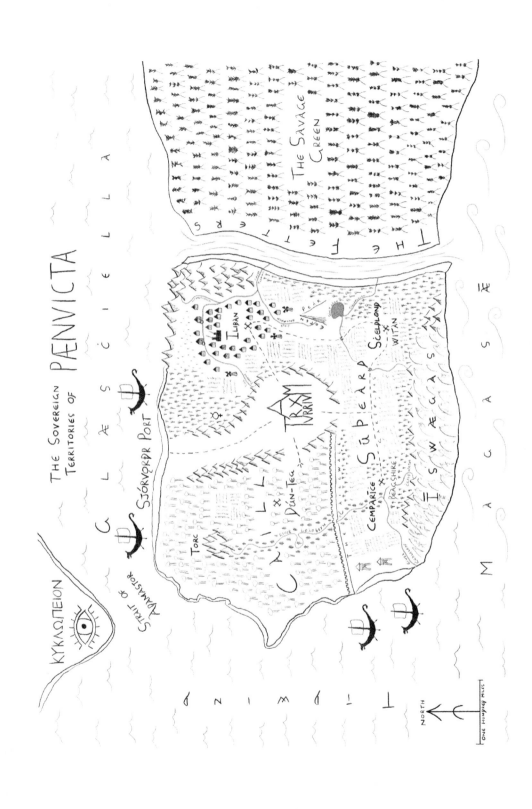

The Sovereign
Territories of PÆNVICTA

KYKΛΩΠΕΙΟΝ

Strait of Adamastor

Sjórvǫrðr Port

G L Æ S Ċ I E L L A

The Savage Green

The Fetters

Ilban

Torc

Dún-Tea

TRXM VRRIVM

Sūþeard

Scelplond

× Witan

Cemparīce

Pleaġshire ×

River Leaðbry

The Catullway

M Æ G A S S Æ

S W Æ G A S S Æ

Tidwind

North

One Hundred Miles

COLLABORATED CALENDAR
OF PÆNVICTA
XXXIII A.A.D.
ANNŌ AUSTRĀLIS DISCORDIAE

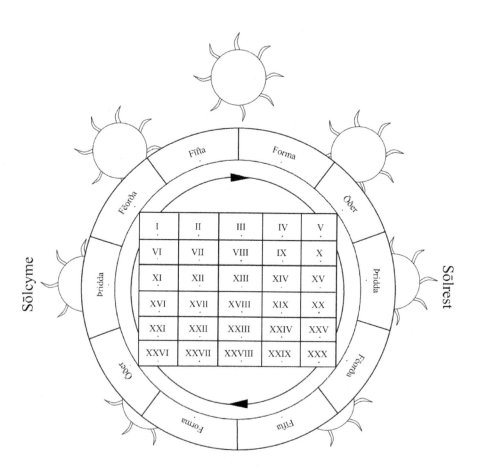

ACT I

"Death in itself is nothing; but we fear
To be we know not what, we know not where."

- John Dryden, *Aureng-Zebe*

XXXIII A.A.D.

Sōlrest-Ōðer-XV

It is a harrowing countenance that stares back at me from the mirror these days. There is something beyond the mere ravages of time; the haggard face, the bare scalp, the wispy white cobweb of a beard. The years have been long and many, but they have not been kind. No, there is something else. Some creeping loss of humanity; ghostly scars lingering just on the edge of my perception, like watching soil shift subtly from the unseen worms beneath. Only I can see it, but it is undeniable. The looking glass bears only a stranger to me.

Perhaps this is the sensation of a spirit departing its body. Perhaps I am dying, though I do not yet feel so weakened. Could it be that all of the warnings, all that the preachers across Pænvicta said, was true? I refuse to accept it. After the life I have lived... it truly does not bear thinking about.

Too long have I been mired in this uncertainty. Too long have I procrastinated, watched the world go by as each passing year tolled that it would soon be too late.

But it is not. Not yet. The time has come for me to make my final journey. My last pilgrimage, so long planned but never undertaken. My existence has served to guide me to this single moment of eminence. The penultimate full moon dominates the night sky overhead to exhort me to action. Am I to acquiesce to annihilation now? If my soul is already forfeit and my years all but spent, then what have I left to lose?

All that remains is to finish my preparations and gather my travelling gear together. I shall need to purchase supplementary supplies and ensure my affairs are in order before I disappear.

A return in this life would be only the result of drastic failure. Regardless, I leave tomorrow. May the gods have mercy, though considering my intentions, it probably would be wiser to expect precisely the opposite.

Sōlrest-Ōðer-XVII

The ancient stone tower is locked, and is as secure and hidden as it can ever be. The library's full contents have been transferred to the concealed space, along with all of the laboratory equipment I have been forced to relinquish. Looking at it now, any onlooker might believe it to be as abandoned as it was the day I found it, stood as it was in the wilderness. The town, whose outskirts include the location of my tower, will remain nameless. The resultant... publicity, should this journal be discovered, would be unforgiving.

I spent the daylight hours of yesterday ensuring that I was provisioned enough for a prolonged journey, or at least until I might restock. The equipment I have deemed necessary to bring along is far more than a single man can reasonably carry, especially an old one; to that end I purchased a nag, ashen in coat, called Felicia. She is aged but strong, and bears my trappings and I without complaint. After my time at the local markets, I returned to my tower upon my new horse and dug up the hoard I keep buried on the grounds. It contains coinage relevant to most of Pænvicta, and on this occasion I emptied it of the pressed square coins known as *Scūta*. The circular punched hole in each piece allowed me to thread them onto a string, and I have seen shopkeepers and bankers use fixed vertical dowels mounted on desks to make the counting and storing of them easier. The other currencies, being as good as dead weight at my destination, I reburied. I spent one last, mostly sleepless night in my own bed, and now, after conclusive checks, I am finally ready to leave.

The road is long, but the first leg of it is safe, even by a commoner's standards. It is ultimately this which means I have to leave to complete my final project; prying eyes are everywhere, and today's friends could be tomorrow's enemies. My work demands a quiet refuge, and I believe I have found the perfect place. Should my journey remain uninterrupted, I expect to arrive within two weeks, hopefully less.

Sōlrest-Ōðer-XXII

I feel sufficient distance has been traversed from my origin to divulge my current location without concern. Making good time, I have managed to find my way to the westerly side of the Republic of Sċeldlond. The weather was more than amicable, especially for middle Sōlrest. Avoiding main roads in favour of farmers' paths was evidently the right policy. What seemed like a consistently downhill desire line through pleasant countryside made for easy travel. I was wholly unmolested and was even able to bother a cheery, sun-ripened farmhand for directions. Before too long I could see Gārfeldas in the distance, appearing almost as acres of burnished gold coins rolling over the horizon. It was only when Felicia carried me closer that the chaff became visible, each stalk standing more than twice my height.

As the situation stands, I have made a stop at a lodge ('The Westing Spear') just on the edge of Gārfeldas. From here I can no longer keep to empty trackways, for the heavily trodden road through that region also happens to be the main trade route to Cemparīċe.

As such, this inn is significantly busier than I prefer, even at the late hour of my arrival. It is a large and proud establishment, cutting an impressive silhouette against the sun as it sets over the flat horizon, and standing significantly taller even than the high-stalked Sōlcyme wheat. Good, solid timber makes up a majority of the structure (including a connected stable wherein I left Felicia), and the interior is densely decorated with many of the knick-knacks often seen in the rural homes of this region. Hunting trophies and pelts, small hand-whittled figures, hanging strings of garlic, dried flowers and stuffed rabbits and game birds. All of this plays second fiddle to the respectably sized roaring fireplace, which I sought immediately to combat the evening's creeping chill.

These days, my old bones suffer the whims of the climate. Ever it is a reminder of my task's urgency.

While the lodge was busy with all manner of people from farmhands and landowners to merchants and even mercenaries, the atmosphere was undeniably jovial when I entered. After warming myself beside two other new arrivals, I eased myself through the crowds to reach the counter, exchanging pleasantries along the way. Eventually I was able to lean on the bar and await service. After handing three tankards of golden, frothing ale to a burly, bearded man, the landlady turned to me.

The woman introduced herself as Edmonde Aelfric. She is a short lady with a head of untamed tawny hair and modest attire. With her scarlet cheeks and face full of laugh lines, the joyful atmosphere of Edmonde's business was an extension of herself. A lull in patrons as people began to sit and quiet down saw me engaging the woman in conversation. I spend so little time communicating with other people that I surprise myself in still knowing how. Nevertheless, I paid for a tankard of the same ale I had seen earlier and we talked. Two Scūta, which I quickly learned were colloquially known as 'Scutes' by the inhabitants of Sūþeard. The woman was surprisingly well spoken, still accented but definitely more eloquent than a majority of her clientele. She asked where I was headed and what my business was, and I told her a practiced alibi; that I am a dye maker, travelling to Cempariċe to collect dyestuffs. I began to talk about all the various sources of colourants and detected an involuntary note of feigned interest in her voice. Far from offended, it was precisely my objective to deflect; the less I had to fabricate, the more likely the story would hold.

A gaunt, tall man in a long coat politely interrupted to order an ale. It seemed strange to me that the establishment offered only one beverage, but I brushed the thought aside. As the man stalked off cradling the tankard, Edmonde and I both eagerly changed the topic of conversation. I instead enquired about The Westing Spear and its history. Apparently the family-owned business is at least a century old in one form or another, persisting on this important nexus and somehow avoiding the political strife of the region.

For those blissfully ignorant of Pænvicta's turbulent politics, the dual factions of Cempariċe and Sċeldlond, which together make up the Sūþeard region, are currently enjoying an extended period of peace. The two were once one country and under one king, but a monumentally bloody revolt against the monarchy tore its populace apart. A breakaway faction of disenfranchised individuals endeavoured to bite the hand that (had not) fed them, resulting in civil war. The schism's endless violence was only stifled when the royalists were forced to concede a portion of the country, three and thirty years past (an event marked by the commencement of the new calendar, *Annō Austrālis Discordiae*; Year of the Southern Discord). The king, and those loyal to him, kept the far richer and more fertile lands to the west, while a new republic of revolutionists inherited the east, confident that their leadership could renew the land and enrich its people.

And it did, for a time. Sċeldlond's partial democracy brought forth competent people to solve issues efficiently, more so than the opposing monarchy's nepotism could possibly hope to achieve. The stalemate between the countries soon began to fray, however. In the allocation of lands, many on both sides had been disinherited. Lands significant to certain family lines exchanged hands. Entire estates were divvied out to others, and compensation was often inadequate or nonexistent. People were understandably concerned that what began as a temporary wartime resolution would become a permanent arrangement. That the western country had vacated itself of dissidents, and the eastern one was populated primarily by malcontents, likely stoked the flames. Soon, growing tensions became untenable, and unauthorised military actions (starting with the occasional raids and escalating into small-scale exterminations) plunged the now separate lands into constant skirmishes and meaningless bloodshed. It was only the interjection of Arx Turrium, newly exerting itself on Pænvicta's political stage, that strong-armed cooperation between Cempaṝīċe and Sċeldlond. But that is another story.

The Westing Spear was founded just before this most recent major conflict began, and persists to this day. Given its proximity to the border between Cempaṝīċe and Sċeldlond, the lodge came into contact with warriors from both sides and, remarkably, served as a haven for both. Men that may have been fighting the following day would drink together on the previous evening without so much as a heated argument.

As Edmonde Aelfric relayed this part of The Westing Spear's history to me, my scepticism began to chide. But looking around, it was true; this menagerie of vastly different people were talking with each other in groups, with nary a single peacekeeping hand in sight. I have never seen the like in my long life.

I asked her what secret could keep the bitterness and hatred of warring men in check, especially in the presence of drink. She smiled, uncharacteristically oafishly, and gave an infuriating non-answer along the lines that 'it was just the way it had always been.'

As frustrated as I should have been, I did feel strangely pacified. Instead of arguing or interrogating, I played coy, accepted her answer and changed topic once more. I asked her which brewers were responsible for the ale I had just polished off. She tapped her finger on her nose and winked.

"You shan't know, I'm afraid," she mocked playfully, "but you won't find it elsewhere, I can say that much! Certainly keeps the punters coming, though, eh?"

Sure enough, just as she was about to go on, a flurry of boisterous and happy customers ordered another two rounds of the golden brew. As she finished with the rush and headed back to continue our talk, I exaggerated a yawn and announced that I would retire, requesting my keys and a drink to take to my room. Edmonde placed both on the bar, smiled and, with a polite curtsy, wished me goodnight.

Once upstairs, it did not take me long to discover the secret of The Westing Spear's good natured patrons. I distilled a small sample of the drink over a lantern and found traces of a strange sediment. While I am no alchemist, I strongly suspect that the Aelfric family are as such, and that the ludicrous good will in the lodge's customers is brought on by some sort of tranquiliser or sedative in the drink. It could be mildly addictive, even, to ensure their recurring patronage. Perhaps I am not the only one to have found this.

I feel there is no reason in saying anything. Evidently the worst that comes of it is that one establishment grows fat on bringing peace to a small part of Pænvicta that desperately needs it.

And she does not even charge over the odds.

Sōlrest-Ōðer-XXIII

The Westing Spear and its mysterious ale ensured I could resume my journey on a good night's sleep. I bade Edmonde farewell as I left and asked if she had any of her ale bottled for purchase, to which she replied that she had tried but that it would not keep.

I expected as much, so I ordered a tankard to drink before my journey, pouring it into one of the smaller waterskins the moment she was distracted, then quickly stowing it in my robes. I must remember that it is in the container with the marked stopper. It could prove useful for research.

Just before I left, a large group of Arx Coercitōrēs made their way noisily into The Westing Spear. These were the mainstay of their soldiery and enforcers, both religious zealot and iron fist, and this was not a place I had expected or hoped to meet them. Rarely did the Coercitōrēs ever remove their plate harnesses, and this appearance was no exception; their glinting, gold-trimmed armour clattered stridently as they barged their way through patrons and furniture alike. Their enclosed steel helmets portrayed a certain coldness matched only by their purposeful, wordless gait. Thankfully they made no attempt to block the exit, and I felt no desire to wait and discover the purpose of their visit. I slipped out as they approached the bar, hastily making my way to the stables to saddle my keffel and put distance between myself and whatever was about to transpire behind me. The Coercitōrēs' magnificent white chargers snorted at me contemptuously from the next paddock as I bundled my belongings onto my mount. Felicia was as glad to avoid the barded warhorses as I was their riders.

Though Arx Turrium seeks to portray itself as the benign guardian of Pænvicta, the reality of their protectorship is very different. From what I have seen and heard, the 'peace' treaties they enforce seem to ensure only that the protectorate territories are guarded against hostilities from the Arx itself. And by that, I mean only the direst hostilities. Frequently do the Coercitōrēs engage in racketeering, extortion and general browbeating of their subjects. I have yet to observe any punishment of this outrageous behaviour enacted by either the subject nation's lawmen or anyone else. The balance of power is clear as day, and no king will risk his sovereignty, or indeed his line, to challenge it.

With this mistreatment, as well as the significant raising of taxes characteristic of finding oneself firmly under the thumb of Arx Turrium, a silent rage is building in most of Sūþeard. I do not believe the current situation is sustainable; it is only a matter of time, I would wager, before the downtrodden begin to loudly demand change or seek to bring it about themselves, even despite knowing the appalling odds stacked against them. Inevitably, the result will be the same. It always is. Blood.

But for now, men and women who value their heads keep them down in the presence of these tormentors for good reason. Perhaps rebellion is the objective sought by the Arx Turrium; all the better to excuse the annexation of Sūþeard entirely.

The Westing Spear was eerily quiet as I was carried away at a brisk canter. A few others, pale-faced, had seemingly followed my example and began filing from the doorway to go either separate ways or retrieve their horses from the stables. They made special effort not to seem too eager to evade the Coercitōrēs. I myself headed west through Gārfeldas along the main thoroughfare to Cempariče. This is called 'The Golden Road' by some. In ages past it joined the two Sūþeard cities of greatest import directly; now it is the primary link of all three southern powers, making it presently the single most valuable trade route in Pænvicta. The road itself gave the impression of marching a royal parade, the tall wheat on both sides reminiscent of warriors' spears. While the flat cobbled road through Gārfeldas is well kept and known to be one of the easiest and safest roads in Pænvicta (indeed, a watchtower was almost always in sight along the whole way), I must confess that I do not find it to be particularly reassuring. The crop which unceasingly flanks travellers stands higher than one's head which, in myself, instils claustrophobia and unease. Were it not for the presence of the watchmen, it would be the perfect road for brigands to ply their trade.

An irrational fear, to be sure. If I were alone enough to be targeted, then I would be able to defend myself with my preferred methods untroubled. Any bodies would likely remain hidden until harvest. Still, for one of my calling, it pays to maintain a healthy paranoia.

It is indeed a very busy road, trodden by either travellers such as myself or traders on heavily laden carts, their goods always covered over against the weather and inquisitive eyes. Smaller, tributary paths along the road feed it with ever-increasing traffic, and with the four lanes of the highway nearly always packed, the din of horseshoes, cartwheels and boots echoing off the cobbles is at once musical and somewhat maddening. I have set myself down at the roadside to take a rest and let faster commuters by while I write this entry.

There will not be another opportunity to record my progress until I cross the three-way checkpoint which joins Cemparīċe, Sċeldlond and the Arx. Even to the most innocent of travellers it can be a treacherous crossing. Assuming I am not apprehended, I shall write again on the other side.

Sōlrest-Ōðer-XXV

There is no doubt now that the Arx hunts for someone, though I know not which unfortunate soul.

The checkpoint, as I approached it, was congested. Long lines of people had formed and lost their definition, resulting in an amorphous and disorganised crowd. And yet, despite this, the body of people possessed all the life of an undisturbed grave. They were deathly silent, save for the intermittent shout of "Come!"

I had assumed that farmhands travelling for the Sōlrest harvest had been the cause of abnormally high traffic (many such people were hired seasonally for work in both Sūþeard territories), but the periods of stillness between the checkpoint's calls were definitely longer than the norm. At first I was merely irritated, but I soon began to grow nervous. What if my tower - or worse, its secret stash - had been discovered? What if an Arx Turrium agent had charged across the land to spread word of a manhunt? What escape could I possibly make if I was actually seized? It was highly unlikely, I assured myself, and I was able to relax. Outwardly, at least.

It was a few hours and some short showers of light rain before the crowd started to move faster. When the tall iron-barred fence of the checkpoint was in sight, people were more orderly and the queue was clearer, and I was finally able to peer around the side to see the cause of the delay. Two fully armoured Arx Coercitōrēs were manning the large wrought-iron gate, while the usual regiment of neutral Sūþeard border guards stood by the wayside, dejected and impotent. The Coercitōrēs and the travellers they spoke to were out of earshot, but it seemed to be a relaying of information. A wooden signpost, hammered into the road where they worked, seemed to be of great importance; the Coercitōrēs, with multiple gestures and explanations, ensured that every wayfarer and trader was made thoroughly aware of what was displayed upon it. The travellers then wrote their names and made their marks beside them, and were only then allowed to move on. I was confident, upon observation, that it was not an interrogation.

That is, until I first saw how they reacted to a migrating woman. The Coercitōrēs called for the next in line as they would normally, but as soon as the woman was within arm's reach, one would clasp his gauntleted right hand around her right wrist and push it up her back in order to restrain her, and with the left hand he would take all of her hair together and pull it back to keep her face exposed. In this degrading position she was inspected by the other enforcer; I realised then that the woman was being forced to stand next to the signpost, the inspector looking intently at it and her repeatedly as he checked her face, wrists, belly and shins. Any impeding clothing was rolled up or otherwise shifted without ceremony or care. When the Coercitōrēs were satisfied, they released her, allowed her to briefly compose herself, then explained the sign as they had with the men. This process was repeated with each and every woman that passed through, including those travelling with men. Quite often the women seemed understandably upset by the ordeal, though they dared not complain. A few stoic individuals remained stone-faced from start to finish, to their credit.

This continued methodically until I neared the front of the line. The man directly ahead of me, a very tall and bald brute sporting a face full of scars, glared and muttered under his breath as each woman was abused. When it was his turn to be called, he marched furiously to them and, shouting in their visored faces and pointing ahead to the victimised women now on their way, chastised the Arx Coercitōrēs for their cruelty. Scarcely had he begun his tirade, however, when one of the Coercitōrēs stepped forwards and slammed a steel fist into his gut. The air left him immediately and he crumpled, writhing on the ground. He coughed up a gobbet of blood and swore as loudly as he could manage. Though the armoured man was at least two hands shorter than the giant, the former had neither fear nor patience for the latter's attitude. The Coercitor seemed to consider the unfortunate for but a moment before he lifted his leg and brought down the heel of his sabaton onto the man's exposed temple. The report of his skull cracking between polished metal and flinty stone broke the uneasy silence. A few horses far back whinnied in surprise. The Coercitor nonchalantly called the regular guardsmen over to clear the ground of the man's body and what remained of his head. One of them retched as he filled a bucket at the pump and brought a mop to clear the now thickly pooled blood and cranial debris. The queue behind me tutted and shook their heads; not at the Arx Coercitōrēs' brutality (that was fully expected), but at the dead man's brave yet foolish attempt at small justice. That a mere two men can feel safe to enact such open cruelty in front of such large numbers without fear of recompense speaks volumes of their tyranny.

Scarcely had the last remnants of their latest victim been swept away when I was called to the fore. I dismounted Felicia and lead her over by the reins. I feel that the horse shared my growing nervousness.

The language of Sūþeard is commonly known as Sūþstefn, and was clearly not the first language of the two armoured figures. Arcāna, the language of Arx Turrium, is a different animal, and their speech was thick with accent as they wrapped their lips around the unfamiliar vowel sounds. Their voices rose and fell in alien intonations, but they were capable enough in Sūþstefn to make their simple message understood. One of them spoke matter-of-factly and without emotion, except perhaps boredom.

"You see picture, *nōnne potes*?" he pointed at the sign, leaving his plated finger hanging until satisfied that I had studied it sufficiently. "Remember picture of witch, remember ink on skin. You see, find and tell Sōlis Mūnus, get reward of gold."

Sure enough, the sign had several parchments nailed to it, displaying an artist's impression of a woman's face and several examples of tattoos which supposedly could be found on her body, though it did not detail where. The so-called witch, whatever she truly was, seemed at once quite young but also wizened and grey. Certainly it was an unnatural countenance, if the artist was to be believed. The tattoos were almost definitely from Caill, with swirling, dreamlike designs of vines and other plants.

"Make name and mark here, no forgery," said the other Coercitor, shoving a parchment and quill in my direction. I signed one of my many names and inscribed one of my many marks, which was checked for legibility. I noticed that many of those before me could not write, and had made pictographic marks in place of signatures. The parchment was glanced at by both Coercitōrēs before I was waved past with no further words exchanged.

As soon as I crossed the threshold into Cemparīċe, I mounted up and managed to reach a steady canter, the traffic alleviated on this side by the slow checkpoint. Travellers to Sċeldlond seemed unhindered... perhaps the quarry's movements were known to the hunters? Ah, but truly, it is not my concern. I have no interest in furthering the Arx's goals, nor in the gold they offer for doing so.

Had I not crossed through a checkpoint, I likely would not have even realised that I had traversed into a different country. Outwardly, Cemparīċe is so similar to Sċeldlond as to be indistinguishable. The watchmen's shields have changed, now displaying the fearsome hawk, symbol of King Ricbert's lineage, but they wear the same tunics, masked helms and disinterested faces. It is a long journey to my final destination. I shall write again when I reach it, or if something interesting happens, whichever first.

Sōlrest-Ōðer-XXIX

The journey *was* continuing seamlessly, but I suppose the ideal weather could only hold out for so long so far into Sōlrest. I would estimate to have traversed around half of the distance between the end of the Gārfeldas and my destination in Cemparīċe; Stilneshire. The Golden Road continues west unswerving until it terminates in Bēagshire, seat of Ricbert's kingdom. I instead diverted to the north for a less-travelled and more covert avenue. Along the way, the crowds and watchtowers thinned as my path became more and more obscure, until I was finally completely alone. I had borne northwest as the roads opened up and was now travelling somewhere near alongside the Caillwall, though it was not in sight. I was moving westerly along a steep and wooded hill which climbs sharply to the north and drops precariously to the south. Now I find myself stopped only for the whims of the sky. A great storm began to loom on the horizon a short while ago, and on this backwater path there is little in the way of buildings. I had no time to travel further along the road to find one, and am thus taking cover under a particularly large and ancient oak.

Under one of the great leafy branches I can say that I am faring quite well, well enough to write this entry without blotching my parchment. When the storm quells, I shall be continuing my journey towards the Ġeolwǣt Hundred, the most north-easterly region of Stilneshire County. I am actually unsure as to what county my current path belongs to, if any. The land is far too uneven to be farmed without a great deal of reshaping. That, and its proximity to the Caillwall to the north, make it an unlikely place to be truly settled.

I have, personally, little to fear from Caill. The stories of raiders climbing the wall to capture villagers for their druidic rituals are, by my reckoning, highly exaggerated, and even in those tales lone travellers seem to be exempt from their exploits. I always considered the Caillwall to be more of a border marker than a necessary defensive structure. Caill's xenophobia is more substantial than their supposed raids. People who stray too far into their lands are rarely seen again, especially not alive. Trade with them is a rare thing indeed, and scarcely can their painted bodies be seen outside of their sacred forests.

Still, they have been this way at some point. A little further back on the path I found a piece of antler from one of their great stags, carved with intricate patterns all over its surface. I could not bear to leave such a fine piece of craftsmanship to be neglected, so I took it with me. Studying the piece now, it is almost hypnotic to look upon, such is the fine detailing... I shall have to remember to study it again in better light.

The flashes in the sky and rumbling thunder grow more distant, and I can hear the rainfall lessening. The weather remains quite warm despite the precipitation. I shall prepare to leave and write my next entry once I have reached Stilneshire.

Sōlrest-Þridda-II

It truly took longer to encounter danger on the roads than expected, although this evening did demonstrate that footpads are capable of commendable creativity in their predations of innocents.

Night had begun to draw in and brought with it a frightful chill. Wolves called to the moon and their mournful howls pierced the dense woodland. I have slept rough, as it were, on a number of cold nights throughout this journey and my life in sum, but when I found a sign at the roadside for lodgings the temptation of warmth and comfort was irresistible. Heeding the marker's direction, I followed a beaten dirt path until the forest parted to reveal a cottage whose windows were all aglow and its chimney emitted constant voluminous smoke. It was at once welcoming and disquieting, but another frigid blast of wind prompted me towards the door regardless. A mound of recently turned earth up against the edge of the clearing, barely visible in the dusk, caught my attention. A midden? Or a grave hastily dug? I have seen and created them often enough to recognise the latter. Curiosity and low temperatures overcame my caution, however, and I dismounted and tramped my way through the doorway.

It was a warm enough greeting I received on the other side, but experience had heightened my senses to the charade. The three men who welcomed me had the look of deserters, from Sċeldlond if I had to guess. They appeared strong, square-jawed, and with a military bearing. Their ages, too, were around the appropriate mark.

Yes, almost certainly they were ex-soldiers; for while the wealthy elites of Ricbert's armies were comprised mostly of his household and personal retinue, the rebel faction was forced to hire men as professional soldiers. This army was dedicated, disciplined, well-drilled and effective, but only for as long as there was money in their pockets, for war is an expensive business and Sċeldlond's coffers were not deep enough for the protracted conflict. Many soldiers left for banditry when their salaries were short or defaulted on entirely, but the worst of it was when the war was over. Ricbert's men (those that had survived with their properties intact) returned to their estates relatively content. Sċeldlond's paid swords suddenly found themselves destitute and often vagrant, and so they repaid their country's abandonment of them in kind. To this day the eastern half of Sūþeard's countryside is more dangerous to wander than the western, and many do not restrict their villainy to their true malefactors, straying far to find the most vulnerable and lucrative targets.

These before me were three such men, and although they had obviously abandoned their wargear, they were betrayed at once by their mode of speech and a subtly anxious disposition. I continued their game in the knowledge that mine would always be the winning play, allowing them to stable Felicia and lead me to their hearth. At that point I found that my plans were sullied by the presence of four others that I presumed had yet to recognise the ruse: a moderately wealthy-looking young merchant, dressed well in vivid blue silk; his two large and roughly attired mercenaries, hired for his protection; and a lone traveller, athletic and equipped well for the outdoors, probably a hunter. Beyond a few lazy acknowledgements, none of the ragtag group spoke, seemingly regarding each other with suspicion. The atmosphere was tense, as if I had wandered into the aftermath of a heated argument. It was little aided by the soup that was offered to us, for it was barely lukewarm, utterly bland and unseasoned. Evidently, none of the impostors had been their encampment's chef. The loner ate the concoction reluctantly, but it was more than the merchant could tolerate, and his went untouched even by the giant men at his sides. Mine, too, was ignored; I doubted the value of eating what could have been little better than gruel, instead deferring to my own rations later.

Eventually, we were politely ushered to our personal spaces. By this point, I had long anticipated their endeavour to extend our slumbers indefinitely. I dared not try to warn the others, lest they panic and prompt rasher action from our captors; such events would likely necessitate the elimination of all parties. No, they must rely on their own wiles and protection. Perhaps the merchant stands a fair chance, having been granted a large room for himself and his companions to share. The outdoorsman rests alone, poor fellow. Hopefully he sleeps with an eye open as I do. One might call our perils shared, but I am isolated only among the living.

Sōlrest-Þridda-III

Despite the brief interruption, I was able to steal some needful repose. Tragically, I proved to be the night's only survivor. If the lodge were stumbled upon, I would quickly be absolved of inculpation, but I shall choose relative prudence and vacate shortly. Similarly, I shall not interfere with the other guests and our hosts; there is little I can scavenge from them that would be of any value to me, and I would prefer not to bloody myself for naught.

Sōlrest-Þridda-VI

As I found my way into Stilneshire County, the ground began to level out and the path became easier. I eventually joined a better-kept road which led the way to the cleared land of the Ġeolwǣt Hundred, and I was greeted once again by great fields of wheat that swayed in the soft breeze. A quaint stone bridge granted me passage over the meandering River Leafbrym and, immediately afterwards, the path turned left sharply. Following this new road south-west, the terrain soon began to roll upwards in a series of graduating hillocks but, just a few hours later, I reached the edge of a basin. That crest provided an ideal view of a sizeable, but sparsely built, settlement.

Laid out before me were structures formed around a single, wavering road of a dozen or so major lateral undulations. At the furthest point, three grand old works of masonry faced each other. Following that way east and located near the southern boundary of the basin was some kind of partition, obscured by a carefully maintained stockade of living trees. Opposite there was a concentric series of stalls. Further still, situated at the first major curve, was an instantly recognisable temple of the Sōlis Mūnus, its distinctive mirrored dome rooftop dazzling me even at this distance. On the section of the path nearest to the northern edge of the basin was a tall tower of stone. These were the most prominent features of the settlement; in addition to those described, more than a gross of timber and thatch houses and many acres of crop fields were scattered to pack every remaining space.

Thus in the early morning had I reached my destination of the Gerefwīċ Hundred, the centre of Stilneshire County. Despite being arguably the most important hundred within Stilneshire, it is, by any other county's standard, a small rural place. Its population can number no more than half a thousand, give or take the occasional traveller, more often lost than not. A majority of the people are farmhands who remain busy working fields and herding animals throughout the day.

All in all, an ideal place for one so inclined to settle and practice necromancy in secret.

Necromancy is, ironically, a dying practice. There is not a single place that I can recall in which the art of raising the dead is not illegal. Whether by state law or religious edict, from the frozen southern glaciers to the sophisticated cityscapes of Iliban, the punishment for even contemplating the use of a cadaver in magic ranges from exile to execution. Related manuscripts, too, are highly contraband, often locked away under guard at local temples, if not simply burned upon their discovery.

So how then, if at odds with the rest of Pænvicta, can one acquire the written knowledge or tutoring necessary to practice this ancient and powerful craft? The truth of the matter is indeed grim; with that endeavour I can offer you little help. If you have come into possession of this diary, then you likely have one of the ever-waning number of already endangered texts dealing with this subject matter. If I am to be completely honest with myself, this document is more likely to find its home in a brazier than in a collection, statistically speaking. A sobering thought.

That, I suppose, is why I am keeping this journal. For years have I practiced in secret, not daring to write a word lest it be discovered. Now, though, as I am old and grey and my body fails me, I have safely hidden my most important tomes and relocated for the last time in order to embark on the most ambitious and complex ritual I have ever attempted; my last gambit to finally, and permanently, cheat death. I shall record every step of my journey, on which I shall surely find use for every form of necromancy I have mastered. Provided I remain undisturbed and uninterrupted, this diary will serve a dual purpose of posterity and education.

The next question to ask myself, I suppose, is why risk exposure for the sake of a text which may never see light? The truth is, if I am discovered before I succeed, I shall be damned regardless. If I am discovered after I have succeeded...? Then I shall mourn my would-be aggressors whether it be a mob or an army. But for now I must remain quiet, diligent, and hidden away in a place that perfectly straddles the line of assets and secrecy. A place just like Gerefwīċ Hundred, Stilneshire.

Of course, nothing could be so perfect. The presence of the Sōlis Mūnus in the area, however small, is troubling. Theirs is the primary cult which overtook the peaceful and reclusive precursors of Arx Turrium like wildfire, twisting them into the violent imperialists that became the premier movers in Pænvicta. No one can say for certain whence the doctrine originated (indeed the usurpers made sure to destroy all records of their predecessors) but it spread through brutal

25

absolutism, taking undisputed rule of the Arx around a century and a half ago. The clandestine Sōlis Mūnus established itself amid unsuspecting populations under the false pretences of order, generosity and divinity, only revealing their true intentions of utter subjugation when opposition was negligible. I believe they are trying to repeat this process more widely in their novel protectorate territories. Here I would guess that their success so far has at least been minimal, and that they would not be so militant as where they have a strong foothold. Thankfully, the likelihood of a fully armed banner of Coercitōrēs knocking on my door is mercifully low, and the worst one could expect from the presence of this temple is some pairs of eyes that pry just that much closer. The local watchmen, on the other hand, are few, friendly and seemingly oblivious. Put bluntly, I have worked under more trying circumstances.

After paying a modest amount of coin at 'The Old Boar' tavern, my newest temporary home has been secured. I stabled Felicia and paid enough for her upkeep for the foreseeable future. I immediately set out to allay curiosities about my presence here, repeating a practiced cover of plainly being a retired old man, using his remaining time to explore some of the world. When assuming an identity in this... profession, it is most important to choose one which accounts for spending a majority of your time away from your place of residence. In this case, I would be out for hours exploring the simplistic wonders of nature and architecture, as far as the peasants were concerned. In my prime I would merely carry a bow and a knife and pass as a hunter, but now, at my age, the image of a man who can barely hobble chasing a buck raises either eyebrows or laughter. A trapper might be more realistic, but then would be expected to bring back a hare or two on occasion; an activity I do not have the time to indulge.

The purpose of this necessary layer of subterfuge is a key rule of practicing necromancy. That is the old adage, 'do not soil your own nest.' In this craft, adhesion to this mantra has two main incentives: firstly, your workplace will be saturated with evidence that betrays your true nature, and the aforementioned high illegality of your actions will assure a hasty and unpleasant end to your career; secondly, on a more personal note, neither the sights nor the aromas of a fully provisioned necromancer's laboratory could be described as 'homely' to any but the most desperate ghouls. Perhaps a practitioner with a stronger stomach would argue, but although I am capable of enduring that assault on the senses from dawn to dusk without refrain, the very thought of eating or sleeping in that grotesquery gives me tremors.

The innkeeper, named Alton, is a middle-aged man with thin brown hair and a permanently drowsy look, meaning either that he does not pay much attention to anything or that I had successfully bored him. Just as The Westing Spear was an extension of Edmonde's personality, so is The Old Boar relatively small and tired-looking, but homely and comfortable, and most importantly, quiet. It is spacious, not due to being an especially large building, but for its lack of adornment or decoration. There is a counter with a few kegs in a line at the side, a decently sized table opposite, and a rather small and sad-looking fireplace. Regardless, having spent most of the day exchanging niceties with the locals and exploring my immediate surroundings for amenities and useful stalls, I shall retire to avoid arousing suspicion. Tomorrow I shall scout for the potential location of a sanctum.

Preferably, of course, in the graveyard.

Sōlrest-Þridda-VII

They say fortune smiles upon the brave. One dedicated to the powers of un-death in this era can certainly be considered so. My search for a secret space has borne the ultimate fruit, and I have already arranged my workplace as to my liking inside.

Budding practitioners would be wise to take notes here; when scouting for subjects and a place to work on them, the graveyard should be your first point of call. Here I give lease for the younger acolytes to be envious; when an elderly individual spends a few hours ambling around a cemetery, a passer-by will assume without question that he or she is either visiting any number of dead friends or relatives, or reflecting on his or her own mortality. A young person may wish to feign a motive and bring some tributary flowers or the like.

What you will ultimately be looking for is something very specific and quite rare, but so valuable is the reward that it is always worth the search. A crypt makes for a perfect necromancer's laboratory, but one must always investigate a few variables: firstly, that the entrance is not too exposed, as you must be capable of entering and exiting regularly and unseen; secondly, the family interred must be either relocated or extinct. If you can risk a hasty exploration, carefully pick the lock and ensure all of the sarcophagi are dated to more than a century ago. A healthy layer of dust on all surfaces is also a good portent. If all of these factors ring true, you have a secure and blissfully lonely station in which you can leave your equipment, as well as your first batch of loyal servants readily available. Graveyards, for superstitious reasons, are often kept separate from the general populace. Indeed, the wall of giant willows I had seen from the ridge seems to have been left standing for this very reason, and will serve to conceal my activities.

If such a utopia is unavailable (as often it will be), you will have to search further afield. A cottage or cabin nearby may be open for rent. Abandoned mines or natural caves are other likely candidates. Improvisation will be important here, but remember; a lack of corpses in the vicinity of your workplace will necessitate more active grave robbery. This is a risky business, as I am sure a few of the guests at your local gallows would have told you. Given that you will almost certainly have to do this at night, additional alibis will be required in order to avoid suspicion and subsequent investigation. Remember, too, that haunts preferable to yourself may also have use for common criminals. They should pose little threat, but always remain vigilant and *never* leave living witnesses.

In this instance I have been fortunate enough to stay at the pleasure of the 'Blōþisōdaz' family, a line which seems to have abandoned its legacy *at least* three-hundred years ago. Indeed, their arched mausoleum holds quite a nobility even having fallen into decrepitude, and the name itself is written in archaic runes that few can now read, even among the educated literate. It dominates the graveyard, topping the large central hill, which itself is dotted with the oldest headstones. The crypt's entrance is marked with a once intricately carved giant eagle's head, whose fine details are all but weathered away. Doubtless when I start my work here I shall learn a little more about them from their remains.

Not wishing to push my luck past its limits, I secured the crypt's gate and shall visit Felicia in the stables. After that, I think I shall have a few drinks to celebrate the day's successes before retiring. Tomorrow I shall be raising the first of my new friends. An additional pair of hands is always useful, even if they are lacking flesh.

Sōlrest-Þridda-VIII

I am now necromancing with the assistance of Rēdawulf Blōþisōdaz. Of course, he doesn't know that exactly.

Let me explain from the beginning.

At early dawn, just before the farmhands began to empty out of their houses and into the fields, I stole away to the graveyard (well out of the way of anyone's morning route) and found my new home-away-from-home. After climbing the hill and defeating the padlock again, I slipped inside and, fitting my hands through the bars, reset it outside to leave no trace of my presence. While a gated entrance is less useful than a solid stone door, the Blōþisōdaz crypt is deep and with multiple corners. At least I can enjoy some fresh air.

In a dangerous situation, a proficient necromancer can quickly imbue nearby remains as bodyguards. For more intelligent and long-lasting soldiers, the use of a little more care in choice of remains and during the ritual itself will improve the result threefold. On this occasion I needed servants to be able to guard my station without my supervision overnight, as well as additional hands for both delicate procedures and manual labour.

Hence I began scanning the dates on the sarcophagi, seeking rhyme or reason to their placement. It seems that whenever the crypt needed more space, it would be tunnelled further at the back. Any previously buried remains were dumped into a charnel pit just to the right of the entrance. The most ancient and resultantly dilapidated remains were closest to the front. Conveniently, the freshest of those interred, being just over three centuries ago, would still be decayed enough for my preference. Here I am sure there is a division among acolytes as to whether they prefer their risen creatures to have flesh remnants or not. While there is definitely an element of subjectivity, there are some measurable differences. To better explain these opposing traits I shall first portray the nature of the un-dead we create.

Unlike revenants (which occur, for lack of a better term 'naturally' and under conditions which are unknown and cannot be reproduced), the dead we raise either accidentally as necromantic fallout (known as wights) or purposefully for our uses do not possess their own souls. The manna with which we infuse the remains reanimates the physical body with a mind composed of the intents of the master and the means of trace memories. In layman's terms, the bodies remember the skills they had in life and will use them at your command. They will not, much to the grievance of those trying misguidedly to win back their loved ones, retain personal memories or even sentiments; it has been attempted by many individuals to achieve a perfect resurrection, but the brain is always written over by the manna.

Rēdawulf (or Rēd, as I have dubbed him) was a model example of this phenomenon in practice. I could tell even from his inanimate remains that he was an accomplished military archer in life, evidenced by the extra ossification and bone spurs on his left shoulder and arm. His sarcophagus also contained all of the trappings and equipment expected of a bowman. The tunic and cuirass had largely deteriorated, but the coned helmet was still secured well enough to stay fast on his skull. I opted not to remove any of the gear lest they had become structurally integral.

Now, onto the procedure of his enslavement. For this ritual, I refer heavily to the *Canticum Chorōrum Ossōrum*. It is a tome I could probably recite from beginning to end if it was necessary, but I have brought it with me and find it invaluable as it often continues to provide insight. The author, who kept himself necessarily anonymous, writes primarily in metaphor when describing the works of manna. The passage on raising an un-dead minion translates as follows:

The best results come from gathering and applying the oils yourself. You must apply them evenly and carefully or the result may be patchy and shoddy. Too much may cause pooling which wastes an expensive commodity and creates mess.

The instructions are fairly clear to one who has even a basic understanding of manna. The last sentence describes the finesse of the process; 'spillage' through haste or carelessness results in a product of more imperfections. These can range from physical weaknesses or, if performed badly enough, total disintegration. If I were to make a criticism of the author's directions, it would be that too little emphasis is placed on the element of control. On this topic they write:

Use warm, natural flesh tones so as to not lose the character of the puppet. Try to match the shade to your own skin.

Put simply, it is imperative that the necromancer maintains a link to the manna even as it imbues the cadaver. This is the most difficult and important skill to learn and master. Consider the price of failure an incentive to temper your ambitions. I shall forever recall my first attempt at necromantic resurrection. Many years ago, I had found the decomposing bloodhound not far from my hideout at the time. I laid it out for the spell much as described in the *Canticum Chorōrum Ossōrum* and began to energise the remains as I thought correct. I only came to realise my error as the thing sunk its putrid fangs into my forearm even as it sprang into un-death. Twelve days of agonising fever and a permanent, extensive scar from the blood rot marked my mind as effectively as it did my body. Little did I know then that revived animals are even more challenging to maintain control over than revived humans, something the tome failed to mention. That said, were I to have attempted this with a human corpse (especially with a weapon within its reach) it could have been a worse outcome still. My advice is to restrain the subject of your first attempt; a wound attained from any dead creature could easily prove fatal, eventually if not immediately.

Now, given that I had struggled to even move the lid of Rēd's stone container, I had no wish to try and move the whole thing from its shelf. Instead, I could perform the spell directly into the sarcophagus. The methodology is quite simple once the successful technique is recognised, and will improve with practice and repetition. I raised my hands over the skeleton, my arms as wide apart as I could stretch them. The focus is then, much as the tome's author describes, to draw all energy from your immediate surroundings and 'pour' it into whatever remains you wish to manipulate. The entire process bar preparations can be completed in around an hour. Note that side effects are a slight drop in temperature and the possible death of small insects, birds and rats in the area. The sapping of life and heat energy and its conversion to manna is very efficient in necromancy because of the subject's previously being alive. When an enchanter animates a golem of living clay or an elemental, giving life to a body that has never known it requires a much larger injection of manna. Raw energy must articulate limbs from solid structure. The capability of a necromancer to cast a mass raising spell in a graveyard or recent battlefield for an immediate and sizeable horde cannot be matched by the intricate spell of an enchanter. To even make a sprite from a candle's flame requires a greater supply of energy than that needed to raise an un-dead minion. Not including a Construct, of course. I shall describe this creation another time, but hopefully it does not become necessary to engineer such a monstrosity before my work here is done.

As I transferred the manna into the remains, Rēdawulf jerked back into wakefulness, just like one would from a deep sleep. Immediately he climbed from his resting place, stood at attention and retrieved his rotted longbow and string. Bemused, I watched him attempt to string the bow, obviously a practiced technique; but as he forced it into place, the weapon's limbs exceeded their diminished limit and snapped spectacularly. It is always surprising just how expressive a skull without a face can be, and on this occasion it portrayed to me a look of deep confusion and disappointment. I shall remember to find a new warbow for him. He would make a fine watchman or, if the situation arose, a formidable warrior.

Returning to the item of contention among necromancers that I mentioned earlier, Rēd stands generally at attention when approached and, given a spare moment, tends to perform maintenance on his equipment. He acknowledges orders with a silent and subtle nod. I can see his jaw move in answer, also, but having no lungs, vocal cords, or even lips, he cannot be understood. If Rēd had been better preserved or buried much more recently, he may have possessed these things along with other fleshy parts. In my experience, reanimated creatures tend to have lacklustre mastery over these now seemingly vestigial pieces; they will breathe out of habit, but their torn windpipes and tattered lungs often make an unpleasant noise, not only maddening to listen to but potentially betraying others to your presence as well. Similarly, the remnants of sentences they speak with stricken voices may soon make you wish that they could not speak at all. While a fleshy servant may pass for living at (very) long distances, I do not consider the risk of their discovery worth whatever tasks they may be able to perform independently.

I decided to test the strength of my spell and have Rēd slide some sarcophagi from their shelves. Evidently having accomplished some heavy lifting in his lifetime, he near effortlessly extricated the stone packages containing Ermunahild and Haþuwīgą Blōþisōdaz, settling them onto the floor in preparation for their awakening tomorrow. Not wishing to overly tax myself (a risk in any form of magic), I decided to spend the rest of the session refining my work area, giving new candlesticks to the wall fixtures and refilling my oil lamp. I left Rēd there to guard the depths of the crypt, which he did diligently with his hand on the pommel of his sheathed seax. I exited and secured the crypt as usual, quietly slipping back to the town.

I think I shall retire early. I plan to transcribe some of the symbols on the Caill-carved antler onto parchment, to better study their complexity for my own interests. Then I should sleep. If I am to make multiple servants tomorrow I shall need to be well rested.

Sōlrest-Þridda-IX

This morning, by pure coincidence, I met with the Reeve of Stilneshire... in the graveyard, of all places. He is a tall, well-built man, rough-faced and straw-haired, somewhat imposing in stature (surely contributing more than a fair share of farmwork himself). His name is Ewin Falken, and he was in the graveyard to mourn the tenth anniversary of the natural passing of his father, Eamon Falken.

The reeve is a position of relative importance in Cempārīċe. They are elected to the office by majority vote and organise most of their county's administration. This contrasts with the ealdorman, who is chosen by the king himself and presides over the military workings of a shire should the need arise, as well as enforcing the collection of tax and tribute should expectations not be met. Reeves such as Ewin tend to reside in their own county; ealdormen, as a rule, stay in Bēagshire for the king's convenience. I introduced myself politely, offering condolences and company. I had not spoken to anyone from this region in some time, and it took a while for me to adjust to his strong west-Sūþeard accent; short, sharp vowels, dropped consonants and rapid, unbroken sentences were abound, but this is essentially what he portrayed.

"Thanks for the kind words, friend," he acknowledged with a heavy heart, "but I can never linger long, truth told. No rest for the wicked, isn't that what they say?"

Ewin chuckled, nudged me gently and winked, despite his eyes being still visibly swollen.

"Still, you seem a decent enough chap, and well spoken too. We could always use a new quartermaster, should you be looking for work, by chance?" he said, wiping his face on his sleeve.

It was a generous offer which a small part of me was sad to respectfully decline, citing my well-practiced alibi. Ewin smiled, shrugged embarrassedly and wished me a good day, to which I replied in kind. It is times such as these when I wonder what a life of normality would be like; whether I could abandon my works and simply live the rest of my days out in peace. But no, I rebuke myself, I know too much now to cast off my chosen destiny.

Nevertheless, to establish so excellent a rapport with a man of such authority is, in my opinion, a worthy goal of anyone new to a town, especially if they plan to be unseen by anyone for lengthy amounts of time. Better to be collared into an unwanted conversation by an acquaintance than silently followed by a curious stranger. At least, that would be my opinion, and have I not outlived most other necromancers?

Vanity aside, I waited for Reeve Ewin to be out of sight and entered the crypt as usual. Following the corridors to my workplace, I found Rēd exactly as I had left him (though he had heard my coming and taken it upon himself to light the candles), and the sarcophagi of Ermunahild and Haþuwīgą lay neatly on the floor. Having already wasted enough time with the reeve, I decided to inspect Ermuna in preparation for her immediate raising. As I slid off the lid, I was greeted with an interesting sight; at first I thought that she might have been a noblewoman, given the amount of gold jewellery she was dressed in. As I looked more carefully, however, I noticed a few important details. Under the tattered and half-rotted shirt was a vest of scale armour, and over her left hand, a shield boss bereft of board bore the same sigil as the one above the crypt itself. Half clouded in moss and weathering, perhaps, but still unmistakably the same symbol. A hawk-like head looked up at me with piercing eyes. Above its head it sported a halo. I shall have to seek some information on the Blōþisōdaz family heraldry. Ermuna, meanwhile, must have been a shieldmaiden. All the better. An un-dead shieldmaiden would make for a better fighter than an un-dead housemaid.

I set to raising Ermuna exactly as I had done with the archer (I could see Rēd himself peering over in the periphery of my vision). When I was done, the shieldmaiden rose up elegantly, stood at full height and retrieved a bastard sword that I had previously not noticed due to it having fallen beneath her body. She looked down at the now useless shield boss and discarded it carefully back into the sarcophagus. Finally, she turned to face me at attention. Looking at the pair of them, I considered that female fighters are a sure sign of a strong military family background... and yet, by their numbers, they seemed prosperous to the point of flourishing even. Though I cannot complain about what could be an effectively limitless supply of soldiers to draw from, I am now deeply interested in the original nature of my growing army.

Still, after pondering on my subject for a while, I realised that inspecting Haþuwīgą's remains may provide me more clues. I put my fingers under the sarcophagus' lid to move it and... I could not. I had Rēd attempt to lift it with me, and still it held fast. I might have abandoned these remains and moved on to the next ones but for my building intrigue. It took both Rēd and I levering the iron crow to finally move the lid, and it came apart with a great crack and landed with a crash. A quick inspection revealed that it had been sealed by some process of cementing in addition to being heavier than the other two.

Haþu's burial, however, was grand to behold. She was very ornately dressed, wearing a long dress of seashells linked with thin bronze rings. Even in death she held her staff close in front of her as if for comfort or protection. She appears to have been either imprisoned alive or carefully posed posthumously. The stave itself was a precious artefact; an ivory rod with enamel insets, an eagle's talon carefully carved from bone at its head. Further repetition of this motif confirms to me that it must be a persistent symbol of the Blōþisōdaz family. I am now certainly resigned to somehow slake my curiosity.

Something about the interment still felt unusual. I stood staring at the skeleton, trying to place internally what was amiss. I had the sensation of lingering magic, of residual manna, that I could not explain. It did not originate from the staff, or Haþu herself. My deep feeling of unease was then overridden by another sensation. I had lost track of the time, and I checked the entrance to find that I had indeed lingered too long in the crypt. It was dark out.

I collected what I had to as rapidly as I was able and had Rēd and Ermuna snuff out the lights while I locked the mausoleum behind me. Perhaps my concern was somewhat unwarranted. Alton barely stirred as I entered significantly after my normal hour. I made my way up to my room to set down my things and decided to distract myself with the antler, but copying the patterns seems to be taking forever. I am impatient and the mysterious presence at the crypt is consuming my thoughts. It feels like the illustrations on this piece are deceptively numerous, and I have covered two sheets of parchment with them already.

Bah. I am going downstairs and having a few ales before I exacerbate my headache.

Sōlrest-Þridda-X

I awoke today with a fresh mind, full of ideas and optimism. I could quite easily, I realised, use the skills and equipment at my disposal to solve the puzzle in the crypt. I had been fretting unnecessarily.

I packed my things, locked the room and left, Alton barely glancing upwards from his breakfast and murmuring a greeting in my direction. Passing a couple of drowsy farmhands, I wandered towards the mausoleum, trying to guess at what stalls were being erected by the traders. I noted the carpenter's and decided I would come back during the day to see if there was anything suitable for Rēd and Ermuna to equip themselves with.

Upon seeing a couple of local watchmen methodically collaring the passers-by and verbally engaging them, I thought it better to avoid the guards and quickened my pace slightly. I had no idea what their conversations pertained to, but I had no desire to be drawn into their troubles. So I hastened to the cemetery and took a moment to glance about before making my way inside and closing the way behind me.

I was greeted first by the damp, musty smell of the ancient dead before rounding the final corner and being acknowledged by the two I had raised. The chamber was exactly as I had left it; the skeletons had turned to face me, but Haþuwīgą's sarcophagus lay with its lid turned over on the floor next to it, her remains still inside. The magical presence, too, had not dissipated, so I set about with the method I had devised this morning.

Removing the chalk from my bag, I drew a fairly regular circle on the stone floor and imbued it with a trace amount of manna. The chalk of the circle shimmered softly with a spectrum of colour before intensifying on around forty degrees of its circumference. In that direction, I knew, would be the source of this phantom magical energy.

It seems pertinent to here explain some of the processes of manna. While the author of *Canticum Chorōrum Ossōrum* describes manna as a fluid, I find this to be helpful as a tool of imagination, but ultimately an imperfect comparison. Water, for example, will never flow upwards without a force behind it. It has weight; its trajectory is generally predictable even when not purposefully guided by man or by result of its own processes. Of manna, none of these things are true. But it can be guided by other means and it does seek favourable paths. By giving an area the lightest touch of manna, it can be persuaded to prioritise this place foremost.

This is what is accomplished through the drawing of these shapes on surfaces. The markings themselves are not inherently magical as the uninitiated often believe, but are merely a visual aid for observing and controlling the flow of magic. Chalk is often used for the mundane reasons of being easily acquired, applicable to most surfaces and providing a plain, bright colour against which the refractions caused by concentrated magical energies may be clearly visible. For less complex systems, it is possible to project a purely mental image to manipulate the manna's path. Really, nothing could be simpler than this device of detection; the resonance from the energy's source radiated from that direction, and therefore was visible in the corresponding segment of the circle most strongly.

I shall note here that I was privileged enough to have played spectator to some experiments in the Science Quarter of Iliban. There they have harnessed and are finding applications for a new kind of energy, one that travels along lines of metal and causes objects to be attracted to one another. While I know little about it, I did observe that it seemed superficially reminiscent of manna, but that it was more... rigid, with both the benefits and deficits of what that brings. Doubtless good use will be made of it; invention is rarely squandered in that remarkable city.

Returning to the mausoleum, I found that the errant manna was not coming from the sarcophagus itself, but the heavy lid that had been removed from it. I looked again at Haþu's adorned skeleton. Could she have been magically imprisoned? If this was to be a sadistic punishment, it would seem to me that she had been dressed and treated very well. And indeed, if that were the case, why would she be buried in the Blōþisōdaz crypt at all? I stared again at the posture which she had retained even in her final rest. Her hands clutched her staff which, other than in its craftsmanship, was unremarkable. At first I had interpreted it as self reassurance or even safeguarding the artefact, but looking at it again...

I created another detecting circle between the sarcophagus and its lid to test my hypothesis, and found that it was correct. The side closest to the cover shimmered strongly with the myriad colours of magic, their entrancing hues shifting and dancing above the pale chalk.

Some device was evidently hidden within that stone segment, and the posture of the interred was defensive; she was positioned as if to protect herself from whatever was emanating such power.

Other than the presence, the lid was unassuming, appearing to the naked eye as a plain surface of stone. It would be a simple concealment, though, to seal something within a void using some form of concrete. I hesitated a little before endeavouring to recover the object, for could it not be a trap left for thieves? The decision was made not to risk myself in removing whatever protection was there, so I slinked around one of the crypt's corners and willed Rēdawulf to do it in my place. I peeked over and watched the skeletal archer take the iron crow, aim carefully, and strike the centre of the surface. It was to my relief, and to Rēd's if I let my imagination get the better of me, that there was neither explosion of corrosive grit nor flood of choking gas into the tunnel. The worst to say of it was a slowly settling cloud of grey dust formed from the surface's disintegration. Suspecting that the primary threat was gone, I nevertheless returned cautiously. Rēd stepped aside and stood back at attention, and in doing so allowed me to get close and peer into the opening, to see better my prize.

And a strange prize it is! The mysterious manna-focal device takes the form of a rod, nearly the same height as myself, and made up mostly of two distinct metallic substances. The main body of the rod is something like a dark steel, cold, and even after its long storage, shines as if freshly polished. Inset into this dark metal is a lighter one, a brilliant bronze, taking the form of a twisted bar. It climbs spiralling from end to end, emerging barely above the surface like a brazen serpent stalking a lake of quicksilver. At each end the bronze-like bands concentrate into tight coils like bundles of neatly stored rope.

I remember gasping audibly, for I could not even fathom how such a thing might be forged, and to such exacting perfection. Even still, there is more at work than meets the eye. The core must be composed of some matter beyond my knowledge, for it passively attracts and absorbs manna from the surroundings, just as the hole in an unplugged basin forms a gentle vortex in the water. Were I not mindful of its influence, I expect that in holding it I would be slowly, almost parasitically drained. As it stands, it is clear to me why this glorious thing was made; it was surely intended as a magical focus, and would serve to provide its wielder fantastic control over truly awesome quantities of manna.

Heedless of any further peril, I could not help but to reach in and grasp this treasure with my own hand. The inlaid twists made for a secure (but also smooth and comfortable) grip. I expected a struggle to lift it, but although this new staff is somewhat heavier than my walking stick, it is significantly lighter than its appearance would suggest. I believe that it is either made from metals unknown to Pænvicta, or that its construction was yet more intrinsically magical than I had initially reckoned. It was designed for function first, and in this way it is phenomenally potent; its resultant pleasure to behold stems from nothing other than its quaintness and efficiency, for it lacks any extraneous decorative adornment. This contrasts with the purely ceremonial and aesthetic piece held by the interred priestess.

Except in very remote and secret places, magically crafted artefacts, or objects created for the manipulation of manna, are incredibly rare, and scarcer now than they were a millennium ago. This is, in part, due to the sowing of mistrust towards magic in all its forms, especially through the teachings of the Sōlis Mūnus; not all schools are as illegal and dangerous as necromancy, but wizards, mages, tomes and magical foci are still safer if kept a respectful distance from public spaces. The other major factor in the slow diminishing of supranatural artisanry is the dissolution of its mastery. Such crafts were refined and honed over untold generations, and the growing persecution of its practitioners causes the already small pool to shrink evermore. Thus is the arcane art maintained only in a few bastions so hidden and precious that I shall not mention them even here; thus are ancient devices like the one I hold now treated as either incomparably precious to the knowing, or dangerous and eldritch to the ignorant.

Irrespective of its insofar unknown origin, I shall make use of this miracle of craftsmanship. Unlike the superstitious, I know that inanimate objects themselves carry no agency. The sword in the hand of the invader or the defender are no more good or evil than the sword in its sheath, or the iron from which it was forged. Still, it would be interesting to know where such a thing was made. Also when, for that matter. But these are likely lost to the sands of time; I may never have the answers.

I must continue my work. I shall write again later and log my findings. Perhaps the staff will aid my progress.

Later...

Having finally rid myself of the tension of the phantom presence, I could examine the remains of Haþu at length and in greater comfort. With the ceremonial staff and iridescent dress, she would certainly seem to be a non-combatant. This, ultimately, may make her less useful as a guardian. However, an inspection of her bones revealed a mostly undamaged skeleton, and I resolved to make a minion of Haþu nonetheless. One should never pass up a corpse in good condition - who knows what the state of all the other individuals will be?

I decided to experiment with the focal staff, to see if its use was intuitive enough for me to improvise my expected result. For all the complexity in its design, its function seemed simple enough. I held the shaft on my right side with both hands, angling one of its heads so that it hovered about a finger's length over the subject's ribcage. I then willed manna to travel into the opposite end. Immediately the staff surged with power; energy was drawn in as if into a powerful vacuum and swirled its way to the other terminus. From the core of those tightly wound coils it poured in frightening concentrations. Even without the chalk I could see the flares of manna pouring from the staff's end and into the waiting sarcophagus. The remains absorbed the required magical energy in a matter of minutes. The greater challenge, in fact, turned out to be the necessity of stifling the staff once it had been activated. I quickly found that cutting off the source at its 'input' end worked best and resulted in the rest of the energy dissipating in short order.

So distracted I was with operating the staff that I barely noticed when Haþuwīgą climbed from her resting place and stood before me. With her now standing, I could see that she held a strong, noble posture, holding her stick like a symbol of office; it was certainly no mere walking aid. As her dress of shells shifted and glittered, she impressed upon me the undeniable air of a leader. I would be willing to guess that she was above any of the other dead in this mausoleum. She was made to take position with the others and stay similarly on-guard.

I paced down the corridors until I was at the final corner before the entrance. Looking at the wall, daylight was fading into the gentle dark of evening. The days were growing shorter with each passing. Not unexpected, but I feel that I should direct my efforts towards my final task before the full moon. Further procrastination than that simply cannot stand.

There were a few chores that could be accomplished before I retired back to The Old Boar. I decided to direct my three minions in an effort to remove more sarcophagi from the shelves. They could be made ready for tomorrow morning, though I may take a slight diversion to see to finally acquiring Rēd and Ermuna's bow and shield respectively. I snuffed out all the lights and made my way to the gate cautiously, as it was earlier than the normal time, still barely dark. It would seem that none of the farmhand's routes home pass through the graveyard, so I could unlock the padlock, slip out and reset it behind me without excessive concern.

When I bustled my way into The Old Boar, I found it to be an entirely different place to how I had ever seen it before. There were more patrons now than the sum of every visitor since I first arrived, and the largest group of about fifteen burly farmhands sat around the largest table, talking and laughing loudly. Alton was not only active and rushed off his feet, but also seemed to have a helper; a scruffy young man ferried coin back and drinks forth, chatting with the customers on the rare occasion when a spare moment presented itself.

"Bayldon, my lad," a gruff voice half-laughed, half-shouted above the din, "tell Orman here about the time you found a dog in the outhouse!"

Already smiling at the recollection, the boy placed the tray of full tankards on the centre of the table and took a seat next to them, leaning forwards. Some, it seems, had heard the story before and were already grinning in expectation. The dark-haired one I had guessed to be Orman was immediately rapt and sat still, listening intently.

There was a window of quiet as Bayldon narrated (and occasionally, re-enacted) his story as they listened, so I was able to take a seat at the counter and order a drink for myself. Alton himself served me, and for a change he seemed alert, awake and talkative. In fact, he said the most words he had ever said to me. His dialect was dense like that of the inn's patrons, but in general he spoke more softly and slowly than did the others.

"Sir, I don't mean to cause alarm, but I'm afraid the watchmen have been around here, and they seem sharp on finding you."

"Thank you for letting me know, but I am a little confused. Did they say what it was regarding?" I replied, hiding my unease.

"Oh Sir, I wouldn't be overly worried. I doubt it even concerns yourself. Seems there was an incident right near here and the watch are struggling to make a whole picture of it. I've heard nothing of it myself, so I can't tell you what it was all about."

"The watchmen said nothing?"

"I did ask, but they explained to me that they had to keep it hush-hush so as folk don't go making their minds up before the hearing. And so folk don't just repeat what they've eavesdropped, if you get me."

"I see," I said, giving a contemplative scratch of my beard before continuing. "I wish I could be of assistance, but I know truly nothing of whatever has transpired."

"That's what I told them, Sir, that you were up and well clear of the place hours before the thing's supposed to have happened. They said then that they still want your word on it, but you're alright till after the day of rest."

Of course, I thought to myself, *that explains the inn's suddenly booming business.*

"Thank you very much, Alton. I would guess that the courthouse is the wide stone structure?"

"You'd be guessing right, Sir," he said with a warm smile, his complexion easing with the passage of the difficult subject. "Only masonry here, except the guard house and the prayer house. Truth is, anything 'administrative' is done at the place you said. Reeve's office, one," here he counted on his fingers. "Courthouse, two. And three, something a smart one like yourself may like, if you don't mind my saying so, they have the Stilneshire Books, supposedly the whole history of the shire. I'd like to have a read myself, only it isn't all in Sūþrūna. Fair bit's loads older, so I reckon."

"Very thoughtful of you, Alton," I bowed gently, "I know not what I would do without you." I beamed at him, genuinely grateful.

"People around here, Sir, they'll help you whenever they can, as will I. Now, what say I fix you a drink on the house, for putting you through some upset at such an... *advanced* age?" Alton winked and gave a mischievous grin as he poured an ale from the keg by his side. I chuckled with him as he handed over the brimming tankard, and its aroma was most welcome.

Just then a raised voice from the table shattered the relative silence. Bayldon had reached the climax of his anecdote.

"So I say to the bloke; 'For all our sakes, man, didn't your mummy ever tell you to chew your food!'" As the men collectively exploded into bellowing laughter, Bayldon was among them, slapping the table triumphantly. Then he jumped up from his chair to fetch another round for the happy patrons, just as Alton passed me another drink unbidden. I must say, before I retire, that it has been a more joyous evening than I have experienced in a long, long time.

Sōlrest-Þridda-XI

I awoke with a start, unsurprisingly late given last night's frivolities. My head was splitting and my eyes could barely open, but I forced myself out of the bed and made myself ready. Upon leaving my room to make my way to the exit, I was greeted by a quite bemused Alton.

"Why, if it isn't our resident souse! Looking for a morning tipple, are we?"

"No, that is quite alright, Alton," I managed the wry smile of a cruel jab accepted, "though I should bother you for some clean water, if you know the meaning of the word."

"And which word would that be, Sir?" Alton retorted, forcing an educated accent to mock me. "Would that be 'clean' or 'water' that I might lack understanding of?"

"Both. But I am sure you will manage to deduce a meaning, especially if you have finally repaired your diction."

"Right you are, Sir," he laughed, relinquishing his facade. "Piss and vinegar, on its way!"

With that, Alton turned about and filled a tankard from one of the casks. The spigot was noticeably more stubborn than the others. When he turned back and placed it on the bar in front of me, I could see that it was, indeed, commendably pure water, and its taste did not disappoint. I could almost immediately feel my headache melting away. After greedily gulping down half the tankard, I asked him whence the water was drawn, to which he replied that it was taken from the greatest well in Gerefwīċ Hundred. The River Leafbrym, he explained, was too impractically distant for regular water acquisition, and so a remarkably deep well had been excavated to service the settlement. When I asked him how long ago that might have been, he confessed that he knew not, but postulated that it was probably made by the same architects which made the other stone structures in Stilneshire.

As this point was made, I greatly desired to ask about the still standing mausoleum that had become my laboratory, but I thought better than to outwardly show interest in that particular place. I instead asked if the archives would be open today, to which he replied that, while most of the commerce was actually at its best on the holiday, he knew little of the Stilneshire Books' workings.

"Thank you, Alton. For the drink and the wisdom," I bowed my head as I stood.

"Very welcome you are, Sir. Always nice to have some polite company, unlike *this* riff-raff..." He made a soft chuckle and pointed at someone I had previously not noticed; Orman lay prone under the large table, his chest rising and falling gently in slumber.

I raised my brow in amusement to Alton and made to leave, only to be stopped at the door by a raised stage-whisper.

"Don't go now, Sir, you'll miss the show!"

"Have your fun, Alton, I must be off. I shall see you later." With that, I left. Just as I was outside the door, I heard Alton shout Orman's name with a surprisingly authoritative bark, and a great thump when the latter's head struck the table as he presumably bolted upright. I walked away to the sound of Alton's infectious laughter.

Looking about the street, what I had learned in The Old Boar proved to be true. Nigh all the stores were selling their wares, and they were indeed busier than I had previously seen them. Compared to how it had been, the street was positively thronged with people, even some outsiders from the neighbouring hundreds. From what I have heard, Sceoppaton is the most important hundred for trading within and without Stilneshire, but it may be that Gerefwīċ is a close second in providing for its closest tithings.

Curiously absent were the priests of the Sōlis Mūnus, who elsewhere use rest days such as this to preach publicly; but it seemed that here, today, they were all shut away in their temple for reasons unknown. Though the people were busying themselves with commerce and conversation, they did seem altogether... subdued, watchful perhaps. For that reason, and the general crowding, I decided that visiting my laboratory today would be much too conspicuous. I nonetheless accepted the prudent deferment only with disappointment. Accounting for tomorrow's mysterious business and now today's crowds, the delays are quickly amounting to potential ruin.

Still, there was business I could attend to outside of necromancy, given that those activities were struck off. I decided to find the carpenter and attempt to acquire replacement equipment for my servitors.

It had apparently rained a little overnight, and the heaving crowds had turned the main thoroughfare into a quagmire. I began to push my way through the masses of people, soon finding that most were polite enough to give way to an elderly gentleman, much unlike on the Gārfeldas road. The ground itself seemed ill-suited to the traffic, and my footwear ill-suited to the ground. Several times I almost slipped on the trampled mud.

I eventually reached a great cluster of stalls, on the forefront of which was a game butchery with a blacksmith to its left. I used the opportunity to purchase some vittles from the young trapper. Just as I had finished the exchange, I found myself eavesdropping on a conversation taking place outside the next stall, where a group of men were waiting on their carthorses being shod. It was difficult to hear over the din of the marketplace and the hammering from the smithy, but what follows is an approximation of what I could make out:

"-Hasn't got no chance, has he? Going up against the temple on his lonesome. I've yet to see one of them face any kind of recompense, much less for something like this."

"'He had no choice though, did he?'"

"He had every choice, Hardwin! He had every choice, and he made the wrong one!"

"Made the only one, I says."

"Oh, you 'says' does you, Hardwin? And how loud does you 'says' it? Loud enough for you to tell them at the judgement?"

There was a shamed silence, the man's fury quenched just as was a newly shaped horseshoe.

"Feeling a bit bilious now, Hardwin? Truth is, I don't blame you. By what's proper, he has done right. But for the sake of his kin, he done wrong. The temple won't take it lightly, they never does. And when he's done away, what do you reckon will happen to his wife and child, eh?"

"*They* haven't done wrong by the temple, they'll be left out of it!"

"Now you knows it don't take a great deal to slight them, does it? Look at what the bastard done to poor Camden, for *discourtesy*! Sad truth is, they does what they wants, and isn't one of us can stop them. The man would have better kept his mouth shut, and I bet he wishes he had done, now."

If there was further communication between the two, it passed into whispers. I headed to the right around the central stalls so as to avoid the men and their cart which would presumably be pulling away imminently. Rotating around this circle of wood and canvas structures, I came across a leatherworker, a potter and a baker. The aroma of the freshly baked goods from the latter was too tantalising, so I could not resist paying for a sweet roll to nibble. For a short while I lost myself, unused to the concept of a leisurely day, before continuing to circle the stalls.

A butcher, a furrier and a tailor were passed by until I found the trader for which I sought; a woodworker. Inside the entrance I could see that the stall extended surprisingly far back into the centre of the market, and indeed must have had far more space than the trapper's, and perhaps a little more even than the baker's. Looking about, however, the place was something of a mess. Odds and ends were scattered everywhere, and it seemed that the owner was a purveyor of second hand goods as well as a craftsman in his own right. Despite the chaos and difficulty in moving, it didn't take long for me to set eyes on one of my prizes, that being a small, circular table. Half-walking, half-climbing my way to the quaint little stand, I got a hold of it before realising that the merchant was nowhere to be seen. Were I not remaining here for some time I might have pilfered it without much of a second thought. As it stands, it would be best not to sour relations with the locals if it can be avoided.

I called out for the owner and was answered immediately. A clatter and hasty footfalls on the planking preceded the emergence of a fairly diminutive man, aging, his silver-flecked mousy beard tied into two long braids. He was kind enough, but seemed hurried for some reason I knew not. He sold me the table for a mere three Scutes and I departed with nary another word from either of us. I never even learned of the man's name, most unusual in this region when doing business. Still, I did not dwell. If I were in Iliban I would have thought nothing at all of it.

When I had exited the stall carrying the new table over my shoulder, I went to complete a circle around the cluster so as to return the way I had come and find the Stilneshire Books. I then noticed that, further on ahead, the crowds were parting. A group of the Sōlis Mūnus priests had finally showed themselves and were slowly marching in their solemn yet authoritative way, the frontmost one swinging an ornate thurible to the timing of every second step of the procession. It seemed as if Sōl itself emerged to pay heed to them, for just then the sun breached through the clouds, causing their flawless white robes to glow and the fiery golden embroidery upon it to dazzle those who looked. Their outfits were reminiscent of their more violent brothers; segmented, covering of every inch of flesh, with gauntlets and epaulets beautifully etched but cruelly shaped. In place of an enclosed helmet, they wore high-peaked hoods that hid their faces, and a finely detailed robe ran all the way to their ankles instead of greaves. This part of the raiment trailed in the mud, but they cared not, and they were strikingly surefooted. They wore sabatons that sank deep into the sludge, but never struggled. The priests, their path cleared, moved inexorably and in silence to the town hall, and would be slowed by nothing.

I was not alone in standing awestruck. Every man, woman and child that had hastened from their path took their place at the side and stared wordlessly at the spectacle. The Temple of the Sun certainly spare no expense on their aesthetic. I wondered, and wonder still, if the people know or care just how valuable even the raw material alone of their regalia is. Do the common folk begrudge them the taxes they pay? Do they find their insubstantial message of purpose a comfort, or do they find their stringent damnations upsetting? Would they even answer truthfully if I asked them these questions? I doubt that they would have sufficient trust to be candid, to me nor anyone else.

When the priests were out of sight, commerce began to resume normality. The low murmurs rose into a crescendo of conversations returned to in unison, then died back down to the regular din. There being a few hours remaining until sunset, I had ample opportunity to complete the day's tasks. I remembered then that I had yet to find a longbow for Rēd, nor even any kind of purveyor of weaponry (the blacksmith being purely domestic), so I returned to the trapper on a hunch. The young man stepped forwards with a smile, clearly recognising me and hoping for repeat custom, but was visibly confused when I asked him if he had any old bows for sale. I explained to him that it was for a friend, one who hunts large game. With that, his face of confusion was replaced by one of thoughtfulness.

"Well, truth is, mister, I had made one myself, but I done it dead strong. Too hard for me to even string, it is... my dad, who were a bowyer before, said it were like one for hunting game that was wearing mail and helm rather than a pelt and antlers, if you take his meaning, mister," he chortled. "He gave me a right hiding for wasting good yew on it. If your mate's a big one, you can have it cheap and be doing me a favour, all told!"

Perfect, I thought.

We made a deal and I passed him three Scutes. It was only as he handed me the weapon that he informed me of his father's estimation for the bow's draw weight of one hundred and fifty pounds at least. I managed to swallow my astonishment and play it off that I was sure my friend would be strong enough. Frankly, I am actually curious to see if my creation is capable of stringing and loosing from the thing. As it stands, it is sitting next to me with its string tied about it, much like a tremendously tall, thin and subtly curved stave. It will take a more recognisable shape when (or if) it is successfully strung and bent. I could not possibly complain about the quality, however. The finish is excellent and the straightness is without flaw. The trapper even provided a quiver of arrows, themselves a high enough gauge to withstand the force of the release. I find it impossible to entertain the notion that the maker had created a warbow accidentally. The miscalculations would have been ludicrous. More likely it was an attempted boast gone awry. Still, I shall not gripe. It will suit Rēd well enough, I hope.

I parted then with the trapper and, carrying the day's purchases, made my way back to The Old Boar to deposit them in my quarters. As I carefully squeezed my way through the door, I found that Alton was not there. Instead, Bayldon was manning the bar. He waved sheepishly when he recognised me, red-faced and clearly suffering after his own night of merrymaking. I retired long before the rest of them in the end. He half-heartedly offered to help with my burdens, but I waived the suggestion. Neither items were particularly heavy, just awkwardly shaped; I saw Bayldon wince at the edge of my vision whenever I bumped something on my surroundings, but it was not long before they were in their place and I was back outside, progressing to my last task of the day.

Leaving the inn and turning left, I could see a fair distance down the pathway, and could make out one of the stone buildings. The road was much less trodden this way, and beyond the periphery of the market traffic, I could actually trace the muddy tracks that the priests had made before. Following those, I came upon a courtyard which had three major works of masonry surrounding it and facing inwards. All are of a similar architectural style; multitudes of great stone slabs shaped carefully to fit together and sealed with cement, and doorways marked out by arches of impressive size. To my left, or south, was the archives building, the 'Stilneshire Books'. Straight ahead on the western edge, the town hall. To my right and north, the primary guard barracks, which is complemented by a stylistically similar but much smaller watchtower on Gerefwīċ's east side.

Now, while all of the buildings were seemingly constructed around the same time and with the same methods, they do have marked differences. The archive is essentially an enormous block and features no windows. Perhaps this is to prevent wind or excess sunlight from interfering with the delicate parchment inside. The overall effect is that of a vault, and indeed was it closed to me today, much to my disappointment.

The town hall appears far more welcoming, being a wide building with a triad of domed rooftops. It has many windows, though they are placed too high to see in through. Either the floor is raised inside and they can be used to view the outside, or they are solely present to permit natural light. This place, too, was closed to me, though I could see the hints of torchlight inside. The priests' tracks led to this doorway, and I do not believe they had left at that point in time.

The barracks, on the other hand, had a fair few watchmen gossiping in its doorway. Their headquarters are a marvel of defensive design, albeit small; it is no castle, but a solitary four storey keep might describe it better. The walls are sheer, with arrow slits systematically located along where the spiral staircase runs within. The large wooden door has a retractable steel portcullis, and above that are holes which defenders could utilise for projectiles or other deadly traps. The roof is accessible and lined with parapets, commanding what must be a spectacular view of the relatively flat settlement. Amidst the barracks' mightiness, the guards seemed most inadequate, like a child wearing his father's war gear; I doubt that they could defend it properly were there ever truly a need to do so.

So it seemed the tasks planned for today had been cut two-fold, and I was left with an hour or so before sunset. The town hall was casting a looming shadow over a majority of the courtyard, its three rounded peaks well defined on the mud.

Another intriguing thing is that these structures definitely seemed to be of the same origin and vintage as the mausoleum I now occupy. When I can access the Stilneshire Books, I may find that they do, in fact, have records regarding the very beginnings of the settlement. Therein may be the answers I seek.

I decided to trudge back to The Old Boar and check on Felicia in the attached stables. She seemed to be well kept, but appeared happy to see me nonetheless, so I sat with her for a while. However, I soon heard the deep rumble of not-so-distant thunder overhead, and my brave steed slunk back to the recesses of her pen and lay down. I took this as my cue to leave her be and settle in for the night.

As I left the stables, I could already feel the first droplets of rain. The streets had rapidly emptied of people, and the sunset was accompanied by inky stormclouds, bringing about a frighteningly abrupt gloom. I hastened into The Old Boar and almost slipped on the way in. The ground outside was already becoming slick.

Inside, Alton once again manned the bar. He seemed to relax as I greeted him.

"If you hadn't sauntered through that door just then, Sir, I daresay I'd have sent the lad out to search for you!" Bayldon, sat at his side and wearing a heavy cloak, was visibly relieved. A fair response too; for even as the young man shed the extra gear, a most tumultuous downpour began to hammer the roof as well as the western wall.

"You'd have caught your death in that, I reckon, Sir!" the barkeep said with a dramatic exhalation.

"You need not worry so much after me, Alton," I tried to reassure him. "I am quite capable of caring for myself. I have lasted this long, have I not?"

"Still, Sir," he persisted, "you're away nigh all decent hours, and while this place may be friendly as you like, there'll be plenty of villains and desperate men using the dusk to ply their trade, so to speak. And with you speaking the way you do, why they might be thinking they could get something good off of you!"

"O hush. I am not so helpless, Alton." At this, he raised an eyebrow, obviously sceptical, then dropped his cleaning rag on the bar with a sort of stubborn finality.

"Well, if you ever *do* stop feeling so young and foolhardy, Bayldon'd be happy to keep you company without a second word."

At this, Bayldon stood with a silly grin and performed a comically exaggerated bow.

"I shall protect thee from the most vicious of stray dogs and beggars, my lord," he announced, "but anything scarier than that, rest assured that I will call out for someone bigger and uglier!" Bayldon did arouse my sense of humour with his ridiculous display, but I must admit; from his bearing and looks, and despite his attire, he might have passed for a noble. I thanked him through stifled snorts, and Alton permissed him to retire to his quarters for the night.

For me, it was much too early to sleep. I stayed a while and talked with Alton. I asked if Bayldon was his son, and was corrected; the innkeeper explained how the boy was his son-in-law. Alton's brother, Warin, had died from a terrible fever. Bayldon's mother followed soon after, leaving him in Alton's care since he was very young. Alton had clearly raised the boy to be strong in body and mind, and I congratulated him for his efforts. Bayldon was midway through his seventeenth year now, already clearly popular among the other labourers, and was even learning literacy. I could easily see him becoming the Reeve of Stilneshire when he reaches the proper age. Alton agreed with me, and we drank to it. I had no plan to repeat last night, however, so I resolved to put the metaphorical lid on it, bid goodnight and stay in the confines of my room.

I gave another hour to copying the inscriptions on the Caillic antler. I understand that the complex shape gives it a deceptively large surface area, but this is becoming ridiculous and I must be making some mistake. Eight pieces of parchment joined, and apparently the design has not yet met back on itself. Perhaps it was crafted purely to drive some poor soul to madness. Or perhaps I am just drowsy. The sound of the rain has become hypnotic. Yes; I shall sleep now to wake early, and so have time to visit my laboratory before attending the town hall.

Sōlrest-Þridda-XII

My bid for a more productive day met with success, and I arose a little before the sun. The precipitation had concluded as I slept and clear skies promised a fair day. This time it was I who winced as I carried the table and the bow, the former over my right shoulder and the latter in the opposite hand, through The Old Boar's public area. Neither Alton nor Bayldon were present, so each knock risked an unnecessary and possibly awkward conversation. In the end I went unnoticed.

Slipping through the doorway, I found the streets to be comfortably empty and was able to make my way to the graveyard without fear. Similarly, no one was present among the headstones either, so I tarried not and made my way into the mausoleum. The inside was not as I had thus far known it, this being the first time I had seen its state immediately after heavy rain. A good portion, certainly that closest to the entrance, was untouched; deeper, I could hear the dripping and trickling of an imperfectly sealed ceiling, and some large, murky puddles had formed on sections of the floor, particularly about the corners. The gloom and the dinginess of the water made them appear deceptively deep, though in truth I reckoned the deepest at no more than an inch. The scent of damp earth and stones was almost heady. The echoes of the moving liquid resounded down the corridors, imparting the eerie sensation that the tunnels were flooding. I stayed myself to confirm that this would not be the case. Fortunately, it would seem that the floor was sealed just as imperfectly as the ceiling was and excess was being drained away at an acceptable pace.

I splashed through the puddles (much more loudly than I would have liked) and soaked my shoes and the hems of my robe until I finally reconvened with the unliving Blōþisōdaz family. I relieved myself of my burdens and sat out of the way, willing Rēd and Ermuna to take their gifts.

It was fascinating to see, really. The un-dead can show a surprising amount of agency in their actions if they were well practiced in life. Many years ago I experimented with having a skeletal weaponsmith forge me a hunting knife to replace the one I had lost, and it turned out to be fine work indeed, being the one I still use today. This case was similarly impressive; Rēd took the longbow from the table, hooking it between his legs and expertly bending it against himself, bringing the end of the string up to the limb and readying the weapon. As it turned out, Rēdawulf had no problem at all in drawing back the string. He was evidently an archer of significant veterency in life.

Ermuna's challenge was a little more abstract, and I initially thought I would need to take some part in it myself, but a mere nudge of intention was the only requirement. She kneeled, put the little table over her raised knee, and forced the top free from its stand. After discarding the unneeded pieces, the warrioress walked over to her own sarcophagus and retrieved the shield boss from within, dented but stainless, still shining. As she manipulated it in her bony hands, I realised that the boss had a handle set into its recess underneath. It would seem that Ermuna would have to make modifications to her would-be shield. I left her with that task while I focused on my own.

I had some time before dawn was upon me, and felt a need to increase my security. Everything must be in place before the full moon. To that end, I considered that, using the stave, it would be possible to raise two new servants before attending my appointment. Rēd placed down his bow (seemingly with great reluctance, if only in my imagination) and worked with Haþu to shift a couple of the sarcophagi with inscriptions of Hildirīks and Helparīks. I levered the lids from them both and found that they were in quite good shape, certainly better than reasonable considering their age. The two wore mostly rusted chain coats and the last scraps of some rotten leather. They were buried with spears whose shafts had miraculously, but barely, survived. The keen-edged spearheads still glinted with the promise of a deadly skewering, but the poles may break on their first use, if it comes to that; and I hope that it does not. If the decayed wood fails them, they might use the spearheads as lethal daggers. My fascination with this family has led me to be more observant than I would usually be otherwise, but with these two individuals I found nothing overly intriguing. Their bodies were laid very straight as if at attention, though decay had caused their jaws to fall open in the perpetual scream of the forgotten dead.

Sensing no magical anomalies (another phenomenon I shall meticulously feel for), I first angled the conduit staff over Hildirīks and allowed the manna to flow. I have established a technique with this new tool and it made the process feel truly effortless. I found myself able to transfer the terminus over to Helparīks' sarcophagus and began anew even before Hildirīks had set his skeletal feet on the ground! Before long, both had marched over to the others and taken their places on the flanks. The stance they took, however, was strange; they held the spears high and rigid (even moreso than the stiff rigidity of the un-dead), more like banners than weapons. Perhaps they *were* standard-bearers, and the fabric for the flags had disintegrated. Or perhaps they had been removed before their carriers were interred so as to preserve them. Either way, such a pity. I would like to have seen what devices they might have borne in life.

I may be loitering too long here. I was given no definite hour for when my presence was required... In fact, precise time is seldom used in rural Cemparīċe at all, the population preferring to estimate by the movements of the sun. Perhaps a sundial exists in Sceoppaton, just as it does in the capital, to facilitate more consistent business.

I shall hopefully have the opportunity to return here after my summons.

Later...

Apparently I made a better impression on the shire reeve than I thought. When I met him at the doors of the town hall, he described me as a man of 'commendable character', fit for the duty of serving the jury. Imagine if Ewin had known who he was truly endorsing.

Alongside eight others I shall help to settle a minor dispute between two men (details further than this will be concealed until the trial). I might have refused in other circumstances, but all jurors remain anonymous, and a lack of knowledge regarding the event in question and the individuals involved are preconditions of the selection process. In reality, I was probably chosen due to my unfamiliarity in a shire of endemically familiar folk. And I was so hoping to begin my campaign for election as reeve in the new year! O well. Inflexibility of trades is a risk of overspecialisation, after all.

In any case, I shall note the date of the trial here as taking place on the seventeenth of this phase, giving me six free days including what remains of this one. From what I understand, the court can and does operate with less than nine jurors, so should I find myself... indisposed, I can always rescind my attendance without notice.

After bidding farewell to Reeve Falken, I turned and began to head back to the graveyard. On the way, I glanced to my right, at the archives. While I contemplated entering and attempting to find some illuminating history, I realised that I would probably need some sort of direction from the resident archivist. Finding a specifically relevant document will surely be no mean feat, especially if it is vague enough to have disappeared from public consciousness entirely. It occurred to me that I would have to be subtle and indirect in my line of questioning. It will be carefully planned so as to misdirect in case of investigation. One can never be too careful when leaving a paper trail.

Given that it was not yet midday, the streets were still quite empty, though a few women - the older wives of the farmhands and their younger daughters - were about the town, greeting each other, catching up on happenings and completing their chores. Accompanying them, too, were the boys too young to join their fathers and older brothers; the ones grown enough to care seemed most embarrassed by the whole arrangement, but were snapped at by impatient mothers and sisters until silent. Such divisions are not the case throughout Pænvicta: In Caill, women hold a religious significance and tend to be trained in those practices; in Iliban, they hold professions just as the men do, and are considered equals in society; and within the walls of the Arx Turrium, even a young boy holds authority over any woman he might encounter, and upon reaching adulthood may take as many subservient wives as he pleases, enabled by the multitudes that are captured and enslaved by the Ultōrēs.

In Sūþeard, the women do not seem so miserable as in the lattermost case. The society at large appears to mimic the royalty, in a way. While the king is undisputed in his rule, his chosen queen in past cases has had important roles in family dealings, social functions and diplomacy. In short, the women here tend towards running the households and definitely hold their own power. Indeed, many in Cempariċe fear that the near future may hold uncertainty. The king has not yet taken a queen and some reckon the solitary rulership to be impossibly strenuous, especially as Ricbert seems adamant to avoid delegation whenever possible. He has never been called incompetent, but he seems old beyond his years, and his subjects are concerned about his lack of an heir, and what that could mean if he passes. If Ricbert possesses any relatives valid for succession, they are certainly well hidden from both the public and the court. I myself am quite detached from these issues; this comes from the luxury of nomadism. I have travelled in order to eschew political turmoil before and would readily do so again, but the prospect of such excitement here seems far, far away.

So it seemed the meagre remnants of my day had been unknowingly squandered once again thanks to the good people of the Gerefwīċ Hundred. Anyone might think I had important work to do! Realising a return to the graveyard would be much too public and prone to observation, I briefly dropped by the stables to see Felicia before sulking my way back to The Old Boar. I do not know why I was especially drawn there. It could be that a hidden part of me sought Alton's company, for I found myself cheered a little by his smile and wave as I crossed the inn's threshold.

"Afternoon, Sir," he greeted me warmly. "I wasn't expecting you till later, I'll admit, but I am glad you're here!"

"Why is that, Alton? Do you not get enough of my coin already?"

"Not nearly enough! You could have awoken the dead with the racket you made this morning!" We both laughed, but probably for slightly different reasons. I made my way to the bar and sat opposite to Alton.

"So you heard me moving about then? I apologise if I woke you," I spoke while pointing out my desired ale. Alton nodded and began to pour it as he answered.

"Nonsense, Sir!" he brushed the apology aside. "Even if you had risen before me, you'd find I don't cling to my bed so much as some. Some like Bayldon." I looked, but Bayldon was nowhere to be seen. A few women had seated themselves in one corner to take some refreshment between their tasks, but I saw no trace of the boy. Alton guessed at my confusion and informed me that he was out running errands for the reeve.

"So why *are* you glad to see me, Alton?" I asked.

"Well, I didn't want you caught out in the rain as you nearly were last night, Sir," he said, a touch of confusion in his voice. "I had thought you well travelled, Sir, truth is I'm surprised you hadn't read the sky."

The truth is, he was undeniably correct. I had been so absorbed in the day's business that I had scarcely glanced skywards. As much taken aback as he was, I strode over to the door and looked outside. Alton, even though he had probably spent the majority of his day under a roof just as I had, was without fault in his prognosis; gloomy clouds on the distant horizon were converging above Stilneshire once again, and they certainly appeared wrathful.

"Didn't believe me, Sir?" Alton called with mock hurt.

"At this moment I can barely believe *myself*, Alton. Even a blind man might have smelled the rain in the air," I sighed.

"You seem all... taken up, Sir, is something the matter?" Alton questioned, always perceptive.

"I have much on my mind, that is all. Too much for a man of my years, I fear."

My response startled me for its sudden, cutting honesty. It might have been half a century since I confided in someone, and even this small admission alleviated some of my burden. Alton seemed nonplussed, too, and was silent as I returned to my seat at the bar. Part of me wanted to excuse myself and seek the solitude of my lodging, but a recently growing concept of loneliness bade me stay.

"Mayhap I could help, Sir. Sometimes it helps just talking things over," Alton posited. It was a clumsy effort, but genuine, and did give me pause for thought. My problems are myriad but abstruse and especial. I was lost for words and my eyes began to search unbidden for a new topic of conversation, always avoiding Alton's gaze. They did, however, drift over his workings; an inventory and a long-running ledger. His script was neat and flowing, the labour of one who finds satisfaction in his literacy. The evenness and regularity of the letters was downright artistic, and it inspired an idea in me.

"Actually, Alton, there is something you might help me with. Wait here," I said, leaving him with a curious look on his face as I went to my chambers.

When I returned, I held in my hand the Caillic antler that has troubled me since I found it. At first sight of it, I would guess that Alton's face was much akin to mine when I happened upon it; his eyes grew wide with wonder at the thing's beauty and intricacy.

"My goodness Sir, that *is* a pretty thing! Where in the world did you find that?"

"On my way to Stilneshire. I almost tripped over the thing when I was just south of the Caillwall. I can see by your face that you too might have kept it," I said, pleased that it had obviously aroused his curiosity.

"Could be a lucky charm as well, Sir," he whispered as he stared at the object, then glanced up at me and added, "if you trust in such things."

"I tend not to place much faith in them. What makes you say that, anyway?"

Alton lowered his voice further, leaned in close and looked about furtively, ensuring the conversation was private.

"Well, Sir, if you were on the road I reckon you were following, there's been some ill tidings from there. Rumour has it that bandits had done away with the owners of one of the hostels up that way, and were tricking folk into sleeping there so as they could..." he became quieter still, so that his next words were nearly inaudible, "*rob and murder them, Sir.*"

He stayed close and stared, evidently waiting for an opinion on this grisly news. If my face held a fearful look, it was, once again, for different reasons than he might have guessed. I had realised too late that I should have left my route vague or fabricated. A few uncomfortable moments passed before I could answer him, and I noticed the first lashings of rain commence their rhythmic siege of the roof.

"So, did someone survive the encounter? Have the criminals been apprehended?"

"Well, that's the strangest bit, Sir," he croaked. "It was another traveller found the aftermath of their latest deed. Only, the brigands were dead too, like their luck had turned-" he briefly interrupted himself to acknowledge one of the women who had decided to brave the gradually worsening rain to get home, "-like their luck had turned, and no one can see exactly *how*."

"I would imagine robberies go badly as often as well, surely," I shrugged.

"It's true, Sir, but not so often like this. Looked as though their wicked plan was working out well enough; they'd done in three already, all quiet like, and they was about to finish the last one in the same way, only that last helpless, unarmed fellow... well, the rumours say he looks like he's slain them all dead, Sir!"

The tale must have truly disturbed Alton, inspiring the darker parts of his imagination; he was wide-eyed, pale and quaking despite the cosiness of his establishment.

"Well, these 'rumours' sound quite farfetched to me, my friend," I tried to reassure him. "I would not fret over them. Besides, has anyone found this demigod of a hero and congratulated him?" I jested, despite already suspecting what the answer might be.

"Well, seems he fell from the hurts he got in the scrap-"

"That *is* a pity-"

"-Except he'd done a fair bit of the fight short an arm and a *head*, best as they can tell."

"Oh, don't say he's talking about *that bollocks* again!" The sudden, sharp interruption jolted us both. As we turned to face the origin of the interjection, we were met with the mischievous face of Bayldon, soaked from head to foot yet barely containing his laughter. A few of the younger girls in the room giggled to each other and were met with disapproving looks from the older ones.

"Well how do *you* explain it then, you soggy smart-arsed stray?" Alton managed through flushed cheeks and a relieved sigh.

"To rights, you old clod," Bayldon began with a dismissive tone, "there's nothing to explain, because it's bollocks and that's that. All made up, the lot, and I reckon you're double the fool for swallowing it hook, line and sinker. I'd have thought a man would know better at your age!"

"Or could be you're too young and foolhardy to think there's things you don't as yet know of!" Alton shouted across the inn, but there was no venom in the words; it had become a mere playful round of banter as much as it was a debate, and the audience were very much entertained by the to-and-fro.

"So what beastie's to blame for this one then, o lore-master?"

"Mark my words, o fresh-weaned piglet," the innkeeper announced with a grandiose and ridiculous flourish, "when I say a *Sċucca* is the cause of those evil happenings, or call me dotard!"

Sċucca. I did not yet know that word as he spoke it, but I observed the varied responses it elicited from the locals: the children were visibly upset at its mention; the young adults sneered and rolled their eyes; and the elders looked down at their feet.

"Dotard!" Bayldon ejaculated with a wide grin. Alton shook his head, but his ward's retort was loosed with an air of finality that forced the argument's conclusion. The dynamic was lost on me until Bayldon made his way over and sat beside me. His impish demeanour had faded and he murmured softly, almost apologetically.

"You know talking about the *Sċucca* will upset the punters, Alton. The ones that don't believe it will call you a dolt, and the ones that do say it's bad luck to name it. You can't win."

"I know, I know..." Alton said, wiping his brow. "I just got a bit carried away is all." Noticing Bayldon was upset, he brightened up and shoved his shoulder playfully. "And don't think I need *your* bloody help to make myself look thick! Go on and get dry before you catch your death." The gesture coaxed a smile from the lad, and Alton filled tankards of ale for the three of us. Bayldon took his drink over to the meagre fire and crouched down close to it, while Alton and I sat in meditative silence for a time.

It was I who finally broke the sleepy calm that had descended on us. "I have never heard of a 'Sċucca' before. What does it mean?"

"Oh!" Alton seemed surprised at this hole in my knowledge. "Well, it's a sort of a grim omen, you see," he hesitated and contorted his face as if carefully selecting the right words, "I suppose folk in *other* places might call it a 'devil' and be right enough. But it's just stories, like as not; in a lot of the old, *old* tales they tend to be behind anything nasty and mean. Snatching little ones and the like. Scary, beastly things, shape-changers too so as they can trick folk," he shivered visibly.

"And you think such a creature responsible for the slayings you mentioned earlier?"

"Oh, I don't know really, Sir. The lad's probably right about most or all of it being a tale in itself. Mayhap I lend my ear too much to strange folk and stranger gossip."

"Well you could not get much stranger than me, my friend," I said, trying to raise his spirits. "Besides, rumours can be exaggerated, but you never know what truths may be hidden - I am certainly glad about dodging the footpads, Sċucca or no!"

"I'll drink to that, Sir!" he agreed, raising his tankard. I brought mine up to meet it with a resounding 'clack' and we both drank deeply.

"So, as to that lovely antler, Sir..."

"Ah, yes!" I blurted. I had managed to completely forget about the thing laid out on the bar directly before me.

"Well, are you looking for a buyer, Sir? I know a few folk that just might hand over a few dozen Scutes for it..." Alton picked up the antler and inspected it thoroughly, barely disguising his personal interest in its acquisition.

"It is not coin I seek, but your talent."

"Now are you sure you have the right man, Sir?" he chuckled.

"It might not be appreciated as much as it deserves here, but you have a fine writing hand, Alton. If I provided parchment, ink, and maybe a few extra Scutes beyond the rent, could I ask you to transcribe the carvings for me?"

Alton blushed at the compliment and raised his eyebrows.

"Keep your coin, Sir, if you don't mind my saying so. I'll give it a go, if you really reckon me capable!"

"I do. I am in no dire need, so do not feel too pressed. Though I *shall* say; good luck to you!" *you poor man,* I added inwardly. Alton appeared to be confused, as if feeling he was on the receiving end of an elaborate practical joke that he did not yet understand. Nevertheless, he took the Caillic antler, gave it a last admiring once-over, then finally tucked it somewhere underneath his bar.

A deep growl of thunder overhead gave me a distraction to capitalise on. I stood up before he could ask any further questions and decided to attempt a gauge of the time and to check on the weather. What I observed at the doorway did nothing to allay my concerns; the rain had progressed into a storm yet again, and I was beginning to grow concerned that the mausoleum would completely flood. I left a fair amount of my equipment - including my necromantic tomes - there, and it may be damaged should the rainfall persist. Additionally, Stilneshire had once again been plunged into a murky abyss by a shroud of thick stormclouds, and the sun's concealment meant that I could make little reasonable estimation of the hour. I noticed the fleeting wisps of mist as my voiceless curses met the outside air.

The ringing of a small, handheld brass bell caught my attention again. I turned to see Alton gathering the stranded patrons together.

"On account of the weather, everyone here is free to spend the night in this room at no charge," he announced, receiving a collective murmur of gratitude and approval. "Or, I have a few more private rooms at the ready that I'm happy to lend on credit if you haven't got coin to hand."

A few hands appeared above the group, surely more than there were available rooms.

"Now I'll not be playing favourites or raising prices, but them that want a room and have little ones will have first pick - to help us *all* get a good night's rest!" he added. It was an astute manoeuvre; the young children, boys and girls alike, were growing tired and agitated. It had become noisy and Alton was inundated, so I decided to leave covertly for the privacy of my own chambers. I overheard a remark from Alton just as I closed the door.

"Young Bayldon's room is second on the left and isn't often locked through the night, in case any of the ladies were thinking of- *OI! I was just joking!*"

I never did find out if it was one of the women or Bayldon himself that had so expertly hurled the boot.

Sōlrest-Þridda-XIII

I was vaguely aware of movement within The Old Boar in the small hours. It roused me, but not sharply enough to persuade me away from my bed, so I drifted back to sleep despite the muffled voices and footsteps. When I opened my eyes of my own accord, I collected parchment and ink vessels from my own supply and made to give them to Alton.

I opened my door to find that the inn had been all but abandoned. There was no sight nor sound of the women and children who had lodged here overnight, and I surmised that the disturbance I had noticed was the men having come to find their families now that the weather had cleared. Alton's arrangement of The Old Boar doubling as a sanctuary for stranded townsfolk must be a pre-existing one. Unsurprising that they would choose the inn over the nearby temple. While the latter does usually accept those imperilled or otherwise needful, it is often on the precondition that they are subject to endless sermons and obliged to return in the near future. Personally, I would rather take my chances in the thunderstorm.

Alton and Bayldon themselves were also absent, so I deposited the writing supplies on the bar and left. I emerged into a pleasant day, still a touch frigid from the night but with the promise of a warm, clear afternoon. Stepping out further and into the mud, there was not a single cloud to be seen on the entire horizon, nor one other person walking the miry street. My laboratory was long overdue a visit; I postponed my review as minimally as I could.

Looking into the familiar grey mouth of the mausoleum, I could see that the flooding had worsened beyond that of the previous day. At its lowest level the stone floor was, in fact, completely covered by a layer of glassy, pellucid water, reflecting the minimal light like a surface of polished marble. It was aesthetically pleasing in its own right, though discouraging in all but one extrapolation; that the liquid was steady and silent because it had ceased to swell from above. From this point it could only linger or decline. I know now, of course, that it does slowly recede, but if a downpour endures yet longer I shall be forced to devise a system of drainage.

Holding out hope that the further end of the tomb, being raised a little, might have escaped the creeping pools, I decided to wordlessly project my will to the servants. Four came to me then; Rēd, Ermuna,

Helparīks and Hildirīks, wading noisily through waist-high waters. As they grew near to me, they made an even square to support Ermuna's circular shield above them. Being too close to the entrance to be comfortably private, I scrabbled into a crouching stance upon the shield and they bore me across the now churned waters. My idea originated from an illustrated representation of a Caillic coronation I had once seen. The noble Caillic king had stood proud atop the targe, borne aloft both literally and metaphorically by his mightiest warriors, himself resplendently crowned and brandishing his claymore. I, in contrast, was kneeling and tightly gripping the rim of my makeshift podium so as to avoid either concussing myself on the ceiling or losing my balance and submerging myself. It also cannot be denied that my warriors, while mighty in their own right, truly are 'all bones' as the locals might say.

Thankfully, no shameful incidents befell me on my uncomfortable but mercifully short ride, and my puppets lowered my platform to the ground dutifully. Haþu had busied herself with lighting a lantern and I was momentarily panicked when I saw that my things had vanished; I was, however, enormously satisfied when I saw that the skeletons had transferred them into Rēdawulf's sarcophagus and reaffixed the lid. It was an impressive display of autonomy, and a fine example of how effectively a distant minion can enact your will if due care is taken in its creation. Rēd himself, still dripping rainwater profusely, strode over and levered the lid free, returning to me access of the irreplaceable tomes.

"Thank you," I said, shocked with myself even as the words left my mouth. Rēd, of course, made no response.

I leaned in and hoisted the tomes from their storage, covering my nose and mouth with a sagging sleeve as the corpse dust billowed free of where it had settled. The two I took hold of were *Kýkloi Dunámeōn* and *Zich Suthina*. The former is in itself not even a particularly dangerous book to hold; it is not specific to necromancy and pertains to magic very broadly. My annotations within, however, would likely send most men to the gallows or the stake if it was discovered in their possession. The latter grimoire, for which I have a great deal of bittersweet pride, is a unique scripture and may well be the last of its kind. I shall not reveal the identity of the one from whom it was provisioned, nor can I fathom how it might have been acquired. It does, however, bring me copious joy in having the Sōlis Mūnus' seal, an instruction to the censor which reads in Arcāna simply:

'CŌNSECRĀ ŪTERE FLAMMĪS,'
or,
'SANCTIFY WITH FLAMES.'

I have copied the contents twice and ensured their safety, but I find myself far too attached to the original to leave it behind. While the cover is assembled from discoloured burial wrappings and the pages are flush with maniacal ramblings and frantic scribbles, its forbidden, enigmatic contents will soon be invaluable.

But not yet. I have waited this long; a couple of days longer means little, and I am not ashamed to admit to a sensible degree of anxiety now that the time approaches. For the moment I decided to further improve my security and raise more guardians. At this point I could barely fathom what they might defend me *from*, but I had, and still have, a consistent sense of apprehension. Perhaps things have felt too easy, too forgiving? Regardless, I shall not provide that snare a chance to spring.

Continuing to work my way along the inner crypt towards the entrance, I still had a few potential servants before reaching the first corner. I had Helpirīks and Hildirīks bring down the nearest sarcophagus. It grinded awfully from its shelf and nearly tumbled over as it landed at ground level. I looked it over with disappointment; this one was clearly in an ill state of repair for whatever reason. Perhaps the water had trickled in from above and slowly eroded the features, for I could not make out more than '----AWALD' for the name. Upon its opening, the individual interred was revealed to be equally degraded, with nary a few fragments of softened bone within. The individual's equipment, too, was corroded beyond recognition. There was naught at all to gain from this one.

I did not hesitate, having fully expected a few incidences such as this. I instead progressed immediately onto the next and had it shifted down by the same pair (they seemed to work well in unison), but they struggled and I had Rēd and Ermuna assist them. The results, at least, were fruitful. Audaward, his name was, and a true brute he must have been in life. At nearly seven feet tall, covered shoulder-to-shin with a hauberk of mail, and wearing a helm with eagle-eyes that sported a veil of chains, he would most certainly have been a dreadful sight on the battlefield. The ax by his side was appropriately fearsome too, with a haft only a foot shorter than its wielder and a bladed head as wide as my chest. All of this would stand on leather boots, mouldy and rotted, but nonetheless gargantuan enough to give our feet the comparative appearance of hooves. I could see why his remains had taken most of my retinue to extract. The weapon and armour were in incredible condition and must have been treated somehow to prevent their decay.

Needless to say I was jubilant with this latest discovery and could barely restrain myself from raising Audaward immediately; but in necromancy, as in all professions, a methodical approach is best. Given the amount of weight this creation would need to bear perpetually, I was to feed it a greater portion of manna than I did the others. A simple concept, really. A man who is far taller in stature and expends more energy through burdens will inevitably require more food, and this principle persists for energy and the un-dead. Fortunately my relic staff made this a triviality, and Audaward was standing among (and over) us within minutes.

Even taking into account the ruined sarcophagus and the extended heaving of Audaward's container, the pace was more than adequate and I was much encouraged. I rushed over to the next one, kept on the highest shelf, and decided to test the power of my new giant. In doing so, I made my first real mistake.

Audaward reached skywards, his freakish height allowing him to grasp the two closest corners of the container with his feet firmly on the floor. But just as my enthusiasm momentarily lacked restraint, so too did those bound to my will. He slid the sarcophagus too fast and uncontrolled, and it would have upended lengthways were it not for the low ceiling, which it struck heavily. I realised my error as soon as response allowed and manipulated my henchman into supporting the stony casket from underneath. It worked in that I was not utterly pulverised; but I was left with no answer prompt enough for the dislodged ceiling slab which smote my head as it fell.

When I awoke, I did so sluggish and groggy. Memories assembled themselves slowly. I looked around to find myself thoroughly soaked in blood. The still-draining water to my left had a varying carmine stain. I started as I noticed Audaward still holding the sarcophagus over me, looking almost as if he were ready to flatten me underneath it. Thankfully he had remained in that position during my bout of unconsciousness, a constant intake of energy preventing his magical bindings from tiring as would a man's muscles. A creak from my right had me glance that way. The action was too brisk and proved painful, but that was quickly forgotten and replaced with wonder. Haþu was kneeling next to me, her hands open, and from them issued the *unmistakable* hue of manna. The empty eye sockets of her skull watched intently. This was no spell of mine; in fact, it was a craft I was absolutely unfamiliar with. *Restoration*. Not my brand of false life with which I inflict my will onto the lost, but the healing of bodily trauma. Thanks to the actions of this ancient priestess, I had not died; then, I would have been beyond even her evidently profound abilities. But I live on, saved from a most ignominious end by one who would ask neither for pay nor gratitude.

While she finished her work, I remained supine; not from persistent injury, but in a state of perplexion. Seldom do I encounter novelty at my age and expertise. Yet with mages being as rare and vigilant as they are, I had never before raised one into un-death. It had never occurred to me that they might retain their skills in magical manipulation. A realm of possibilities began to consume my thoughts; even *I* would refuse to duel, say, a pyromancer or cryomancer. Such individuals are rightly respected or feared by most in whatever communities they might accommodate themselves. The idea of *owning* the aptitude of such people *by proxy* is... tantalising. Were I not currently engaged in a task of far greater importance, I might have proceeded to investigate where prominent spellcasters might have been buried. For now, I shall content myself with the control of Haþuwīgą, who has repaid my damnation with salvation.

Finally the healing spell drew to a close and my doctor stood. She and Rēd helped me to my own feet, and I found myself unstable but capable. Scarcely had I straightened my back when I was hit by the pungent malodour of my own gore. Coughing and retching, I tore the robe from my back and tossed it with repugnance into the pool. I had my assistants help me towards my pack and washed myself as best I could with water and my washcloth, then attired myself in a spare robe. I had no way to tell how much time I had lost until I could see the sky, and I decided to escape as soon as possible. Most of the water had thankfully drained away at this point, and I was able to lift the hems of my robe to keep them dry as I shuffled along the wall. On my way out, I willed Audaward to replace the sarcophagus into its original alignment for the night. He joined the others, on guard and ever watchful.

It had clearly been some hours since I entered the mausoleum when I arrived at the gate. Dusk had already set upon Stilneshire, and I could just make out the flitting shapes of bats against the sapphire sky. I stole away from the crypt and into the willows as quickly as I dared, and from there strolled casually to the lights of The Old Boar.

I had no inkling of how I appeared after my accident and so, when I noticed that the bar and seats were devoid of people, I took the opportunity to sneak into my room.

I slumped against the door and exhaled.

After a moment's steady breathing, I walked over to the beckoning looking-glass. There I inspected my head and face, as much as I could see of them. If I might venture to say so, I think Haþu may have mended a few years of weathering from my face, as well as whatever grievous hurt I was dealt by the rubble. Most impressive...

Sōlrest-Þridda-XIV

I was stirred, most unusually, by a knock at my door so restrained I could barely decide if it was real. It repeated itself, then was followed by Alton's voice, uncharacteristically timid but recognisable.

"Sir? Are you alright in there, Sir?"

"Yes, of course I am, Alton," I answered, my own voice meeker than I anticipated. "Why do you ask?"

"Begging your pardon, Sir, but you've kept to your chambers far longer than usual is all. I was starting to worry!"

"I told you not to do that over me, Alton. I am as tough as old leather, as you might say," I scratched my head. Memories from the previous day swam disorganised through my mind. It occurred to me that I could not recollect retiring to bed after writing yesterday's entry.

"How late is it, anyway?" I asked.

"Noon, last I checked, Sir."

Noon! I must have slept more than half a day! I thought to myself. Fearing the worst, I had Alton confirm the date, which he did with obvious concern. Thankfully I had not lost a full day.

I began to read my journal to recapitulate. Apparently my body had needed time to recuperate from the accident, even accounting for Haþu's intervention. Not that I am complaining; I have no misconceptions of how very fortunate I am to be breathing.

"Shall I leave you to it, Sir," Alton interjected uncomfortably, "or can I persuade you out with some food?"

It was then I realised that I was *famished*. I assented and dressed myself, making sure I remained steady enough to stay upright. Maintaining a veneer of composure (trembling more than I cared to admit) I eventually departed my quarters to meet Alton at the bar. On it I could identify a plate of ham slices and a loaf of bread, a tankard of water and, further along, a wide section of parchment. I sat down and began consuming the former while being thoroughly captivated by the latter.

"A meal and a mystery, eh? If I didn't know better, I'd say I was getting to understand you, Sir!" Alton proclaimed with triumph. I certainly could not call him wrong.

Alton had succeeded where I had failed. All of the Caillic antler's engraved designs - every swirl, coil and vague animal shape - were laid out in ink, clear as day. I took up my drinking vessel as I stood to take it in more thoroughly.

"And take a peek here, Sir," he pointed to a particular spot. "I had guessed some Caill-folk might know our runes, but who might've guessed they'd know the Arx letters?"

I started to turn the parchment around so I could see better, astounded that I had not noticed these things myself, as Alton went on.

"Now I see it there says *Leafbrym*, like the river over yonder," he waved his arm in a vague direction, "but what do you suppose this reads?"

There, irrefutable beside the river's Sūþrūna title, was a word in the clandestine script of Arcāna. A word which shook me to my very core; for it was not a word, but a name. My name. Not the one by which I am known in Stilneshire, but my *true* name, known by none that live. Or so I had thought.

Time seemed to freeze as paranoia devoured me wholly. *Someone* knew who I was. *Someone* knew I would travel the precise road that I did. *Someone*... may have been watching my entire journey. That same individual anticipated my interest in their curio, and depended on my knowledge of both scripts. *Someone* knows *who I am*.

I could feel my heart hammering and, though still on the edge of monumental panic, forcibly collected myself. The Caillic article was genuine, the intrusive characters woven into the patterns too seamlessly to be a later addition. Yet there they were, just as Alton had indicated. How had I not seen them? The object *must* be magically shifting its shape with a technique subtler than mine. These details aside, my adversary (or admirer...) is more likely to be of Caill than of any other place, and capable of both remarkable craftsmanship and powerful enchantments.

Whether they were actively stalking me or possessed the clairvoyance to foretell my path, a deadly and inescapable ambush would have been a trifle to arrange. And quite beside the point, as it occurs to me now; the most trivial way to have me slain would be to publicly identify me as a necromancer. I feel I can tentatively conclude that my prowler *does not want me dead*.

Then *what*? The riddle was maddening. Had they a desire to meet with me? Then why the games?

A hand on my shoulder brought me back to the present with a gasp. The drinking vessel fell from my hand and landed on its side, rolling as it spilled its contents. I looked up to see Alton's face, brow creased and eyes wide with concern.

"Are you alright, Sir? You look as if you've seen a ghost!"

"I am... fine, Alton," I claimed despite the clear tremor in my voice. "Just bad dreams."

"If you say so, Sir, I'll not argue... but..."

"I do speak and read Arcāna. That is what the Arx calls their language from both mouth and hand. I know not what it represents. A name, or nonsense perhaps. *I do not know.*"

I may have been more curt than I had intended and Alton deserved. He was understandably slighted.

"Right you are, Sir. I'll leave you with it, shall I?"

"No, Alton, I am sorry," I said to him as he turned to leave. Again I surprised myself. Seldom have I conversed with anyone for long enough to truly offend them. Never in memory would I have actually cared if I did so. But the sight of my... acquaintance, turning his back in dejection, had me choked with remorse. Thankfully, he turned around; but the smile he had for me was a dismayed one.

"I can tell something's bothering you, Sir. And I can tell it gets worse every day," he said sadly. "Are you in some sort of trouble? Bayldon and I, we want to help, but to do that we must know what we're to help *with*."

"I cannot tell you. You would both be far safer and far happier not knowing," I stated gently but firmly.

"I get everyone has their secrets, and trust me," he whispered with a wink. "I'm old enough to know the older they get, the more secrets they tend to keep up their sleeves." With that, Alton drew up the hem of his tunic from his waist; and there, underneath the cotton, a long, pale, disfiguring scar ran straight the full width of his midriff. It reoriented my perspective of him instantly, for he seemed a man of minimal violence; yet here was the cicatrix of an all but mortal wound.

"A sword," was all I could muster, "but whose?"

"A secret, Sir. A secret someone's life depends on, truth told," he covered his belly again. "So you'll have to excuse my discretion on the matter."

"I see," I conceded. "Then what would you have me do, knowing that my lips must remain sealed?"

"I'd have you not risk yourself for nothing, Sir. If you're into dodgy business, it isn't mine and don't mistake me," he brought himself close and whispered, "but watch your back and make sure you know the folk you're dealing with. And if you're in too deep, *then for fuck's sake, tell someone.* You could be the king's spymaster under that robe and beard, but if some bastard's fixing to put you in a ditch, then all it takes is a bit of cunning on his part or a bit of bad luck on yours, and then you're stitched up good and proper."

It was sage advice, and poignant. Once again, this 'simple' innkeeper had given me pause, and I began to ponder whether he might be concealing secrets darker even than mine.

"I propose a deal," I said, extending a hand towards him, "that before I end my tenancy at The Old Boar, we shall keep no secrets from each other. I am tired of keeping secrets."

It was, and still is, true. A consuming sense of futility has begun to envelop me. What Sōlis Mūnus and others teach about the price of necromancy being one's soul is propagandistic drivel, but the environment it has created for my ilk is all too real. I tire of this life of absolute solitude, of confiding in no one. I am so close to exacting my ambitions, but with whom shall I share my victory? Even if it makes an exile of me, I am beginning to believe it preferable to nesting in this web of lies. Raising the dead bears no spiritual cost; but I fear that such is not the case for dishonesty.

"We have a deal, I think," Alton grinned as he took my hand and shook it vigorously. "You're a queer one to be sure, but I've a fair few things to get off my chest too!"

"I look forward to it, Alton. I just hope my secrets are not enough to put you to flight. Who, then, will serve me horse piss in a tankard?"

"I don't know, mate," he managed through relieved laughter. "It's hard times and you're probably keeping me in business nowadays. What am I going to do if you skip on your bill, eh? I might have to start serving my own brew!" He took a swig of frothy ale and acted out a spluttering retch to illustrate his jest, and the tension was mercifully eased between us.

"I wonder why it has 'Leafbrym' on it, and if that *is* someone's name," Alton mused aloud.

"Could it be a map of some sort?" I asked.

"Now I did check that when I'd finished it," he scratched his head thoughtfully, "but I couldn't match it up to anything, no matter which way round I put it. Besides, what could it rightly be a map of? It's a pretty thing, but I couldn't see it making for a practical road."

"No, you are right. Just an idea," I shrugged. Truly I was at a loss, even in the knowledge that *my* name was the one branded upon the thing itself. The only conclusion at which I could arrive was that I was to go there, to the River Leafbrym... to do what? To meet with its creator? To exchange words? To return their item? To be assassinated?

It *could* be some form of extortion, a (successful) attempt to accentuate my vulnerability and an instruction to attend a parley. Should this be the case, not acquiescing could prove as ruinous as compliance.

"How far is the River Leafbrym from here?" I questioned, dragging Alton from his own workings.

"Oh! I would say, around a day's walk to reach its nearest part, then the same again to get back. Why's that?"

"I may go there to search for answers at some point..." I trailed off in thought. Leaving immediately would not be an option; I have a vital appointment to meet on the fifteenth. In fact, I thought, I really needed to draw our conversation to a close. It would be the first test of our new understanding of each other.

"Do you want Bayldon to-" Alton continued until I interrupted.

"No, no. I cannot make the journey now at any rate. And I have no desire to put Bayldon - or yourself - in any danger when I do. I promise; I shall return safely."

"What makes you think I care about that? I just want a cut of whatever treasure you're digging up!" he joked, breaking into infectious laughter.

"I doubt very much that you do," I grinned, "but if I find anything you *would* like, perhaps I shall bring to you." I caught myself. Alton was very easy to get mired in smalltalk with, and I had important preparations to make.

"Alton. You have my word, I shall let you know when I visit the river. But for now, I must be going; sleeping in has made me late enough without chattering with you all afternoon!"

"Fair enough, mate!" Alton sniffed, smiled and patted my shoulder gently. "You take care of yourself. Don't be back too late if you can help it."

"Yes, *mother*," I quipped to his great amusement as I snatched up the engraved antler and made for the exit. "But if I want to stay out late with my friends, then you cannot stop me!"

"Well, when you find someone that'll admit to being *your* friend, we'll talk!" Alton called after me as he waved.

But I *do* have friends, and they were eagerly awaiting my late arrival.

Moving to a sanctum in the daylight is generally more dangerous than I am comfortable with. Normally, I would not consider it worth the risk; few tasks are worth the increased likelihood and ensuing consequences of discovery. However, it now appeared that my hand had been forced and the final preparations for tomorrow could be delayed no longer.

I feared the worst as I joined onto the street. Someone had used a workhorse to drag a roller over the surface, making it far less treacherous. Traversing the ground was easier. Unfortunately some of the traders were preparing their stalls for tomorrow already, resulting in a multitude of busy people. They were unwanted eyes, but they were also occupied eyes, and I felt confident that I could slip beneath their gaze. There is nothing unusual about an old man visiting the graveyard. That he does not emerge until nightfall is reasonably likely to go unnoticed. To that end I made for the willows, casually but briskly, and ducked inside. Then, seeing that the partitioned area was devoid of people, I made for the mausoleum unhindered.

What I found at the entrance was less convenient. The water from the rainfall had now completely drained away to be replaced by a long, erratic trail of blood, barely perceptible at the limits of the sunlight, leading further into the crypt. Panicking, I reached for the padlock, only to find that it was not there. Had I forgotten to set it after yesterday's concussion? Or had someone picked it? The thing was not on my person where I normally kept it. I entered warily, closing the gate behind me and silently praying for it to maintain its illusion of security.

I proceeded further inside, following the still-wet blood. Here and there were small areas of higher concentrations and larger pools. At one point, when rounding a corner, a simple linen hat lay in one such puddle; once beige, now carmine from the dye it had absorbed. I had made myself ready for combat with man or beast, my hands aglow with the shimmer of manna.

As I rounded the final corner, I discovered the origin of the grim trail. A man lay there, slumped against the wall and slain. His ultimate visage was one of terror; unsurprising, given what I can extrapolate of his conclusive circumstance. I had initially worried that this was some variety of threat visited upon me by the Caillic antler's creator, but these ideas were swiftly swept away by the evidence. An arrow, expertly aimed, had pierced the man's throat, impaling his windpipe down to the feathered fletchings. He had then been dragged, as best I can tell, into the recesses of the catacombs. There, probably in order to silence the man's obstructed but nonetheless desperate wailing, Ermunahild slashed at the man's neck with her sword. A fine cut it was, too, worthy of Rēdawulf's precise warbow shot that had preceded it. Her blade had damned near decapitated the poor bastard, biting deep but ultimately snagging on the rough material of his rags. But a few exposed sinews persisted in linking his head to his shoulders, leaving it lolling at an awkward and unnatural angle.

The man was clearly drenched in gore and it was, at first, difficult to make any kind of analysis of his attire. As I inspected it more closely, however, the questions began to find themselves answers. The man's outfit was stitched together from a patchwork of linen and wool, underneath which was an emaciated frame. The teeth, visible inside his ajar mouth, ranged between thoroughly rotten and completely absent. He had aged terribly, far beyond his years. Lastly, and most importantly, was a bag of burglar's tools (also containing the padlock which I then retrieved) by his side, dragged along with him in his final moments. These factors led me to the reasoning that the man, who had been killed so cruelly by my own minions, was a simple graverobber. Likely he had predicted that some of the sarcophagi might contain valuables; certainly he had earned more than he had bargained for. A similarly brutal punishment as he would have received at the hands of the watchmen if he had been found out, but I pitied him still. After all, his represents the barest minimum of my own crimes.

It was not so disastrous, then. My servants had performed flawlessly, and if the intruder *had* managed an audible call, it had obviously not attracted any further attention. I had Helparīks take my waterskin and a rag to clear the blood from the entranceway. The unfortunate vagrant, at least, would have a burial unthinkable for his station, even if he is incorrectly named. I had Rēd and Ermuna, the man's collaborative killers, lift him into the latter's sarcophagus and replace the lid. There I hope he finds whatever peace the grave may offer.

The graverobber's death may have been unlucky and avoidable both, but today's schemes will help to prevent a repetition. *Kýkloi Dunámeōn* truly is a fantastic tome; it is ancient beyond ancient (rumoured to have been originally formulated by one of the distant isle's fabled Cyclopes whose name is long lost), a contender for the oldest existing treatise on magic, and remains a staple for every variation of spellcraft. It has been translated and reinterpreted ceaselessly for feasibly over a millennium. I designate it as I do for respect of its timeless origins, but most understand its title as '*Circles of Power*'.

As mentioned, *Circles of Power* is more concerned with the fundamentals of basal manna manipulation than it is with the end products. To make a simplified comparison; if it were a guide to metalworking, it would involve exclusively ore locating and mining techniques. In this way it remains universal and wholly endemic to magical practices. In summary, the text teaches how manna flows and how to alter that with greatest efficiency. These methods include, but are not limited to, the eponymous 'Circles'. They are what some of the uninitiated might mistake for a language or ignorantly interpret as 'demonic', but conversely they are more accurately akin to machines. The marks vary in form according to purpose and are too numerous to list here, but I shall be making use of one particular sigil known as the 'Sapping Circle', or sometimes 'Fear Aura'. The basis is simply to draw manna from a wide area and focus it into a central point.

Although this is a necessary skill of all mages unaided, the use of a sapping circle is the difference between a city allowing floodwater to drain away of its own accord and the introduction of an intricate sewerage system. What the energy is used for, and how, is dependent on your preferable craft; I would venture that, with my own personal modifications, it is with necromancy that these devices find their greatest use, as I shall demonstrate.

I began to draw a simple circle upon the ground. As always, the physical presence of the chalk is technically optional; however, given the intricacy in some of the forms, I would recommend the use of a visual medium, at least until the manna flow is fully actuated. I myself still made use of the chalk in this instance.

After the primary circle was done, equalling approximately my full length if I were lying prone, I began to add the tertiary devices. These took the form of multiple instances of converging pairs of lines, about the size of a hand, pointing inwards and separated by a finger's width. These consisted of two concentric circles, one inside and one outside of the primary band. Functionally, these serve to channel energy from the surroundings into the inner section, then to the centre (and whomever or whatever occupies that space); the partitioning primary circle serves as a dam, preventing a catastrophic and uncontrollable manna overflow.

These markings, in concert, form a basic sapping circle. Its flow can be stifled or spurred by the operator, and one who stands within the nucleus will be the recipient of any and all power gathered. Of course, the surroundings may suffer if the flow is too aggressive; as the energy is drawn from a greater area, the regularly visible effects of a powerful spell will be even more so. Plants and animals are likely to suffer in a wide tract around the event. Conscious, sentient creatures will find the sensation of this phenomenon repulsive, the slow ebb of life-force being lost to an unseen vampiric presence, and it will manifest itself to them as *dread* (hence the device's alternative title of 'Fear Aura'). All but the most disciplined, or magically capable, will consider it intolerable for reasons beyond their understanding and take flight. Thereby do I hope to avoid further intruders; perhaps the instinct of a 'haunted' crypt will be enough to dissuade any chancers.

So, the sapping circle was formed; the next stage was to improve it with my own additions. *Kýkloi Dunámeōn* is ubiquitous not solely for its instructions in basic manna manipulation, but also for its tutorials in more advanced and specialised formations. Following its guidance, one can design the unique, personalised schematics that will serve them best. An addition I have made excellent use of on many occasions is a method of dispersal. This is not to say a shedding of excess manna, but the sharing of it among my minions, thus empowering them.

The un-dead, being ultimately a creation of magic, is capable of accepting and utilising a waxing energy source. Whereas so fed a magical flame might grow more intensely hot, bright and voracious, so an un-dead might grow more intensely strong, agile and skilful. The soldiers I create, given the time, push the boundaries of capability; even then, by 'overfeeding' them, I can increase their effectiveness twofold again and encourage them to superhuman, terrifying feats. Seldom have such extreme measures been necessary, but now - *especially* now - I should like them available.

The modification is, in fact, rather simple. I return to the outermost edge of the sapping circle; there I add a shape akin to the bell of a brass instrument, no larger than my outstretched hand. I illustrate as many of these devices as I have active minions (at this time six) spreading them equally about the exterior circumference like the cap of a mushroom overreaching its stem.

And so, my necromantic sapping circle was complete. Not only would it aid me in gathering the manna for any spell I might choose to perform, but it could be incited to parasitise any antagonists with arrant rapaciousness and feed that sustenance to both me and my guardians. In short, their growing fatigue would become my retinue's vigour. All that remained was for me to activate it; but therein I made a considerable error.

Occasionally, a sapping circle can prove troublesome to initiate. A variable as simplistic as a cold day, as was today, might create considerable abnormalities in the required input for its quickening. I therefore foolishly decided that I might use the relic staff to further trivialise this minor inconvenience. I positioned myself inside the circle, holding the staff close and vertically. I focussed a manna flow into the rod to act as a primer and, with all the caution of a drunken youth, I touched the terminus to the ground.

A quake shuddered through the tomb, shaking crumbs of earth and other small debris from the ceiling. At first I thought it a mere abysmal turn of fortune, but then the circle emitted a glow so bright that I was blinded by it. The myriad colours of raw manna were temporarily burned into my now tightly shut eyes. I tried to remove the staff, but it and I were seemingly locked together, and it to the circle's centre. After a few seconds I was capable of forcing them open, but the earth's angry rumbling persisted. Then, faster than I could react, my strained eyes saw a huge figure hurtling towards me. It was all I could do to shrink back weakly. The rod was promptly ripped from my grip and sent clattering down the corridor, and the quakes and lights ceased as suddenly as they had begun.

Slowly I lifted my robe's sleeve from my face, terrified of what I might find there. Perhaps an Arx Coercitor had discovered me and was lining up a fatal blow. Perhaps the Caillic antler's mysterious creator had sabotaged me and was now positioned to subject me to his will. As my vision cleared, however, I could distinguish the mighty frame of Audaward, who had knocked the troublesome rod clean from my petrified grasp. Almost certainly had he saved me from a humiliating demise for the second time. As I started into those empty, uncritical sockets, I shook my head and vowed inwardly that such an intervention would not be necessitated by conceitedness again.

The sapping circle was active and behaving normally after its initial atypicality. I only prayed now that somehow the disturbance was localised and had gone unnoticed by Gerefwīċ's people.

I crept towards the entrance to find that dusk had crept up on me again. I could hear no shouts of alarm that might have accompanied a cataclysm's aftermath. Instead, I found another consequence wrought by my incompetence; the colony of bats, which inhabited the nearby willows and sometimes the mausoleum, had been devastated. A dozen or so of their tiny bodies lay in the entranceway, emaciated and drained of all vitality. A regrettable outcome... but it did provide a touch of inspiration.

I felt it would be injudicious of me to attempt a return to The Old Boar tonight. With tomorrow being market day, it will be populous. Coming back here unseen, as I have learned, may also prove impossible on such a day. This time failure is an unthinkable outcome. I must take the only logical path and remain here, in certain discomfort, overnight.

With that in mind, I imbued a little un-life into one of the bats and sent it carrying a short epistle to Alton. It read, in Sūþrūna, simply:

'Alton,
Worry not, returning after tomorrow.'

I sealed it with my assumed mark and commanded my diminutive messenger away. It was to stealthily deliver the shred of parchment to the inside of the inn's doorway, then find a hidden place to continue its eternal rest.

Alton will likely find it all very strange, but what matter is that? I am sure he has come to expect some strangeness of me these days.

Sōlrest-Þridda-XV

Daylight streamed in, warming my bare face. Despite my back aching from lack of comforts, the sensation was pleasant and I lay still to bask for a while. It took me that long to remember where I was; then, I leapt upright faster than I thought I could manage and pointed my staff towards the light's source. My skeletons' weapons were at the ready, prepared to lunge at the very moment of my command.

When my eyes had adjusted to the brilliance, I cursed myself for a fool. The light was natural, and indeed was shining through a recently created hole in the crypt's ceiling, located above where I had been knocked unconscious by the rock. I had not noticed it yesterday due to the overcast sky and the torches being lit on my arrival. In the full glow of today's sun, however, it was painfully overt. I had Audaward lift me onto the highest ledge so I could peer through it; thankfully, it seemed to penetrate behind the hill on which the mausoleum sat and looked out at the green southern edge of the basin. Thick turf helped to conceal it from the exterior and it was not in a place that people tend to tread.

Though the temptation of having clean sunlight rather than flickering torchlight in my laboratory was near irresistible, I thought better of it and instead resealed it. I reached through to pull some of the overgrown grass over the space before lowering myself down, then allowed Audaward to push the corner of the sarcophagus into the gap. It would have to do for now. My more pressing concern was that of today's ritual, for which I have travelled long to find the most ideal place. And it is true; though setbacks have shown themselves on occasion, I can think of no other place that could provide me with such safety as this.

To preface what I shall shortly be attempting, I must contextualise it with some history:

The oldest and best kept chronicles tell of a time, commonly calibrated to be three-hundred and eighty-six years ago, when a new danger threatened to conquer Pænvicta. While many sovereignties have sought to unify and dominate this land, none were so close to success as a single entity whose name was *Velthur*. Bodiless and pitiless, the being was almost universally thought to be a demon or malicious deity, and there were many who believed him to be the world's divine reckoning.

Velthur appears to have originated from nowhere at all; in a time of relative peace, a small settlement was attacked in the south-east of the Kingdom of Sunþrardiz (now the region of Sūþeard). While blamed initially on brigands, the refugees swore to being descended upon by a horde of walking, implacable corpses. They were disbelieved as even then necromancy was little known or understood. Regardless, the forces of Sunþrardiz were marshalled to face this band of marauders. What quickly became apparent was how unbelievably *fast* this invading army could march; in the time it took to collect a meaningful resistance, six more villages were put to the sword, each with rare survivors reporting the same events. They must have moved ceaselessly, day and night, and their numbers seemed to swell with each victory.

The unknown raiders were gathering recruits just as a rolling snowball gathers mass. What started as a gang of miscreants quickly became a veritable host, but their nature was still not fully identified until they were first met in open battle. Andaswar, the King of Sunþrardiz himself, had led the army in order to make an example of criminal enterprises in his kingdom. Battle reports describe how the defenders took up a strong position on a hilltop, with good visibility and a literal uphill struggle for those that would assault them. The attackers came brazenly, in broad daylight... so no man could deny what was seen on that day.

Those that did not meet their end there recounted how the numberless hordes charged towards them in utter silence. There were no battle-cries, or even shouts of pain, when the volleys of arrows struck them; in fact, though they were unarmoured and dressed only in the simple clothes of village-folk, the projectiles seemed not to stop or even slow them. The warriors were shaken already when the attackers, having now indefatigably surmounted the difficult slope, collided with their shield-wall. They swung and stabbed with makeshift weapons - clubs, forks, scythes - and grasped with determined hands when nothing more deadly was available to them. The defenders hacked with swords and axes, severing limbs and splitting heads, but that did not faze those indifferent masses.

Waves of panic began to spread through the ranks when the first of the king's men were slain. They slumped, momentarily; then, ignoring whatever injury had dispatched them, they would become renegade and turn their weapons on their former comrades, slaying indiscriminately. Their victims, too, would join this epidemic of turncoats, and the odds of what seemed like a winnable confrontation soon became an unsuppressed bloodbath.

Though the field had become chaotic, the king was a seasoned commander and sensed that a rout was imminent. Knowing that the grievous casualties from such an event would leave the invaders unchecked and Sunþrardiz lost, Andaswar personally made a valiant attempt to rally his men. It is recorded, then, that the master of this invincible legion chose to show itself. Just as the king stood in his saddle, a shape coalesced before him. An indefinite shape of ephemeral light, man-sized, levitating and incorporeal, a shimmering paleness with vague suggestions of a disembodied robe and a skull beneath the hood. It was faint and insubstantial enough that many witnesses would think themselves deceived, but all denial left them when Velthur spoke.

Though none could recollect the precise words that the apparition used, its inimical, oppressive voice purveyed a message thus: that it was called Velthur; that surrender would not be met with any indulgence of mercy; that all would join its soldiery, whether as volunteer or conscript; and that they would aid it in claiming all of Pænvicta and beyond as its rightful empire. These commandments it gave to the quailing masses even as their flanks were butchered.

King Andaswar was brave, to his historic credit, even in the face of doom. He made to answer the dreadful thing, but it raised a ghostly, robed arm to him and his words caught in his throat. Before his bodyguard's own eyes, he began to writhe and contort himself in obvious agony, but unable to cry out. The sole survivor from his personal retinue claims that his liege aged decades, then centuries before him. The monarch turned weathered, wrinkled, decrepit, then to dust in the space of four breaths. The gilded mail, thus emptied, collapsed in on itself, thereby leaving a horse riderless, an army headless, and a kingdom kingless. The battle was over, and Velthur had won effortlessly. It is said that those few who survived the rout would never forget its maniacal laughter as their world crumbled around them.

Velthur continued on its path of destruction, but it was not entirely aleatory; always it tended north-west towards the mountain civilisation of Zeritmia (where now stands Arx Turrium). Why so was anyone's guess. Zeritmia was of negligable political importance, had but a small population and fielded no standing army. It kept some wealth, yes, but Velthur had so far shown no interest in such material goods. With no other organised or especially worthwhile resistance, Zeritmia pulled together a pitiful collection of its peaceful monks, as much a symbolic dissent as anything else, and from their high walls they awaited the arrival of the flood of un-death.

Velthur itself mustered its forces below them. It is said to have seemed distracted, as if taking leave of its senses, and was showing uncharacteristic caution for what would surely be its easiest engagement yet. Finally, the moment came and the frontmost ranks began their advance. The monks readied themselves to join them. All was surely lost...

Then, Velthur's ethereal body *dissipated*.

For no discernable reason, Pænvicta's ultimate adversary simply drifted away as vapour on the wind. No sooner than its shape was completely lost, the shifting mass of the un-dead were felled in unison and returned to inanimate, rotting corpses. The men and women of Zeritmia gave thanks and sacrifice to their numerous gods and made it their solemn duty to cremate the countless victims of Velthur's conquest.

Such ended what many would come to call the darkest period in Pænvicta's recent history. Though Velthur's reign in truth lasted but a few fortnights, its effects were deep and widespread. Given that the entity was soon to be recognised as some product of necromancy, the practice itself was banned and its practitioners executed. Materials relating to the skill were systematically destroyed. Wizards and mages, who had suspiciously proved just as helpless against Velthur as the worldly, would never be trusted among men again, and magic as a whole was shunned by society at large. Such is the legacy of Velthur, Baron of the Damned; Velthur the Unforgivable; Velthur, Blight of Pænvicta. Thus the chronicles make no further mention of it, preferring to forget.

Velthur may have vanished, but in the darkest corners of the most obscure taverns, its name is still spoken in hushed whispers. People ponder grimly the inevitability of its return, or the rise of another just like it. Some guess at its nature, whether it be a fiend, a master prestidigitator, or even once a simple man; and in the latter's case, what dark gods he must have bargained with to obtain his peerless abilities. Fearful folk wonder how it could be stopped if its ilk rose again, and indeed, how it was even thwarted the first time.

I believe, spurious as the claim sounds, that I can provide answers to all of the above questions *and more.* The key to Velthur's power lies within the leaves of *Zich Suthina,* for I suggest that it is nothing else but Velthur's *personal memoirs.* It is written in Ancient Zeritmian, a language now known by but a few scholars and once known only by the monks of Zeritmia itself. In that monastery extensive libraries were kept and maintained, for the monks considered it their sacred duty to preserve knowledge; but given that this tome deals quite explicitly with the secrets of un-death, it must not have been housed there. The Zeritmian monks were known to be both wise and learned, so the book's origin would surely have been deciphered and the dangerous works destroyed. Where it was hidden away and how it came into the hands of Arx Turrium's censor I cannot fathom, but these outlying issues aside, I would wager that *Zich Suthina* is genuine; that it *is* the last written words of Velthur before *he* (for yes, he was once mortal) began his massacre. I have spent significant time verifying and validating, and only after overcoming my own profuse scepticism did I deem it the most feasible conclusion.

So what secrets can *Zich Suthina* bestow? Between the pages of disjointed ravings and vitriolic tirades, a wealth of teachings and unique perspectives can be gleaned. I am under no illusion that I have but penetrated the very surface of his mastery. I found myself impeded by unwillingness to reproduce some of his depraved experiments... I shall not repeat them here.

The high degree of illicitness within the tome necessitated its translation by my own hand. I had no experience with Zeritmian, so my task was not without tedium; but for every passage of useless choler, another would provide helpful refinements to my techniques, novel applications of the art to expand my necromantic repertoire.

Even without the final pages it had proven invaluable. Within *those* lay the *real* trove. Velthur had recorded his path to immortality, the spell which granted him the incorporeal form which would be known and feared by the entirety of Pænvicta... and fortune had not only placed it upon my desk, but also given me the means to *recreate* it.

Even as I translated it, word by word, I began to feel nauseous. The section had proven beyond doubt whose manifesto I was pouring over, and while Velthur's abilities were undeniably superlative, I have no more love for a wanton slaughterer of innocents than the next man. I was simultaneously disgusted and enthralled. The lust for the ultimate secret of apotheosis was consuming, and I forwent meaningful sleep for three days while completing its rendering. Even when it was done, I was too craven to follow the instructions; Velthur was a madman who found no virtue in caution nor restraint, but my faculties were, and are I should like to think, very much intact. I bided my time to hone my control... and to trim my losses should I fail. Now I am as ready as I ever shall be.

So what does one stand to gain through this dangerous ritual? The state, as described by Velthur, is one close to godhood. The best translation I could propose for this ascended form is an *Arch-Lich* (one who has dominion over corpses), and the benefits of abandoning the flesh and its frailties are many and varied. An Arch-Lich will never die from a natural passing nor, being incorporeal, can it be harmed directly by any means physical or magical. Only through destroying its phylactery can it be undone (no doubt the fate which befell Velthur himself). Being essentially invulnerable, an Arch-Lich need not fear an overcharging of manna, for it has no body to suffer the burning and breaking of failed containment; it is therefore capable of wielding unparalleled quantities of magic, limited only by the individual's tenacity. Its indefinite form is unchecked by any obstacle, and it may immediately locate itself wheresover it chooses.

There *are* negative traits, however. One becoming an Arch-Lich abandons utterly the experience of physical sensation; pleasure, pain and touch itself will be as distant memories to them. There is also no prospect of returning to a living vessel, neither by reinhabiting their own shell nor by stealing another's. Lastly, an Arch-Lich will be forever bound to its chosen phylactery, and its relative proximity to it seems to affect the useful extent of its powers. Doubtless I shall learn more through experience just as Velthur must have. That is, if I meet success just as he did...

The theory of it, when simplified, is to bind one's force of will to an artefact. This item, entirely of the necromancer's choosing, is known as a 'phylactery' and, according to Velthur, must be at least the size of a human heart. The binding is a comparable process to raising a closely aligned un-dead, but the objective differs; one is not attempting to infuse life into the thing itself, but to use it as an anchor for a reverse projection, like reflecting oneself in a looking glass. To meet with success, the necromancer must create a self-feeding loop of manna containing all of their willpower. The eventual intention is the elimination of the need of their physical body altogether. The ordeal cannot be too hasty, Velthur notes, as one's body could quickly and agonisingly warp itself into unrecognisable, bloodied pieces in a maelstrom of pure manna.

How very reassuring.

I forced my thoughts *away* from the price of failure and set to inscribing the necessary shapes on the ground. My phylactery (which I shall obviously *not* reveal the character of) has been given its own sapping circle, albeit adapted as a receptacle for my manna projections. A multitude of chalk arrowheads indicate the energy to the phylactery. Thick lines of channelling run from my circle to its, fortifying the flow and preventing any errant pulse from causing a disruption. At the halfway point, curved paths have been added on each side of the main channel, diverging like an enormous flower before meeting once again on the phylactery's furthest end, completing the cycle.

Most importantly, and most concerning, is that only trace drops of this considerable manna investment return to me. I shall be slowly draining away, starving myself of the very energy which grants me motion and life. A few times I paused for thought at the prospect, but something occurred to me then which served to strengthen my resolve; is that not what old age inflicts upon me with each passing moment? Do I choose death within the decade? Or the chance of immortality?

I walked slowly to the mouth of the Blōþisōdaz mausoleum, taking in what might be my last few breaths of cool, refreshing night air as I gazed at the full moon. Many of the wise theorise that the sunlight reflected by the moon is imbued with an additional, mysterious energy. Many, as Velthur did, as I do now, choose to perform their most important rituals on the night of a full moon for that reason. I knew that the time was right and, steeling myself, I paced back to my audience of un-dead minions as they watched the unravelling spectacle with indifference.

My choice is made, and there can be no turning back.

...

I had thought the ritual was going well. I was *so sure*. I stood within my sapping circle and forced forth my willpower and every ounce of manna I could call upon. The shapes at my feet glowed as they worked hard to feed my gluttonous appetite for power. The patterns before me were a magnificent sight, throbbing with escalating potential. The phylactery was visibly imbued with the necessary anchorage, and I felt the undeniable draw of my spirit and self being ripped away from my body; painful, yes, but also somehow *liberating*. All seemed to be transpiring exactly as expected and, though the struggle was punishing, I was elated with the sensation of approaching success. *I could feel it*.

And then, the spell died.

It was not the worst of failures. Immediate death would have been the result there. No, *something* seems to have gone awry. All the feelings of disconnection, of displacement, were gone, and I feel as old, decrepit and *pathetic* as I ever have. The humiliation burns at me, but not nearly so much as the vacillation. I cannot reattempt it now. The ritual took *hours*, and the cursed dawn is already creeping forth. It cannot be that I have accomplished *nothing*. I could feel the process working, but where now do I stand? What should I do?

What now?

ACT II

"Sleep, but a short death; death, but a longer sleep."

- Phineas Fletcher, *Amorum*

Sōlrest-Þridda-XVI

I went over everything. I checked my geometries, then my annotations, then my translations; I can find no errors within those parameters. There was surely enough input of manna; the ritual was progressing smoothly throughout, only cutting itself short when it was nearing completion. Or perhaps it *had* concluded? Velthur's last written words in *Zich Suthina* pertain to the ritual's instruction, but end rather abruptly afterwards. What if he had failed and refined his method without writing of its amendment? What if he had succeeded, simply by merit of being a greater necromancer than I, and felt no need to record it?

Maybe that is not the case. From the rest of Velthur's writing - and certainly evident in his later lack of respect for *any* life - he held the very pronounced vice of *arrogance*. If Velthur had ascended his form, I have no doubt in my mind that he would have indulged in gloating, even if he could find only himself to listen. It is a mystery to me, I fear. I know only that he was provably successful, ultimately, and that I must be his inferior in some aspect. Velthur was the pinnacle of cruelty as an Arch-Lich; it is certainly not beyond the realms of possibility that his enchiridion is deliberately incomplete so as to selfishly guard his accolade. If that be the case then I am thwarted; a thousand times a thousand permutations on the formula are plausible, and that is working on the assumption that the one provided is not outright fabrication. Besides the point, all of this postulation is irrelevant! Yesternight was the necessary full moon, and the Ilibanese astronomical calendar indicates that there will be no further opportunity within my lifetime. I have essentially, through my own shortcomings, consigned myself to death.

My skeletal servants looked upon me with consummate neutrality as the skies opened overground in a show of pathetic fallacy. I knew it to be no more than coincidence, of course, but in my state of self-pity it was enough to evoke a reaction deep within my soul. Before I knew what was happening, my servants were fighting among each other viciously. Helparīks and Hildirīks duelled with their spears, attacking and parrying each other with frightening speed. Rēdawulf and Ermunahild were working in tandem against Audaward as they kept distance and avoided wide swings of his battle-ax, arrows and sword-blows clattering noisily but ineffectually against his mail. Haþuwīgą watched on from the side, avoided by the others and seemingly uninterested in this impromptu melee. I spectated with satisfaction, these long-dead warriors venting my wrath against one another. They were extraordinarily skilled and beholding their tireless combat was cathartic. My aching head was beginning to cool, and I thought about many things while I played audience to their mock war.

Perhaps, I considered, I had been offered an opportunity. A last chance to die with dignity, peacefully, making amends for my life of birthing nightmares unto Pænvicta. The thought had never occurred to me before; death, as I had known it, was seldom, if ever, *dignified*. Men and women die screaming from war, murder, accident, or even childbirth. They beg for their lives' continuations as they bleed outwardly or are consumed inwardly by maladies. Or, they outlast their usefulness and burden their offspring, losing sense and faculty in their twilight years. And yet, why do we not think this of kings that have ruled well and lived long? Is not every man that does right by his family and holdings deserving of as *dignified* a passing as a king is? We are born to different lives and fates, but do we not become equal in death?

My considerations drifted to those I had met recently. Reeve Ewin is an unapologetically simple man, yet has advanced to a most respectable position due alone to popularity among his peers. Although he has gained the favour of many people, he will be granted a less ceremonious funeral than the ealdorman, who has gained the favour of but one. And what of Alton, who took on an orphaned child and has foregone a family of his own creation in order to better that child's prospects? Bayldon could well attribute his already promising future to his adoptive father's efforts. I hope the lad realises the good fortune he was met with, helping to redress the unpropitious lot of his earliest years. I hope, too, that some percentage of Pænvicta feels the true loss of Alton's passing. That, now, will surely be long after mine; and I would not find complaint should I evaporate quietly and forgettably as the morning mist. Mayhap it would be the best outcome.

As I was levelled by my resignation, the fighting among the un-dead slowed and drew to a close. The rattle of bones and the clatter of arms was replaced by the soft patter of rain on grass. I had Audaward, who was as unscathed as the others despite challenging two opponents, shift the sarcophagus he had used to close the breach and lift me to the shelf. I peered through the hole, watching the showers dampen the emerald grassland and the forested hillside beyond. The late morning sun shone bright and defiant between the clouds, making each numberless raindrop glisten as it fell before me and vanished into the verdure. I was overtaken by a tranquillity of acceptance that I have never known; my life, though long, was still but a brief droplet in the history of the world, but perhaps there is no shame in that.

The arrival of a new instrument to the natural orchestra prompted my turning about. The water had already begun to seep through some parts of the crypt, and the repetition of beads tapping on stone soon transitioned into the splashes of tiny puddles. It seemed as good a cue as any to take my leave. To what end, I wonder? I have still not decided on my next move. I resolved, for now, to keep my tomes and servants safe, having the former sealed away as they were and the latter covering the hole before lurking in the shadowed corners. Some... *intuition* has prevented me from reinterring my retinue. I may later return to erase my presence here. The ritual patterns will soon be washed away in the flooding and the remaining evidence can be tucked away from whence it came.

I took one last glance at the would-be phylactery and left my station with a heavy heart. Creeping up the stairs, I scouted the graveyard for any signs of the living. Sure enough, a woman walked among the headstones. She wore a great brown deeply-hooded cloak and looked this way and that, searching, I guessed, for a particular name. I waited until she left, her task apparently fruitless. Are there any other graveyards in the area that I do not know of, meaning that she had been misdirected to this one? Certainly it is a possibility, and one I may investigate. For the moment, I escaped the crypt once she had left eyeshot and was soon enduring the rain and the slippery grass to make my descent from the hilltop. It was precarious and challenging, but manageable, and although my own cloak was hooded, I found that the sensation of the soothing rain on my scalp was helping to further counteract my headache. It was not until I reached the willows that I turned to look back and shuddered; a clear circular area of the graveyard was *blighted*. Not unmissably so, but around the base of the mausoleum's knoll could be traced a clear discolouration, a hint of reddish-brown amid the green. The ritual had clearly consumed *tremendous* power.

How could it have failed? The thought buzzed around my mind like an agitated insect trapped within a glass jar. I shook my head and turned about before leaving the cemetery, hoping only that the land would heal before it could be noticed and scrutinised.

I ducked underneath the lowest branches of the willows and headed back to The Old Boar. The street was empty but incredibly disordered. Yesterday's market had clearly been a significant event; the dirt road was more upturned than I had ever seen it and refuse littered seemingly every nook in which it could sit. Footprint-sized puddles were everywhere, and the whole scene was reminiscent of a flooded delta in miniature. I gave the mud as wide a berth as I could manage, bypassed the stables and plodded my way into the inn. It was vacant but for its owner, deeply involved in his chirography.

"What ruinous battle befell the town in my absence!" I called out to Alton, who seemed pleased to see me.

"Hark at you, back from the dead! I had assumed you trampled under the stampede, old and frail as you are!" he hollered back. I had been nostalgic for his personal brand of light-hearted mockery, and it cut through a little of my sorrowfulness.

"It seems I took my leave at about the right time," I said, taking a seat in front of him at his counter. "I can seldom bear people at all, never mind in swarms."

"Well, that's a smart stance to take, if you ask me," Alton sniffed. "One bear-person would be dangerous enough, I'd have thought!"

I stared at him blankly as he struggled to contain himself after his cringe-inducing wordplay. Finally, the pressure in his reddening face met its breaking point and he burst into a series of rapid, restrained snorts. The stupidity of it all had me - shamefully, I admit - joining him in laughter. When we calmed and he had wiped a tear from his eye, he began to pour a drink for me.

"I got your note," he commented as he filled the tankard to brimming, "and I must say, the bloke you hired must've been *real* quick. I was watching the door as he showed up, and I reckon I caught sight of his hand and that was it!"

"He did not stop for tidings?" I asked idly.

"Nope! Nor water, nor *pay*, for that matter!"

"Ah, see!" I said knowingly. "I had paid him for *two* missives; one mine, and the other a reply. I suppose he fancied twice the wage for half the effort."

"From outside the hundred, was he?"

"Yes, I would say he was from outside Stilneshire, even. A travelling merchant, so I thought."

"And *you* trusted him?" Alton raised an eyebrow is disbelief. "Well, you don't *look* like you were born yesterday, yet here you are with your Scutes pocketed..."

"*You* trusted *me*, did you not?" I shrugged. "I could have been *anyone*."

"Aye, mate," he conceded, "and when I chuck your stuff onto the midden, you'll wish you hadn't paid *me* up front, too!"

"Quite alright, Alton. I have saved a small fortune by paying you with counterfeit money, anyway."

"Oh, you thought I didn't know about that? Bayldon's too green to check his share of the earnings, mind!"

We shared a laugh and a drink.

"Where is Bayldon, anyway?" I enquired over my ale.

"He's helping the reeve get the court in shape for tomorrow. Rumour has it, an important guest will be attending, so to speak."

"An 'important guest'? Who might that be?"

"Your guess is as good as mine, mate. If Bayldon knows, he hasn't let on. All that's been told to *him*, so he says, is that he's got to help get the place spick and span, so to speak."

"How curious!" I proclaimed. "I wonder what all the fret is over! Still, I suppose I shall learn that tomorrow."

"You are... attending that then, mate?" he said, glancing nervously about the inside of his establishment.

"Is there a reason I should not?"

"Well," he began, now apparently satisfied that we were alone, "between you and me, mate, I think a fair few people will... *forget* the date. I'd hoped you'd have heard it from someone else by now..."

"A controversial trial, then?"

"Well, yes, and by no small measure neither, I might wager," Alton went on, lowering his voice despite our apparent privacy. "Word is, the temple's involved, and that's always bad news, make no mistake."

I could not help but let loose a bark of a disbelieving laugh. It was an apparently inappropriate reaction, for Alton wore an expression of utter sincerity.

"I am sorry, friend. But you must have misheard, or your source must have; the Arx's preachers *never* stand trial. Sōlis Mūnus is as good as sovereign in Cempaīĉe."

"It's what everyone's saying. *Everyone*."

It was clearly no jest of any sort, and my sense of intrigue was stoked. I had never heard of such a thing.

"Of what are they accused?" I queried. Alton put both hands flat on the table in a gesture of defeatism.

"I know as much as you do, there. Does it matter?" he sighed. "Naught'll come of it, I'm sure. No one has the bollocks to tell it straight."

"Would you?"

"No. For Bayldon's sake, not my own, mind."

"And many people have their families to consider..."

"Exactly," he conceded, slapping his hands on the surface for emphasis once more. He seemed morose and helpless, and I felt badly for him. I was struggling to gather comforting words, but Alton began to speak in the sorriest voice I have ever heard from him.

"It wasn't always like this," he began, sniffed pointedly, then continued. "Used to be, folk trusted in their ancestor's spirits to look over them in hard times. They asked for respect, and that was that. Sure, things were tough during the big split, and after it too, but it was... different."

"Different how?" I prompted, keen to explore this new and outspoken facet of Alton.

"Different because of Sōlis Mūnus, and the Arx. Folk don't know who to turn to no more. The priests bleed us with their 'holy' taxes and don't offer much back, just calls for our *obedience* and the like."

"It that so different to living beneath a king?"

"Well, yes and no, I suppose. Before the Arx things seemed more... *private*, if you get me."

I nodded in agreement and we both took another drink before he persisted.

"Past the law, the king's men were never that fussed with your lifestyle, just your *loyalty*," he pointed at an imaginary place on the table, "and taxes," he prodded another spot. "They don't even watch *over* us as the king did, for all they ask..."

"What does Arx Turrium demand that is so different?"

"*Adherence*, I suppose. *Doctrine*. It's strange to us that they feel the need to watch us *that* close, and make sure we think what *they* think. They push for our kids to learn it, too. What's meant by it all?"

"*They* might tell you," I suggested, baiting a reaction, "that it was to teach you wrong from right."

"And they, of all people, would know that! Would they?" Alton was righteously angry in a way I had never seen him before. Certainly I was glad that no patrons were present, but I was also astounded and entertained both.

"Anyone might think you did not like them, Alton."

"They're like a fat, greedy leech," he deflated a little, as if relieved to have the words pass his lips, "and I know a few good folks who'd sure as shite like to burn them off, make no mistake."

"Can you be so sure about tomorrow's verdict if some of your *good folks* are my fellow jurors?"

"I do follow," he said, raising his open hands from the table and regulating his breathing to relax himself, "but the fact is, we're angry, but we aren't stupid. The king protects *them* now, not us. Not his own. Ricbert has a lot to answer for. We came out on top in the split, the way most would reckon it. But he should've had the bollocks to say 'No!' to those pious pricks when they came to stick their beaks in."

"They would have *killed everyone*, Alton. And made *slaves* of those they did not. It has happened before."

"Happen that, I know; but at least there would've been a *fight*. Good King Ricbert's made geldings of us all, and now we're being bled, slow and easy like. There's no dignity in it whatsoever."

"So long as you retain that defiance, my friend, you are destined to throw off whatever shackles they clasp onto you. I may be dead before it happens, but so long as they remain unbroken, *no* peoples can be held to ransom indefinitely."

They were motivational words, and I believe I delivered them with conviction, but they were in truth uncertain; Arx Turrium is wealthy and powerful well beyond the means of most states. Their rise was as meteoric as it was unexpected; not even the finest political prognosticators in Iliban were able to foretell the rapidity of their ascent. Who could have known that little Zeritmia, the peaceful, secluded monastary of knowledge and enlightenment, would transform so quickly into the zealotous military juggernaut, the subduer and master of Pænvicta, that we know it as today? Not since Velthur himself has the balance of power in these lands been tilted so inordinately. The Arx could well prove to be Pænvicta's terminal conquerors.

"If you're right, mate, and I *do* hope you are," Alton answered, evidently unsold on my hopeful message, "then it had best happen soon, before the reins are passed to our sons' sons. If it's left *that* late then folk won't know that there was better, and I reckon there won't be a Cemparīċe, Sċeldlond or Sūþeard worth defending no more."

"Grim! That *these* should be my last years on this world!" I declared, banging my now empty tankard on the bar.

"Lucky. That you don't have to see it get any worse, mate," he retorted sullenly, refilling our ales. The keg dribbled and sputtered a few drops before giving out entirely.

"Could it become any worse!" I cried melodramatically. Alton guffawed and patted my shoulder over the bar.

"Always, mate. Always," he managed once his laughter had sufficiently subsided, "but we do have more ale. Let me just grab another barrel." With that, he took the empty one and carried it around the corner and out of sight, leaving me alone with my imaginings.

Or so I had thought. Bayldon, at that moment, walked into the tavern and sat ungracefully beside me. He was damp and dishevelled, but his usual playful attitude was unabated.

"Whose funeral have I stumbled in on?" was his opening gambit. I had little immediate answer for his facetiousness, but before too long I was able to reply through a weary sigh.

"Worse. Alton and I were discussing our age."

"So you've been here all day, then?"

I rolled my eyes at him, much to his amusement, but before long he seemed discouraged by my meekness.

"Sorry, Bayldon. I am presently with heavy heart and without direction," I admitted.

"Things not going your way, mate?" he grimaced sympathetically.

"Not by half."

Bayldon evidently had less experience in humouring old, disconsolate men with conversation, and I felt slightly guilty for his obvious discomfort. Thankfully, Alton chose this moment to return, and was struggling to carry a fresh keg of ale. His ward seized the opportunity to escape my gloomy aura and rushed to help his adoptive father with the burden. Together, with the fluidity of routine, they hefted it onto the counter and shunted it into its correct place.

"You two might need something stronger if you're planning on drinking yourselves to death," heckled Bayldon through steadying breaths. Alton, still flushed and heaving from his exertions, made a gesture to cuff him on the side of his head (in mock only; he struck nothing but air).

"Have some respect, you little gobshite," Alton followed up his feinted blow. "Our aged friend here's on tomorrow's jury."

Bayldon whistled a descending note of condolence. Reassuring it was *not*, but the lad went on heedlessly.

"So you're sticking it out here, then? We can bring food and drink to your door if you want to stay low."

"I have not yet decided what to do," I clarified while flashing Alton a dirty look, "but I should like my role to remain as confidential as it can be."

"Begging your pardon, mate," apologised Alton, "but I can promise it won't go further than the three of us." He placed his hand over his heart and Bayldon nodded in agreement. Decades of distrust from a clandestine existence fought with a desire for personable connection, but recalling recent events, suspicion gave way to apathy. I made two decisions in that moment: firstly, that I would mindfully permit myself the simple, gratifying sensation of trusting the two men before me, for good or ill; and secondly, that I would use any presented opportunity to personally condemn a priest of Sōlis Mūnus, regardless of the improbability of any supporting verdict, or of any true consequence for the guilty... or, indeed, for myself. It seems that my conscience has concluded that the *least* I could accomplish with my remaining time is with honesty, now that I have scant to lose. I had sought to maybe right some of Pænvicta's wrongs, but alas; my pivotal tools have been stripped of me, and I am almost as powerless as any other man of unremarkable birth. Worse, I must carry the secrets of my ignominious life of desecrating the dead to my *own* grave. Any other course would brand me a monster to these innocent people, and they deserve better than to know that betrayal.

"Fret not, you pair. I do not doubt your word."

"Well, that's good!" Bayldon chuckled softly with relief. "I don't know what it is about you, but I always felt like it'd be a mistake to get on your bad side!"

"Yes, you are right to be careful, boy," I warned, conjuring my most sincere tone. "You might find yourself bored to death with tales both ancient and tedious."

"A fate worse than death!" Bayldon grinned.

"Well, we won't go out of our way to wake you tomorrow; if you decide to attend the court, then on your head be it, mate. But don't say we didn't warn you," addended Alton. I waved my hand dismissively to this, diffusing and redirecting the dourness of his counsel.

"What will be, will be. For now, I wish not to think of such things. If only there were some draught that might help to ease a troubled mind..." This last part I contemplated loudly and obtusely, pointedly tapping the rim of my empty tankard.

"Alright, alright!" Alton snatched the vessel away from me. "Anyone might think I was a barkeep, the way you go on!"

We rediscovered our senses of humour and set about ousting the troubles from our minds, drinking throughout the afternoon and speaking of a great many trivial things, lost now to the impenetrable fog of insobriety. However, Alton and Bayldon have once again proven my significant betters in handling 'the hard stuff', and I have been sent to bed. Like an infant! I could have sworn someone pulled the stool from underneath me! I am quite surprised by the legibility of this entry, but I have taken some water and inebriation has given way to a most vile neuralgia. I am haunted, too, by a persistent restlessness and insomnia that spites my exhaustion. Perhaps I can find something to induce sleep...

...

I have just awoken from a vision. A dream? Actually, I am not so sure. The details were vivid, precise; a stark memory whose events I can affirm, but the perspective was not my own. From whose eyes am I watching, and for what purpose does my troubled mind exemplify me so? As I shifted my quilt, something small fell to the floor, bouncing and rolling in tiny circles. I recovered it by the candlelight and found it to be a stopper; the marked one from The Westing Spear. Apparently, though I do not remember doing so, I consumed the narcotic beverage in an attempt to find slumber. It could very conceivably have caused some hallucinogenic effect.

Still; I cannot recall when last I dreamt, so as a matter of interest and posterity I shall record its substance here, just as I experienced it:

The room is dark. The old man laying in the bed does not draw the sheets over himself despite the cold, but he lies on top, still dressed in his brown travelling robe. His eyes are wide open; he is listening, alert. He hopes that whatever is going to transpire does so soon. Then, he might be able to rest.

Suddenly, there is a noise. It sounded to be from the farthest room and might have been missed by the unwary, but it was the muffled drumroll of rushing unshod feet.

These men are competent, *thinks the old man. There comes another barely audible noise from the same room.*

"Please!" *the old man can identify, then silence.*

There goes the merchant, *he supposes. The veteran deserters had planned their crimes well. They had placed their victims in descending order of likely trouble: the merchant's two mercenaries shared quarters with him and would surely be capable fighters; the hunter might be able to injure or even kill one of them in his defence; and the senile old man, probably unable to wield any kind of weapon efficiently, could be slain at their leisure.*

Conversely, their chances might have been better if the eldest was their first target. It is just this type of misconception that he capitalises on, again and again and again. It is another palpable armament he has come to rely on with his age. Underestimation. Assumption. Of the utilisation of these tools he is an incontrovertible master. The deserters' odds would have remained unfavourable should they have attacked him first, but now he could avoid personal peril and therefore possible incrimination entirely.

The old man continues to listen, this time for activity in the chamber directly beside his and going so far as to lay a grizzled ear against the wall. Timing would be paramount to success. The tiny creak of the hunter's door would have been enough, but what follows is difficult to listen to.

"No! Bastards, get away! I'll kill you!" the hunter cries, likely brandishing a knife or a seax.

"Why don't you make this easy, you little shit?" growls one of the footpads in a merciless tone. Something happens which draws mocking laughter from the others.

"He's dead slow! Soon just dead!" says one.

"Looks like this'll be an easy job after all!" chimes in another. There are further sounds of a desperate struggle, then a shriek. More laughter.

We shall see an end to that, muses the old man as he places both palms on the wall and closes his eyes in concentration.

"Oh, he wants some more, does he?" jeers a callous voice. There is another succession of thumping and shuffling. A startled yell denotes one of the men receiving a cut.

"Die! Die, damn you!" screams one of the men.

"Your... turn... coward..." rasps a morbid retort. The bravado had all but left them, but a desperate warcry shakes the timbers. Even the old man can make out the reverberation of a heavy blade cleaving the air, followed by a dull boom, then an uneasy silence.

A breath or two later cacophonous, unrestrained, terrified wailing fills the entire cottage. The men start to hammer on the door they closed behind them.

"Open the door! Open that fucking door!"

"I can't, damn you! There's people on the other side!"

"What do you mean, what people?"

Realisation dawns on them even as they struggle.

"Don't open the fucking door! Shit, what do we do?"

Their panicked exchange gives way to hysterical caterwauling. It gets louder. Then it gets quieter as it is gradually overtaken by the repetitive, sickening thud, thud, thud of a dagger biting deep into flesh. It takes minutes before the helpless wailing ceases and the frantic stabbing slows to a stop.

The old man continues to listen. The next room issues the rumble of the hunter's falling body. Shuffling from the corridor indicates the merchant and his two companions returning to their chamber, and to the precise situations of their murders.

The elder allows his eyes to open and withdraws his hands back into his robes. He congratulates himself grimly, wearily, for surviving another brush with death. He wonders whether having the hunter talk to his killers was an excessive cruelty, then reprimands himself.

If only others so murdered could thus requite themselves, *he thinks as he disrobes and clambers into his bed. Wrapping himself in his sheets, he closes his eyes and sleeps soundly.*

...

Feeling disorientated, I quietly unlocked my door and crept through the tavern towards the exit, only to find Alton and Bayldon snoozing in the chairs, snoring and drooling profusely. The indignity of it was hilarious and it took a strong will not to lose my composure, but in the end I was in two minds whether to wake them or leave them undisturbed. I resolved to choose the latter option, continuing on my way out. There I found, as I looked out over the dimly moonlit dirt of the trampled road, that the night was still young. I could barely make out the flattened grass of the opposing market grounds and the occasional cloud of bats flitted overhead.

Initially I was pleased by the discovery; I had not overslept, or missed much sleep at all. The night air was brisk and refreshing. The aggregate was positively meditative; that is, until I caught sight of the waning gibbous moon, still near-full, and I felt the overwhelming sensation of *mockery* as its argentine celestial lineaments leered downwards with smug condescension. Irrational as it was, it quickly soured my tenor and sent me retreating back to my chambers.

The moon, once signifier of my salvific hours and paragon of superlative spellcraft both, has become a symbol of my rawest failures.

Sōlrest-Þridda-XVII

As today may have indeterminate ramifications for all Sūþeard, I have determined to record the events as meticulously as I am able.

My day began early, being roused in the company of mild anxiety. Curiosity and nervousness exchanged blows and I lay quietly in bed for a while, internally deliberating. Finally I arose, determined to satisfy my inquisitiveness, and prepared myself for the day. I had been instructed to arrive as soon after dawn as possible (for the early seating of the jury was considered important for maintaining anonymity; those on trial were to enter when preparations were complete), so I dressed, ate as much of a breakfast as I could stomach in my state of crapulence and packed my stationary. The reeve had informed me in passing that it was permitted for a juror to create notations as desired; seldom invoked due to the quite high illiteracy rates in Sūþeard, but by happenstance useful to myself. I drank from my waterskin and was refreshed, then I made my departure. Alton lay sprawled on the ground by the hearth, young Bayldon having fared the morning better. Seeing that I was in a hurry, he offered an apologetic look accompanied by three words, much subdued;

"Good luck, mate."

I found that outside it was a bright and mildly chilly day, but there was already a commotion under way when I left the tavern. A murmuring crowd had gathered before the courtyard of the stone structures, apparently audience to a fervid confrontation. It was not until I approached closer that I could make out the words in the angry voices, or the nature of the contraption that they argued beside (and indeed, as it transpired, over). A few clever children had perched themselves up on a slight rise between the road and the barracks to see over the heads of the taller adults, so I attempted to join them rather than excuse my way to the front of happenings. I struggled at first, but one of the older boys offered a hand and helped me up beside him, whence I watched the spectacle unfold just as they did.

The newly erected device in the centre of the courtyard was, in fact, a *gibbet*. At its fore, Reeve Ewin railed furiously at a Sōlis Mūnus representative (one of those I had seen in the march that market day, I would wager), heedless of the now rapt and steadily growing audience.

"Frāter Cato," the reeve began in a fresh tirade, "you *will* have this thing taken down *at once*. The trial hasn't happened yet, and you won't sully its like with your sick gestures."

"I am merely saving us all time, Reeve," Frāter Cato, who was dressed in a black robe, answered in the surest of tones. His was a clean Ilibanese accent, even and regulated, and hearing it here and from one so young caught me by surprise. His complexion, too, was decidedly of that region's norm, for he was light-skinned and dark-haired. The Arx was disseminating its advocates further by the season, it would seem.

"*None* shall be hanged by this judgement, *none* of the accusations are *nearly* so serious!" the reeve went on, seeming to lose further patience with every wasted word.

"The punishment for heresy is death," Cato said plainly, "and the heretic shall hang as surely as the sun sets."

"This is your last warning, Cato. Have this *thing*," Ewin gesticulated his left arm frantically in the direction of the gibbet, "taken apart and taken away right now, or I'll add its threat to the charges against your man. I *promise* you that."

I was most impressed upon by the reeve, and I saw him then in a new light. He was a completely different animal when officiating compared to when I had conversed with him personally; his authority was undeniable and his leadership impeccable.

Frāter Cato seemed to consider for a moment then, astonishingly, conceded.

"Carpenter! Remove the gallows and take them away. But..." he added with a cruel grin, "keep the posts at hand, won't you?"

"You're showing up your order, *Frāter* Cato," Ewin checked him.

"Is that so, Reeve? I do *so* hope you aren't incorrect. Because if you *were*, this would reflect poorly on yourself, *and* Stilneshire as a whole..." Cato's words trailed into inaudibility as he wandered away and towards the temple. The crowd parted hastily to allow him undelayed passage. The same carpenter from the market emerged then from behind the gibbet, looking at once terrified and ashamed.

"I'm sorry, Reeve," the carpenter's voice whined like a begging hound as he wrung his hands, "I knew it was wrong, but he offered to pay me and I was afraid to refuse, and-"

107

"Don't worry, Torr," Ewin interrupted, speaking softly to calm the groveller before him. "Just get it gone. If you do it as fast as you can and burn it after, I'll cover your expenses."

"Thank you, Reeve. Thank you!" With that, Torr the carpenter began to pull at the posts of the gibbet unceremoniously, levering joins free by use of an iron crow. The sounds of splitting timbers and nails tearing away pieces of woodwork left no doubt that the thing could never be mended or reassembled.

Reeve Ewin sighed, trundled to the administrational building's door and disappeared as the audience began to disperse. As I was leaving the perch, a fair woman caught the attention of the boy who had helped me up and they quickly became immersed in conversation.

"Why are those temple folk so mean all the time, mum?" I overheard the boy ask.

"I don't know, son. Maybe their mothers never held them as children," was her reply. I tittered under my breath as I made my way around to the side door of the town hall (a far less grandiose entrance) and slipped inside once confident that I was not watched.

The town hall's interior is remarkable for its architectural style; the stone ceiling of every room rose high in a series of groin vaults, each arch intricately carved into feathered patterns in a demonstration of matchless masonry ability. Reeve Ewin Falken was present to greet me and showed me then to the room of the judgement, which extended further sideways (I estimated eighteen yards) than it did back (about twelve yards). Here the ceiling was highest, and the elevated window slits I had seen from outside permitted a pleasant degree of natural light. They were, however, too far up to see out from, and thus could not serve as a distraction for those within or a viewing aperture for those without. The central floor was slightly raised into a podium of sorts, with tall wooden seats to the left and right, each opposed to the other. These, I correctly supposed, were for the ones that were to be audited. Along the entire back wall was a sizeable timber structure consisting of a row of nine doors, giving it a superficial resemblance to a series of segregated gaol cells. On closer inspection these were, in fact, quite ingeniously designed; each led to its own enclosed space (of six by six feet) containing a seat and a small desk. Each cubicle's door had a thin slot, like a visor, through which proceedings were observed from a position of anonymity. These openings could be covered over with hinged slats from the outside as were four of them upon my arrival. This ensured that the jurors' identities could be hidden even from each other. Another interesting feature found on each one of the doors was a protruding vertical lever, operable from inside the cubicle. When the verdict was called for, a tiny, connected iron preventer would be detached, thus allowing the arm to be rotated to the left or right and enabling the juror to indicate their favoured disputant speechlessly.

Tangential to the function of the room but nonetheless notable was the huge statue above the juror boxes. The front of an enormous eagle, talons outstretched as if frozen at the very moment of plunging itself upon some massive prey, loomed over me, its gargantuan wings spanning the full length of the room. Behind the deadly curvature of its beak, glowering, lifelike eyes were focussed on the dead centre of the podium. Once again it was a demonstration of the incredible talent for sculpture present with the Gerefwīċ basin's previous occupants. There were, however, criticisms that could be made; whether by design or mistake, the portrayed bird had been given an impressive crest of plumage atop its head. Beautifully etched from the stone, be not mistaken, but alien to any of the normally sleek, streamlined birds of prey I have seen or heard of. Its nape and mantle, too, were noticeably exaggerated and bulky, almost mane-like, such that I know no precedent for it. Strange it was that such otherwise perfect chisel-work might be marred with inaccuracy when a life model had clearly been used to capture the detail. I would very much have liked to see the artist's rendition of the raptor's fanned tail, but alas; behind the legs and the tertials was where the avian beast finally merged with the wall. Sadly, the statue was long finished but forever incomplete.

Thus was the stage set for the events of the day. The reeve handed a lantern to me and led me into one of the empty juror's cubicles (the third from the left), shutting me inside. The slat was closed and I was left alone in the glow of candlelight. I waited then for what seemed like an hour, hearing the remaining four jurors being corralled into their spaces and additional furniture being brought in and shifted about. Finally a great deal of bustling could be heard, concluding with my view into the chamber being returned. The *clunk* of nine moving slats, including my own, was the last sound to precede the opening announcements. This was my experience of the following case, the exchanged words recorded in isolation and later duplicated into this journal with supplementary description. For reasons which will soon become evident, Reeve Falken would come to beseech me for the original transcription, and it was all I could do to oblige him.

The Judgement of Frāter Rūfus and Wurt of Stilneshire:

Light streamed into the cubicle as the obstruction was removed, lighting a stream of swirling dust particles and forcing me to squint while my eyes adjusted. When I could bear to do so, I moved close to the slot and peered through to find that the chamber was surprisingly quite crowded. I counted thirteen individuals all: two were seated about the podium; two sat to my right, one of which was the reeve, with four armed Cempaŕīċe men with their backs to the wall behind them; two seats were occupied on the left and, seemingly placed in an attempt to partially mirror their opposites, three men of which two were clearly heavily armed Coercitōrēs, stood tall.

The reeve, dressed ceremonially in a blue robe for the occasion, stood then and, striking the end of a straight rod of authority against the stone floor, summoned silence and attention.

"All present shall let their names and titles be known," he announced. "I am Reeve Ewin Falken, of Stilneshire." He then gestured to the occupant of the podium to his immediate fore.

"I am called Wurt, of Stilneshire," said the man. He was in visible discomfort, and had been unable to acquire anything fancier than his labourer's garb. His physique was lean and his skin bronzed from his work in the fields, but his shaved face was pale in contrast and the stoicism in his voice was forced. He stumbled inadvertently as he reseated himself and, from that point on, his eyes scarcely quit his own feet. I could not help but shake my head; the Sōlis Mūnus priests would *eat him alive*.

The reeve pointed the staff to the one at his own left, who stood resplendent in burnished mail and an embroidered cloak.

"I am Ealdorman Heorot, of Bēagshire. The king's own," barked the man. He was tall and broad-shouldered, equal parts noble and commanding, and entirely demonstrated his military bearing. "These are my chosen men," Heorot went on, nodding in the direction of those at his back, "Snell, Īsen, Warian, and Scŭr." The men affirmed themselves sequentially as he named them, from my perspective furthest to closest. Each seemed a heroic figure in their own right, coated completely in hauberks and masked helms, and holding four foot hafted battle-axes at their sides. In them I was granted an inkling of Audaward's appearance in life, though they were not nearly of his freakish stature.

Next, as the ealdorman returned to his seat, the reeve prompted the man opposite from Wurt.

"Fräter Rūfus, of holiest Arx Turrium," he answered confidently. Despite his suggestion, the accent with which he made it was clearly local, barely more refined than Wurt's (and I could swear to the latter glancing upwards with a hurt look). In addition, his skin was as pasty as a Sūþeard salt miner's, and his hair was ginger, thick and untameable; the very antithesis of the mostly olive-toned, dark-haired and somewhat shorter men at his rear. Still, he wore the traditional attire of the *Frātrēs*, just as those that I had seen in the procession days ago; a flowing white robe, trimmed with gold thread. The peaked hood had been removed, but the steely segmented gauntlets and sabatons remained present and polished.

Ewin indicated the man seated behind and to the right of Rūfus, the one closer to my side of the chamber.

"Fräter Superior Jūstus, of holiest Arx Turrium," he answered without hesitation, his features and tongue leaving no doubt of his Arx origins. His robes were much akin to those of Rūfus, but were further adorned with aureate chains and pendants. In the face he looked older and sharper, and his head twitched about as he surveyed the chamber like a wary rat.

The man to Jūstus' left stood then, and I suppressed a gasp as he did so; for he had previously been mostly obscured by the former and difficult to see, but now he was revealed in full and I truly began to pity Wurt. The man was of high station, that much was obvious; his raiment was a full plated harness, elegantly fluted and etched with gold filigree. His cuirass was covered over with a tabard of royal purple with radiant yellow chevrons. Under his right arm he held a sallet which bore an ornate spiked crown, and his left hand rested conspicuously on the rounded pommel of a fine longsword sheathed at his side. The bevor at his neck obscured the face up to the nose, but fierce, dark eyes topped with scarred eyebrows and a closely-shaved scalp peered over the steel.

"Episcopus Urbānus, of most divine Arx Turrium," said the man, slowly and deliberately. The reverberations from the facial armour lent a metallic quality to his voice and he spoke with the barely restrained menace of his intent. But far beyond *all* of those fearsome physical aspects, the most intimidating was the man's station by which he introduced himself. At a mere *three* degrees of separation from the highest position in the Sōlis Mūnus order, *Vīvus Sānctus Apollo*, Episcopus Urbānus wielded awesome authority, likely beyond the true understanding and reckoning of all but Ealdorman Heorot. *Then* I understood why one of King Ricbert's esteemed men was personally attending. *Then* I was absolutely affrighted.

The remaining introductions passed mostly unheeded by myself, being still reeling from the prior revelation. Against the left wall was Frāter Cato, whom I had seen outside, now changed into the same garb as Rūfus. He, too, claimed to be of Arx Turrium, spurning his true birthplace of Iliban. Cato was flanked by two Coercitōrēs, the nearer being called Rēmus and the further named Lūcius. Both were sealed in the full armaments of their rank, their faces obscured by helmets and their hands occupied by murderous pollaxes.

"The judgement shall proceed," the reeve said finally, "with each man's account of the events. Who would like to speak first?"

Wurt's gaze remained at his feet, and he seemed solemn beyond all cares. Nevertheless, Rūfus wasted no time in standing and articulating his priority.

"I shall speak first, being the maltreated party."

"That has yet to be decided," Ewin chastised mildly. He looked to Wurt with something that might have been commiseration before continuing; "but stand and recount, Frāter Rūfus."

"A simple matter, I am sure. The man before you struck me, a representative of Sōlis Mūnus and his superior. I still bear the mark of his assault. Behold;" with that, Frāter Rūfus turned his face to the jurors' boxes and indicated the cheek to our right. Sure enough an ugly, swollen bruise darkened it from eye to jawline.

"What repayment should you wish for this... attack?" the reeve asked.

"It was an act of heresy, and the penalty for heresy is death."

Rūfus' answer emphasised the division in the chamber. His side stared with unmarred sincerity, barely blinking. From the right came an eruption of disapproving murmurs. Reeve Ewin tapped his staff to restore silence.

"That will be dealt with in due time," he remarked, "as will a great deal of other things. For now I shall ask my last question, if your statement is done; what do you believe caused his hitting you?"

"I know not," he answered with a casual shrug. "Perhaps he begrudged me the tithe I had come to collect."

Wurt, transformed, sprung up from his seat and pointed an accusatory finger.

"That's a damned lie, you slimy bastard!" he growled, fiery and scarlet-faced. "Tell the truth!"

Ewin tried to regain control of the situation but seemed unsure precisely of how that might be accomplished. He had not long before Rūfus, acting the very picture of innocence, made his hurt response.

"I have *not* lied, by Sōl! Pray, what falsehoods have passed my lips?"

"You've cut out the guts of it, and what else, you know *exactly* why I hit you, you cocky shit!"

"Stay yourself, Wurt. You will be allowed to say your piece, in *full*, soon," interjected the reeve.

"By all means, let us hear the heretic condemn itself," goaded Urbānus. The others from the Arx made noises of affirmation and approval. Ewin sued once again for quiet, then bade Wurt give his narrative.

"Well," he began, for the moment containing his obviously simmering rage, "that day someone rings the bell to my house. I was busy mending one of my boots and my wife was busy with the stew, so I send my boy Camden to answer..."

"What age is Camden?" interrupted the reeve.

"He's on his sixth Sōlrest, Sir."

"I see. Go on, Wurt."

"So Camden goes to see who our visitor is, most folk are friendly enough here that he does it plenty; he's a friendly boy," he added with tempered pride. "Then I remembered it was collection day, so I stood up and went to the door, boot and all. And what does I see but *this bastard*," his anger boiled over, "swipe his sword across little Camden's face!"

113

Rūfus seemed nonchalant, which only served to further fuel Wurt's discontent. Ewin was forced to comment.

"Do you not deny this happened, Frāter Rūfus?"

"I do not. I reasonably reprimanded the boy with the flat of my blade for his disrespectful greeting."

"*Reasonably*! Reasonably, indeed!" roared Wurt. "Why, I was more than 'reasonable' when I introduced my boot to *your* snide features!"

"Wurt! *Enough!*" the reeve intervened. "Camden is outside, is he not?"

Wurt took several deep breaths with his eyes closed, calming himself before nodding his confirmation.

"Snell, please fetch the child," ordered Heorot. His man tapped the butt of his ax on the ground in acknowledgement before marching from the room. A moment later he returned, leading Camden by the hand. With the ax held close to the head in his right grip and the boy's tiny paw in his left, the pairing was a dichotomy of protectivity and vulnerability.

"Don't be shy, little one. Show the boxes," assured Ewin, but the boy was timid, shrinking at the sight of Frāter Rūfus especially. Snell lowered his helmeted head to the child's ear and may have whispered something; the exchange was out of earshot, certainly for us in the boxes. But whatever was said succeeded in persuading Camden, and he allowed himself to be taken onto the podium by Heorot's man. The boy looked about so that all present might reckon his damages, drawing particular attention to the right half.

Many sounds of disgust and disbelief could be heard from the Sūþeard group and even the jurors as the extent of the boy's injuries were revealed, and for good reason. Camden might not have been recognised by his own mother, so thoroughly had his face been overtaken by contusion: his eye was lost beneath the swelling; from ear to mouth his skin had been split, perhaps as the tip of the blade nicked on its path across; and I suspect the blow would have loosened more than a few teeth, especially in one so young and fragile.

"And what did he say to earn him *that*, Rūfus?" scathed Wurt through his bruxism.

"He addressed me improperly," the priest answered unabashedly, "and so I corrected him appropriately."

"Best for you if it were a dire insult indeed. Repeat it before us, so we can be left with no doubt," Ealdorman Heorot requested in measured tones; yet even he was becoming manifestly agitated, his disciplined demeanour cracking.

"The cretin called me..." Rūfus began hesitantly.

"Tell them, Rūfus," Cato called from the back.

"He addressed me as *'Rēad'*!" he forced, as if the very syllable made him retch. "*'Rēad'*!" On this occassion the Sōlis Mūnus were the ones generating susurrations of disapproval. Camden slipped from Snell's grip and scampered from the chamber, welling up with tears as he went. Snell made to retrieve him but he was too swift, so the man returned to his post. The Sūþeard caucus looked positively baffled, convinced that they were ignorant of some deeper meaning, until Wurt himself broke the bewildered silence.

"What's Rēad to you, *Frāter Rūfus*?"

"A profanity! A foul relic! What does it matter? I feel no compulsion to dissect the viscera of that vile blasphemy for the likes of *you*!" he erupted, spitting on the chamber floor as if ridding his mouth of a foul taste.

Ealdorman Heorot erected himself and raised his voice to a startling din. The man was of a masterful bearing to say the least and, even in the relative safety of the cubicle, my heart skipped a beat.

"You *will* have your man disclose the source of his offence, Episcopus, even if the evil of it summons demons to hear it for *themselves*," was his order. Urbānus, however, was unmoved from his seat, answering with the patient neutrality of a father refusing to entertain a tantruming child.

"He will *not* say, for it opposes our rites to do so."

"His *name*. My son's crime was using the man's *name*: Rēad," said Wurt, turning now to make his appeal to those behind him. From the Sōlis Mūnus came much hand-wringing and muttered prayers.

"That is not so, wretch! Not any more!" snapped Frāter Rūfus in incontinent, frothing frustration.

"Since when, Rūfus? Since, what, last Sōlrest?" pursued Wurt sardonically. "I find it hard to think, these days, that you were once *Rēad*; a man I drank with, worked beside, played games with as children. To think, we were probably about as old as little Camden when we first knew each other, weren't we?"

"*Rēad*," said Rūfus with fresh revulsion, "is dead. His unholy, *simple* life of debauchery and toil died with him, and his like shall not taint our lives again."

"Would that his killers could be brought to justice! For the two of them stand with us now, and a few of their gang have thrown their weight in, too!" declared Wurt as he gestured first to Frāter Cato and Frāter Superior Jūstus, then waved his hand across the chamber's whole left side. He was forced to shout over the fracas that followed, but from my cubicle he could be understood well enough: "A good man was lost in Rēad! Rēad would never have struck down his friend's child! Rēad would never have shown such disrespect to the name his parents had given him!" Wurt's voice grew louder still, emboldened by his righteous harangue. "The truth of it is, *none* of you poisonous toads would have been worth *Rēad's* measure *by half*!"

At this Episcopus Urbānus was finally roused, dropping his decorated helmet and drawing his longsword with a flash of steel. He flourished it in a series of whirling strokes, quicker than perception, testing its balance before bringing it to rest over his shoulder. Ealdorman Heorot in answer unsheathed his own weapon from beneath his cloak, a *Mēċe*; it was a shorter, broader blade of the Cempariċe fashion, though no less keen. He made no gaudy show of martial prowess, but held the edge forwards and across himself in a guarded stance.

"Restrain your dogs, Reeve. *Both* of them, before I put them down myself," Urbānus threatened with impeccable surety. Wurt's courage was spent and he shrank back, inadvertently collapsing into his chair with a whimper. Urbānus' comment had Heorot ready to put him to the proverbial test. A stinging comment it must have been, to suggest that an ealdorman would be subject to a reeve's orders, and to be referred to identically to a commoner. In that moment I was unsure of who would be victorious were they to duel, but the harnesses of the Arx have been tested to be impenetrable by most weapons, and I can see no reason why an Episcopus would not be better trained even than the Ultōrēs they outrank. The armaments worn by Sōlis Mūnus are never done so solely for aesthetics' sake.

"Men, I beg you," pleaded Ewin, "let us finish the judgement *peacefully* and shun bloodshed. Allow justice to be dealt by the word, not cold iron edges."

Heorot acquiesced and sheathed his Mēċe before sitting uneasily. Urbānus retrieved his helm and lowered himself into his chair, but held his sword by the blade and rested its pommel on the ground, pointedly ready at a moment's notice.

"If that is all then the judgement, dear jurors, is a simple one," the reeve explained. "Either Frāter Rūfus of Arx Turrium was justified in striking Camden, in which case the sum of three-hundred Scūta is owed. Or, Wurt of Stilneshire was justified in enacting vengeance upon Rūfus, and as such will receive half of that sum as recompense for the latter's initial and unjust offence. May you choose your favoured man with honesty and objectivity."

"Indeed," added Jūstus with a meaningful smirk. "Choose well, for Sōl watches over us all."

And so the time for judgement had arrived, and my odium for the conduct of Sōlis Mūnus' advocates had only deepened. Frāter Rūfus, or *Rēad* as he was born, left me not only unconvinced of his moral premise, but also certain of his lack of remorse.

'Clunk!' The sound of a shifting lever. A response had been chosen.

Wurt might have picked his actions more moderately and carved a better case for himself-

'Clunk!'

-But if an assault against one of the *priests* had not occurred, would this trial have ever been organised?

'Clunk! Clunk!' The third and fourth votes had been cast.

Had the jurors been successfully cowed by the intimidations of the Arx?

'Clu-Clunk!' The fifth and sixth, simultaneously. A rising clamour begins to flood the room.

Justice clearly favours Wurt, but what of-

'Clunk!'

-Reason? What consequences could be faced by Wurt, his family... Gerefwīċ Hundred... Stilneshire... Cemp]arīċe itself, even, should Frāter Rūfus be found guilty?

'Clunk!'

All votes had been cast but mine. My hand was slick with sweat as I gripped the lever's handle: it is to my lasting chagrin that I dressed cowardice as pragmatism, turning the device to the left, wincing as I shamefully demonstrated favour for Frāter Rūfus and his band of sanctimonious warlords.

'Clunk!'

"At a vote of seven to two," Ewin called over the worsening tumult, "the jury has ruled in the favour of Wurt of Stilneshire."

As I was still reeling and questioning whether I had heard correctly, the climate in the room transcended its flashpoint. Urbānus and Heorot once again drew their swords, the Coercitōrēs brandished their polearms and the ealdorman's guards their great axes. Cato, Jūstus and Rūfus produced long, lethal daggers from the recesses of their robes. Reeve Ewin looked about himself in distress before taking a lengthy, angled seax from the horizontal belt holster at his back. Wurt was by this point hysterical with dread, gibbering tearfully and preemptively shielding himself from potential incoming blows. The ealdorman grabbed him by his shoulder and forcefully flung him backwards towards his retinue, away from the Arx men who were watching him with predatory eyes.

"*Stolidī*! Do you not know that we are above your petty, primitive notions of justice?" mocked the Frāter Superior venomously. "No Scūta will be given to this pathetic worm be it not reforged into a keen point and driven through his ribcage!"

"Sōl will damn your souls," added Urbānus, taking a purposeful stride forwards, donning his sallet and holding out his blade, "but I, *Episcopus Urbānus*, shall carve your bodies."

"The king will hear of this affront to his law, and he'll collect your heads before the twentieth! Go on your way before rash actions bring rasher consequences!" called Heorot. The chamber's occupants seemed set to engage each other in a bloody melee, both sides awaiting merely the first move.

During this standoff Jūstus spoke again, but this time he did so in some dialect of Arcāna, much too rapid for me to attempt to understand. Urbānus spoke the language in return with grace and fluidity, most unlike the slow drawl with which he voiced Sūþstefn. I could tell from anxious expressions that it was lost entirely on every Sūþeard-born man (including Rūfus), and Cato seemed to be concentrating deeply, attempting in vain to follow their conversation. They deliberated for some considerable time - or perhaps it was the tension that made it seem as such - until finally, Episcopus Urbānus sheathed his longsword. His adherents followed his example and the room slightly, imperceptibly, relaxed.

"We shall leave," said Jūstus with resignation. He went on as if making painful concessions. "No blood will be spilled today. Wurt will have his reward. May you all die warm."

And, with those last words, they nodded their heads and filed out of the room in order of descending station. Only Frāter Rūfus, trailing behind, glanced back through the exit with an ambivalent look before shutting the door. The trial was over, and Wurt had won; but beyond a collective sigh of apprehensive relief, there was suggestion of neither cheer nor celebration from anyone who remained. Only a hollow, taciturn solace.

...

The slats were once again sealed over as the jurors were released from their cubicles individually. My box was the third to be opened and the flood of light left me squinting for a moment, after which I found that only two others remained in the chamber. Ealdorman Heorot was sat hunched over and using another stool as a table for the penning of a hasty but lengthy letter, paying no heed to his surroundings. The Reeve Ewin Falken, on the other hand, intercepted me, speaking with urgency but not discourtesy.

"Might I kindly ask if you could spare a copy of your notes there?" he asked, his eyes fixed on the parchment on which I had recorded the judgement's events.

"Of course, Reeve. I would be honoured if you are able to put it to good use," I answered, "but I shall have to translate it from my shorthand first, else I am afraid it has only meaning to myself."

"Of course, of course. Thank you. Be sure not to include your name on the parchment," he sniffed and wiped his brow on the azure sleeve of the ceremonial robe, leaving dark stains from his sweat. I was suddenly consumed by another resurgence of contrition. Ewin was the only man who knew which box was mine, and that I had, at the conclusion, favoured the despicable Frāter Rūfus.

"Reeve Ewin, I-"

"I know, friend," he interrupted, stifling my confession. "Don't worry, I understand why you did it. The Arx wield fear and the threat

119

of violence as a skilful warrior would a shield and sword. Who knows? If their defeat had been total, it may have been too much insult for them to bear and leave without causing some *real* trouble. You and the other fellow might have saved us from our own stupid idealism."

"Still, that poor boy. I cannot believe I-"

"*'Don't worry,'* I said! I know your heart and all is forgiven. I am honestly surprised that not more played it as you did, but at least Wurt found justice today," he said with a reassuring smile.

"Your Stilneshire homes braver men than you realise! And braver men than I!"

"Maybe, maybe. I'd be lying if I said I wasn't a little proud," admitted the reeve as he bowed his head. At first I thought it a gesture of humility, but he had a concerned expression as he looked up and continued. "Or perhaps they lack our perspective and foresight. Time will tell, I suppose, if they acted with wisdom or foolishness..."

I could find no words of reassurance for Ewin. He was correct; whatever was to happen now, it would be out of our hands. Instead I grimaced and patted him firmly on the shoulder, making to leave.

"One more thing, friend," he caught me just as my fingers met the door's handle. "*'May you all die warm'*... what do you suppose it means?"

"I have never heard it," I said, shrugging. "It sounds almost like an amicable 'farewell' of sorts, but I scarcely believe in their capability of a graceful parting."

"Isn't that the truth?" he chortled, shaking his head. "I guess we may never know. Go on, friend. Give my regards to Bayldon and his father."

We clasped hands briefly, then I left the reeve and the ealdorman to their business. I was sure they had plenty to discuss.

The outside air was gloriously refreshing after my suffocating confinement. I was pleased to find that the clouds had cleared to reveal an unseasonably bright and warm Sōlrest sun, and Alton had set some chairs out in front of The Old Boar. I took the opportunity to sit for a while and enjoy the breeze, and for a brief moment I had the sensation that all would be well in Pænvicta. It was, sadly, a fleeting one. A great cloud moved to blanket Gerefwīċ in weird, shifting shadows, bringing with it a sudden gnawing chill and a harsher wind. I sighed deeply and entered the tavern.

Alton and Bayldon were sat either side of the bar there, and the former greeted me with a wave and the faint traces of a smile. It was only as I went to sit beside Alton's ward that I realised the lad was quite beside himself with consternation. It was a sight which deepened my own dismay to see; from what I knew of Bayldon, he was seldom disheartened by much at all. Believing that Rūfus and his band of thugs had committed some atrocity after leaving the judgement, I asked the youth sympathetically:

"What has happened, Bayldon?"

"It's nothing, I..." he began, then turned to look at me. His maudlin expression was replaced by one of recollection, and he exclaimed, "You were there, weren't you!"

"Bayldon!" Alton went to reprimand him, but I raised a hand, indicating the innkeeper to let the lad continue. He was ready to protest, but I insisted nonetheless.

"We are all friends here, Alton, are we not? Come, I want to hear his take on things. I was in the third cubicle from Wurt's end."

"I was right up against the wall, right next to the Arx men," he said, struggling through stammers and wagging his head. "They're real pieces of shit, aren't they?"

"I could not have put it better myself," I agreed, and we both shared an uneasy, awkward laugh.

"You know," Bayldon started anew, "I really thought I was going to die in that stuffy little outhouse."

"Would true fighting have broken out, we would have been trapped and at their mercy, I expect."

"It's not just that," he said, staring at a distant fixed point as if remembering something deeply troubling, "it's that Rēmus. I swear he kept looking sideways at me, trying to get a look at my face and leaning his spear-ax my way. I think he was fixing to kill me if I voted against Rēad. Rūfus, I mean..."

"So you were the other to back the Arx?" I questioned him gently.

"You judged Wurt as *guilty*?"

"I was *afraid*, Bayldon, and now I am ashamed of myself, more so than you can shame me yourself; but it was not a decision made without reason, also. To what extent did Reeve Ewin inform you of Episcopus Urbānus?"

"He said that he was an important bloke, that I should avoid him if I could, and that I should be as polite as I can if I couldn't."

"'Important' does not *begin* to describe the impact the man could have. King Ricbert *himself* might hold his tongue in the presence of the Episcopī."

"You really think so?" he squeaked through a diminished voice as he turned a sickly shade.

"I would certainly think it unwise to take him lightly."

"Maybe you're right. Done now, isn't it?" he queried (though it sounded more like a plea for comforting words). "Can we just think ourselves lucky it didn't get any worse?"

I exhaled and could not look him in the eyes. What could I say? I had as little an idea as anyone else of what events had been set in motion by that jury, only that there could now be no stopping of them. Uncertainty, inevitability and irrevocability are rarely comforting concepts.

"Even should we both have shown favour for Rūfus, the conclusion would have been beyond our revision." Even as the sentence left my mouth, the sentiment seemed unavailing. Bayldon appeared fraught still, and Alton, too, was melancholic. It was almost as if the forlorn mood of the chamber had disseminated beyond those walls and pervaded The Old Boar like a virulent pox.

"I suppose you're right," he said, resting his head on his palms and his elbows on the bar's surface. "Wouldn't have made a difference this way or that."

"Sometimes life's like that, Bayldon my lad," Alton spoke suddenly but softly. "Some things you just can't change, no matter how much you want to. What *really* matters is what you do about the things you *can* change." He took his adopted son in his arms and held him tightly. I saw that Bayldon's eyes were squeezed shut, barely visible with his face pressed into his parent's shoulder. I felt deeply touched; it was the first time I had seen Alton show all the tenderness of a loving father, unrestrained and unashamed. The innkeeper's sentiment had inadvertently struck me like a spark of lightning and given me much to consider in regards to my recent dolour.

"I'm scared, dad," I overheard Bayldon whisper. "What if that Rēmus comes to find me? He'd stick me without a second thought, I'm sure of it..." He began to sob in gratuitous heaves, dampening Alton's tunic.

"Now don't you worry, my lad!" he answered, patting Bayldon's back. "I'll keep you safe like I always have; your old man's tougher than he looks! I'd even bet our guest has a few tricks or scary friends at hand..." he added with a wink directed at myself. He was jesting, of course. I expect that, if either of them were to meet my '*acquaintances*' in person, the angst which the Arx inspired in them would be soon forgotten.

"My walking stick has certainly defeated troublesome children in their dozens," I touted, playing along. "*Dozens.*"

It was absurd enough to elicit some genuine merriment from the pair and I smiled to myself, finding repose in my provision of this minor succour. Alton and Bayldon, much restored, set themselves to changing over one of the barrels and conversed together exuberantly as they did so. I was left alone with my thoughts for a time, my mind set to wander abstract notions previously unexplored. Had my existence brought a positive effect to these men's lives, this hundred's inhabitants, or Pænvicta as a whole? Unlike Alton, and on account of my recent failure, I would likely leave no meaningful legacy. The silent question arose of whether I should destroy this journal before the end and complete my erasure. Perhaps, I mused, it could be gifted to Alton at my parting.

Parting. Had I truly chosen to stay here, to slowly approach my mortality in Stilneshire? Or, if I should travel again, would I candidly reveal my nature as I had promised? That line of imagination saw me again bludgeoned with indignity. I had already today exhibited my addiction to survival, that I prioritise it above any honour or values. It is an indomitable compulsion; throughout my life it has served me well, but now, when there is no purpose in running, it bids me '*Run.*' It aggrieves me profoundly that I might so readily abandon my compeers to save my own hide should I be truly tested. Alas, a veritable lifetime of selfish instinct is a difficult habit to counteract. Hopefully the necessity never comes.

The duo returned with a cask between them and stood it behind the counter. The moment it was secure, he moved briskly to the door.

"I'll be back in a bit," called Bayldon cheerfully, then he swept through the portal and was gone.

"Why does he hasten so, Alton?" I asked.

"He's gone to collect an order of firewood and wants to be back before dark."

"He fears murder at the hands of the Coercitor..."

"He does. I think he wants to leave, if I'm honest. Only for a little while." Alton scratched his scalp and kneaded his face with his fingers. He looked overwrought by the state of Bayldon's low spirits.

"Were you going to see the Leafbrym soon, mate?" Alton posed.

"I may do so. Why the curiosity?"

"I have a big favour to ask..." Alton began hesitantly. "Could you take the lad with you?"

"I am sorry Alton, but it is out of the question," I dismissed the suggestion outright. "I know not what I expect to find there, and it may well prove dangerous. I could not forgive myself if Bayldon were harmed. No."

Alton was disheartened, but was not without his own suasiveness.

"Let me ask you something, mate," he said with a grimace. "Would your journey be any more dangerous to the lad than staying here?"

"It could be," I contested weakly. I could sense the heading of his argument.

"*Please*. He just needs to get away for a day or two. The walk would do him good, and you can't tell me you couldn't use the company."

Alton's words once again rang true. While solitude was as much a part of my being as necromancy itself, the apprehension of treading knowingly towards potential entrapment seemed somehow eased by the presence of an extra pair of eyes that might spot pitfalls and hidden foes.

"You have convinced me. I shall accept Bayldon's accompaniment, but only if certain conditions are met," I declared, giving Alton a stern look and enabling no doubts of my sincerity. "Firstly, he must bring a horse and provisions enough for four days rather than two, lest there be complications. He should also be armed and, if at all possible, armoured."

"Well, I'd best see what I can do, then!" Alton beamed and busied himself with writing an inventory immediately. He then turned to me and added earnestly, "Thank you for this, I really do appreciate it. We'll put everything together so you can leave tomorrow."

"That is quite alright, Alton. Go! I am certain you have much to do!"

And with that the innkeeper left his post, ecstatic, darting from one room to the other on a grand exercise in scavenging. I had much to do myself, for that matter; I would ensure that Reeve Ewin could be in possession of the transcript tomorrow. To find the Leafbrym in good time, we would have to depart at daybreak. I bade Alton a good evening and asked him to say the same to Bayldon on my behalf, then departed for my lodgings.

Here I set now to translating my shorthand, then I should sleep. I shall likely require as much vigour as I can muster if I am to travel alongside a young man.

...

More dreams, more memories. Why must they trouble me so?

Gone! Gone! *The old man scrambles about frantically, moving faster than he has for at least a year. His robe's hood bobs up and down as he traverses stair and threshold, scanning shelves and loose joints in the dilapidated stone walls. The structure appears somehow simultaneously ancient beyond time and presently inhabited. Dark corners and spiral staircases connect a series of spaces vertically; the masonry is old, but the timber floors it supports are recent. A wealth of tomes seems to blanket every available surface, varying infinitely in their designations and the extent of their dust and cobweb blankets. Even with the sizeable fireplace and numerous tallow candles dotted about the place, it is a dismal setting.*

After a long, clockwise climb, the old man reaches the uppermost terminus of the staircase, panting and wheezing from his exertions. This level has in it a desk (clear of objects, unlike the rest) and a makeshift bedroll on a heap of straw. Both are, as the old man had suspected they would be, unoccupied. He kicks the bedding and pulls it apart in an embarrassing display of impotent frustration. He finally collects himself and reclines on the table's accompanying seat; a large, comfortable-looking study chair, quite out of place with its surrounding aesthetic.

For a moment, it looks as if he is on the verge of sinking into it and drifting into slumber. But then, he hammers the arm of it with a tight fist and rises, walking over to the wall. While difficult to see among the clutter, dust and debris, a square wooden board, almost the height of the man, conceals a window slit. He rips it away and discards it carelessly behind him, causing it to crash noisily into the desk, toppling it. Blindingly white light chases every last shadow from the chamber and the man pulls his hood down to shield his eyes. He then peers out, scanning the terrain for his quarry.

An ivory landscape stretches out before him, and his view of it is unmatched from this high vantage point. From a perch of nearly one-hundred and thirty feet he surveys the snowy clearing in which the tower stands, projecting outwards about half a mile from the structure at its centre. Beyond its limits a sea of tall, powder-topped trees obscure the land and hide any path there might be.

A frosty gale batters the tower and slips through the window, causing the old man to shiver. He rubs his hands together, then cups them and blows hot breath into the space. A flurry of drift heralds another gust, worse still. The man shakes his head, dismayed. A snowstorm is coming and visibility worsens with each passing moment. He withdraws a spyglass from an inside pocket of his robe and puts it to his right eye, sweeping it carefully this way and that. Then he stops, fixated by something. His hands shift uncomfortably as he attempts to modify his grip on the device, but they are pink and numbed by the cold, and he drops it. The delicate thing bounces on the sill, then tumbles over the edge and plummets. The old man curses, then hastily replaces the board over the opening before rushing down the stairs as fast as possible.

He passes through numerous levels of multifarious purpose: a library; a storeroom; a kitchen; a disused barracks; another library... but he pays them no heed, nor does he any of the grimoires nestled on shelves or strewn about over floors. He knows which one has been taken; it is the only one he would consider worth chasing with such futility.

Finally he reaches the ground floor. He pauses and slumps against the newel, trying desperately to recover himself.

It will do me no good regardless if my heart fails me, *he thinks to himself as he gasps and coughs. Under the lowest coil of steps is a cupboard, and he swings the door open to collect as many of the furs inside as he can carry, draping them over his shoulders. He covers his head and ties them about his waist until the robes underneath can scarcely be seen. His pursuit has been further forestalled by the theft of his Sōlrest cloak, but he has no time to dwell on the hurt of betrayal. Now he opens the main entrance and once again is blasted by the icy draught and bleached glare.*

The old man traverses the egress and closes the way behind him. He begins to despair, but then catches sight of what he had spied from the pinnacle. Deep tracks left in the snow by the traitor, faint and quickly fading to indefinity as fresh flakes line the impressions. They lead off in an unwavering path to the nearest treeline; a clever ploy to best avoid both exposure and capture.

The old man sees no other option than to follow the footprints. He trudges through the snow, lifting his legs high and sinking deep with each step. He realises that he has forgotten his staff, but it is too late to retrieve it; to abandon the trail now would be to lose it to the weather. Progress feels painfully hindered, yet he is driven and determined to reclaim his most prized possession. Eventually he reaches the relative cover of the forest and finds some respite from the worsening blizzard. He looks back at the tower he has left behind. It dominates the skyline undisputedly, for now. But he knows from bitter experience how easily it is lost behind the dense canopy of this unkempt woodland. Its remote, enshrouded location is part of its charm, but to wander is to invite danger.

He steels himself, turns away and continues. The tracking is a little easier now, the footfalls being more persistent without the unimpeded snowfall. He follows for a while, his hope eroding as each moment brings no sign of gaining ground. His quarry would almost certainly be moving faster than him, so his only salvation may be his target's need for pause. They were burdened, but not greatly.

Suddenly, the old man detects a change. Something additional. A new set of prints merges with his objective's. The pawprints of a dog? No, much too large; a wolf. *Further along, two more bestial pursuers join the hunt. If the fugitive is wily, they have more than enough ability to slay or dissuade the pack, but the confrontation may be enough to slow them down.*

Anything that weakens them, should it come to a struggle, *the old man thinks,* would also be very welcome. The chase is already drawing out too long, *he worries.* If it grows dark, I shall be forced to fall back and concede. *The thought brings him second wind and he increases his pace. Before long, there is another significant development.* Blood. *A few spots of it stain the snow around the bootprints. He initially wonders if one of the wolves has been injured, but there are scraps of cloth scattered about also. The red trail continues as a complement to the tracks, which have grown more erratic. A large depression in the snow signifies a fall and a struggle, and the remnant gore increases in magnitude for the remaining way; but the pursuit does not persist much longer. The contest terminates with a corpse, ragged and rendered, the surrounds melted into a vermillion sleet by the recently-hot contents.*

The old man takes in the scene without joy or particular mourning, but an element of confused sadness. The once handsome and young face had been torn free from its anchors, and here and there could be found a finger, a gnawed bone, a scrap of unidentifiable flesh. The ribcage and entrails had been fully excavated and consumed, and the limbs were wrenched into unnatural, broken positions. Indeed, there is little remaining of his former apprentice at all.

This was the source of the old man's confusion. His apprentice had been an eccentric, uncomfortable man, far from unusual for a necromancer. It had been an experiment of sorts, to seek him out and offer him sanctuary and tutoring. It was an opportunity he had never even imagined for himself, and the young man seemed enthusiastic, if initially suspicious. All told they remained in cohabitation for two years, the younger's meagre (and in truth, essentially worthless) tome collection being added to the elder's vast library, a lifetime's work in gathering forbidden knowledge. And the apprentice was given full access to study this necromantic repository, and academic aid from its collector if it was desired. Only a token monetary contribution towards living costs was asked, which came never short nor late. The older necromancer provided the paradise he himself never had.

In the first year, the young man had been friendly, courteous and eager. His drive and thirst were infectious, and it was joyful to teach him and provide answers to his burgeoning curiosities. Soon, the master began to find the different perspectives valuable in themselves, for collaboration is a nonexistent resource in necromancy. It seemed a symbiotic relationship, refreshing when compared with the usual solitude.

Then came the second year, which bore the beginning of a transition. The apprentice started to become withdrawn and reclusive, no longer seeking his master's input. They shared the tower still, but not each other's company. Eventually it came to pass that one would not see the other for days on end. They were not hateful of each other, merely disinterested. Today's events, the old man considers, are the culmination of that creeping alienation.

But why? *he asks himself, treading carefully among the giblets as he searches for his stolen property, hoping against hope that it has not been destroyed.* Perhaps a necromancer's distrust is simply too caustic to overcome, *he contemplates inwardly. He knows all too well the paranoia and psychosis that accompanies the practice. The apprentice may have feared some betrayal from his master, though to what end the old man had no guess. He would have had little or nothing to gain from slaying his apprentice, and everything to lose by exposing him.*

The once-master feels some tempered elation as he comes upon his apprentice's pack. It had been dragged a few yards away from the body, but was otherwise mostly untouched. He explores the contents and pulls out the pilfered tome. 'Zich Suthina' *reads the cover in the letters of a language long dead, a wax Arx Turrium seal demanding its incineration just underneath. Its untarnished condition is eerie, as if the predators had sensed the* wrongness *of its contents and decided it was best left well alone.*

Perhaps it was the other *thing which inspired the apprentice's perfidy.* Megalomania, *another trait inherent to many necromancers. They seek power over others, if only the dead; it is therefore unsurprising that they hold such an aspect. Maybe the apprentice, then, found his perceived subordination intolerable. He had been following the master's gradual translation of* Zich Suthina *all too closely, inquiring after every fresh leaf of painstaking work. The apprentice may have suspected that clearly visionary secrets were being withheld to maintain the state of affairs. While it was true that the old man had increasing concerns - the young one's disregard for the potential perils of following the mysterious (and clearly insane) author's instructions, for one - no such divide was ever enforced, at least intentionally. It*

129

could have been in a fit of impatience that the decision was made to steal the tome, even though its translation was incomplete and the youth had no experience of the Ancient Zeritmian in which it was written.

Yet, this mistake was evidently only the first in a string of errors impelled by rashness. From the cursory glances around the tower, it seemed as if he had taken few, if any, provisions. The robed man checks the pack again; there is nothing edible, nor any equipment for making a fire. Secondly, a season of frost is doubly dangerous for one whose primary defence is magical. There is less energy in the environment to draw from, and especially in a panicked state one's manna can feel 'stifled'. Only a cryomancer, whose craft specialises in the sapping of power to shape frozen moisture into solid barriers and impaling or striking projectiles, would be able to flourish in this arena. This student of necromancy, put simply, should have gathered as much manna within himself as possible before attempting his escape. Then, simple canines would never have gotten the better of a talented individual such as him. The master had been chiefly proud of his apprentice, once. Now he looks down at the mangled cadaver with abject disappointment before turning to follow the trail back.

The howling of a wolf drifts through the forest. At least four more join the portentous chorus, their cadences overlapping and continuous. Whether through the amplifications of echoes, the illusions of stress or simple grim truth, the pack sounds ominously near. The old man grits his teeth and readies himself, backpedalling calmly towards the remains of his late companion. His gaze flits incessantly between the gnarled trunks, ever wary.

"It seems you have been granted an opportunity for redemption, boy. Let us aspire for you to perform better this time," he grunts, the telltale chromatisms of manna beginning to emanate from his hands.

The visitants of that day haunt me still. Sleep will not return easily tonight.

Sōlrest-Þridda-XVIII

I feel no compulsion to confront my subconscious mind yet. I shall write the day's entry by candlelight instead, as awkward as it may be. I must remember to find my other inkwell come the morning. At least I had not yet unstopped it.

I awoke distempered and irritable after an intermittent, fitful night's rest. The dreams lingered on the periphery of my imagination as I was dragged into wakefulness by Alton's calling through my chamber door.

"You'll want to be up now if you're going today, mate."

"My eyes are open, Alton. I shall be but a moment," I answered, barely audible through my vocal fry. I had no indication of just how long he had been trying to rouse me, whether I was sleeping softly or soundly. I still felt as exhausted as if I had not slept at all. Nevertheless, with much complaint from my aching joints, I straightened myself and stood, dressing myself in warmer undergarments before covering them with my robe. Clothed but unsteady, I took up my walking stick and joined the others in the main room.

Alton crouched in front of the bar among a heap of saddlebags and packs, sorting some last odds and ends into each one. He seemed to be of a most cheery and helpful disposition. Bayldon sat on one of the stools, and lo! Such a sight he was that I did not initially recognise him. A helm upon his head masked about his nose and cheeks, the young eyes peering out from twin elliptical hollows. The rear of his neck was guarded by an attached aventail which draped down over a fine mail hauberk. The protective coat reached from shoulder to knee, including both sleeves. Splinted iron greaves and vambraces defended his shins and forearms respectively, and toughened leather laced boots complemented the look of a regular Sūþeard folk hero. The image would not have been complete, of course, without the straight sword at his waist, the sturdy roundshield slung at his back and the cocksure smirk on his lips.

"Well, come out with it then; how ridiculous do I look?" he blurted, becoming bashful at the stunned silence.

"Oh! I was waiting for you to introduce yourself, I had no idea it was you I was staring at!" I said with mock apology. "In truth, I believed Alton had hired a hardened mercenary for our journey!"

"Hah! Like you'd be so lucky for me to spend a fortune covering *your* sorry arses," teased Alton.

"You should know the grumpy old turd better by now, mate," Bayldon agreed. "If you think *I'm* armoured, you should see this man's purse!"

We shared a hearty laugh and I sat by them.

"To be serious for a moment, Alton; the services of a mercenary might have been less expensive than all of this wargear. It surely must have been a costly purchase. And besides that, I have seen no weaponsmiths or chain-linkers in Gerefwīċ. From whence did you obtain it?"

As I raised these questions, I noticed Bayldon turn attentively towards Alton. It seems that he was equally curious, even if he himself added nothing.

"Now, now, old fellow," Alton said, winking and tapping on his nose with his forefinger, "a man's got to have his secrets, as you well know. Could be I'll fill you in another time!"

"Fair," I admitted flatly. It would have been entirely hypocritical of me to insist otherwise, but even through the helm's mask I spied Bayldon roll his eyes and subtly sink with disappointment. He was apparently keenly aware that his adoptive father kept deep secrets from him, and I had the distinct sensation that he had pursued answers many, many times prior to my attempt. My own curiosity was further intensified, but I am nothing if not forbearing.

"All set, I think!" Alton announced after a time. He hoisted the bags over his shoulders (no mean feat of strength) and walked with us to the stables. Among the many other horses there was Felicia, who flinched initially at my approach but soon recollected my voice, and another that was to be Bayldon's horse; Feran was how he was addressed, and he was a skewbald colt of brown and white with a playful temperament. He seemed every bit Bayldon's equine match. We burdened the steeds with their tack and our supplies, then led them through the gate by their reins.

It was still twilight outside. I suspected that I had been cheated of an hour or two of my bed's comfort, but I made no cavil of it; likely it was Bayldon's preference to depart under cover of darkness for fear of watchful, antagonistic informants. The young man stepped into his stirrup and swung his leg over effortlessly.

"Easy there, blowhard!" Alton quipped sarcastically, prompting a puckish snort of derision from his young ward. Alton then approached

Felicia and I to offer his hands as a mounting block. I prepared myself for the effort, but a lingering thought was bothering me.

"Just a moment," I uttered, already walking towards The Old Boar. Once inside, I stole into my chamber, took the Caillic antler from its resting place on the bedside stand and hurried to rejoin the others, waving it at them to demonstrate the object of my delay.

"Ah!" Alton nodded with approval. "Someone might be wanting that back."

"Have you got my furs, dad? It's a bit nippy, actually," Bayldon interjected.

"Here you are, my delicate little flower," jibed Alton, taking the thick coat from his own back and passing it up to his adopted son. Bayldon removed his shield, hooking it over his saddle's horn so he could adorn himself with the substantial pelts unobstructed. When finished he replaced the shield, sliding the carrying strap about his shoulder until it rested comfortably upon his back once more. The hairy bulk added to his silhouette made him seem broader and just a touch more fierce.

I accepted Alton's aid in mounting Felicia and, then unquestionably primed, we bade him farewell and set a steady pace on our horses.

We headed east, following the undulating main road of Gerefwīċ Hundred before it began to twist into an unfavourable direction. From that point a more minor but still well-trodden dirt track provided a winding way up that edge of the basin. The path was steep and occasionally difficult, but the animals proved themselves hardy and carried us without grievance. Finally we reached the peak of the basin, concluding the most arduous segment of the journey there.

As our heads rose over the elevated circumference, we found that the sunrise had just begun proper, dyeing the sky and wispy clouds with all the colours of calendulas and golden perennials. It was an undeniably beautiful sight, and we could not help but remain a while, wrapped as we were against the chill, to appreciate it from this sublime vantage. The dawn's rosy fingers spread forth, gradually revealing the features of the awaiting landscape before us.

Cemparīċe is, when all is accounted for, a rather flat country. Its shallow hills, practically imperceptible from these heights, blanketed the topography like a vast ocean of faded green. Forests occupied much of its surface but, in this region, farmland was clearly the dominant terrain. Bayldon pointed out the fields, dividing them between which shire and hundred they belonged to and how well the Sōlrest harvest was progressing, even the ways in which the River Leafbrym interacted with each. The thorough extent of his knowledge was astounding and I found myself quite lost in the manifold names of people and places. He had studied them well, and such understanding would serve his political aspirations nicely.

Beyond the specifics of our immediate surroundings it was I who proved to be the more knowledgeable, so I returned his favour of a brief education: from where we were situated, to the south-east was King Ricbert's home of Bēagshire, and to the west, concealed by the opposing edge of the basin, was Westfæsten Hundred. Further still, the watchful county of Sǣrimshire, guarding the coast against the constant threat of the Sjórvǫrðr's raiding incursions.

To the distant south and occupying that entire side of Pænvicta's continent, the hauntingly pulchritudinous Īswægas began to unveil themselves in the advancing glow. The permafrosted glaciers arose high, the frozen peaks overarching like the crests of mountainous ocean waves. They seemed always set to crash down at any moment, but they are, in truth, timeless and unchanging. Only the snow that settles about them is subject to frequent and deadly avalanches. The Īswægas harbour no life, and it is not for many years now that pioneers have ascended into them to find only a rimy, frostbitten demise. The currents of the Magasæ at the escarpment's roots, too, are treacherous beyond reckoning, toiling always to dash wayward ships against the sheer face of the southern cliffs. Myth nor legend knows of a soul voyaging that way and surviving the ordeal.

To the north is a country only marginally more hospitable than Īswægas; the mystical, ancient forest-kingdom of Caill with its hillfort capital of Dún-Teg. It is from here that the great Leafbrym flows, so called for the continuous verdant flotsam of fallen leaves that bestrews the otherwise flawlessly pure stream. A fortified border partition, known as the Caillwall, extends west to east from the Tīdwind Sea to the crags which surround the Arx. Though Caill remains a dangerous place to visit (as much a result of its perplexing maze of trees as its hostile druidic tribes), relations between them and Cemparīce have remained peaceful for decades now; Arx Turrium's increasingly bold slaving missions represent an existential threat to the Caillic peoples.

Despite clever use of irregular soldiery and an unmatched mastery of military deception and ambush tactics, their free numbers are ever dwindling. Caill could ill afford war on another front, and Sūþeard has its own collection of problems.

Of course, to the north-east and central to Pænvicta is Arx Turrium, capital city-state of Sōlis Mūnus and the enterprising overlords of every sovereignty it nestles within. The 'Citadel of Spires' is all but unassailable behind its chasmic curtain-wall and standing army of devout and well-equipped psychotics. The mountain range surrounding the primary seat of the Sōlis priesthood serves as a complimentary natural defence, obligating any meaningful attack to utilise the narrow passes at each of its cardinal points. Such a siege has yet to be attempted since the Arx's conception, but one need not be a distinguished captain to speculate on the most probable outcome.

I might have continued to speak about the further territories: the young Republic of Sċeldlond and its administrative centre of Witan to the east; the industrial cityscape of Iliban, north of there, past the Arx; the insurmountable ravine known as 'The Fetters' that lies beyond those places, severing Pænvicta from the larger landmass; and even the misty, estranged isle across the north-west Strait of Adamastor, which separates the Tīdwind and Glæsċiella seas, rumoured to be home to a race of one-eyed giants. I might have divulged the length and breadth of Pænvicta, for my art has seen me travel far and wide in search of forgotten lore, and hearsay completes where I have yet to prospect; but hearing the Arx mentioned seemed to dull Bayldon's appetite for adventure and dampen his joviality, so I decided to shift to another, easier topic at the first opportunity.

"Have you received any training with that blade?" I asked.

"Reeve Ewin has me do some sparring with the watchmen," he said with disinterest. "They say that I'm a natural, and one of them reckoned I should have asked Ealdorman Heorot to train me up when they found out he was coming."

"It sounds like you might have a talent for it!"

"I wouldn't trust what they say, they don't like me very much. They kick my arse every time, then kick it again when I hit the dirt. *Reeve's pet*, they call me," he complained. "One of them told me I should ask Ealdorman Heorot if I could practice with his guard for a fairer fight. Probably just wanted to see me beaten to a pulp, the git."

"They are attempting to rile you, I suspect. So that you fight harder; more honestly."

"And that's what *you* think, is it?" he questioned with profound disbelief, his eyes wide and his mouth agape.

"Come now! You are a clever young man, Bayldon, but you must learn to perceive things with greater nuance. Otherwise, you will find yourself manipulated."

"You sound just like my... just like Alton," he caught himself. "That is, if he'd swallowed a lexicon."

"It is at your own peril that you reject the wisdom of not one old man, but two!"

"I *do* get it. But what am I to do about it?"

"Acquiesce your tormentors; hold nothing back as you fight. They provoke you so as to take a full measure of your ability, which they evidently do not believe you are demonstrating."

"And if I hurt one?"

"My friend," I chuckled, "*if* you attain that accolade, they will surely *congratulate* you. More likely you will fail regardless, but more admirably and with a significantly more convincing show of passion. Only then will they treat you with respect and your training with sincerity."

"What if you're overthinking it? How can you be sure they won't just beat me harder?"

"Perhaps they will," I shrugged, "but if that were to be the case, what do you truly gain - or, more importantly, stand to learn - from restraint?"

"True..." Bayldon trailed off thoughtfully, digesting the idea. We sat back in our saddles and enjoyed the perspective for the remainder of the dawn.

"Just my luck," I proclaimed finally, "that my 'protector' is too frightened to swing his sword with vigour, lest he 'hurt' someone!"

"Yes... yes, well," Bayldon coughed, "at least you have a brilliant guide! I've got the lay of the land, and I'm ready to go if you are!"

"By all means lead on, friend," I prompted, and our horses started to walk as we began our descent.

The way down from Gerefwīc's basin was more gentle than the way up, the slope being at a far shallower incline. For all my jocular derision of Bayldon, I was grateful for both his company and his guardianship. We enjoyed some witful small-talk as we rode and, despite my previous words, I assert that he would be of not insignificant worth in a threatening situation. Certainly he *looked* fearsome in his wargear, and even a guard dog with no teeth might set a burglar to flight with its bark.

We followed the path downwards until the hill broke gradually onto level ground. From there a metalled road stretched forth, flanked on both sides by wide ditches and intermittent, naked birch trees. The fields surrounding our way were populated sporadically with cattle; stout, domesticated aurochs with long horns and dark coats that meandered absently as they grazed. We conversed irreverently, avoiding mention of yesterday's events or the persons involved, but were still anxious; at one point a loud, throaty bellow from one of the livestock, lying out of sight behind a nearby mound, spooked us as well as our mounts and nearly saw us both thrown. After recovering control we decided that the incident was really quite amusing.

As we continued, I noticed a recurring phenomenon in the scenery that inspired a short discussion.

"How much history have you studied, Bayldon?"

"Somewhere between *slim* and *none*, I would say. Why do you ask?"

"What do you make of these grassy knolls?" I posed as we passed one just across the ditch to our right. It was one of the smaller ones we had encountered, having a diameter of only ten or so feet and a height of around six. They tended towards roundness and a slightly bell-shaped profile, with a shallow depression that traced the circumference. Occasionally a truly massive one would breach the surface and exceed the dimensions of most local homes.

"Looks to me," Bayldon said bluntly, "like a hill."

"There is more subtlety at work than that. *Look.* Have you not heard of them before?"

"A mound, then?"

"They are *barrows*, boy," I disclosed to deny him any further opportunity for flippancy. "Inside them are the entombed remains of men and women who lived many centuries ago."

"Really? Every one of them?" he pursued, his interest now piqued.

"A majority of them, most probably."

"What sort of people were they?"

"People from here, from the time of Sunþrardiz-"

"No, I know that much," he interrupted. "I mean; *who* were they?"

"I see..." I paused to think before continuing. "Well, they would be individuals of import; at minimum wealthy enough to afford the construction and votive goods of their tombs."

"*Votive goods?*" he rolled the phrase around his mouth. "Like what?"

"Anything that they valued in life. Weapons, armour, jewellery... loved ones..."

"*Loved ones!*" he let slip with shock and disgust. "They'd get buried with their wives?"

"Sometimes," I shrugged. "Their wives and servants. Rarely their children, if they were also slain. Oh! And quite often, their horses, occasionally with chariots, even."

"How disturbing..." Bayldon shifted in his saddle uncomfortably before perking up. "Hear that, Feran? If we get stopped by villains and you don't get me away fast enough, I'll make sure you're put in the hole *with* me!" He reached down to pat his mount's neck. The colt's ears swivelled at the mention of his name, but Feran otherwise proved unresponsive.

We kept a steady pace along the road, the sun now providing some meagre, but comfortable, warmth. Before it had reached its zenith, we came upon a fork in the road. Here a wooden signpost stood, and upon it was written 'Sceoppaton' in Sūþrūna. Nearby, too, we had our first encounter with another traveller. A merchant, called Sutton, sat upon a horse-drawn cart brimming with colourful groceries. He was a middle-aged, good-natured fellow, wearing only simple farmer's attire. After exchanging pleasantries, he offered us (and our mounts) a healthy carrot each. With our hunger nagging at us, we graciously accepted the gifts and savoured each bite of the flavoursome purple taproots.

"I'm just dropping by Sceoppaton today, catching the afternoon trade, you see," Sutton explained through a dense Sūþeard accent and a mouthful of carrot. "Seeing what business is like. Then tomorrow I'll be roving on to Gerefwīċ and getting myself ready for the twentieth's market day."

"You'll make a lot of Scutes there; that is, any of these manage to make it there between you munching them and giving them away!" Bayldon grinned, raising the remaining stump of his carrot and triumphantly flailing it by the stem. "We should be back there by then too; I'll be sure to put in a good word for you!"

Sutton tipped his hat, smiling broadly, and drove his cart onwards along the divergence. Our short reprieve finished, we instead spurred our horses down the path from which he had come. We resolved to give ourselves, as well as Felicia and Feran, a more meaningful respite at midday.

It was only a short stint longer until we judged the tree's shadows to be at their minimum, so we chose a pleasant space at the roadside, tethered our horses to a nearby birch, and took seats for ourselves upon a felled trunk. Bayldon removed his helm and set it by his side, running a hand through his now matted hair, relishing its temporary freedom.

"Have we far to go?" I asked as we unpackaged some of our rations.

"Not too far, we're making pretty good time. It depends, I suppose, if you fancy showing up there in the dark or not."

"Will waiting until morning delay our homecoming considerably?"

"Not really, why?"

"I had believed you might have a wish to postpone our return."

"Why would you think that?" Bayldon interrogated, his eyebrow raised in confusion.

"Alton had suggested that you had a compulsion to escape Gerefwīċ for a while, fearing for your safety."

"Is *that* what he told you!" shouted Bayldon in outraged disbelief. "He told *me* that *you* were scared and wanted to get away for a few days!"

"Then your old man has outfoxed us both, it would seem!" I surmised equally incredulously. "Perhaps he worried over *both* of us and sought a joint retreat for us to plan, with one another for companionship."

"Typical. That sounds just like him," Bayldon despaired. "And to think *you* were lecturing *me* about being manipulated too easily!"

"I offer my apologies, Bayldon. I had not fathomed your father having such nous for deception..." I stopped. The young man seemed dejected, so I added earnestly, "... but I am glad of your presence."

"I'll admit, I'm having fun," he smiled. "It's been a nice ramble. And I'll never admit it to him, but dad was right; it was good to get out of the hundred for a change."

"To your dear father..." I declared, holding a shred of dried meat aloft in a toast, "... the bastard."

Bayldon joined my impromptu dedication, raising a chunk of sweet loaf before rudely and pointedly cramming the huge piece into his mouth. After finishing the meals and stretching out our legs and backs, Bayldon reluctantly donned his helm, untied the now lazing horses and climbed onto Feran's back.

"Come on, you fat beast," berated Bayldon as he pulled a full feed-bag from one of his packs, leaning far forwards to fasten it to the animal's face, "we can be moving while *you* eat."

Being no longer quite so nimble, I affixed Felicia's nosebag before mounting her, doing so while she lay on her front. She was easily able to lift me as she stood and we were soon continuing our journey, this time savouring the relative stillness of the countryside in blissful quiet.

The pastoral fields on either side began to give way to a growing frequency of birches, and the ditches cornered off, partitioning the aurochs from the denser woodland. The slender branches became thicker and more encompassing until, eventually, the chaotic tangle was enough to hide considerable swathes of the sky above. Though the birch bark was of a plain white, our surroundings became noticeably darker under the enveloping arboreal shade.

"What is this place called?" I asked, squinting to see in the new murk.

"Bircweald I think," answered Bayldon, screwing up what I could see of his face as he racked his brains. "On the off-chance I'm right, make sure you don't kill any animals. Not that it looks like you're about to..."

"Why would that be?"

"It's one of Ricbert's hunting reserves. So; trap a rabbit and be hanged or gelded as a poacher, that's the order of Bircweald."

"I see. And where are the grounds' limits?"

"I think it's when the birches run out."

"So the territory encompasses more ground every year?"

"Now you're thinking like a king!" Bayldon answered with a quick burst of laughter. His voice echoed unevenly through the trees, deflected this way and that by the erratic acoustics. In truth, some aspect of the forest set my nerves on edge, and the resounding cachinnations only served to deepen my sense of unease.

"Shall we be in this place for long?" I enquired, my tone portraying more anxiety than I had intended. If Bayldon took notice, he made no mention of it.

"We won't be in here long. We're only crossing the thinnest part," he explained, "then we'll be on the last stretch before the river. We'll be able to find a place to pack it in for the night down that bit, if you like."

"A fine plan," I assented, and we spoke no more while within the boundaries of Bircweald.

It seemed altogether too long before we emerged from the birches, and we did so to find that the sun was descending apace at our backs. We had only a couple of hours' travel time available to us, so we urged our horses to an exigent trot. The road ahead, once we had left the trees behind, was not characteristically dissimilar to the one before we entered them; prolonged and unerring, although the auroch-fields had been exchanged for natural, uncultivated swarth and the road itself was a simple beaten track. The barrows were present here, too, but were better disguised beneath overgrown tufts of grass and myriad wildflowers.

"I wish you hadn't told me about these bloody things," grumbled Bayldon as he pointed at the nearest concealed monument. "They didn't creep me out as much when they were just mounds!"

"I refuse to apologise for shattering your ignorance," I retorted, sniggering under my hood. "It is only appropriate that you are acquainted, after all; between them we might find the optimal place for our fire."

It was soon after that when our light was diminished, for a slew of clouds had chased us from the west to blot out the sun. The rapidity of the transition was staggering.

"You *must* be *joking*," Bayldon cried. "Looks like we ought to find a place soonish, too. I'm blaming you if it rains."

Seeing a location of potential usefulness we forthwith departed the track, exercising care to note the route of our improvised steps. The place we had spotted was as ideal as we might have hoped for; two youthful oak trees in close proximity at the far side of a massy barrow.

We dismounted there. As Bayldon took the horses to the first of the trees to tether them, he removed and packed away the feedbags. He then withdrew a tinderbox from Feran's pack saddle, opening it to reveal a flintsteel and a portion of dried parchment tinder. After gathering a selection of loose stones (not difficult among the ancient and often structurally compromised tombs) to make a circular firepit, the young man set himself the painstaking task of striking the tool with a sharp flint. I watched intently, eager to heat my hands against the worsening cold.

Eventually the repetitive sparks coaxed an ignition, and we were fortunate enough for the flames to catch before the sun abandoned us utterly. My companion, after relieving himself of some of his armour, gathered bunches of broken sticks from the vicinity as I retrieved the bedrolls, and we soon had a salubrious campfire whose embers wisped upwards into the blackened night.

"When can we expect to approach the river tomorrow?" I asked casually.

"Actually, it's probably a bit less than an hour," he managed through a wide yawn. "Given that we'll be bedding down early, we can probably get up early, too."

The logic was credible enough, although considering my recent experience, an extended sleep may prove undesirable. We opted to remain wakeful a while longer and have supper. To that end I offered to share some of my supply of salted pork with Bayldon, and it was politely received. The clouds rolled over and devoured the stars but, mercifully, there was no downpour; only an increasingly claustrophobic tenebrosity. I lit my lantern in a vain attempt to maintain our light's influence, but its candle's flare was limited. We enwrapped ourselves in our thick bedrolls, both of us struggling to find warmth and comfort.

"I'll be surprised if I can sleep here," said Bayldon as he inched closer to the fire. "It's damned creepy."

"You should hold no fear of the dead. They have no malice for you."

"Just how would you know?" he grumbled doubtfully.

I confess here that I could not resist a modicum of tormenting.

"Trust me," I affirmed with a deliberately evocative tone, "*I know.*"

"Be like that if you like," Alton's ward squeaked, "but I won't talk to you any longer so you can give me nightmares. Good night to you, you old rotter!"

"Good night, Bayldon," I responded cheerily, and heard only a dismissive huff in return. His bedroll twisted and shifted briefly, then stilled.

Thus I lie here now, dreading what sleep might deliver me unto. Yet, I must recuperate before tomorrow; I could swiftly find mys-

Ah. Bayldon has just unconsciously slurred at me to 'stop that damned pesky scribbling', followed by a vague threat of hurling either my book or my person into the fire. I feel it only equitable and courteous to oblige his request.

...

The aging man, deep-cloaked and grey-bearded, watches lazily from the window slit. He places a spyglass against his eye and gazes down at something small within the encompassing fields of overgrown grass below. It bounds about this way and that at incredible speeds. From an unknowing perspective, one might mistake the man as following the thing's movements; but he is, in actual fact, governing them directly.

Another small shape appears at the edge of the distant treeline. The man catches sight of it and refocuses his vision. It is a hare, its tiny head and perked ears twitching about warily. The first object is accelerating towards it now, building up to a staggering pace on an unerringly straight course. To attempt to track its pursuit would be hopeless, as the aging man knows from previous attempts; it would be barely a blur among the verdant blades. Instead, he keeps the spyglass pointed upon the hare and waits.

The impact comes like a bolt from a rampart crossbow. The hare perceives its danger too late, and its doom explodes from the brush with a monstrous velocity. In the blink of an eye the hapless prey is being suffocated within the attacker's clamped jaws.

It is the first time the creature stands relatively still, and its details become clear. It is, or was, a diminutive sighthound, though patches of its fur and flesh have long since sloughed away to reveal segments of the yellowing skull and disarrayed ribcage beneath. The hare, held by its scruff, sporadically bursts into moments of struggle in an attempt to take its antagonist off-guard; but the canine remains steady and firm as a vice, only shifting to precisely counteract the exertions of its prize's turmoil.

The aging man begins anew his experiment. He slowly, ever so slowly, relinquishes his control over the un-dead whippet's mind. As expected, he sees no change until... until...

There. The change comes like the precipitous hostility of an agitated hornet's nest. The decaying sighthound begins to thrash its head from side to side, incorporating the power from its hunched shoulders to rip the hare to shreds. The smaller animal is already dead, its fragile spine having been immediately snapped by the torrent of opposed, wrenching forces, but the un-dead beast shows no sign of quitting its violence. It flails and threshes until the many scraps of its victim's corpse are scattered far and wide, the only remnant in its grasp now a piece of bloodied gullet. This it drops, suddenly disinterested, and tests the air for new scents. Deep inhalations are drawn in through a mostly disintegrated nasal cavity. It seemingly detects something and pounces again into the undergrowth, disappearing from the sole spectator's sight and leaving only a gory area of minute innards and displaced limbs.

But the aging man, similarly, has lost interest, and instead appears in deep thought from his perch in the ancient stone tower.

Why does this happen? *he ponders to himself. It is a replicable procedure, 'successful' in at least nine of ten repetitions. But* why? *For what purpose do unfettered and mindless un-dead tend nearly always towards violence? He has observed, as have others before him, that those arisen 'free' are driven by some underlying instinct, a dim reflection of how they were in life. A skilled necromancer is capable of utilising this mysterious trait to grant his servants 'intuition', for lack of a better term. In this way, they might antithetically exhibit proficiencies beyond their master's own. However, when left to their own devices, most have a propensity for lashing out at any nearby living being. It is this behaviour that the aging man has been studying these past few days. It flies in the face of reason and imparts a void of understanding in the essence of the un-dead, which he has decided to attempt to fill as a break from his Zeritmian translations. It has, though, proven a more frustrating problem than the one from which he has temporarily escaped.*

The man moves from his uncomfortable perch, accompanied by the creak of his stiff joints, and reseats himself at the nearby desk. Violence is certainly a strong aspect of nature, but is it truly the primary motivator of all living things? *A bleak conclusion, if true. It certainly felt as if he was vainly attempting to disprove something already thoroughly established. In his recent experiments he had raised a number of un-dead from a variety of backgrounds, both human and animal. He had raised pacifists who had never in their lives fought with their fellow men, and he had raised intemperate tavern brawlers after their latest fight found them slain beside the establishment's doorstep; he had raised wolves and the sheep that they had predated on. All, if incompletely broken to his will, became furiously aggressive and consumed utterly by a speechless, frothing rage. They fight as does a cornered and desperate creature against its captors, but their frenzy seems to extend towards* life itself.

Their conduct, needless to say, does not allegorise with the model of an unthinking animated carcass. The aging man found the implications... disquieting. Had the un-dead more autonomy than was popularly ascribed to them? And were they filled with resentment *for their condition? Just how unwilling* were *they as servants? It was a conundrum that he was determined to solve, but the answers might cost him his sanity, as much as he could still claim to possess that. He throws his notes on the floor with a flutter of parchment, slumps back and closes his eyes. A scientific method would not help him here. Perhaps some more philosophical erudition was in order.*

The un-dead, he has noticed, are irrational in their anger. They target only the closest being, and (while they are often, in practice, one and the same) make no special effort to destroy their 'patron' necromancer, to whom a rational mind might assign blame. Neither, if they were dispatched by a killer of any sort, do they prioritise vengeance against the one responsible for their untimely death. Additionally, they will not spare those they loved in life, even (as he had witnessed in one tragic incident) their families. If their apparent hatred is unconditionally inclusive and generalised, can they truly be designated 'sentient'? Could not a wildfire be imagined as emotionally compelled if subjected to that reasoning?

Mayhap such anthropomorphism is misplaced. It could be that the anarchical un-dead are simply a naturally destructive force, that they are to life as torchlights are to the shadows; ever seeking to extinguish that which is within their reach, not through a conscious labour but because it is merely what they do.

Yes, that is a convenient enough answer, *the aging man concludes inwardly and tentatively,* A force of nature. Or unnature.

A low, guttural rumble emanates from the doorway at his back. He turns slowly to find the sighthound; it is crouched in a combative stance, the scraggly remains of its hackles standing on end. The face, decomposed as it is, retains a permanent snarl. The sockets stare back at him. At times like these, it is difficult indeed to consider the un-dead solely as inadvertent and ambulatory cadavers. He is initially overcome again by curiosity, but the thing prepares to lunge at him, necessitating the exertion of his will before it seizes the initiative. It stops instantly and sits still as if rebuked by an authoritative trainer. At another inaudible command, it stalks forward and curls up at his feet. The aroma of the grave rises to meet his nostrils, but he ignores it and looks down at the thing with a hint of sadness. This is how little Beorc was in life; a lapdog, a loyal friend and, through laziness or softness, incapable of harming a living thing. He knew its owner well and had met Beorc on many occasions, and even disregarding the physical degradation he could see nothing of that beloved companion in the hideous, twisted mimic before him. It is acting like Beorc because he has made it do so, not due to its own volition.

The aging man decides that he will soon free the poor wretch from un-death. He has come to find its presence quite upsetting.

I awoke, once again, during the night. Tonight's dream had actually left me with a sensation of mild contentment, but I was soon disillusioned as I became more aware of my surroundings. My conscious reality was to be more nightmarish than the memory I had left behind.

Bayldon was still sleeping, his bedroll occasionally squirming as he adjusted himself, but the campfire was dying out and the chill felt dangerously frigid. I cursed myself for not insisting on a rotating night watch, but resolved not to rouse the youth, instead taking up my lantern to collect additional firewood myself.

It was then that I sensed what had probably roused me from my slumber. A disturbance nearby; the undeniable feel of necromantic energy, but not my own. It pulsed from deep within the nearest of the barrows (the one by which we slept), a repetitive flare of un-life from the occupant. Could it be... the birth of a revenant? I had never been within this close proximity to such an event, and had no point of comparison... but also no alternative explanation. I uprooted a patch of grass from the mound and listened to the bare soil beneath, only to hear *footsteps*. I leapt back with horror upon realisation that the revenant was pacing back and forth; searching, perhaps, for an exit.

I hastily gathered some spare sticks, tossed them to the flames and set to work on a warding spell. The ambition was to create a subversive ethereal redolence, one that would be anathema to any revenant in the vicinity. The simplest methodology, given the absence of an area to inscribe a sigil, was to imbue the flames themselves.

I believe we shall be safe now. The campfire now resonates with the faintest shimmer of manna refractions, but Bayldon is yet soundly sleeping. I think I shall strive towards the same situation for myself.

Sōlrest-Þridda-XIX

We were greeted in the early morning by an invasive damp; the overnight dew had frosted over to form a crunchy layer of hoar on the heath. In the prevailing light of dawn it was aesthetically pleasant, but warned of a potentially pernicious temperature. It is likely fortuitous that I had chosen to contribute more fuel to our campfire. Still, we sat before the flame's remnants and, rubbing our hands together as our breaths misted the air, we tried desperately to warm ourselves before going on.

"Have you slept well, Bayldon?" I asked, seeing if I could improve the young man's injured humour.

"Yes, I think. For the most part, at least," he answered thoughtfully. "Had a few odd dreams, mind."

"Oh?"

"I remember turning over and opening my eyes to see... *strange colours* dancing in the embers, so I watched for a while before drifting off again. I guessed it was a dream, or a trick of sleepy eyes," he shrugged.

"A good omen, perhaps?" I suggested tentatively.

"Could be."

In truth, I believe he was discomforted by the experience. Not a surprising reaction; I had ensured that the ward would draw its power from the fire only, but gazing upon the dancing aberrations of manna is seldom pleasant for those of a more mundane background. I can find solace not only from the fact that we were not (gods forbid) accosted or otherwise approached by the revenant, but also that Bayldon thankfully remains ignorant of its abhorrent existence. The horses, on the other hand, may have sensed something. They were incredibly skittish as we went to them, and indeed had done their best to maximise the distance between the offending barrow and themselves, having pulled their tethers to their limits to stay behind their anchoring tree as they slept uneasily. We were all four of us in a mood of lethargy and irritability, but we mounted up and pushed onwards out of necessity, hoping the activity would aid in keeping us heated on this frigid morning.

Our resumed path across the moors was largely uneventful, and we remained silent for a long while. I myself was miserably cold, and I suspected Bayldon was beginning to regret his coming with me. The dour march through drab fields was eventually punctuated by the emergence of a line of trees, very different from the gaunt specimens we had encountered on our way. A line of mighty peaked evergreens stood proudly, shadowy jade spruces stretching away to the north and south, following the landscape beyond both horizons.

"That's the Leafbrym Colonnade, so they call it," Bayldon announced as he pointed, finally renewing some of his positivity. "It's only three or four ranks deep, not far to go now."

It was still a lengthy approach given that such massive conifers were as a modest hedgerow against the grey sky, but with a clear and visible objective we rediscovered our enthusiasm and went on. In fact, I was in a state of exceptional alertness. I glanced about in internalised distress, half-expecting to find tracks, or refuse, or piles of ashes. If we were to be ambushed, treading our way wilfully into the noose of a snare, here might be our last opportunity for precognition. Alas, nothing. We were to be equipped with only our wiles and reflexes. After resigning myself to this possibility, my thoughts progressed to the recitation of a dozen scenarios of prospective ruin. I had no un-dead available to me, a limitation applied by my present company. While I do have other powerful defensive measures, they are of a similarly unnatural origin. Disregarding even the immediate issue of traumatising the young man, Bayldon's knowledge of my ability could prove catastrophic. He would likely on discovery of my practice consider me appalling, betraying me to others at the first opportunity he might consider himself guarded enough to do so. I evaluated the concept that, if Bayldon were incapable of standing his ground against whatever adversaries might oppose us, I should be incentivised to slay him after calling upon my dark craft to extricate us; but the thought made me sick, even the action's very imagining made untenable by its repugnance.

I have been altered, I fear, by Stilneshire. I do not yet know what to make of these changes, but at that moment I realised just how thoroughly I had compromised myself: I had restricted my primary *and* secondary methods of protection; instead, I had placed my survival in the hands of this young acquaintance, well equipped but greener than a fresh recruit; the mysterious stranger, or strangers, can be assumed to understand my abilities, and thus are likely themselves magical, or else confidently skilled; and my only option should my life be truly endangered is one I find too unpalatable to contemplate. In short, I have become foolish and sentimental, and therefore vulnerable.

My only hopes of survival were, I soon calculated, that I would either revert to my baser survival instinct when my limits were tested, or that the summoner meant me no harm. But I was in such deep and anxious thought that, by the time I came to my senses, we had made short work of the distance to the spruces. Our destination was before us and the flattened road had faded to nothing. It seemed altogether too quiet. If the Leafbrym was so close now, why was it not yet audible to us?

"Well, this is it. What's your plan?" Bayldon asked with a hint of nervousness.

"How much has Alton told you?" I countered (a temporary deflection).

"He told me about that pretty antler, and that it had the river's name scratched into it. Why?"

Ah, I thought, *I suppose I never asked Alton to keep the item a secret.* In retrospect I pray he has not leaked the information further, though that would be something of a departure from what I know of his constitution.

"My answer to you, Bayldon, is that I have no plan," I confessed. "That is why you must remain here."

"Bollocks to that, you're not getting rid of me as soon as I might be useful!"

"It may be dangerous-"

"A bit of danger is just what I need to test my mettle!" he ejaculated. "I've been a boy for long enough."

"For many, their first battle soon becomes their last."

"Well, what kind of worth would I have if I let an old man wander off alone to die?" he remarked stubbornly. I realised that, once again, I had been tied by my own self-imposed compromises. Bayldon must be allowed to persist in his belief of my feebleness, and his virtuous nature predisposes him to watch over those he perceives as indigent. Even when faced with probable harm, it would seem.

"Have your way, Bayldon, have your way," I conceded grudgingly. "But I provide no assurance that you will consider this a 'victory' should adversity befall us."

"Can't live a life so full of doubt, can you? Come on, let's get to it."

And so we tethered Felicia and Feran, delving into the thicket to trace a route beneath the needled skirts of the spruces. Bayldon's hand ever flexed apprehensively over the grip of his sheathed blade as we followed the youthful dawn hidden behind the canopy. I wielded only my walking stick in my right hand and the Caillic antler in my left, holding both more tightly, I am sure, than was strictly necessary.

The evergreens were of an impressive enough height that we could walk beneath their branches with minimal crouching or diversion of the tree's limbs. This side of the colonnade proved to have a file of only five or six, so reaching the river itself did not take long.

Once we had emerged from the trees and into the Leafbrym's clearing, we absorbed the scene about us, shaded as it was from the low sun. The river at this section was fairly narrow, only about sixty or so feet wide, but it was immediately obvious why it was so uncharacteristically mute; its surface had completely frozen over to leave a deadly, but undeniably beautiful, translucent veneer. Its stillness was uncanny to observe, almost as if one were standing within the canvas of a talented artist; looking over the reeds which protruded beyond the bank and over the water, the assorted verdant debris which gives the Leafbrym its title could be seen embedded sporadically within the ice. If one peered closer still, they might glance an occasional lonely leaf through the verglas, speeding downstream as if propelled by a strong gale. To the attentive, the prophecy of a sealed fate for any who might unwittingly breach the frangible plane.

And there we stood, our eyes scanning the opposing bank and below the umbrous boughs for emerging figures, but we saw nobody. I had ever been under the assumption that the antler's creator had been watching my movements. Certainly, they had been for a substantial count of years - many decades, perhaps - if they held as meticulously expurgated a secret as my true name. Had they suffered from a sudden lapse in vigilance and missed their opportunity? Had I misread their intentions? Could the entire debacle have been an elaborate hoax? The concerning thoughts were propagated and fed by every passing moment of fruitless idling. I had anticipated a meeting. An ambush, even. But nothing at all was somehow more disconcerting.

"Well, this is shit," Bayldon muttered softly, the words passing his lips as expanding, vaporous clouds.

"Have you a useful suggestion, boy?" I nudged him, now becoming positively exasperated.

"Why don't we just shout for them and get it over with?"

For a brief time I found myself caught between the urges to laugh and to weep, so obtusely ridiculous the idea seemed. However, upon scrutiny, I found that I was unable to suggest a more elegant proposal. I could think of no better way to honour its sensibility than to effectuate it instantly, prompting Bayldon to jump with fright and loose a rapid string of curses in my direction.

"Hark! Come, antler-carver, and reclaim your trinket! Let us parley!" I called out to the trees. My voice is not what it once was, but it carried well and seemed to echo along the ice in both directions.

After expecting no response, the swiftness with which one was given disheartened us both, I think; for out of what we had taken for a pile of fallen, colourful leaves, laying by the trees beyond the opposite bank, arose a shape. At first, it appeared to be simply growing and shifting, as if a sizeable animal were burrowing up from the ground it was piled upon. It began to take a more defined form; person-like, with the leaf litter revealed as some manner of gown. Then a set of features issued from the recesses; the fair and elegant face of a woman, young but wise, whose sleek, flowing tresses were whiter than the hoarfrost. She opened her eyes which, with such clarity as to be perceptible even across the width of the river, glowed like twinned viridescent fireflies at dusk. Yet, for all her extraordinary characteristics, she embodied an air of nature, wholesomeness and a familiarity that I could not quite place. Bayldon was entirely awestruck by her grace, his previously cautious stance wavering.

"Who calls for me? Who so kindly comes to return my charm?" she probed, her melodious, honeyed voice emanating warmth and benevolence. She spoke in Sūþstefn but with a strong Caillic inflection and a dancing timbre, sweet enough to turn a blade.

I did not understand. Was this some manner of riddle?

"You know who comes," I answered awkwardly, intending more but producing nothing.

"Perhaps, once," she said, pausing to giggle coyly, "a long, long time ago."

"What is your name?" I sought.

"My name is like yours."

I promptly took her meaning of mutual anonymity and persisted no further.

"Ah, but that matters not. I have something for you, for bringing me my charm!" she declared. Her smile never faltered.

Much as Bayldon, I found myself so overcome with curiosity and uncertainty that I was disarmed. He and I exchanged glances, finding no answers in each other's perplexed expressions. The strange woman apparently took our silence as consent and proceeded towards us. Her leafy gown rustled as it swept across the grass behind her, and it seemed as if her very presence encouraged verdancy in the vegetation around her while she strolled forth at a leisurely pace. The undergrowth flushed with colour and surged in height, and a multitude of flowers defied the season to bloom incongruously. Enthralling and divine... but otherworldly enough to momentarily break her previously soothing aura.

She soon reached the riverbank and paused, granting us an opportunity for a closer inspection. This was when I was able to establish a partial recognition; here, definitely, was the witch that had been shown to me by the Coercitor at the Garfeldas checkpoint. Evidently she had evaded them and their bounty-hunters thus far, so was presumably able to assume a more subtle countenance than the one presented to us then.

Unexpectedly, she took another step, lowering herself onto the precariously thin ice, and continued on towards us undeterred. Bayldon's growing trepidation was forgotten and he rushed to intercept her, pausing only when I grasped his shoulder tightly.

"Stop, man! This is folly!" I implored. He turned to look at me with confusion, eyes wide and wild with panic.

"She'll drown, I have to save her!" he cried.

"By adding your weight, you will more likely doom her *and* your asinine self! Stay your ground and do not take rash leave of your senses!"

Bayldon whimpered fitfully, but acquiesced without argument. His mind was not entirely lost, but it seemed then as fragile as the brittle, thinly frozen surface of the Leafbrym. The witch was undeniably potent, but magical manipulation of a living mind is an impossibly complex undertaking, and in reality exists only in fabricated tales. *Truly* attainable methods of influence are found *without* thaumaturgy;

charisma, coercion, deception and seduction. Bayldon has, somewhat predictably, demonstrated his susceptibility to the lattermost category, possibly without even being intentionally targeted. The sources of my immunity were twofold: firstly, her allure to myself was somehow chaste, and its precise essence remains difficult to explain; secondly, I have seen many young men lose so much more than merely their innocence to a beguiling damsel. I would endeavour to defend Alton's ward from a similar fate.

The witch was disinterested by Bayldon's rescue effort as it sank back into barely restrained anxiety. Her attention was unquestionably trained on me. She continued to amble across the ice, barefooted, beaming as if indulging in the humour of a freshly recalled witticism. She drew close enough for me to become cognisant of her eyes' radiant intricacy. The two coronas pulsed gently and rhythmically with a throbbing emerald luminescence; the drum of a restful heartbeat, at once hypnotic and asseverative. Despite this, some unknown aspect had me requiring considerable willpower to maintain a necessary mistrust. Some fleeting reminiscence...

But in that moment, my time to think was curt. The witch had soon, without incident, arrived on our side of the Leafbrym, and was then pacing gradually to me. My imagination buzzed with the potential adverse consequences of allowing her to continue unabated. She was within a few yards when - to his eternal credit - Bayldon finally unsheathed his sword and thrust it forth between us.

"No further! Don't force me to do something regretful, you hear?" His throat was shaky but his bearing was firm, and lo; the witch was given pause. Her simper, however, survived undaunted, and she turned her head as if noticing the young man for the first time before returning her gaze to mine.

"The boy, is he yours?" she asked.

"He is not," I stated simply.

"Such a pity," she sighed poignantly. "A brave and handsome one he is, too."

Bayldon twitched his eyes towards me with an uncomfortable look and his sword-arm slackened minutely. I decided to hasten the encounter along, to better preserve his nerves.

"I have the antler. It... has been a pleasure to appraise," I told her, presenting it to her. Bayldon lowered the weapon to provide easier access, but the tapered point was now trembling.

"And I have something for you, also." For the first time, her face darkened. Through sleight of hand she appeared to produce the object, some flattened thing about a foot long and of an outlandish ochre pigment, from thin air; but she bestowed it inchmeal, wary of our suspicions - or, perhaps, reluctant to relinquish it to me.

Our trade was completed in unison, the both of us giving with our left hands and taking with our right. Bayldon stared with inquisitiveness as the mask crossed above his barrier; for a mask it was, and not dyed with ochre but shaped from pure amber, so feather-light that I well-nigh dropped it in my surprise. As I held it, it seemed to radiate delicately in spite of the scant sunlight. Its design is Caillic, a bulbous, misshapen visage complete with a sculpted moustache, grand and etched as to be finely groomed, and the material over the eyes is sanded thinly enough to grant the wearer a yellow-tinted perception of their surroundings. The shaping and condition are superb and appear as new as if it were finished only yesterday, but somehow it seems as ancient as the eternal forest itself. The witch, seeing my fascination, began to speak as she herself looked over the antler.

"It is a relic, a gift from our eldest god. The one who has no love of man; the one who rarely gives, but always takes."

"But why do you give this to me? What is its purpose?" I queried, my mouth agape, my angst transformed to wonderment.

"Be wary of whose footsteps you follow, and do not follow them too closely. You must take the critical turn," she answered grimly.

"What are you saying?" I pressed.

"Don the mask in the pivotal moment. That is all I can say, for yours is not a path I have taken, nor one that I envy," she paused, studying me as if perceiving beyond the flesh with those lurid green orbs, "and I have not yet decided whether I can condone it, nor whether it is my place to do so."

"Shall we, then, be called allies?" I interrogated.

"We may share enemies aplenty, but the manner of the company you keep proscribes a shared alliance."

"I see."

I harried no more, acutely aware of the perilousness of my position. Bayldon already seemed uncertain of the relationship between the witch and I, and I doubted her allusive riddles were doing much to ease his suppositions. I felt that inducing the meeting's swift conclusion had become imperative; but before I could suggest the like, the witch herself conferred an identical proposal.

"It is time we parted, young ones," she said, smiling once more as she addressed Bayldon *and* I, "though I should like much to speak further, time hesitates for nobody."

"Agreed. Let us part on... *good* terms. Farewell."

The three of us said no more as she turned and strode back across the ice. On this occasion, Bayldon made no move of urgent heroism, instead opting to scrutinise her every movement until she had stepped up onto the opposite bank. From there, she appeared to blend into the spruces and scattered leaves, and was gone. I realised, forlornly, that she had created more questions than she had answers, and I could feel the accruing pangs of another baneful headache. Bayldon pivoted away and cut a path through to the exit. I stayed close behind and kept his sedulous pace.

Bayldon was either jarred or irked, but it was impossible for me to catch him as he pushed and kicked his way through snagging branches and moistened detritus. He did not cease until he broke from the treeline and inhaled sharply. I feared the worst until I was stood at his side.

"I don't think I took a breath the whole time that witch was there," he gasped, his chest heaving as he struggled for air. "I didn't know in the least what to make of *her*."

"There is no shame in being afraid; you acted commendably, better than I might have at your age."

"It wasn't like that," he sniffed, thoughtful rather than offended. "It was as if the trees were as much a part of her as her white hair. Was she... human?"

"She was. Sōlis Mūnus might call her a witch, but Caill would know her as a druidess. Regardless of your perspective, she is certainly a powerful individual."

"Could she have killed the two of us?" asked Bayldon straightforwardly.

I was taken aback by the cold, unemotional manner of his question, but it was not one whose answer I had not contemplated for myself. Her magical specialisation of *life* was the very antithesis of mine, and I have little experience of it. I pondered if it could be used offensively, or if a duel between us would have constituted only of her mitigations of my onslaught. One of her potency might well have inventive and unpredictable means of aggression, something far removed from my knowledge. Also, while such an ability is exceedingly rare, the witch may have mastery over multiple schools of magic.

"I am honestly unsure, though I suspect that, even if she had the faculty, she had not the inclination."

"You believe I could have slain her?" Bayldon scoffed with disbelief.

"The surest blows can vanquish kings and sorcerers alike, so long as they are struck first. Please do not misconstrue me when I emphasise; I am relieved that we were not impelled to discover the answer through a mortal confrontation."

"Oh, I agree..." he nodded and seemed sated, then started as he remembered his next query. "But what was all that about 'shared enemies' and 'following footsteps' and such? And that weird mask?"

"As for the first example, I believe she may refer to the Arx's minions; she is of special interest to them, if I correctly interpret the likeness on their bounty boards. Though in truth, I understood little else of her Caillic ramblings," I replied. A half-truth, at least.

"She is hunted by them and considers us allies!" Bayldon laughed. "I'm not sure if I should feel comforted or upset!"

"We have an accord there, my friend," I grinned and placed a hand on his shoulder.

"Still, maybe we should keep all of this, and *that*," he pointed to the amber mask, which I held in such a manner as if it might burst into flames at any moment, "between us. Folk might take badly to it."

"Brave, handsome *and* wise! No wonder the witch was besotted!"

"Shut it, you," he chuckled, a bashful flush deepening the shade of his already scarlet cheeks. Then, his face and voice became serious. "One last thing. Do you know that woman, or did you know her before?"

"She suggested as much, but no; I have no recollection of encountering her before today."

"Promise?"

"On my old bones, I promise." And this truth, dear reader, was unadulterated.

Convenient it was that Bayldon had suggested a vow of secrecy before I did. I had, in part, expected that he might require significant persuasion, but the young man was fortuitously canny. The whole affair seemed not to have shaken him but, as I would later discover, his was a temporary courage supplied by his nerves, soon to fade once the initial threat had passed. Inauspicious but entirely inevitable, and blameless; for one so fresh, it is astounding that he kept his nerve at all when in the presence of such a mystical, imposing being. His valour, even if fleeting, was deserving of substantial praise.

We had departed the cover of the trees to find that deceptively little time had passed during our encounter. The sun had newly begun to climb over the spruces and turn the hoarfrost within its reach into a grey slush. The sky was clear for the moment, but distant clouds were crawling their way towards us, so we resolved to commence our return journey without delay. We had not exited the trees from the same direction as we had entered them; briefly we panicked in the belief that Feran and Felicia had freed themselves from their tethers and bolted, but a shrill whicker a little further south honed the search and our mounts were soon carrying us in their saddles. We started - and remained - at a trot, exchanging the occasional sentences but mostly preserving a pensive hush.

We rejoined the path on the moors with little to note. The weather had progressed into an overcast sky, the ineffectual tepidity of the sun already erased and forgotten. We had hitherto resigned ourselves to a tiresome, frigid day's travel when we happened within sight of the previous night's campfire, now a smouldering heap of dampened ashes. Something, however, was amiss; the side of the neighbouring barrow, the one that had demonstrated some activity, had caved inwards to create a sizeable hole. I instantly remarked that wild animals occasionally attempt to burrow into the side of the mounds, but Bayldon was plainly dubious, his unspoken speculations much darker than my weak rationalisation. In fact, his direst imaginings were probably slightly too near to the distressing truth; the revenant, after having bided for my warding flame's expiration, had opened a way for itself and was now roaming free. It was a singularly rare phenomenon, one for which all reports suggest unpredictable results. I may have been as perturbed as Bayldon for our remaining time on the moors, but we found Birċweald in merciful absence of any noteworthy occurrence or sighting of the anomaly.

We were following the road through the birches long prior to midday, opting not to pause for food or rest beforehand. During the illusively lengthy hike through that reserve, we came to regret that decision; we had reattached the nosebags onto the then permanently masticating horses, but we ourselves were painfully hungry and sore. Bayldon, having minimal experience with long periods of uninterrupted riding, was developing excruciating blisters on his posterior and thighs about which he complained constantly and loudly. This lasted until a dense lowland fog crept through Birċweald, smothering the surroundings in an impenetrable grey haze. We could see only as far as the nearest trees to our left and right, the distance of a few yards at most. From that stage we adhered to the path uncompromisingly. I insisted on a minimisation of distraction (with an outstanding emphasis on *noise*), and Bayldon subdued his lamentations to intermittent gasps and pipings.

The environmental changes did nothing to ease my ideations of the king's hunting grounds, and more than once I swore to catching the sound of an additional set of hooves just beyond our reduced sight. I had thought it to be merely echoes until the presence began to scatter screeching birds and the horses grew bothered and chary. We ignored the chilling signs as best we could, but were pushed beyond our tolerance when the presence passed very near our fore, causing Feran and Felicia to rear and whinny into their oats. It was all I could do to keep track of the correct direction as the beasts twisted and bucked. We elected to dismount and tether the animals so as not to be forcibly thrown, then to wait, vigilant, anticipating whatever might approach from the brume; but nothing came and the sounds grew fainter. Being frustrated by his inanition and sores, Bayldon forgot his worry and theorised that our tormentor was probably a stag, and that we should move on and leave Birċweald so that we could take a meal without being accused of poaching by a particularly fastidious game-warden. I was inclined to agree if only for his peace of mind... and, of course, the excuse to leave as speedily as our mounts could manage. If my companion detected the far removed creak of distant *wheels*, then he was as voluntarily ignorant as I was. We mounted and galloped, making as short a labour of the remainder of Bircweald as was possible.

Relief overcame us as we left the birches behind. The fog was no less claustrophobic (we could not even find the sun and had no guess as to the actual time of day), but we were able to rest and eat. Firstly freeing the horses of their feedbags and again securing them, we proceeded to indulge in a fulfilling and much-needed luncheon, taking leave of some of our previous day's conservation. Our consensus was not to dither in the cold, and so we were moving again before long.

Traversing the road soon proved itself still more ominous than Bircweald. While the metalled surface and deep banks on either side made accidentally straying an impossibility, *nothing* of the surroundings could be seen, making the road appear endless and isolated. We might have chosen not to travel in such conditions, but were determined to return to The Old Boar before dusk and spurred onwards by the promise of hot drinks and soft quilts. Once Bayldon confirmed the presence of a number of brass bed-warmers kept in one of Alton's pantries, we knew then that we would not settle for another night on the bare ground. It may have been highly ambitious, but our pace had improved since the outgoing journey and we were far less concerned about approaching Gerefwīc Hundred in the dark.

We passed the signpost and diversion for Sceoppaton some way along. I wondered aloud whether it would be more prudent to take that route and pay an innkeeper there, but Bayldon shook his head.

"I see what you're saying and why you're saying it. Problem is," he said, "it's damned expensive and about as far as Gerefwīc, now, anyway."

He was correct, of course, having superior local knowledge to mine; but something else was afoot in the surrounding countryside, some menace just out of sight. We were granted a detailed illustration of it when we passed through a rift in the fog, and would have been decidedly happier if we had not.

We saw only the aftermath of the disaster, but that was more than enough. The many barrows dotted about had *every one of them* been similarly exhumed, the disgorged stones of the interior cairns and the dark, heavily rooted topsoil that encapsulated them spilled from the wounds. The rubble was heavily trodden, leaving traces that stretched far from their origins; tracks of men, of horses, and most disquieting of all, the twin rutted marks of a *chariot*. A number of aurochs had been driven together and cruelly slaughtered, stuck with lances and pelted with still-protruding javelins. Great sport had apparently been made of their hunting, but they had not been butchered or skinned, being instead left to rot. Rivulets of darkened gore matted the fur in trickled lines. A few of the beasts' entrails had spilled from terminal wounds. One head had been severed and tossed some distance away. Felicia and Feran were deeply unsettled.

"*Shit*," choked Bayldon. I met his gaze to find his eyes wide and wet with fear, his skin, for all the brisk cold, still clammy.

"What a depraved assemblage... I had never expected such brigands to infest this region," I remarked with feigned disbelief.

"A band of fucking reavers is what they are. How can they be desperate enough to rob old graves, but well-off enough to leave the meat?" Bayldon spat. "Bastards."

He unsheathed his sword and rustled in his pouch for something as he watched the landscape. His hand eventually closed on the needful item, which he withdrew and revealed to be a fist-sized whetstone. This he set to work on his blade, drawing it along its length in slow, deliberate movements.

"We should continue and attempt to reach the safety of the settlement," I whispered.

"Yes, of course," agreed Alton's ward. "Once there we can raise a hue and cry... get a manhunt on."

I nodded my assent and we restarted our trot. The thick fog once again submerged us but was now more irregular, providing us with occasional unwanted glimpses at the continuing devastation. In one of these windows I was forced to position myself in such a way as to partially shield Bayldon's view, for within the steep ditch on my right side was an upturned, ruined cart whose owner, a man I could scarcely recognise as Sutton, lay brutalised and mangled over the axle. He had been pierced many, many times; far more than would kill a man.

For the first time, I believe that I was more afraid than the young man at my side. I had never known revenants to be so abundant, nor to act in this way, so coordinated and galvanised. More often they wander, solitary and unconscious of others, as if seeking a meaning that none can contemplate before either disappearing or eventually embracing death once again. Only active hindrance might provoke the lonely wayfarers from this un-dead trance. This... this was something different. The barrow's occupants had arisen, that much was certain; the area was saturated with the tinge of their unnatural presence. But it was all so abnormal, exceptions clad in exceptions. What did it all mean? Had another, more careless and malefic necromancer taken up residence nearby? What was the purpose of this wanton violence? These questions and their unpalatable answers inspired - and continue to inspire - a most sickening dread within me. A pilgrimage of revenants, I may be capable of deterring; but a talented necromancer commanding a relentless horde of un-dead cavalry? I would be less sure of my ability to wrest away their control in a surprise attack. I was susceptible; more so than I had been for decades. And I was not enduring the sensation well.

Our pace was quickened when we resumed it, the trot escalated to a canter. It was difficult to maintain considering my age and Bayldon's raw saddle-sores, but the hidden sun was dropping below the horizon ahead and the light was slipping away. The horses were pushed to their limits, their bits foaming and their breathing laboured. We were relieved indeed when the steepening ground evinced that we were climbing the edge of the basin. We slowed only hesitantly as we reached its peak. There the horses were allowed to recover, and the sun fell away entirely to plunge us into a murky blackness. Were Bayldon not now on a familiar path, we might have been utterly lost. That is, until another interval in the drifting fog showed us Gerefwīċ Hundred, lit up with an abundance of tiny lights: stationary ones from hearths that shone through the apertures of houses; and ones that moved gradually along the paths, the torches of the night watchmen. It was a welcoming enough sight that we started our descent that very moment and without a word of conference.

The way was treacherous due to its harsh incline and sharp turns, but so heartened were we by our propinquity to home that it was quickly negotiated. Bayldon greeted the watchman, who recognised him and permitted our passage. Before progressing, my young companion whispered something to the guard. Then, unaware and unheedful of the time, we traversed the final, straight trackway like happy drunkards, with exasperated laughter and joviality. It would have been impossible for Alton not to hear us, and so he met us at the entrance to his tavern with an enormous grin across his face.

"Glad to see you, gentlemen!" he called to us. "How about some hot mead?"

We made eager noises of approval, dismounted and handed the reigns to Alton. Bayldon also removed his helmet and cloak, making a deliberate nuisance of himself by piling them onto his elder's other arm.

"Did you miss me?" he teased, then adopted a serious tone. "We're going to have guests shortly. Stable the horses and meet me by the fireplace."

"Guests? Guests?" interrogated Alton as he raised a suspicious eyebrow.

"I've - I mean, we've - got to report something to the watch."

"I see! Well, I'll keep the mead hot, then, shall I?"

"Thanks, dad. I'm really glad to see you again."

Alton was taken by surprise and flustered by this last comment. It may be a sentimentality that is rarely shared so directly between them, but I expect his adoptive father dwelt often in Bayldon's mind during moments of danger. The innkeeper mumbled something as he led Feran and Felicia to the stables. His ward and I did not wait for him, craving too urgently the warmth of the flames. We sat promptly on the sheepskin closest to it and held our fingertips as near as we could bear to.

"Don't worry, I won't mention anything they don't need to know," uttered Bayldon under his breath.

"I trust you completely," I assured him, "though I may leave you to make the report yourself. You are more familiar to them and they will have greater trust in your words. My aging joints are creaking, and I should very much like to sleep in a comfortable bed. These previous few days have been much too exciting for me!"

"I think I've gotten a hint of how you feel, mate," he said, smiling and lightly squeezing my shoulder. "You slouch off, I'll sort things here."

"Thank you. For the tolerable company, too. I appreciate it. Also, I would prefer to avoid attempting to provide an explanation for *this*," I said, mischievously flashing the amber mask at him from between the folds of my robe. The gesture elicited a playful nudge and a scoff from the young man.

"Go on, you, I think I hear the guards. I'll have Alton bring you your drink. Sleep well!"

"Likewise, assuming you are not interrogated throughout the night."

With that, I departed from him there and hobbled to my chamber to find it just as I had left it. I shed some of the more cumbersome layers and replaced them with a wrapping of blankets. Alton soon knocked to provide me with my heated mead and to check my wellbeing, which is now quickly improving. I indicated that we could discuss details of the journey tomorrow. I still possessed a vestige of energy, and I thus might have proved capable of regaling the account then and there; but the truth was that I was exhausted and I had much to write while the memories were fresh. Now I shall seize some well-deserved sleep, even if I *can* discern the incomprehensible, muffled discourse of the gathering outside...

...

Bright eyes glower at the cloaked, aging man from the shadows, reflecting the flickering torchlight. They watch curiously from the inky darkness until the illumination proper reaches them; then they skitter further into the cave and recommence their vigil from another, more distant crevice. Bats, rats and vermin of all kinds linger here, but this may not always have been the case. This was supposedly once the home of something... different.

There were discrete rumours of this place among the Ilibanese aristocrats. It was akin to a fable, a frightening tale with which parents could infuse children with obedience and caution; but there was something more to this one. Some fringe groups had come to refer to it with a certain element of respect or veneration. The Timeless Cavern. *The aging man had asked a great number of these ideologues where they might theorise its location, and he had marked a target area based on correlations in the results. Now arrived, he is not entirely certain what he should be looking for.*

The exterior was inconspicuous enough. Caves are not exactly common to this region, though mineshafts, both active and abandoned, are quite pervasive. A natural limestone cavern, contrastingly, would be a unique landmark; but this one was well hidden, buried as it was beneath a thick, tangled mesh of overgrown rhizomes and ivies. A pair of raised skeletons, who now shuffled behind him in the narrow passage, had taken considerable time to hack a way through using their keen falcatas. Now they are pressed closely into the tight corridor together, advancing into the primordial unknown.

The minions at his back are of limited practical use in such cramped conditions, but the presence of the armed guards provides some inexplicable moral support. The surroundings are wondrous and alien, with every slick, ridged surface the colour of bleached bone. Long, drooping stalactites are suspended as far downwards as his head. Above him in the recesses of the wide, conical roots are more coupled orbs, glinting whence the torchlight cannot penetrate. Their incessant scuttling is one of the few sounds present now that the outside forest has been left far behind. His careful footsteps on the smooth, wet floor are another, as is the subtle rattling of the un-dead frames. The air is humid and his breathing audibly heavy. The ceiling drips constantly onto the explorer and into tiny, eroded reservoirs. The acoustics amplify these otherwise minor noises into an echoing cacophony. Most rarely, the clack of an especially prominent dripstone, incidentally snapped as the aging man blunders through it, persists repetitiously for several moments.

The cloaked man breathes a sigh of relief as the cavern widens. He steps into the space and relishes the opportunity to rotate his shoulders and flex his arms. The animated servants take up positions on his left and right, falcatas at the ready against the gloom. But nothing comes; not that he is seriously expecting adversaries. Every sign thus far has pointed to this being a natural formation and nothing more. Still, the way inside was difficult and he is determined to satisfy his admittedly dwindling curiosity, so he begins to circumambulate the chamber, holding the flame close to the wall so as to check for anything of interest.

He leaves the skeletons where they are and follows the wall on the right, the flame revealing more and more blank, featureless surface. Wait, there - pigment? A pictograph...? No, merely a discoloured dappling of minerals. How droll! This cave could continue for several miles and amount to several miles of cave. A waste of his time. Following rumours regarding black magic had taken him to extraordinary discoveries in the past, but it seemed this one might prove to be a false lead. The cultists truly believed in a mysterious and formidable presence dwelling within this underground system. Perhaps their faith is unfounded.

An unnerving sensation grips the aging man unexpectedly. He spins about and waves the torch, triggering the retreat of a dozen of the diminutive eyes but exposing nothing else. The tunnel may have its own air flow; it is not unknown for a perfectly ordinary cave to 'breathe', causing a candlelight to flutter or even to be extinguished. This is why he bears a torch instead; its larger, healthier flame would be less likely to succumb to such a mishap.

He shakes his head, disappointed with his own fretfulness, and resumes his surveyance. He moves more quickly, not due to any lingering fear but because he is already resigned to the expedition's failure. This is the third of such chambers he has encountered, and he foresees as little of relevance in this one as in those prior.

Aha! Here there is something. Or, rather, there is a notable nothing. A hole in the wall. It is a foot wide and the same in height, much like a window, and offers a view into a new room. The man tries to peer into the umbra but the glare from the torch is too much, so he puts his arm through the opening, obscuring the flame from his direct sight and casting the light over the space below. The details fill out as if lit by a subterranean sun, divulging to the necromancer a vision beyond his wildest speculations.

A vast expanse opens up before him. Much of it is a magnificent hypogean lake, milky in colour and immaculately still. Further out on the periphery of the luminance is an edifice, definitely built by intelligent hands. It is gargantuan, *even if it can be only partially beheld; a line of towering columns featuring a bizarre, organic architecture hold up a triangular peaked roof framed with a ribcage-like motif. It is strangely styled and impossibly scaled. He is both drawn to it and horrified by it. Resisting its temptation is inconceivable.*

Just as he feels he will never be able to divert his gaze, a new distraction pervades his ears. A low, rapid clicking, like a rotating cog-rattle. It recurs elsewhere. An echo? Or an answer? *He twitches his head like a night-owl, trying in vain to locate the origin, but it ceases as abruptly as it began and leaves him doubting his senses.*

He shakes away the trepidation, leaving the aperture to peruse the wall. He is possessed utterly by the need to reach that enigmatic

166

temple, and the desire has caused him to throw some (but not all) of his caution to the wind. He again draws the armed un-dead close as he comes upon another tightening of the cavern; a corridor.

They must lead to there eventually, *he thinks to himself.* What eldritch knowledge must be held in that place?

The passage narrows, then narrows further. In his haste he realises that he had almost become wedged, and he pauses for a few moments to consider his next move.

Suddenly, a frightfully powerful wind nearly causes him to lose his balance. It feels disturbingly like a monstrous inhalation, *pulling him towards to interior of the cavern. A violent clatter cascades behind him; his skeletons have collapsed into scatterings of inert, lifeless bones. Panicked and confused, he attempts to reanimate them only to find that his manna reserves have been wholly* sapped *by the unearthly gale. Terrified, he scrambles to snatch up one of the fallen blades and trips, spraining his ankle and leaving him sitting among the disarranged pieces of his former guards with his face to the corridor. He holds the torch high in his left hand and the weapon ready in the right, questioning inwardly if he is finally bereft of his sanity.*

The myriad eyes rush into the crevice. At first they appear to be routing, but they are, in fact, coalescing. *The many, many eyes, now all in an improbably small cluster, stare at him inimically. Then, they lurch forwards as if of a singular, heavy bulk. The man starts to push himself away and narrowly avoids a giant, hinged spike, blacker than pitch, as it strikes the ground before him and scrapes itself back to score a deep mark into the ground.*

The aging man does not wait for another attack. He clambers, stumbling to his feet, and sprints towards the way out, heedless of the screaming pain from his leg. It is a miracle that he does not slip, or strike a wall, or suffer any other calamity.

The next thing he is aware of is being at the mouth of the cave, blinking his eyes against the daylight. It had felt like half a day in that accursed place, yet it appears as if no time has passed at all. At some point in the escape he had evidently lost his pack, contained in which are his vital supplies and the essential map.

He looks back at the cave's entrance, which appears now to him as a gaping, ravenous maw.

The cloaked man hurls the sword haphazardly at the mouth, turns about and walks in the opposite direction, briskly.

The memories of that place had somehow departed my mind. How I wish they could be forgotten once more! I shall not sleep soundly tonight, and I may be incapable of doing so ever again!

Sōlrest-Þridda-XX

Unable to bear the thought of reliving certain memories again, I spent the remainder of the night reading over this journal by the light of my lantern. This helped me to reorder my mind and brought two things to my attention: firstly, the speculation that the veiled woman who stalked the graveyard might have been the druidess in another disguise, and that she was likely spying on me unnoticed for far longer; and secondly, that I had yet to arrange for a session at the archives.

Both of these are focally curiosities, and the latter I was recently considering the abandonment of, along with my investments in necromancy throughout my twilight years. However, my curiosity was newly enflamed by the vagueries and euphemisms of the priestess, whose words had come to inhabit my thoughts in all waking hours. I may not have been ensnared so directly as Bayldon was, but I now find myself undeniably tangled within a web of intrigue; one which I am surely resigned to investigate. As such, I decided that the most substantive aspect of today's agenda would be to attain access to the archives or, failing that, at least to secure an appointment for the near future.

As I was urging life back into my unrested limbs, I noticed that there were no sounds permeating into my room from the street, not even if I held very still and strained my ears. Not only was this excessively subdued for a market day, it was also quieter than the average working morning. I found my feet, dressed, and left my room in search of Alton or Bayldon for an explanation. Sure enough, the innkeeper sat by the hearth; but he seemed forlorn. His young ward was nowhere to be seen, so I resolved to speak with him to see if I could not improve his mood somewhat.

"An eventful night, Alton?"

"Yes and no, mate," he said uneasily, pressing the bridge of his nose with the fingertips of both hands. "Couldn't dare myself to sleep last night, is all."

"We shared a predicament, then. I should have you reimburse me for such restless conditions!"

"Thank you for keeping Bayldon safe, but I wish I hadn't sent him out there. I shouldn't have tricked the two of you."

"You could not possibly have known about the raiders, Alton," I consoled him. "If I had any supposition of them, I would myself have abstained."

"There was something else, though," he continued sullenly. "Another thing I did which maybe I shouldn't have."

There was an uncomfortable pause wherein Alton said nothing, but rubbed his eyes and head anxiously.

"I have no use for suspense at my age, Alton."

"Sorry. Well, there's a reason I had you both sent away together, and it *was* to keep you both safe; that much is true. But as it happens, I had the two of you sleep and shoved you out of the door on account of something that happened on the seventeenth."

"The trial?" I pressed, his imprecision fuelling my agitation.

"No, after that. When it was all finished with, you were waiting to get out one by one, right? Well at that point, most of the Arx men left for their temple. All except one, actually."

"Episcopus Urbānus." I predicted. A sinking sensation began to fill my stomach.

"Made that sort of impression on you too, did he?" he sniffed grimly. "The bastard decided to go to the stables instead. Got on his steed and left Gerefwīċ Hundred. But not before making one last stop, at Wurt's house..."

"Surely not?" I gasped, mouth agape. The situation was much more dire than I had realised.

"I'm afraid so. Rode Wurt down just outside his own home and ran him through in cold blood, then took off as fast as his charger could carry him."

"Along the eastern road, I would wager."

"That's right, mate. Outrode the guards without a sweat, then bolted. His party are hiding out in the temple still, saying that they can't be held accountable for his doings," Alton sniffed and stared downwards in disbelief.

"What of young Camden, and his mother?" I inquired.

"Gone. I reckon Wurt guessed at what might happen, so he arranged for them to be smuggled away during the judgement. It could have been worse, maybe, however queer it is to say that."

"We can only hope," I remarked.

"Why do you say it like that?" he asked, worry creeping into his voice.

"Let us simply acknowledge that Arx Turrium is not best known for its measured responses."

"They surely aren't," agreed the innkeeper.

It was an assuredly gross understatement. Sōlis Mūnus considers any threat to its authority as personally insulting, so on reflection it should have been of little surprise to me that Wurt's 'reward' would not be to his liking. The question now is; who else do they consider responsible for their humiliation?

"You were wise to send us away, my friend," I said with a subtle nod of appreciation.

"I'd like to have thought so, mate. I thought I'd done some good; so you can imagine the look on my face when I heard about that roaming gang of bandits!"

"We saw only the aftermath of their presence. Fields of looted barrows and slaughtered livestock, and at least one dead merchant."

"And the rest, mate!" he piped, exasperated. "The roads are *deadly,* it's a wonder the two of you made it back in one piece! At least a dozen of the market traders have been found killed, and probably a fair few more on top of those, too."

"When did they first reveal themselves? Who are they?"

"The 'when' is easy, because we reckon showing themselves might have been one of the first things they did. Supposedly, a party of the bastards were spotted on the eastern ridge. They were on horseback and had a *chariot* of all things! That was the afternoon of the day you both left. Then, the stories started coming back of what they were up to..."

"And the who?" I interrupted, not necessarily eager to learn more of what I likely already knew.

"Well, that's the big question, isn't it? We thought that Westfæsten might have let some Sjórvǫrðr slip past by accident, but they looked all wrong. Besides, we reckoned the sea-raiders don't tend to make use of horses all that much. Not very handy to have on their ships."

"A reasonable deduction," I concurred.

"Right. So we thought they could be a Caillic warband, come over from the north. But that didn't fit either; they like their horses and a fair few of their drawings even have them on chariots. But they weren't acting right by half, killing random folk and animals isn't usually their game, is it?"

"More astute observations."

"You sound like you know a bit more about this than we do. What are you keeping up your sleeves?" he pushed, his eyes narrowing. Evidently he was growing increasingly suspicious of my furtive tone.

Had I any justifiable reason to keep the nature of the aggressors a secret? I had kept it from Bayldon so as to protect him from unnecessary and avoidable alarm, but did the settlement itself truly require the relative comfort of such a deception? All things considered, defending themselves against a marauding host of revenants would be much the same as with any mortal antagonists. If a necromancer holds some grudge against Stilneshire, there is little I could say to prepare them against such an adversary, though I could provide (covert) succour to the best of my ability if that were the case.

"The pillaged tombs suggest they are desperate men to me," I posited after some time. "I predict them to be either a band of deserters or a collection of roaming vagabonds, armed and thus emboldened."

"What about the Arx? Don't you think it could be them in disguise, settling scores and slights?"

"I suspect not, my friend. Arx Turrium's soldiery behave disgracefully in many ways, but they do retain their own codes of law and honour, if not anyone else's. Military deceit is not something they practice, and they despise Caill doubly for their employment of it.

"No, if anything we might hope for this latest problem to resolve our old one; for these outlaws to have taken and slain Urbānus as he fled."

"I take your meaning," Alton nodded. "I suppose a shepherd might get some bitter-sweet joy if a travelling pack of wolves were to kill a prowling bear! Do you reckon it's very likely?"

"No," I conceded sadly, "that would be much too fortunate. And too fitting a conclusion for him. Fate is seldom so just."

"Too right," he ceded and sighed. "Men such as him are always above us in law *and* luck."

"However, they will fall further than the rest of us when they do so," I hissed. *And I shall ensure that Episcopus Urbānus plummets spectacularly if I receive so rare an opportunity,* I added inwardly.

"Hear, hear," Alton muttered in agreement as he filled a pair of tankards from one of the barrels. Handing one to me, we gently tapped them together and drank. The ale was cool, rich and delicious.

"So has Bayldon informed you of yesterday's events?" I asked, breaking the brief silence.

"Not a great deal. He did mention that there wasn't a 'great deal' to tell, but that you'd tell it. Pretty uneventful until the last leg, he reckoned."

"That is about the sum of it," I shrugged my shoulders in a deliberate show of disinterest. "There was no one to be found as we lingered at the Leafbrym, and I must confess that I foolishly discarded the antler into the river..."

"You *what?*" he exclaimed, amazed.

"Shamefully, yes! I am afraid that in a lapse of reason I postulated that there might be some spell in place, so I tossed it. There it broke through the ice and was promptly washed out of sight. There was, of course, no spell of any sort, and we left disappointed as well as empty-handed."

"You daft old coot!" Alton guffawed uproariously, and I had joined him before he went on. "That sounds as mad as something *I'd* do! Why, I can see why Bayldon left me to hear it from the horse's mouth!"

"Yes, his generosity knows no bounds," I managed between bouts of laughter, "and I shall be sure to give him proper thanks for his discretion!"

The young man in question had indeed proven to be a capable keeper of secrets. He might possibly have made for a fine necromancer, had he not already well implanted himself among Ewin Falken and the other local officiators... though I would not wish my growing pains upon any individual I name a friend.

"So, what are you up to today then, mate? More secrets? Or you can stay in the warm and get drunk," said Alton, the latter part with a touch more enthusiasm.

"I shall be taking my planned visit to the archives and staying for a while should I be allowed entry today. Then, I shall return to your fine establishment to enable your bad habit. Satisfied?"

"Fair enough," he grinned. Alton was of a much more agreeable humour, and I left him feeling I had made a positive impact. It is an experience to which I am still acclimatising.

The conditions outside were reasonably favourable. The cold was less gnawing than that of the morning previous and the fog was all but replaced by a drab, overcast sky and a soft drizzle, tolerable enough to traverse without my heavier cloak. The main thoroughfare, usually churned into a treacherous mire by the market day traffic, was still nearly pristine. The excluded merchants and the news of the extrinsic threat had turned the hundred into a settlement of recluses, many of the people opting to remain in the relative perceived safety of their houses. Few were seen travelling outside, and those that were moved briskly. It was a mute, lonely walk to the archives.

Once there I was immediately discouraged. Again its doors were closed and locked to me, and I was becoming increasingly tempted to succumb to my irritation and gain entry through illegitimate means, but I reconsidered and instead shifted my focus to the town hall. I let myself in and sought the reeve at his office, petitioning the two guards to allow me a meeting. One of them entered, presumably consulted with Ewin behind the closed door, then opened the way and beckoned me inside. Once I had crossed the threshold, the guard exited and left us alone.

Reeve Ewin Falken's study is a fairly decadent space by the local standards and the aesthetics of the building's interior are no lesser in this room. The ceiling is high-peaked and an ornate, blazing fireplace is set into one wall, though the others are draped not with the sort of colourful tapestries that one might expect to see in such a place but with numerous framed charters, plans and maps. It would be easily possible to mistake some of them for duplicates, however they were, in fact, progressive, representing various iterations and changes regarding the settlement's layout and functions. Through the sequences, one can extrapolate the county's transition from quite minimalistic origins to a region brimming with farmland. Shelves are stacked with scrolls and ledgers of documentation, and the grand stone desk (more reminiscent of an altar than a table) is flush with recesses for inkwells and devices for counting. What initially presented itself as an ostentatious, lordly chamber is, in reality, a most practical study. Like a war-room, from it could be organised all of Stilneshire's six hundreds, their pasts, presents and potential futures plotted. Needless to say, I was singularly impressed.

"Sorry to disturb your work, Reeve," I began, commencing a curt bow but interrupted by a firm handshake.

"The pleasure's mine, my friend. I'm glad to see you," he addressed me excitedly, his eyes gleaming. "You've done a great service to us, even if namelessly, and we shan't forget it soon. How can I return the favour?"

"Service?" I looked back at him, baffled and bemused. "Bayldon would have returned safely, perhaps safer still, without my hindrance."

"Ah, the watchmen did see you two leave. When the bandits came we had half a mind to chase after you and bring you back, but it would have either left Gerefwīċ defenseless or sent too small a party to their deaths. Still," he added, placing a hand on my shoulder with genuine relief, "it seems our expectations of your resourcefulness weren't unfounded, thank the gods.

"No, I'm referring to your transcript of poor Wurt's judgement. We've sent a copy with Ealdorman Heorot to King Ricbert, who will surely give it the attention it needs."

"The transcript! I dare say that I had close to forgotten about it. What action do you suppose it will coax from Ricbert?"

"Myself? Nothing," he stated bluntly. "Heorot reckons different, however. He insisted that he might bend the king's ear. That man's been itching to cast off the Arx since taking his place with the king's own, biding his time and quietly gathering all the evidence he needs to paint a sharp likeness of the Arx; and it isn't a pretty picture, I'll say that much. I take it Alton has informed you of Urbānus' parting insult?"

I grimaced and nodded.

"I believe Wurt's slaying was the last quench Heorot's blade needed, so to speak," he surmised.

"He is a brave man," I remarked to the reeve's immediate frown, "considering that the king's court is now not entirely his own."

"That's exactly what I said to him, in as many words. And do you know what he said back to me?"

"What did he say?"

"He said, 'If King Ricbert would do nothing, his subjects would take action in his place,'" Ewin recounted, the volume of his voice diminishing to a whisper as he did so.

He, much as every man, woman and child in his hundred, was fearful. Tumultuous change seemed to be perched above Cemparīċe like a vast, menacing raven, ready at any moment to descend and pick at the vestiges of their once simplistic lives. Not even during the schism of Sūþeard and subsequent founding of Sċeldlond had their ways of life been so close to the brink of dissolution. The folk of this settlement were terrified, and rightly so; but it could be that the transpirations of these past few days are to serve as a catalyst for something broader still. The reeve may know his immediate jurisdiction to a fault, but the ealdorman attends a court of many others, making his position far less insular; the ealdormen talk, often in secret, and Heorot must have gauged a mutual attitude to be so certain of his machinations. I wonder... how many leaders of the counties are involved in plotting these potentially treasonous conspiracies? Do the councillors of Sċeldlond's republic share comparable discussions behind closed doors? I have known long of the dwindling patience of the subjects, but I had not predicted such communicable detestation among the elites, whom the Arx permit relative comfort.

"Troubling times," was all I could think to comment, succinct and unhelpful though it was.

"I'm sorry to have roped you into this, friend," he apologised glumly. "I'm quite sure it's not what you came to Stilneshire for."

"Not exactly. But at least I might spectate something important and exciting in my final years," I said, straining partway between a weary grin and a grimace. It was an honest sentiment, but darkened by the inevitable loss of too many innocent lives.

"A ripe tuber beneath the dirt, I suppose," he smiled weakly in answer. "Anyway, let's set that dark business aside for the moment; what can *I* do for *you,* my esteemed friend?"

"I should very much like to do some research in the archives, if that would be convenient and permissible."

"I always did take you for the scholarly type," Ewin chuckled. "I might have endeavoured to warn you about a good portion of it being in Old Sunþrardic, but something makes me think that *that* wouldn't provide an obstacle for yourself. Or do I miss my mark?"

My only response was a smirk and a sly wink. It is far from my most competent tongue, but I happen to have one of my referenced guides with me. Although it is only a self-made and abridged vocabulary, it should prove sufficient alongside some applied grammatical knowledge.

"I thought as much!" the reeve beamed, "I'll have a second set of keys forged for you by tomorrow, so they should find their way to your hands by morning. The bigger key will get you into the oldest section, which I'd guess is where you probably want to be. We had it closed off separate; you'll see why when you get there, but I'll tell you now that it's nothing to do with what's written in the texts."

"Most intriguing!" I declared, my interest doubly piqued.

"It's in the words that the *real* treasure awaits, I expect. I'm jealous, really. To my understanding, no one's ever looked through them properly since they were made, and there's not many that are capable now. I've always wondered what secrets this place was founded on..." Ewin paused to gaze thoughtfully at his majestically decorated surroundings before finding his way back to reality. "It must have been something... *nobler.*"

"It truly is beautiful," I reflected, admiring the masonry alongside him. "Be assured, if I discover anything of note inside the archives, I shall inform you as soon as I am able."

"I look forward to it!" Reeve Ewin beamed again, clasping my hand in his for a firm handshake.

We said our farewells and I departed his office. The guards took little notice of me as I passed them to exit the building, leaving behind the opulent architecture for the steady, restrained rainfall.

The weather was relatively cordial then, but the sky threatened worse. My primary business was concluded as well as it could be for the moment and I had a significant duration of time to use. Gerefwīc's roads appeared still to be trodden only by the ghosts and I, and I was of two minds whether to retire immediately to The Old Boar or to visit the mausoleum first. I decided on the latter option; it had been too long (four days) left unattended, which could result in another emergently dangerous situation.

I tried to keep to the banks of the road, the track itself having become a veritable swamp in the rain. The grassy edges had fared slightly better, the tufts providing static, if slippery, footholds. Soon I was traversing the graveyard's watchful willows and climbing the hill to that familiar, dominating structure. During the ascent I looked about me and was shocked, for the grass in the cemetery was withering, against all reason, as if it were sun-parched. The siphon of my sapping circle must have been drawing substantially more energy than it should, which is, by all accounts, a cause for concern.

At the summit I peered into the entrance, searching for obvious signs of misadventure, but there were none. I noted that the lock had remained intact before I opened it to allow my passage and descent into the gloom. Thankfully I was spared the discomfort of wading through pools, for the light rain was apparently insufficient to overburden the drainage. Still, the pervasive sound of falling droplets reilluminated awful images from disquieting dreams, causing my heart to race at the reminiscence. After rounding the penultimate corner, however, the tension I felt was relaxed; eased of all things by the familiar, hollow sockets of Rēdawulf the archer.

There were no fresh corpses of graverobbers, nor smashed skeletons and pillaged tomes. It was, as could only be the case with an obeisance of un-dead, *precisely* as I had left it. My precious artefacts - the texts, the channelling rod and the failed phylactery - remained mercifully untouched. I looked my un-dead retinue over one by one, remembering their names: Rēdawulf, Ermunahild, Haþuwīgą, Helparīks, Hildirīks, and Audaward. And I contemplated whether the time had come for them to be unmade, to have them climb back into their sarcophagi and cease existing once again.

But, given the situation, do I not owe the local people my protection? I thought to myself.

Why do you owe them anything? spoke another, older voice in my head, one that was becoming increasingly unfamiliar. *It matters not how many 'friends' you make; they would still have you killed if they knew you for what you truly are.*

They were cruel, sobering notions and my rationalisations against them were weak and sentimental. My presence could well become the crux in the face of an invasion, be it one of revenants or a rival necromancer, but would I be offered any further quarter than the enemy should I be revealed in the process of their defense? It would be foolish to assume otherwise. In truth, an encompassing blame would more than likely find its way to my neck. Why, then, should I be encumbered by a sense of loyalty?

They are good people. You know this, the younger aspect chimed. The voice in my imagination sounded so akin to that of the priestess that I instinctively glanced behind me to reassure myself of her absence. No, my mind had assigned that wise, whimsical and benevolent intonation to the sympathetic argument, and I was greatly inclined to heed it.

I took the artefact staff and sat upon one of the displaced sarcophagi, beside my would-be phylactery. The skeletons gathered around, encircling me in a way most other men would consider frightful, but I found it comforting. The un-dead were simple; one dimensional, devoid of moral question or complex choice. Reeve Ewin Falken may be envious of my scholarship, but I had, in some way, become envious of my minions' existential mundanity. At my merest whim they would follow or tarry, defend or attack, slay enemies... or even slay their master. The concept lingered as my eyes moved from weapon to deadly weapon and across the leering skulls. It was not its first occurrence since my aspirations of Arch-Lichdom were dashed.

I shook myself. If my life (though it proved shorter than my intentions) may be of significance to worthy people, I shall require neither gratitude nor validation from them, even enduring their misguided hatred and persecution if I must.

The overpowering aura, meanwhile, required my immediate attention. The chalk guidelines had been distorted and washed away, but these lose relevance the moment the spell is put in place. I moved the phylactery object to the floor and had Ermuna open the sarcophagus on which it sat, then bade her retrieve *Kýkloi Dunámeōn*. This she held open to me, allowing me to rifle through its leaves in search of solutions. It was only on the final pages that I happened upon an abbreviated discourse on so-called 'critical circumstances', most of which detailed rare aberrations with catastrophic outcomes. I had read through this in its entirety before, of course, but the conditions described were apparently rare enough for me to have never encountered a single one of them. The disasters ranged in severity from a circle that consistently fails without discernible cause, to an instant and devastating explosion. Generally speaking, most necessitated reckless technique to facilitate such a calamity; the manner of mistakes that would be far beneath even a journeyman in magic.

All but one fell into the aforementioned category, the exception being a phenomenon known as a 'Manna Glutton'. This peculiar mishap, according to the tome, is the result of an extremely overburdened sapping circle, one that is laboured with the provision of an escalating manna demand. In theory, this could be mistaken for a simple error; in practice, the sheer quantity of manna needed to push an auratic spell beyond its regular boundaries is *staggering*. The three anecdotes (or possibly ancient historical examples, they would be impossible to verify) given in the treatise each involved entire *clans* of spellcasters, all sharing the use of a single 'font' during a period of intense magic use. Two of the three were attempting to bring about an extensive and ruinous meteorological upheaval. The third seems to have been a gambit to destroy the mythological beast known as *Adamastor* in its eponymous strait. All three met with failure mostly due to the accidental emergence of a Manna Glutton. Despite the name's suggestion it is not a living being, much as a whirlpool or a sinkhole is not; it is simply the descriptor for a sapping circle that has begun to drain its locality of essence in *exponential volumes*. This can culminate in one or both of two possibilities: one eventuality is the loss of any semblance of control and consequent annihilation of any who attempt it, at which point the spell tends to dissipate; the other climax is when everything in the vicinity is utterly enervated, the zone rapidly desolating into a freezing, abiotic locus.

I stepped back from Ermuna and looked. I sought with my natural eyes and I sought with my attuned, supernatural senses, and I could detect *nothing* which adequately explained the increased draw of manna. My sapping circle was operating at a steadily mounting capacity and had expanded further than its set specifications, but I could not locate the leak. There was no evidence that the power had been tapped, no trace of an alien perversion of my array. I could feel an influx of magical potency through my veins, but if I were truly assimilating the complete brunt of the accumulation... I should have expected to be *very, very ill*.

I was obfuscated. Such a concentration of manna cannot simply *disappear*. I dared not sever the spell's influence lest it ardently unleash some unseen, pent-up reserve, like a dam breached by floodwaters. I decided that the most prudent alternative would be to open more channels and thus ease the turbulence... *praying* for a cessation of the deteriorating crisis.

To that end I had my assistants clear some floorspace and traced out four further sigils equidistantly. This may seem counterintuitive, but by spreading the labours of the hyperactive one, the sum consolidation may become easier to regulate. The measures seemed successful; with the introduction of each complementary spell, the excess ebbed away before reaching a stage of moderation. I stayed a while, watching for a relapse until satisfied that one was not perceptibly forthcoming. Then I positioned my guards and left, myself burdened with an unshakeable and dilating sense of angst. I can no longer responsibly leave the crypt for days at a time. Not until this strangeness is terminated.

The weather had maintained its merciful restraint for my curt walk back to The Old Boar, and in this solitary aspect did I feel fortunate. When I arrived at the tavern, however, things were quickly rectified. In the short-term, certainly.

"Hail, old man!" came a happy shout over the din. "Come and sit with us!"

I was not unpleasantly surprised by the gathering I happened upon at The Old Boar. Bayldon, or Alton, or the two working in cooperation, had somehow coaxed a small collection of the townsfolk from their homes. The ale and conversation flowed seamlessly, the young men relieved to have escaped the depressing undercurrent - if only for a short time. They were jovial, merry and, not least of all, *loud*. Hearing them from outside, I had expected a group of twenty or so, rather than barely a dozen. Still, their tone suggested that they had imbibed enough intoxicant to compensate for their numbers (and more besides). Their table by the fire was supporting its very own 'miniature' keg, over which they had free reign, carried from the bar. As I sat, I wondered at whether Bayldon had taken undue liberties. It was only as my backside found the bench that Alton appeared beside the storage room, shouldering *another* keg. His face lit up as he saw me, and he accelerated his pace towards the us.

"Evening, mate! Glad you've decided to join us!" called Alton, "You've got a bit of catching up to do, mind, but we can soon see to that!"

In the midst of the plague of threats that loomed over Gerefwīċ, this celebration of sorts made for a surreal experience. Flanked by the father and his adopted son, attempts to integrate me with the others were reasonably successful and the conversation and laughter were soon flowing freely. The ale, too, was flowing freely, and I must confess to hastily becoming quite inebriated. Of the present crowd I recognised Orman and a number of his companions that were here before. This time we were properly introduced, and they were called Durwin, Bearn, Erian, Ramm, Putnam, Grindan, Holt, and Galan; though were I interrogated, I might struggle to connect the faces to those names. We thoroughly ruminated on various topics and, though we oft had difficulty in finding common ground, we discovered some points of affinity. Furthermore, the group was emboldened to engaging in open, unbridled criticism of Sōlis Mūnus, something which I had yet to hear in Sūþeard since its vassalage began. It was *wholly* refreshing to hear their unadulterated opinions on the Arx's extortionate taxes and what the labourers considered to be cultural malefactory. What they felt powerless to do with their hands they accomplished here with words, and I daresay that if words could manifest as physical force, the priests would awaken quite bruised indeed.

Alton had anticipated no further attendance and so had locked the front, allowing his guests to instead use the other way out to relieve themselves. One might imagine how we responded, then, when our festivities were unexpectedly interrupted by a late knocking at the door. The room went silent, our eyes affirming with each other that the sound was not merely imagined. Alton stumbled as he stood, glancing about nervously and creeping towards the closed entrance. Another, louder knock caused us to collectively flinch. Orman and Ramm withdrew small scramseaxes from their belts and snuck into flanking positions on either side of the door. A third, more sustained rapping shook it, but this time the trio were steeled and ready. Alton reached out gradually towards the bolt before undoing it with a mighty heave.

"You bloody shit-heads!" howled a familiar voice from outside. "It's damned scary outside, and you lot see fit to leave me out there to stew?"

"Reeve! Begging your pardon, Sir, but how were we supposed to know it was you?" Alton squeaked, high-pitched but clearly relieved.

"Can't you recognise the 'Reeve's Knock'?"

"'Reeve's Knock'? It just sounded like hammering to me!" called out Bayldon.

"Yes, that's the 'Reeve's Knock'. It means: 'I'm the fucking reeve, so you'll let me in if you know what's good for you!'"

The table snorted with suppressed laughter finally unleashed. Ewin's hooded head protruded around the corner and glowered, but in our drunken state the action only served to provoke more chortling. In the face of such light-hearted humour, however, he was disarmed. He smiled, shoved Alton's chest playfully in order to clear a way for himself and came over to kneel beside me. His cloak was damp from the showers outside and the rim of his cowl dripped on me as he leaned close.

"This is for you, friend. Keep it at hand and don't let it leave your sight," he instructed quietly and sternly, producing a pair of keys on a ring and handing them to me. I stashed them away and nodded, trying hard to maintain sincerity.

"And make sure you're sobered up before you go in there," he added, a hint of amusement in his addendum. "Can't have you throwing up on everything."

"Of course, Reeve," I answered in mock-hurt. "What do you take me for, a souse?"

My audience tittered while Ewin rolled his eyes.

"Why don't you join us, Ewin?" Bayldon invited him, prodding him in the ribs to acquire his attention.

"No, my wife would never forgive me," he declined the offer.

"But the bandits!" warned Galan in jest. "It's not safe to go back out!"

"Frankly it'd be more dangerous for me to stay, Galan. My wife would pay whatever 'captors' I'm hindered by a hefty ransom just to tan my hide herself, I reckon."

The statement was met with a cacophony of groans and booing, to which Ewin shrugged innocently.

"My hands are tied, gentlemen! Stay safe. And *you*, lad," the reeve addressed to Bayldon, "I'll see *you* bright and early."

A fresh tirade of mockery erupted from the table, directed at both Ewin and Bayldon. Among the taunts were crude insinuations of an illicit affair and the cracking of a whip. The ridicule followed Reeve Falken all the way to the exit, his parting retort taking the form of a mildly offensive hand gesture flashed back to the crowd. At his departure the levity returned with renewed enthusiasm and we continued to laugh, sing and drink the ale.

Alas, I seldom partake in frivolous consumption of this kind (being a rare attendee to social events, surprising though it may be to you, dear reader) and among these veterans of booze I was certainly outmatched. As evening transitioned to night, I began to slur like a madman; from what I understood of the others, I became extremely difficult to extract any sense from, and I was eventually persuaded to forfeit and retire for the evening.

Fortuitously, I still possessed the presence of mind to take some water before sleeping. I may have awoken with the urge to relieve myself (I found that the jubilations abided still; only now is the fervency eroding), but my head has recovered enough for me to record this entry. Now I shall sleep more extensively... preferably for as long as my vacillating conscience allows.

...

The cloaked man waits pensively, attempting in vain to hide his troubled breathing. He sits at the table in the dimly lit room, his hand resting on the base of an overturned cup. The rushlight at the table's edge flickers and occasionally flares, revealing the face beneath the high peak of the hood; middle-aged and rough, a few days' worth of stubble coating the lower half. He gives the impression of one who comfortable sleep has eluded for some time. One who is in desperate need of some good fortune. This is a table at which one can put their fortune to the test.

But this man is not relying solely on luck and bluffing. He watches the three others (to his left, right and opposite) with uncertainty. They are as rough-looking as he is, perhaps moreso. Their shaved scalps and faces bear networks of scars and sutures, and the man directly opposing him is bereft of his right eye. Their stature is intimidating, for they are tall and attest considerable brawn, and their tunics are worn and dirty. They express no aesthetic pretence of being respectable gentlemen. *The hooded man is unbearably nervous even as he utilises his tricks, for they are far superior players of this game than he is and their silent expressions are utterly opaque. Bored, even. One might even believe they were entirely unshaken by their precarious proximities to elimination.*

"Sixty-one," says the cloaked man, staring expectantly at the stranger to his left side. A conservative opening to the new round. He slides the cup over without showing its contents.

"Fifty-five," yawns the man, announcing the bid while pointedly disregarding the dice altogether. The cup is passed on.

"Thirty-three. Call me out, you spineless cunts," growls the one-eyed man in a deep, rumbling baritone. Of the three burlier competitors he is surely the ringleader. His remaining eye seems never to blink and is focussed on the cloaked one at all times. No calls were made against what the two dice might actually read, and they are moved along again.

"Twenty-two," bids the next man in a devious, mocking drawl. This one is somewhat less broad than the other two, being instead lean and sinewy. Unkempt hair and a long, pointed nose conjures the mental image of a bedraggled and starving rat, and he is blessed with a comparable personality.

Only two pairs could win the game now, and neither matches the one concealed under the cup. The hooded man's initial roll had, in actuality, scored twenty-two. He notices that none of the other players have called each other out for a number of rounds now, and the terrible truth of the situation dawns on him, freezing his insides solid.

This is it, *the cloaked man realises.* This is the tightening noose which I have tied for myself. They have been experimenting with me since their first suspicions, and now they are cooperating in order to either force my defeat or expose my cheating.

Realistically, he has no legitimate way to win at this game should the others choose to victimise him so. They must be communicating surreptitiously, somehow. He curses himself for a fool as he is hit by a second realisation; at this stage it probably scarcely matters what action he takes. The conclusion is foregone, his coming here had been a mistake, and now there would be little opportunity for escape. Yet still a simmering defiance leaps up within him; he refuses to simply lose and forfeit his last remaining coin. His near-destitution had prompted his coming to this forsaken den in Sċeldlond to gamble. Clearly he had naively miscalculated how effectively these outlaws could detect a cheat, even a supernatural one.

185

Damn them, *he broods, concentrating on the cup under his palm. The dice quiver. The 'one' faces, having been gently painted with manna, are attracted vertically to his hand. The dice settle back down to display their new score.*

"Eleven, you ugly bastards," *he spits, preparing himself for a fight.*

The three faces leer at him. Then, the one-eyed man stands up and begins to clap slowly, laughing as if he had just been told an excellent joke.

"I'd call you a liar, mate, but I'd wager you don't have the knack! You'll have to forgive my curiosity..."

He leans over and swats the hooded man's cup off the table. The twin marks look back at him and his sneer returns with fresh sadism.

"Eleven is a pretty good roll. And a one in twenty-one chance, if I'm not mistaken. But you've rolled that pair... how many times, Tolan?"

"Nine in the last dozen rounds at least, Drefan," *tallies the ratlike sycophant.*

"Nine in a dozen!" *repeats the one-eyed man, whistling in astonishment.*

"Must be beginner's luck," *shrugs the hooded man, a wry smile on his lips.*

"Beginner's luck, that's right!" *Drefan agrees cheerfully. Then he leans closer still, to the extent that his addressee smells his rancid breath and hears his whispered, almost sympathetic words:* "Do you think you're the first magician to try this here?"

The two spectators begin to cackle in a cruel, grating dissonance. The spellcaster evaluates his options; he had guessed that they had recognised a defrauder, but they had also identified him as a wielder of magic and felt fit to confront him undaunted. Once again he had demonstrated his ineptitude for character judgement when his life may well have truly depended on it.

"Shit, I was even thinking of asking if you'd join our merry band," *Drefan remarks wistfully with an exaggerated frown.* "A pet witch would be a good bit of fun, maybe even useful. But then you called my good mates 'ugly', and we can't have that! They're sensitive souls, don't you know?"

More chortling, from all three of them now.

"Surely this is no cause for incivility," whimpered a voice from the recesses of the hood, *"I am sure we can negotiate a mutually beneficial arrangement, can we not?"*

"Well it won't involve your money, I reckon we got the pittance that was left of that already," derides Drefan to more laughter, *"but I'm sure we can sort you out..."*

The thug's solitary eye is distracted by something behind the cloaked man, who turns about and attempts to shield himself from the hinted incoming assault - but none comes. He lowers his arm to see nobody.

Then the blow strikes him hard in the side of the head. He slumps in the chair, the feeling leaving his limbs; and as his vision whirls and fades, his last sight before losing consciousness is Drefan, bloodied cudgel in hand, having smote him from across the table.

Time passes. There is an aroma of burning, and of death. To the hooded man, it feels as if he opens his eyes in the very next moment. He quickly realises, however, that he had been unconscious for hours. He had been dragged outside, and the gentle warmth of the morning light is on his face. The sight he is greeted with as he absorbs his surroundings is only marginally better than the immediate ending he had expected; a wide camp extends outwards, filling up a sandy clearing that has been made in the depression of an old, shallow quarry. There are firepits, weapon racks and armed outlaws in every direction. Despite the odds he is able to spot several avenues of escape, but they are of little use to him; for there are many shackled people here, and he views all of this from the inside of a sturdy iron cage of his own.

"You're awake. Good!" Drefan's smug tones ring behind him. *"Now I'm a busy man and you've wasted enough of my time already, so I'll be brief. Don't try anything stupid, magic or otherwise, or Tolan'll stick you, and he's a good shot."*

The hooded man's attention is drawn to a shrill whistle from Tolan, who is standing on a small overlook some distance from him and manning a sizeable mounted crossbow, possibly a pilfered siege weapon. Its operator waves energetically and resights it on him with purpose. The man in the cage twists in an attempt to show Tolan a rude hand sign, only to find that his wrists are bound behind him. Drefan tuts with disapproval.

"If you ask me, you'd better just sit nice until your collector gets here."

"'Collector'? Who is this 'collector'?" asks the captive.

"None of your fucking business, that's who!" the ringleader barks, suddenly enraged. "The highest bidder! Now shut your mouth and keep it shut. You're only worth a little more alive than you are dead. Any fire, ice or whining from you and I'll have you stuck like that prick."

Drefan points skywards. Confused, the captive shuffles to the bars and shrugs back his hood to look up. Only then does he notice an unusual thing on the cage's top; a charred corpse is pinned above him by an enormous bolt (presumably from Tolan's weapon), the point of which protrudes from the body's chest, ribs splintered outwards from the forceful impact. Its arms and legs hang down awkwardly, outstretched as if attempting to grasp at him or beseech him for release. The cracked face bares blackened, empty sockets and exposed teeth alongside an expression of purest agony. Startled, the living prisoner collapses onto his back and pushes himself into the corner with his legs.

"Every time!" chuckles Drefan as he kicks sand into the prisoner's now lowered face. "I reckon his spell went bad when we stuck him. Either way, I'll see you later. Just don't go to swat a fly or anything; Tolan's twitchy today, and he'd be really very upset if you got run through by mistake!"

Drefan passes close by the cage, taking one last chance to kick more sand at his prisoner. The hooded man rubs his eyes in frustration but, by the time they are cleared, Drefan has disappeared among the tents.

The captive ignores the distraction of the threatening siege crossbow for the moment and seizes the opportunity for a more thorough examination of the area. Being restrained, starved, beaten and broken, the other incarcerated men and women would be making no attempted escapes of their own. A few bodies had already been laid naked in a perfunctory stack, piled high, presumably in preparation for their unceremonious cremation. The majority of the guards are lethargic and drowsy in the hot sun, and seem on the verge of falling to sleep at any moment; but Tolan was superlatively skittish, to the extent that his charge felt totally endangered even when absolutely inactive.

In place of any other options, the hooded man props himself up against the bars of his enclosure and attempts to find some speck of comfort. Seeing the floor of the cage inspires novel distaste as he discovers that he has been resting in the ashes and calcinated pieces of the unfortunate soul above him. He inspects the cage and approximates it to have a square base with sides of eight feet and a ten-foot height, with the cadaver's limbs dangling slightly lower than that. If said corpse's structure maintained stability, and if he were more agile (and unbound, for that matter), he might have been able to hoist himself and cling to the ceiling of his prison, but that seems as secure as any other side.

He thinks again on his torched cellmate. The slavers incinerate those who do not survive their imprisonment. Whether the remains above him had truly belonged to a pyromancer is difficult to decipher. Although the environment is noisy and distracting, the hooded man suspects he can sense a residual trace of manna in the dust that now stains his robe. This is enough to convince him and adds weight to their threats. He does, however, educe something that he can manipulate to his advantage; the slavers may know that he is a spellcaster, but have made it evident that they know not what type. *Any initiate could configure the dice as he had, but the concept that he might be a* necromancer *had obviously not occurred to them. If it* had, *he would most assuredly have been killed in his sleep. Even murderers and slavers would not knowingly suffer the presence of a master of the un-dead.*

More fool them, *thinks the necromancer. His exterior remains very still. Calm. Meditative. But internally, he is now in a state of equanimous cogitation.*

Unbeknownst to the others among the visual and auditory commotion of the camp, something gradually begins to move. From the mound of yet-unburnt bodies, a lonely individual starts to crawl, painstakingly slowly, towards Tolan. The vermin-featured criminal continues to train the heavy crossbow on the cage, oblivious to his flanks. The un-dead creature inches closer, now silently rising to its unshod feet. It stands unnoticed, now only a yard behind Tolan.

Suddenly, the sentry's ear perks and he makes to look back; but the creature lunges forth to grasp him from the rear. With unnatural strength and determination it wraps its decaying left arm about his throat, pressing his windpipe closed. Tolan's hands leave the ballista instinctively, grasping pitifully at his attacker's elbows. He pulls, scratches and hammers to no avail. As his face changes colour, he finally manages to clutch the hilt of a dagger at his belt and, using his last ounce of stamina, plunges it deep into the aggressor's eye. To his chagrin, the creature persists unfazed. It uses its right arm to twist the knife free from its own face and stab it, still coated with the gelatinous remnants of its own ruined orb, under Tolan's brow. He falls instantly limp in his un-dead killer's arms before it drops him carelessly to the ground.

Phase one... *celebrates the necromancer mutely.*

An unwelcome scream echoes across the camp.

"Damn it all," he sighs.

The caterwauling actually originated from one of those in the shackles, seemingly having seen what had transpired and not entirely approved. Now the guards were alerted and his plan would require an acceleration.

Rapidly, more and more disrobed bodies rise up to join the other in un-death. When possible, they arm themselves from the racks with an assortment of makeshift weapons; spears, scythes, forks and the like. Then they descend upon the slavers with reckless abandon. Some fight and some flee, but all of them are misdirected away from the architect of their antagonists.

A strong hand takes hold of the necromancer's hood and pulls it backwards into the bars of the cage. The collision causes his ears to ring and the world to spin.

"A fucking corpse-lord!" froths Drefan in incontinent disbelief. "My contact would give me both our weights in gold if I gave you to him alive. Still not worth it."

The necromancer winces, expecting the lethal stroke to fall. Instead he is wrenched again into the iron and his cowl, along with a substantial amount of his hair, are torn free from their respective moorings. The abrupt removal of the tension flings him forwards just as something hurtles past the back of his head, narrowly missing the cage.

"You sneaky fucker! I'll put you right," snarls Drefan. Tolan's aim is apparently less reliable in un-death than it was in life. The ringleader scampers back upright and sprints over to the cage's gate,

fumbling at the lock amid the madness and confusion. A moment later the latch snaps open and Drefan draws a long, polished sword from his scabbard. He raises it high, ready to bring it down, and... cannot. He glances upwards to find the charred, suspended body reaching down to hold the blade firmly with both of its seared hands.

"Fuck off, I killed you once already!" roars the slaver captain, tugging to retrieve his sword. He heaves mightily; mightily enough for the impaled un-dead to come crashing down atop him. The bolt through its sternum punches into the man's back, pinning him face-down in its own ashes. He struggles weakly, but the bolt has severed something vital and much of his body is unresponsive. Drefan coughs, splutters, and dies inelegantly.

Two of the armed un-dead enter the cage and step over the tangle to their master, helping him to his feet. One saws through his bonds with a scavenged cleaver, and he walks over the shell of his lead captor wearing a visage of utmost disgust. His mood lightens, however, when he exits his prison and shuts the gate behind him.

"Only a hero or a necromancer could escape captivity commanding a new army," he muses under his breath. He turns to commence his flight proper but something catches his attention. He strides towards the shackled prisoners, accompanied by a regiment of shambling carcasses. The chained, weeping men and women shiver at his approach and bow their heads, less out of respect than it is a show of their unwillingness to look upon the dire spectacle unfolding before them.

These are innocents, *considers the necromancer.* They are not deserving of the same fate as their abductors.

Innocents they may be, but an innocent you are not, *he rebutts himself,* and they have seen your face, and will likely remember it forever.

The necromancer sighs again, this time with a fathomless regret, and turns away. The un-dead advance past him on either side with their weapons readied.

Sōlrest-Þridda-XXI

Guilt is a bitter bedfellow, and I was punished with that memory several times last night. Why have I been cursed so? Is this the experience of a newly developing moral conscience? The eidetic dreams began immediately after imbibing the concoction from The Westing Spear. Perhaps the mixture had fermented and I have been poisoned. I shall observe my health carefully, though what I should use for an antidote if I begin to degrade is a mystery. This morning hunger did not touch me and I was unable or unwilling to eat, so I dressed and took water but no breakfast. My departure from The Old Boar went unopposed, and there were no traces of Alton, Bayldon or the evening's patrons beyond a disarray of strewn tankards and chairs. Upon reaching the exterior I somehow felt elated, invigorated even, as if my remorse had been transmuted to raw willpower. Purpose had put aside my life's grievances and assigned me to one of my oldest, most practiced callings; the acquisition of knowledge.

The sky was tearful but worse was brewing in those roiling clouds. Expecting them to open at any moment, I raced to the archives as quickly as my legs and stick could carry me. I twisted the smaller key just as the storm broke and, in a feat of remarkable punctuality, stepped inside 'The Stilneshire Books' before becoming particularly wet. Nevertheless, I removed my gently dripping cloak and hung it up before beginning my perusal. My initial findings, those in the main section, were essentially what I (and the reeve) predicted; a well-organised, library-like collection of entirely mundane ledgers regarding matters of property, production, taxation and law. That the records are so complete is an impressive thing in itself, but they were admittedly not what I was looking for. No, what I found in the 'vault' was far more compelling...

The smaller partition is thoroughly secured against thieves, and I could envisage no way to break into it without the correct key, magical subversion of the lock's tumblers, or siegeworks. The door is thick and sturdy, braced with riveted iron, and each wall is constructed of dense stone slabs. Aesthetically, it is exceptionally unadorned when compared with Gerefwīċ's other early masonry. Inspecting the seams of this chamber with its surrounding structure, I discovered that the 'partition' was actually the earliest part of the whole, and may have existed independently before the rest was subsequently built to complement it - much like the graveyard which expanded concentrically about the Blōþisōdaz mausoleum.

Having entered, I realised why such efforts had been made to ensure the place's impregnability. Many of the tome's covers within were either studded with precious stones or cast from gold. Additionally, they were all atavistic, written in Old Sunþrardic as Ewin had mentioned. These were no simple collated reports, either; here could be found almanacs, anthologies of poetry, biographies and legendariums. A veritable trove of forgotten lore was mine to scour. In here, I was bound to find something invaluable - it would be only a matter of time. As I judged it, Reeve Ewin had repaid his 'debt' to me with substantial interest.

Thus I dived into this repository, the excitement of discovery quickening my probing hands and flitting eyes as I scanned for promising titles. Primarily I sought materials referencing the Blōþisōdaz family and Gerefwīč's earliest occupants, but I also remained persistently attuned for potential covert necromantic scriptures. As with *Canticum Chorōrum Ossōrum*, most published works in necromancy take the form of a more standard topic communicated in a decidedly eccentric style. One might understand, then, when I ecstatically unshelved a tome titled *'Firhiwiz fram Erþōi'* (which I took to mean *'Lives from the Ground'*) and began its transcription at the available study desk. Only when four sides of parchment were completed was I fully convinced that it was simply a treatise on crop cultivation and nothing more. Doubtless it was used to aid the settlement's founders with the establishment of a consistent food source, but it would be of little value to me. Perhaps I will provide a translated version for the reeve as a gift of gratitude. There may be some neglected grains of wisdom buried in there still.

On I went, analysing a number of the decorative spines. Unlike the more recent archive, this one was not ordered so systematically, frustrating my efforts; but this is a challenge to which I am much accustomed. A necromancer, if one is to be successful, is also obligated to be a scholar of some meticulousness. When the object of your study is obfuscated by its proponents as much as it is by its censors, you soon see yourself obtaining a certain talent for finding needles in meadows. Here, one such needle glimmered at me; a set of letters, foreign and wholly unexpected. It was a relatively minute grimoire, written in Ancient Zeritmian of all languages, whose title I transliterated as *'Favin'*. It was not a script I anticipated to encounter in that place and I had not brought my relevant primers so as to extrapolate its context, but I felt it had promise regardless, so I stowed it safely in my satchel alongside *Firhiwiz fram Erþōi* to examine later.

I resumed the hunt, scrutinising the rune sequences for ones that match those on the crypt. And there it was, tucked neatly into the furthest corner on the right and not two yards from the desk! It was a hefty opus with a cover of ochre-dyed goat skin, designated *'Blōþisōdaz: Gamōtą Krumpis'*. Such marvellous revelations were held inside this tome! I shall divulge the sum of it here...

The first surprise this chronicle had in store for me was that the Blōþisōdaz are not a family as I had previously assumed, but an *order*. This much became evident when there were plentiful mentions made of recruitment and training, but none of marriage or childbirth. In fact, it seemed as if the members were actively forbidden from forming families of their own. The reasoning for this was not explicitly provided, but I shall offer my theories later.

The purpose for the order, too, was clandestine. The 'Blood-Marked' (for that is the meaning of the group) had founded the town, which served as a hidden base of operations. The heading, as I rendered it, was unhelpful; *'Blood-Marked: Council of the Curved(?)'* is quite nondescript. Apparently, answers would not be forthcoming and would require a deeper inquiry. Thankfully, such resources were revealed as time went on.

Enclosed within the leaves was a short epistle which, as I deciphered it word by word, left me astonished and eager to continue. It read:

'They who are Blood-Marked,

Your gathering is a great service to the Kingdom of Sunþrardiz and the land in which it thrives. Though all of you have my eternal personal gratitude, you will remain needfully unknown to the world if it is to survive its coming challenges. For this, although there can be no worthy apology, I am sorry.

Your quest is as we discussed in person and must not be repeated beyond the boundaries of the Gamōtą. You may take from the royal treasury as you need it, so long as you do so covertly and by means of your contacts.

Be subtle. Your secrecy is paramount. Your discovery would mean ruin. Your limitless sacrifice will be anonymous and undoubtedly forgotten, but your legacy is the surviving world.

This message arrives alongside my final gift to you; may you put it to good use. We shall not correspond again. I shall pray for the best possible fortune for your endeavour.

-King Andaswar.'

My eyes were opened, and I perceived my raised minions in a new light. Just whose remains had I so unwittingly defiled? These were supposedly unsung heroes of matchless consequence... but for what had they been assembled? I pushed onwards, the flow of my interpretation accelerating as I reacquainted myself with the diction. The format of the volume seems to be a series of reports (almost always some manner of sweeping search, ending with the phrase '...found nothing') interspersed with supplementary materials of another kind. In addition, there are periodical inventories, charters and registries. The latter documents in particular repeat some very familiar names. I sought to learn some of their individual exploits, but the narrative provided was not a traditional one. However, one *can* discern something of a disjointed story through the bureaucracy; when specific men and women became associated, where they were found, which existing member was responsible for making contact with them, and so on in that fashion.

As I turned more and more of the leaves over, their aforementioned searches began to narrow in scale, and though some of the place names are outmoded or changed, I received the distinct impression that their focus was refined to a certain region. That being south-east Sunþrardiz.

Upon that realisation I became truly captivated. I lost myself in my work and my surroundings faded into obscurity. I confess to being quite unheedful of the onset chill when the archive entryway opened, the creak of the partitioning door as it softly rotated wider, the muted footsteps and the dripping of wet clothes as I was stealthily approached... No, I became aware of the intruder only when their hand was set upon my shoulder. I froze in panic, fully expecting to feel the point of a dagger pressing into my throat. Instead, a large tankard of frothing ale was placed on the left side of my desk.

"Sorry, I didn't mean to make you jump!" chirped Bayldon's voice behind me.

"'Make me jump', assuredly so! You should consider it fortunate that my heart did not give out entirely!"

Bayldon brushed aside my admonishment, diverting his attention to my project.

"Looking into some local history, are we?"

"How did you know? Do you read Sunþrardic?" I counterquestioned.

"No," he explained, "it's just that I've seen that same line of runes in the graveyard, on that big crypt on the hill."

"You have an exquisite memory!"

"That's as may be," he chuckled and shrugged, "but I've not the slightest clue what it says."

"*Blōþisōdaz,*" I said to him.

"Well go on, who were they then? Their place gives me shivers if I get too close to it, these days."

The sapping circle is effective, at least, I thought to myself.

"That is what I am wrestling with now, my friend. I can inform you that they were some type of ordained sect, commissioned by the king of that age, Andaswar," I imparted, "but to what end, I cannot yet say."

"To slay the Sċucca!" proclaimed Bayldon as he wore a deliberately oafish smirk.

"Perhaps!" I humoured. The suggestion, facetious though it was, may not have been so detached from the truth. The only question was, what was the nature of this 'Sċucca'?

Bayldon knelt by my side, his wide eyes sweeping over my notes and the subject of my study. He had abandoned his dripping cloak by the entrance door, but his hair, face and other clothes were still damp from his braving of the weather, and he seemed relieved for the building's impeccable insulation, complemented, as it was, by the gentle warmth of the numerous lanterns.

"You have not touched your drink. Be sure not to spill it when you do," I commented, protectively sliding the chronicle further from the tankard.

"Well I'm not going to touch it, am I? It's for you, you old carper!"

"Is it, indeed? In that case you have my esteemed appreciation, young Bayldon!"

"Hold your bloody 'young' talk and you can have some of the stew I brought over for you, too," he hinted with feigned irritation.

"As you wish, though I myself would give much for my title to be 'young' rather than 'old'," I retorted, "*Master* Bayldon."

In truth, it had not passed unmarked that even my one-time apprentice, being the only person in memory with which I have had any lasting bond, had never adopted any responsibility for my well-being. It was an unforeseen kindness which I found to be both charming and discomforting. Bayldon looked as though he would soon be preparing to leave, prompting me to make an interjection which I was astonished to realise originated from my own lips.

"Will you not stay longer?" I asked quietly.

"I don't see why not..." Bayldon began, hesitant but thoughtful, then his face brightened. "Actually, yes, I'll stay. With the troubles there's not much happening in the hundred anyway, and Alton's not busy. Why not?"

"Good! Shall we share the stew and talk for a while? My tired eyes would be most grateful for the reprieve."

"I was hoping you'd say that," he said, grinning. "That stew smells damned good."

Bayldon had left the lidded bowl on a desk in the outer archives, so we brought the tankard and dined away from those precious relics of literature. The stew was of mutton and vegetables, still hot and delicious enough for me to regain a portion of my lost appetite. He explained to me that he had been to check on a number of yesterday's partygoers to ensure that they had returned to their abodes safely. Orman, apparently, had not, and was still unaccounted for. No overt search effort was yet being made lest it spread undue alarm. It was from the last home he visited that he had been gifted the stew, a giving of thanks from the individual's mother for his selfless show of concern. Bayldon, of course, modestly de-emphasised this last point, insisting that the others would have done the same. That they obviously *had not* seemed to be of no importance to him.

When those developments were purveyed and the stew and ale were finished, Bayldon went on to speak of a new topic; a query that he claimed he had been harbouring for some time.

"Would you tutor me in *Arcāna*? For a fair payment, of course," he enquired abashedly.

"No," I said in as stern a voice as I could muster, pausing to watch his heart sink momentarily before continuing. "No, I should very much prefer to do so without charge."

Bayldon's broad smile was heartening.

"You sly fox!" he protested. "That was mean!"

"If you consider *that* 'mean', you should know that my pupils are not spared the rod," I warned in jest.

"Well then, I'll be sure to wear my armour to your lessons!"

We bantered in this way for an interval, then began to make arrangements. It would appear that, from tomorrow, I am to begin the lessons. How capricious fate can be, that my purpose here has so mutated!

We spoke our farewells, I bade him travel with utmost caution and was once again alone among the dusty tomes. I sealed the doors and immersed myself into *Gamōtą Krumpis*, determined to extract the shrouded significance of the 'Blood-Marked'. The documentation provided was esoteric. Ancillary. The experience of attempting to navigate its elusiveness was vexing, akin to swatting a tenacious, droning gnat in the dark, but my intension was redoubled by the emergence of some encouraging titbits: firstly, that the scouting parties of the Blood-Marked began to record encounters with *'Līkō'* (meaning simply 'corpses'), for which they listed tallies and unequivocally assured their 'laying to rest'; and secondly, the introduction of a new term, *'Huntōdaz'* ('The Hunted'). Though the former were never directly referred to as un-dead, the coded words were to me as clear as Īswægas ice. As for the latter, I found myself deeply suspicious of the organisation's objective, but dared not contemplate that connection until it was confirmed indubitably.

There! A sudden shift in the pace of the searches; a novel dating system, one which progressed in reverse and commenced at fifteen, accompanied a literal tripling of expedition frequency. The appearance of the phrase *'Derkô Dagaz'* ('The Dark Day') roughly coincided with this upheaval. The 'hunts' became more and more frantic, eventually peaking at *six in one day* (accounting for travel, the seekers could barely have slept), until the climax of the countdown came to herald the dawn of 'The Dark Day'. Of this, surprisingly little is mentioned. The calendar ceases. Entries become non-uniform, undated and seamless, and their comprehension becomes difficult. After what must have been nearly a fortnight of overturning sites overrun with un-dead, an entire leaf is set aside for a succinct message:

'Andaswar,

May the telling of your rule be unblemished by the evil begotten under it. May your undying spirit guide us so those you leave behind might be saved.'

Beneath this was inscribed a curt addendum from a different hand. A disparate word - a name - in Zeritmian letters was nestled among the Sunþrardic runes, reading in aggregate:

'Velthur be damned!'

So here was the proof I had been expecting for hours. And yet, I could still scarcely believe that which was laid bare before me. Here, at my desk, in this rural settlement that I had picked primarily for its remoteness and unimportance, was the solitary recognition of those who, operating from this very place, were tasked with Velthur's destruction.

Either excitement or fear (I cannot surely say which) overwhelmed me and I was impelled to partake of some of the fresh, cold air outside. I walked over to the main door, swung it open and inhaled with relish. The storm had escalated into a tumultuous, sustained tempest. The strong westerly gale carried the pelting torrent at a severe lateral angle, whence it besieged the wall of the archives tirelessly yet ineffectually. The rain ran athwart the north-facing doorway in such a way that I could stand within it and appreciate the spectacle in the dry.

The black clouds above had utterly enshrouded the sky; if the sun persisted still, it was swallowed behind them. As such I had no inkling of the true hour, and I dared not step out into the freezing downpour and the threatening roars of the thunder. I beheld, too, brief but savage squalls of hail. In essence, I was both willingly and involuntarily stranded, silently thankful for the excuse to abide at the archives a while longer.

The labour slowed as the patterns of *Gamōtq Krumpis* became less repetitious. For the first time, those of the Blood-Marked began to suffer casualties as their opposition increased exponentially. The pretense of *'Līkō'* was soon openly disregarded in favour of *'Un-daudō'* (un-dead), as was *'Huntōdaz'* addressed occasionally by his uncensored name. I would posit that the parties of the Blood-Marked were undeniably zealous, but here that zealotry had grown to be reflected in their once neutral and dispassionate chronicle in the form of a fiery, desperate hatred. Had they been overly optimistic of their timescale? King Andaswar is thought to have counted magical scholars among his advisors and existed in an age of less suspicion; perhaps he had acted upon their advice after they had received some undisclosed forewarning. Could it be that, at their conception, they had underestimated the magnitude of immediate threat represented by an ascended necromancer? How much blame can reasonably rest upon their shoulders when such a thing was starkly unprecedented? I pitied the Blood-Marked as I traced their pursuit of a malignant entity that they did not - *could* not - comprehend.

A rumble of thunder high above spurred me onwards. The leaves of the record were running thin and the conclusion, foreknown though it was to myself, was imminent. As I opened to the final spread and recommenced the translation, I anticipated a confrontation of substantive proportions. I was... disappointed. Velthur, of course, was not in attendance of his undoing; it is very likely he was unaware of those who worked against him in secret. It could be that the distant sensation of his ultimate guardians being vanquished had caused the anxiety he is said to have demonstrated prior to his dissipation at Zeritmia. Certainly, by the account of the Blood-Marked, Velthur was woefully underprepared for their conclusive assault, and the secretive order were leaving nothing to chance, bringing forth every extant combatant they could muster.

This is not to say that they did not meet resistance. The Arch-Lich had set a brutal trap for any who would strive to extinguish him; the scripture detailed two monstrous Constructs unearthing themselves at their approach, *'...forged from the bones of countless men, each gigantic in stature and in possession of multitudinous grasping limbs.'* No further description was offered, and the things were not defeated but instead distracted. Here was 'Krumpą' mentioned again, one of few occasions since the title and possibly the only incidence of it not in reference to the order's name. 'Krumpą', the text recounts, *'...fought valiantly with beak and talon, bearing High-Priestess Haḫuwīgą on its back, but was caught on the wing and mauled alongside her.'* I wondered at what manner of creature 'Krumpą' was. It seemed reminiscent of a bird, though one of impossible size. I pondered on the literal rendering of its name as 'curved' and a host of images flashed through my mind like the lightning still echoing overhead; the eagle's countenance, whose fierce eyes peered at mortals from the stoneworks of Gerefwīċ. The same beast whose likeness, with its *curved, hooklike beak,* scowled inimically at the judgement's proceedings. If this history is to be believed, said statue must have been sculpted at *actual scale.* How terrifying!

After this concise retelling of the critical battle, all that followed were single-sentence epitaphs of the fallen, and a catalogue of the things recovered from their enemy's primary hoard. Chief among the miscellanea, obviously, was the phylactery, which was *'...destroyed implicitly under the scrutiny of all surviving members.'* It was noted that Velthur's chosen object was an hourglass. A droll and brazen preference, if I were one to criticise. There were numberless and ageless necromantic grimoires (all incinerated, tragically), a hoard of weapons, armour and gold that had been taken as spoils and, most intriguing of all, Velthur's prized staff of sorcery from before his infamous ascension. It was designated in Zeritmian letters (like its owner) which I would translate as the *'Hinthial Sceptre'*, an artefact supposedly gifted to Velthur by strange, undetermined benefactors. Suggestions were made that the artificers were also the authors of those rare, mysterious scrolls concealed within the necromancer's manuals. These inserts were covered with unintelligible markings which none of the Blood-Marked could even begin to penetrate and, being etched into the same outlandish metal as the sceptre, were more arduous to deface. Why such toils were undertaken to nullify the scrolls and yet not the Hinthial Sceptre was never clarified, but the former were softened in a furnace, hammered into unrecognisability and jettisoned into the Tīdwind, while the latter was instead entombed with Haþuwīgą. The terminal passage of the logbook is a listing of those interred in the Blōþisōdaz tomb, initially consisting of those lost in the course of their mission (including Krumpą, which served to solidify to me that my translation was at fault, for I had certainly not encountered a sarcophagus that could *remotely* house a bird whose wingspan could brush the bow and stern of a sea-worthy ship *simultaneously*) and amended as the victorious survivors came to expire through old age and infirmity. The handwriting permutes as the crypt is filled until, finally, the record ends.

Such was revealed the source of my retinue and recently acquired staff, the identity of the venators of my twisted 'mentor', and the origin of the settlement's dominant emblem. I sat back in my chair, overcome by my enlightened perception of fate's workings. Since a lifetime ago, when I embarked on the lonely path of the necromancer, my destiny has been instrinsically linked to that of Velthur and the Blood-Marked. With my factual questions largely (but not totally) answered, those that endured were of a philosophical nature, chiefly; have I narrowly escaped sharing Velthur's dole?

Through the eyes of his furtive opponents, one can dissect his methodology for its virtues and flaws. I believe, foremost, that Velthur made enemies of altogether too many people. Even before the ascension and declaration which saw him quickly attaining unmatched notoriety, close informants were endeavouring to counteract him. This also implies that, at least when mortal, Velthur retained some living companions who were aware of his habits. *Zich Suthina* said nothing of such individuals; they were either insignificant to him or already departed by its time of writing. I am reminded of my own treacherous apprentice, the incompetence of whom may have provided a serendipitous protection for myself.

Regardless; by means unknown, I posit that the Blood-Marked were given forewarning of Velthur's ritual, its date, and its intended result. 'The Dark Day' would seem to correlate with the birth of the Arch-Lich, which itself is dependent on the lunar cycle and is therefore somewhat predictable. Some aspect of this bothers me, but I cannot think how. I shall return to this later, preferably after sleep has helped to reorder my mind.

The concept of becoming the keeper of Velthur's staff, the 'Hinthial Sceptre', brings me some unease. Its previous owner is not my concern; rather, that I know nothing of those supposed 'benefactors' who bestowed it upon him fills me with ineffable dread. Who were they whose exotic cipher was innominate, and what stake did they hold in Velthur's intentions? Could they have been the ones who came to him bearing the secrets of immortality, carved, perhaps, onto those bodeful scrolls? The Blood-Marked recognised their continued existence as especially perilous. I had, at first, wished them still available to me; now I am glad that I will never be exposed to their unspeakable temptations first-hand, and I shall not venture to imagine what malefic whisperings eventually drove Velthur towards murderous insanity.

What else can be said of him? A necromancer can choose to rely on either subtlety or an overt presence of power, and his choice was the latter. While it is true that a mortal practitioner, when cornered, is essentially only as powerful as the un-dead he can bring to his defence, one that blends adequately into the general populace need not fear coordinated adversaries. Thus shall I always be a proponent for discretion; for if every fortress can be breached, a hovel in the mountains might harbour a fugitive better.

I have just glanced outside to find a sky clear of clouds but full of stars. I have definitely overstayed and shall be constrained to trusting in the stability of my refined sapping circles tonight; the watchmen patrol the area with torches, and attempting to visit the crypt now would draw too much attention. I shall instead retire to The Old Boar, review my notes and strive for sleep, if my inflamed imagination permits me to do so.

...

It is night, but the lanterns along the empty, cobbled streets pierce the dense smog and banish all but a few stubborn shadows. A large, square enclosure exists within this intersection, containing an immaculate surface of grass, itself covered with standing marble shrines of various shapes and sizes. A rhythmic clapping of hard-soled shoes on the road echoes between the buildings, drawing rapidly nearer.

A man appears at pace, dressed in a hood and an old, disrepaired suit. He vaults the brickwork wall with respectable dexterity. During the action, his cowl falls back, revealing a clean-shaven face with a panicked expression. The covering is brought back up as soon as the man has his hands free to do so. He breathes heavily, constantly glancing behind him, and he appears bedraggled and desperate. The left leg of his trousers has been ripped away at the shin, and dirt stains discolour his previously white shirt.

The man sits and slumps against the wall, giving pause to his retreat in an attempt to regain some of his stamina. He accomplishes a mere two controlled breaths before the shouts of a mob and the barking of dogs rouse him once again into flight. The turf here is more comfortable on his sore feet than the cobbles he sprinted across to reach this district; for Iliban is a city of tall buildings lining complex, intricate streets, and he had found his way here for no reason other than the location's relative familiarity.

The wall represents the enclosing boundaries of a graveyard. Inhumation has become a rarity in Iliban, a practice of the wealthy and the eccentric. The old religions, for the most part, have given way to a competing dichotomy of Sōlis Mūnus advocates and a novel movement of scientific scepticism, as well as some secretive occultist societies. To the former group, cremation is the correct way to honour sacred Sōl in death. To the other denominations, it is primarily a matter of practicality; space is a scarce, premium commodity in the city-state of Iliban, making an 'intact' burial a plausible aspiration only for the very rich.

The hooded man has visited this place frequently over the past fortnight, but never had he been pursued *here.*

His slovenly exploitation of previous graveyards is the cause for the unwanted attention he is currently experiencing. The city's sewers are a veritable dungeon beneath its streets, capable of accommodating the movements of labourers for maintenance and cleaning. It is utilised, too, by the criminal underclass to a plethora of nefarious ends, including the smuggling of dubious goods and, occasionally, the disposal of their more unfortunate victims. This particular lawbreaker had made clever use of a conveniently situated and quite expansive cistern, fairly safe from flooding in the heat of later Sōlcyme, to create something of a nest for himself. From there he had used (and added to) the network of man-made tunnels to access from underground what he could not on the surface; the bodies of those interred in the scattered and sparse burial grounds of Iliban.

The scheme was initially monumentally efficient, allowing for the acquisition of many subjects aged and fresh. The more he collected, the more servants he could put to expanding his operation; and, like an empire which founds colonies in every direction, so had he and his minions spread their influence and silently taken effective ownership of almost every cemetery inside Iliban's southern quarter. His sappers worked all hours and needed no light, food or respite. Petty swindlers quickly learnt to give the mute but industrious men a wide berth and to ask them no questions. Thus did the mysterious hooded man become lord of his very own underworld, for a time.

But then, as often happens with those who swiftly accumulate power and whose ventures seem never to fail, he became arrogant and negligent. He failed to recognise the flaw in his methods or prepare for the eventuality of a needful upheaval. This calamity was, as it transpired, of his own making, and took the form of a devastating collapse in an especially lucrative and evidently overmined graveyard. Continuously excavating its roots in order to rob the burials of the cadavers and valuables therein had finally compromised the structural integrity of the entire area. The resulting sink-hole was inevitable, in retrospect, but the children of the local governor being among those consumed and crushed in the process was spectacularly unfortunate. The law enforcement tasked with removing the rubble might not have been so surprised to find individuals underneath that were dead prior to the cave-in, but the fact that some were supposedly buried in other graveyards, and that an overwhelming majority of them were equipped with shovels or pickaxes, raised questions that apparently demanded immediate answers.

So when the tremor and the sounds of tumbling earth echoed through the sewers, the hooded resident of the cistern had barely minutes before the provost marshals, dressed in their long, blue coats and polished barbutes, began to sweep the tunnels with bar maces and baying hounds. He was disorientated, compelled to act instantaneously and, being uncertain of his numbers after such a calamitous report, chose to flee rather than battle an increasing number of marshals as they coordinated to enmesh him. Once they recognised the manner of their opponents, they would surely call forth every armed man they could. As the hooded one darted through aperture and junction, he soon realised that the provosts were working efficiently to cordon his subterranean realm, thereby preventing his escape. An opportunity arose for him to slip past one of his seekers as they rounded a corner, but it was a narrow evasion and the marshal's beast was more wary than its owner, catching him briefly by the leg. It clamped shut its iron jaws but, thankfully, they met only in wool and not muscle or bone. He was able to scramble away from the encounter with but a flesh wound and a torn garment. Of course, realising their quarry had eluded them, they divided themselves between making short work of the now undirected minions that remained and pursuing their cowardly creator.

And so here some twenty men had been led on their chase; and when it dawns on them just where the fugitive has brought them, there is some trepidation within their ranks as to whether their hunt should continue.

"Shush! Quiet yourself a moment, Indo!" one of the provost marshals scalds his animal. The dog reluctantly obeys.

"There's nothing for it, we'll have to go around."

"That'll be too slow!"

"If we do it snappy, we can close him off in there..."

"Are you stupid, Urcebas? He's a necromancer. He's right where he wants to be. We've got to get at him before he makes himself a brand new army!"

"Leortas, he isn't going to stick around. He can't take all of us with a pack of shamblers, and I'm sure he's smart enough to know that."

"Shut it! Both of you!" bellows a gruff voice from the back of the formation.

"Yes sir, Captain Korbis!" the two shout in unison and stand at attention with somewhat more compliance than Leortas' dog. Korbis' helm bears a great white horsehair crest, a symbol of his office.

"Listen," says the captain quietly as he walks to the front of his men, "he's probably waiting in there to see what our next move is. What we're going to do is go straight after him, but stay low. I want a handler going each way on the outside with their dogs being as noisy as they can make them, so he thinks we're heading him off. Then we jump him while he thinks he's got time. Right?"

The other marshals nod their affirmation.

"Good," grins Captain Korbis, satisfied. "Extinguish your torches and stick to the plan. I'll shout an order to flank, just for his ears. Got it?"

The heads again bobbed in understanding. The captain stands tall and prepares to vocalise.

Meanwhile, the hooded man kneels in the centre of the graveyard. He is astounded that the provosts are not yet upon him, but deeply thankful; he had started his spell, seeping manna into the soil, the moment he had reached the central memorial statue. With his eyes shut tightly in concentration and both hands pressed into the lawn, it is a vulnerable posture - but it seems this last gambit is destined to save his hide.

"Blockade the perimeter! We've got him, boys!" calls a distant voice. It is proceeded by the clamour of frenzied hounds as they gallop along the edges of the square.

The provosts must be slipping if it has taken them this long to reach an accord. Perhaps they are afraid. They should be, *the necromancer laughs to himself morbidly as his spell begins to take hold. This specific graveyard is as yet untapped; in this circumstance, a reasonable portion of its potential can be deployed concertedly. He would raise the whole cemetery and smuggle himself from the city in the ensuing havoc. All he required now was for the things to dig themselves free. They had the necessary* strength, *at this point it was simply a matter of* time...

Leortas creeps between the headstones, slinking behind Captain Korbis. Urcebas had taken Indo for a leisurely stroll, while Leortas was in here *trying to 'jump' a necromancer. He had never regretted foregoing the handlers' training as thoroughly as he did now. The black magician becomes visible. He looks... injured? The captain raises a whistle to his lips, ready to signal the charge; but the subordinate feels a growing, sickening sensation in his stomach. He could swear the ground is churning beneath his feet, the dead readying themselves to pull him under.*

The whistle blasts its high-pitched note and the captain lurches forwards to engage the enemy, but both falter. Korbis coughs in alarm and nearly falls over as something in the undergrowth tugs at his boot. He beats it with his mace, but the creature drags itself out further from the ground in response.

"Kill the bastard! He's over there! Kill him!" screams Captain Korbis in blind rage and frustration.

The contingent of marshals break into a run, following the command of their superior officer, but swathes of them are entangled in a similar way. Decaying hands grasping from the earth hinder or halt them, and the momentum of the attack is completely lost to dismay and confusion.

Leortas readies himself to make his own attempt to reach the necromancer, but he perceives the grave moving before him and realises that it is hopeless. Before the rising un-dead obscures his sight, he momentarily locks eyes with its master - and swears *that he catches a mocking smirk on the villain's face as he turns tail and runs south, towards Iliban's closest limits. Leortas can do nothing but watch his foe throw himself over the wall and disappear. That, and ready his weapon to release his anger upon the corpse now limping in his direction.*

The necromancer moves as fast as his legs can carry him. Buildings and signposts pass him by as he dashes through the maze of streets. He is elated, ecstatic even, for the unlikely circumvention of his pursuers; but his celebration is tempered by the knowledge of how precarious the situation had truly been. He had lost much, forced to hurriedly abandon his laboratory and all of the collected treasures within. Iliban was too populated, too busy, too alert, *he decided. He would never return to the bustling capital, and the news delivered by their printing presses will keep the country's population paranoid for years to come. No, he should reside elsewhere for a while... Although the occult orders were an excellent source for necromantic materials. Perhaps he* will *eventually travel again in this jurisdiction, if he can only find a means to sufficiently alter his features...*

Another night deprived of meaningful rest, and yet I feel vigorous, sharp... what is happening to me? I am subject to no exigencies of repose, no desire for food or sustenance of any sort. I feel disconnected, like an observer anchored to the world by this mortal shell; a tractable tool, but *o, so heavy and inadequate, begging to be cut loose...*

No! I must put aside these wretched thoughts of abnegation. I am indurated against the miseries of the necromancer's lot, the scorn of mankind, and I shall not now be extinguished by the phantasms of memories long forgotten!

Sōlrest-Þridda-XXII

Stultified with my bedchamber, I abandoned my attempts at sleep. I considered the possibility that my rations had spoiled and were responsible for unbalancing my humours, and so my fast went unbroken but for a sparing sip of water. After this, I dressed myself, left The Old Boar without a word and headed to my sanctum. There I hoped to find some solace among the bones of the Blood-Marked. The morning was clear but the watchmen were elsewhere, and so I was able to slip through the willows to the graveyard, and into the crypt, without incident. As I climbed the slope I noticed that the grass had not deteriorated significantly further, indicating that my failsafes had functioned correctly.

Once within the mausoleum, I found an odd comfort in the musty shadows. I felt also... imbued. Potent, as if I might raise the entire population of the cemetery at the merest whim. Somehow it remained persistently dissatisfying; provocative of the sensation that I had neglected an aspect of greater consequence. Small pools of rainwater from yesterday's storm lingered in the corridor's recesses. I walked around and over them until I arrived at the innermost section which comprises my laboratory. All was as I had left it, though I imagined a new and resentful disposition from the skeletons of the Blood-Marked; so quickly would I have been slain by them once my intentions were discovered, if they had by some means retained autonomy. It was impossible to decide whether I was experiencing guilt from the disrespect of their accomplishments, or humour from the irony of their corrupted purpose, more pronouncedly.

In any case, the aims of this visit were threefold: firstly was to ensure the stability of my spellcraft to prevent a possible future calamity. Though peculiarity of this circumstance means that predictions are worryingly speculative, I believe that the manna stream has settled to a steady flow, and that there is presently little cause for concern. Secondly, a cursory verification of the facts proposed by the Blōþisōdaz ledger. To this end, I inspected Haþuwīgą closely, having her shift aside obstructive segments of her dress of seashells and bring herself close to the torchlight. Thus was I able to identify several notable pathologies which served to corroborate the tale of her demise: a number of the cervical vertebrae had been deformed or broken; her ribcage showed evidence of a forced constriction, and many of the ribs had splintered beneath the pressure; and tiny fractures originating from the brow radiated outwards to decorate the whole of the skull. The injuries could reasonably belong to one who was set upon by a mob of strong, determined men... or a single-minded beast of many cruel hands. That I had not taken prior notice of these signs is unsurprising; in addition to the brevity and superficiality of my initial appraisal (as well as the inexorable degradation of the remains generally), Haþuwīgą's frame specifically seems to have undergone a rapid but partial mending at the time of her death. Hearsay exists that those magically adept in healing often leave an unblemished body upon their expiration. Manna, it is theorised, may express itself in a practiced way during such final moments; having witnessed the possible result of a pyromancer's untimely end, the terminal throes of a slain biomancer may yield the previously described abnormalities. I suspect that, at the immediate time of occurrence, her contusions would have been far more disfiguring and hideous than the bones now suggest. Regardless, the twisted neck and smashed head would have offered Haþuwīgą a relatively painless passing.

Hers were not the only remains I scrutinised afresh. While she and Krumpą were drawing the attention of the twin Constructs, the other Blood-Marked present were fighting through a tide of necromantic fodder to reach the phylactery. One by one, I confirmed that their fatal wounds were as stated: Ermunahild bore a terrible gash on her right thigh, which indeed sliced deeply enough to score the femur; Rēdawulf was caught from behind by a volley of arrows loosed by un-dead archers, the diminutive, corroded heads of which clattered to the floor like iron pebbles when the victim's rusted armour was experimentally loosened; Helparīks was impaled upon a spear, which proved to have severed his spine as it ran through him; and Audaward's left knee was utterly disintegrated by a viciously brandished mace, his tall stature only now enabled by the supplementary bracing of necromantic animation as it compensates for weakened bone and rotted muscle.

All of these subtle proofs were once so insignificant! Men and women die and I, as a necromancer, would raise their remains as servants. Whether in the next instant or the next century, so long as their own driving forces were departed, they could be made pliable. The cause of their situation, as it were, was irrelevant. It has come to pass now that, through the reading of their records (minimalistic though they were), some of their humanity and personality has been restored to them. Though they are instrumentally unchanged, I regard them differently nonetheless. The question I now must ask of myself is; can I now conscionably use them in the knowledge that their living will has been so extremely perverted? Perhaps more pertinently, can I justify their continued use at all if my own ambitions have been completely shattered?

This lead to the topic of my third evaluation; should my laboratory be disassembled? It is not a misguided inquest into the welfare of the unfeeling minions, but more an issue of the safety of Gerefwīć's people. As I had seen with the graverobber who resides now in one of the sarcophagi (undeservedly, perhaps, in many senses of the word), the existence of this place represents a potentially deadly trap to any interlopers, unscrupulous or otherwise. The aura makes it a dissuasive prospect to any but the most reckless, but still one might consider it immoral to simply forsake it if there is a chance for it to inflict harm upon innocents.

That said, there is yet another angle of perspective to this quandary; should the settlement come to face further challenges from the revenant warband, this place may be their only source of salvation. I must account for this factor as the situation is precarious, more so than they realise. An occasional trespasser may go missing, but without the guardianship of the Blood-Marked, *every* inhabitant of this quaint farmstead (including myself) could be doomed. The un-dead on the attack would not be akin to any banditry known to the locals, and it brings me substantial dread to imagine just how poorly they would fare alone.

I decided, therefore, to maintain this dour retinue until such a time when this current threat has passed. This neglects to conclude the problem of the Manna Glutton, for which I have yet no sure solution. I shall operate under the assumption that the phenomenon has found an equilibrium rather than fully resolved itself. In truth, I do not know whether the latter option is an actual eventuality. I would prefer not attempting to dismantle the seemingly benign system and risk exacerbating it needlessly, even if its energy consumption is merely consistently inordinate rather than exponential.

A quaternary curiosity arose and niggled at me before I left. I made to retrieve the Hinthial Sceptre that had once been Velthur's. When I sought to take the object in my hand, however, memories that were until so recently locked away in the recesses of my mind were brought forth in quick and discomposing succession; memories of dank tunnels, of an unfathomed temple beneath Pænvicta, and of a nameless and voracious stalker from the shadows. The Sceptre fell from my grasp and struck the floor with an unnatural metallic thrum. I always believed that an object could preserve no malice of its own, and I continue to envision no persistence of Velthur's will...

But of these... *things*... I know truly *nothing*.

I could not bear to touch the Hinthial Sceptre again while the reminiscence of the musky scent of moist limestone pervaded my nostrils. It induced the odious impression that I was reaching out to touch one of *them*, and the miasma of their purest *wrongness* was unendurable.

I took instead *Zich Suthina* with the intention of looking it over again for coded information regarding Velthur's disquieting patrons, and to compare it to my findings in the journal of the Blood-Marked. Lastly, I traced some chalk 'primer' markings onto some of the untouched sarcophagi; those inside should now be ready to raise with minimal delay should Gerefwīċ's perilous affairs become acutely desperate. After this last adjunct, I left contented that I had taken the best measures I could on behalf of the hundred, and of myself.

As a final addendum to my investigative report, I must regretfully inform the reader that I found no giant eagle, nor evidence of any such creature. Krumpą, indeed, would appear to be a thing of myth or exaggeration; perhaps it was an ordinary trained hawk or an icon of symbolic importance, and nothing more.

The surroundings passed me by in a haze as I walked back to The Old Boar. Gerefwīċ seemed dead already, depopulated and desolate. The roads and fields were emptied aside from the sparse watchmen, whose enthusiasm and courage had dwindled to such a degree that they had become similar to my ancillaries; dutiful and efficient, but ultimately lifeless and lacking in character, petrified into monotonous obedience by the looming menace.

At the tavern the atmosphere was solemn, the defiance of the evening before last having been exhausted. Alton's head was propped on both palms with his elbows on the bar, while Bayldon, Galan and Bearn sat by the hearth's ebbing embers in silence.

"Afternoon, mate," the innkeeper greeted me. "Sorry, I can't give you an ale. Or water. Not yet, anyway."

"Quite alright, Alton, I have my own supplies for the moment. Why?"

"Gerefwīċ's really in the shit. The well's tainted, and I've been ordered by Reeve Ewin to keep the ales safe in case things don't get any better," he warned, his expression resigned.

So it would seem that the hundred is truly under siege. The noose of time is tightening, but that hard fact has at least been recognised and acted upon by the reeve. It is my hope that someone outside might have delivered a message to Bēagshire, urging them to gather a capable liberating army; but this cannot be validated in either possibility, and the unprecedented aggression of the revenants could impel them to waylay any living person who lays eyes on them. In this latter circumstance, a breaking of the siege could be long delayed in such a remote location of relative unimportance. I hope otherwise, but to trust in hope is a foolish placation.

"The well is tainted?" I asked suddenly, belatedly identifying the most pertinent point of information. "How? When?"

"Folk reckon they started to notice it when Urbānus made his move. The water got a bit of an... *off* taste, and it's been getting worse and worse. No one drinks it now, as they're worried it'll do them some mischief."

"Has anyone described this unwelcome flavour?"

"I tried it myself, mate," he murmured grimly, "and it's none too pleasant. It looks fine on the outside, but yesterday it was like sucking on a Scute, really nasty and metally. The thing is, no one can think of anything like it, it doesn't seem *natural*. I hear talk of *poison*, and what sly bastards might be so twisted."

"The people suspect the Sōlis Mūnus priesthood?"

"That they do. And I reckon they haven't got long before they'd be better off taking their chances with the raiders than sitting locked in their temple."

"They have overstayed their welcome, then?"

"Not by half, and make no mistake!" Alton revealed with excitability in his voice. "I'd say that Wurt's death was the last feather, and one of the only reasons their temple hasn't been turned into Stilneshire's biggest kiln yet is because some folk think they'll help against the raiders. Personally," he paused and sniffed sharply, "I doubt it."

There was a sombre anticipation in the innkeeper's manner, like that of a footsoldier on the eve of a favourable but decisive battle; the anxiety of participation contrasted with the avidity of approaching a visible, attainable resolution. Should Alton's suppositions be correct or not (the Arx men may be spurred into action once the nature of the enemy is realised, but perceivably not beforehand), their contribution would account for little considering the potential quantities that the revenants field; if one were to tally the opened barrows seen by Bayldon and I on the return journey from the River Leafbrym, their numbers are worthy of an entire army's cavalry contingent.

It is all extraneous anyway. The Arx are not the perpetrators of the well's irregularity, nor is said irregularity 'poison' as such. I might have requested a sample, but I was certain already of its composition and cause. For here was another misfortune I had unwittingly inflicted upon Gerefwīċ's hapless people; a portion of the errant manna has apparently seeped into the ground and affected the well's water supply, infusing it with magical energy. In all honesty, imbibing it would not damage them unless done so excessively. In fact, to do so would empower them, filling them with vigour and mending physical ailments. Alchemists have been known to vend successful distillations of this sort at astounding prices, for the concoction is an uncommon one even among skilled adepts. Reaching an effective and stable balance is a process of masterful precision: if the manna input is too sparing, the result will be unremarkable; too much and the liquid will vapourise, leaving behind a volatile and dangerous crystalline residue. By staggering coincidence, the well has produced a safe medium somewhere between these dichotomies. But the people will not drink it out of an understandable instinctive mistrust, and so will consider themselves relegated to stores and rainwater unless they can somehow be persuaded to overcome their revulsion. Aforementioned alchemists often add pleasant herbs or cordials to their tonics in order to offset the inherent unpalatability of dissolved manna. Could this be replicated here, I wonder...?

214

Despite my awareness of the authentic source of this alteration, I seized the opportunity to feed public rumour. A consensus of blame may aid in stifling inquiries, deflecting from the possible drawing of (accurate) connections between the well's blight and that of the Blōþisōdaz mausoleum. I shall not be shedding tears for labouring the temple with false accusations; their innumerable *real* crimes have gone unpunished for too long.

"They have too few men here to take Gerefwīċ by strength of arms, so they would poison its people!" I cried with feigned incredulity. "Despicable!"

"They'll get theirs, and sooner rather than later," assured Alton with unnerving sincerity.

"Be wary, friend. Animals are at their most vicious when cornered," I reminded him.

"You're right, mate. And there's a great deal of us cornered here, don't you reckon?" he observed with a sharp grin and a sly wink.

This was another facet of the innkeeper which I had seldom encountered, and I came to find it astonishingly frightening. It seemed in these moments that he would be capable of acts of ferity that I would at other times think impossible of him.

"When you speak in that way, Alton, you raise questions for which I only dubiously wish answers."

"Is that right?" he laughed. "I don't mean to make you worry, mate. All these troubles are bringing back memories, that's all. Besides, if you want to learn the latest, I'd talk to Bayldon. Maybe *you* can talk it out of him. Whatever's happened has really got him upset."

I nodded to him and walked across the inn to Bayldon. As I came near, his two friends arose from his flanks and, flashing me a sympathetic grimace, departed The Old Boar. I sat beside him, wordlessly at first, as we stared into the embers together. Such a position is more discomforting to me than Alton's smouldering savagery, but his adopted son mercifully broke the silence.

"Orman is dead," he stated frankly. "He never made it home."

"But how? The raiders?" I guessed.

"Aye, *them*. He fell asleep in the east field, and one of them found him. Put a spear through his guts before he even woke up."

"They were within the confines of the basin, then," I surmised aloud. "Were they caught?"

"They should have been!" Bayldon growled with frustration. "The watchman, Eadig his name was, didn't see it happen with his own eyes. He just saw the murdering bastard getting about on his horse. Riding in the night without a torch, and through a field, too. It took Eadig a moment to realise what he was, but as soon as he did, he yelled out for him to stop. He decides he's not going to, and means to go right for him instead. Charges him. So Eadig gets his spear, sees that the raider's is longer and figures out pretty quick that he'll be lanced if he tries to brace against him, and that he can't get away either. So he throws his spear right at the bastard..."

"...And misses, I suppose?"

"That's the riddle. That's what I don't get. Eadig reckons it stuck right into him, buried it right through his ribs. *Swears* on it. And Eadig's got a good arm and an honest tongue. The way he tells it - and he was pretty damned shaken by it, too - the rider didn't even flinch, just carried on like nothing happened. Eadig has to dive out of the horse's way to stop himself getting speared or trampled. He gets his seax out and tries to get ready for the next pass, but the rider gallops off and leaves him there."

"Orman was beyond treatment, then."

"Eadig didn't know about Orman yet. It was too dark to see what the horseman was doing, so he reckoned they were scouting out the hundred, getting the lay of the land or something."

"How was Orman's body discovered? When?"

"Well, the east field's untended thanks to the raiders - they don't want a whole crowd of folk to get rushed and cut down for the sake of a harvest - but a few got together to sweep the field for him this morning. I think it was his young sister who nearly stepped on him in the end. I'm surprised you didn't hear the scream, to be honest," he sighed tearfully, "I know I did."

"I am sorry. May he find peace."

"I'm starting to get used to it. The thing that's really bothering me is that they never found Eadig's spear."

"What are you suggesting?"

"I reckon there's something unnatural about these raiders, mate. There's something *off* about all of it. Why are they so fixed on Gerefwīc? Most of us don't have two Scutes to rub together, but they won't leave us be to attack Sceoppaton, or anywhere else further and richer. If we were at war, I'd have thought they'd have declared themselves to us by now, or tried to negotiate terms, or even just attacked us, because they could. But no! Nothing!" Bayldon shouted, throwing his hands up in despair and exasperation.

Alton glanced upwards from the paperwork with which he was arbitrarily busying himself, then mutely lowered his head in understanding. I was still fastidiously assembling my response when Bayldon spoke again. His voice was soft, almost inaudible, and he sounded on the very edge of weeping.

"Why are we being punished like this?"

The simplicity and poignancy of the question pierced deeply, and I felt compelled to answer without premeditation.

"Yours is the first hundred, in the first county, in the *entirety of Cemparīce*, to demonstrate open dissent of Arx Turrium. Urbānus fled in fear of being caught and made to suffer for his heinous transgressions, the Sōlis Mūnus priests cower in their burrow like harrowed rabbits... and *you* are panicked by a roving band of *cutpurses*!"

"But what if they're *not* cutpurses?" he whispered, shuffling closer and placing his arm across my shoulders, using the show of affection to surreptitiously exclude Alton from the conversation.

"*Do not be absurd,*" I retorted, though my own volume had inadvertently reduced to a mutter. It was not the convincing denouncement I had intended.

"You know something about these raiders, don't you?" he hissed quietly, his tone both pleading and accusatory. "You knew something I didn't when we saw their tracks near Sceoppaton."

I was silent. Deception was beginning to represent a strenuous effort on my part. Sensing my hesitation, Bayldon pushed his gambit harder, squeezing my shoulder as he made his closing appeal:

"If you know things that might be important and you choose not to tell us, you honestly can't say that you care for *any* of us here. I don't think that's true. *Please* don't prove me wrong."

"Alright," I breathed sorely, already doubting the wisdom of my acquiescence, "but I shall speak no more here, and I shall speak only to you. Follow my lead."

I gave Bayldon no opportunity for protest, instead freeing myself from his hold and ascending to my feet.

"I am sorry to hear of it, Master Bayldon. Perhaps engaging with your language studies will help you to put it from your mind," I said loudly enough for Alton to overhear. "My materials pertaining to Arcāna are in my chambers, and I have a spare chair. Come!"

Bayldon nodded and accompanied me to the chamber. When inside, I gestured for him to sit. Then, after unpacking and splaying about all of the books that could serve to grant a working knowledge of Arcāna, I began to disclose that which I had withheld regarding the revenants. I explained, in detail, that the un-dead that he knew from folklore were very real; that I had suspected their presence since before we encountered the witch together; and that it was they who were the mysterious faction now beleaguering Gerefwīċ Hundred for reasons not only unknown but *unknowable*.

And he listened. At times he seemed indignant. At others, awestruck. Frequently he appeared pale and horrified, his spirit on the verge of failing from the challenges against his perception of the world. I saw a young man's confidence unmade, but I saw it also reforged into something greater. Tempered by the confrontation of his own ignorance, Bayldon began to see Pænvicta through a newly ground lens of humility. He came to accept the proportion of things that exceed the decidedly short reach of his control, and to comprehend the chasm of that which he did not yet know. His reaction, however, was not to recoil, but to embrace; he asked deep, searching questions and accepted only thorough answers, even when such answers disturbed him. I kept only my nature as a necromancer from him, firmly maintaining that my occupation must remain secret. I was pressured to concede only that the name he knew me by was not my original one, but that it would be equally as meaningful as any other I could provide him with.

"But how can I trust you without knowing who, or what, you are?" he would ask repeatedly in a multitude of varied phrasings.

"You cannot. Suffice it to say that I ask and have asked nothing of you, and therefore have no incentive to deceive you," I would reiterate.

"Then why not tell me what you *are*!" he eventually snapped, rising to his feet.

"It is a weighty burden, and not one I wish for you to bear," I said. "At your insistence, I shall tell you. Soon."

This vow seemed to placate him. He nodded and reseated himself, digesting the banquet of rare knowledge that I had laid out before him. He seemed calm, collected, thoughtful; his initial horror had been superseded by acceptance and, I think, *hunger.* And I watched him, fascinated by the alacrity of his transformation. In a matter of hours, he had adopted a maturity of thought that eludes a vast generality of men throughout their entire lifespans.

We were both startled by an unexpected rapping on my chamber door. It creaked open to reveal the sheepish face of Alton peeking through the narrow opening.

"Is everything alright in here, gentlemen? I heard raised voices!"

"Quite alright, dad," Bayldon reassured him. "This Arcāna's doing my head in, that's all!"

"No one ever told you it'd be easy, did they?" Alton chuckled.

"Fair enough. I guess it wasn't what I was expecting, that's all," Bayldon admitted; but as he did so, he gave me an equivocal look.

"It is a pity you feel this way, you show great aptitude. Do you wish to end your lessons?" I replied, the dejection evident in my voice.

"Not at all!" the young man confirmed with a cheerful smile. "Just go a bit slower tomorrow, alright? It's a lot to take in!"

"Of course, that is acceptable. For now I suggest we retire and attempt to sleep, regardless of how difficult these conditions make it. Remaining well-rested may prove a vital policy."

There were no arguments against my reasoning. It had indeed become late during our discussion, and both of them knew that being needlessly fatigued during a midnight call to arms would not be an attractive prospect. Bayldon and his friends had already made the error of misjudging the tenacity of the foes, an act of folly for which Orman paid the toll; none desired a repetition of that regrettable outcome.

So the two men and I bade each other goodnight, and they departed for their own chambers. I, conversely, tidied the Arcāna manuals from my bed and occupied myself with updating this journal. Tiredness has shunned me again tonight, but I shall pursue rest all the same. Perhaps I can reflect on the day's developments in order to formulate a plan of action. Yes, Master Bayldon has *certainly* come a long way...

...

The borderlands of Iliban are characteristically different from the metropolis within. The architectural style is similar but sparser, the population density much lower. There are numerous reasons why people might prefer to live there: the air is cleaner, with less of the smog which is so pervasive towards the centre; land and rent are both cheaper, owing to 'sub-prime' locations and more accessible space; and overall, it is much quieter, and more private. In these ways, the Ilibanese suburbs possess the curious quirk of being occupied primarily by some of Iliban's poorest denizens; the wealthiest tend to seek businesses in the centre and build manors in the expensive open countryside, and those that work for them generally attempt to settle for cramped accommodation in the city. The end result is that (apart from the panhandlers who roam streets across the entire city) the main residents of the middle-ground are those who work for less significant industries, or those who are at a transitional stage in their lives.

This particular suburb is a teeming waystation complex in the day, its many single-storey brick structures outfitted to stable and shoe traders' horses and repair wagons. On a clear, late Sōlcyme night like this, however, the narrow streets and empty checkpoints are as silent as the grave.

At the entrance to one of the connecting alleyways, a man waits anxiously. He is middle-aged, short of stature and bald but for a tiny pointed beard on his chin. With his face of worry-lines and nervous disposition, he is exactly the type of person who one might expect to have no business prowling the Ilibanese streets after dark.

"Damn it, Liteno," he squeaks to himself, "what have you gotten yourself into this time?"

Liteno has been waiting at that intersection for some time now. The alley at which he stands is divergent from a significantly longer, straighter one. He looks to the left, then to the right. Several other side-paths branch off from the same backstreet. His 'client' could emerge from any of them, at any moment. Or from behind him...

Having given himself a fright, Liteno scares himself and turns his head, rolling his eyes at his own paranoia. There was plenty to be afraid of without being needlessly haunted by his own shadow. He pats the satchel at his side, checking that he has packed the item.

"You have the tome?" enquires a new voice.

Liteno nearly faints and looks back to the main path. There, about fifteen yards away on the left side, is a man, tall, his features obscured under the shade of a wide-brimmed hood.

"Y-y-yes, I've g-got your tome, N-N-N-Necromancer," he stammers. "H-have you got my m-m-m-m..."

"Your money? Yes..." chuckles the stranger. "Eighty Śalirk, if I recall. Does our deal stand?"

Liteno abandons his attempts at speech, instead hesitantly nodding his assent. As the cloaked man takes the first few steps towards him, the pedlar begs inwardly for the situation to come to an amicable resolution. He is keenly aware of how precarious this secret meeting is, and exposure is not nearly as terrifying a prospect as upsetting his customer. He regrets covertly advertising the book almost as much as he regrets happening upon it in the first place. He should have asked himself more questions when he found it in that hollowed out stump. He did not have to delve deep into the text before he realised its purpose, but that was already enough to keep him awake at night.

"The tome is mine, hand it over!" barks a woman defiantly.

Liteno's heart skips a beat as he spins his head to see yet another cloaked figure. This one is shorter, more lithe, and, though her face is similarly obscured, flowing locks of silvery hair protrude from the recesses of her cowl. The first necromancer halts his stride. Then, the two stare in each other's directions, mute and motionless. The tension is agonising. The standoff persists for mere moments, but it seems to Liteno like hours, and he soon loses his nerve.

"Take it! Take it! No charge! Farewell!" he blurts, placing the satchel between the two strangers and scampering down the backalley, wheezing as he goes.

The two corrivals barely react to Liteno's retreat. The price of the tome was of negligible consequence to either of them; both would have been willing to pay the asked price, but neither would have accepted leaving without their prize. Their respective presences have thrown that predestined conclusion into uncertainty. Neither dare to risk the distraction of attempted communication, lest the other prove inevitably hostile.

Suddenly, the female necromancer seizes the initiative. A sickly glow forms about both of her hands, and she holds them forth in a clawlike gesture. She fails to notice the clatter on the rooftop beside her until it is too late; a skeleton, bright and pale in the moonlight, plunges down at her from above. Wielding a pitchfork in its bony hands, it combines the force of its fall with a mighty downwards thrust, skilfully and simultaneously piercing both lungs with the twin tynes. The un-dead pins her facedown against the cobbles, adding the weight of its foot into the small of her back for good measure.

The victorious necromancer strolls towards her with a casual arrogance, stopping only to hoist the surrendered satchel onto his shoulder. Upon finally arriving at the side of his defeated opponent, he kneels down to inspect her. She is not yet dead, but unconscious, her cheeks coloured a vivid cyan by her continued suffocation. Her hands had suffered the damages of her unfinished spell, both stripped of flesh by the caustic energies.

An interesting method, *the man muses,* but too slow in its execution.

There would be no saving her; she is dying, and even if he had the medical ability to do so, there would not be the time to heal her. Death is probably the most merciful outcome she can receive, now. He looks at her face, and finds himself unexpectedly distraught. The tome could easily have been shared. No one had to die on this night, but the distrust inherent to necromancers ensured that the culmination of this encounter would involve at least one fresh corpse on the street.

It is not tenable, *considers the hooded man.* There must be some way to dissolve the animosity within our practice...

He almost forgets himself in the thought, but realises that the sooner he departs, the safer he will be. So he walks away, savouring the cool night air. The following morning, three curiosities are discovered in that suburb: firstly, a nearby stable is bereft of its pitchfork; secondly, a witch has been murdered after somehow dissolving her hands in acid; and thirdly, a physician finds fresh blood upon his otherwise completely inert skeletal specimen, used by him for anatomical study. The three occurrences are never linked because, frankly, no one would be mad enough to do so.

It would appear that I sleep only now to dream. I *should* be wretched by now, having taken neither slumber nor subsistence, and yet I feel instead positively *youthful*. I can now be certain that the memories I am being subjected to are regressive, pushing me back to ever earlier events within my own lifetime. Could it be that my physical body is emulating this pattern subconsciously? My exterior has quickly become, if anything, *more* wizened rather than *less*. If I am treading the terminus of mortality's path, I do so with a strange stride indeed.

Sōlrest-Þridda-XXIII

I had failed again to sleep, but rested my old bones all the same. Overnight I had much opportunity to premeditate my objectives for the day, so I extricated myself from the purposeless bed and left the tavern in the early hours.

It was not yet dawn as I stepped into the murky drizzle outside. I could see the glowing lanterns of the unfortunate watchmen as they slowly patrolled the perimeter and roads of the basin, but knew that they would not see me if I adhered to the shadows and lit no fire of my own. My eyesight was of astounding clarity in the gloom (I found myself able to walk confidently with help from neither moon nor star) and I was soon climbing the graveyard's hill. I became distracted momentarily as I reached the summit; a bright object at the periphery of my vision that I initially took for the priestess of the Leafbrym. But it was gone as I turned, and I dismissed it as a flash of distant lightning and a figment of my sleep-deprived mind. That I am conscious at all is somewhat mystifying, so a hallucination or several should probably be expected.

The rain had yet to penetrate the ground and begin its usual process of flooding the mausoleum, but I suspected such events were presently due, and resolved to perform my visit with brevity and efficiency. The un-dead Blood-Marked appeared more decrepit than previously, my examinations of them having revealed some of their more disfiguring mortal scars, but they still looked as formidable and intimidating as they ever had. They were considerably empowered by the excessive stipends of manna from the siphons, and it was evident in their behaviour; they were impeccably alert, immediate in their response and swift in their movement. After observing them as they followed my experimental orders, I have an unwavering confidence in their performance should it fall upon them and their still-entombed brethren to defend the hundred. They will surely make King Andaswar proud once again.

My next task was to reevaluate the sapping circles to ensure their continued stability. Of this, there was no change and therefore little to speak of. Each day of constancy brings me hope of a permanent resolution, but for the moment I am far from trusting of it. Regardless of how the situation changes or stagnates, I shall eventually be forced to gamble, severing the flow of energy and praying that the Manna Glutton has been reversed.

I proceeded with the final task of retrieving the last of my possessions from the mausoleum; that is, *Canticum Chorōrum Ossōrum* and *Kýkloi Dunámeōn*. I have surpassed the point of their usefulness in my current predicament and there was no sense in risking the valuable tomes to the weather any longer. They might find use with another who succeeds me, or they might be stored safely and forgotten along with my other necromantic materials once this ordeal is finished with.

One last artefact remained; the Hinthial Sceptre. It was leaning against the terminal blank stone wall of the corridor, and not at all near where I had left it. I had planned to overcome my foolish superstition pertaining to it, but again I could not bring myself to approach it; the thing has developed the perceived quality of watching me as I behold it. That one of the un-dead could have plucked it from the ground was of no consequence to me, especially considering the manner with which they otherwise seemed utterly ignorant of it. The irrational sensation that it was the Sceptre that commanded them, not I, was too disquieting, and I was motivated to leave forthwith.

The sun was barely rising as I departed the crypt, not that the heavily clouded sky made such a thing obvious. The lanterns were doubled in number, which I recognised to be the changing of the guard, so I descended the slope and hid within the willows for the night watch to withdraw before slipping back to The Old Boar.

The hearth was nearly extinguished as I stepped inside; unsurprising, considering that firewood was commonly collected outside the basin (trees being something of a rarity within) and brought back to be sold. No doubt the remaining supply was being rationed. But with the communal room cold and dim and Alton and Bayldon still asleep, I saw no reason to stay and so retired again to my chamber. There I found scarce entertainment and, being nigh overcome with boredom but unwilling to begin the translation of *Favin*, began to reread my painstaking decipherment of *Zich Suthina*. In part, I sought after a sliver of information previously overlooked which might alter my interpretation of recent developments. I happened upon nothing so fortuitous.

Things were indeed bleak, and I think I took leave of my senses for a while in my state of indifference. I pitied, vaguely, the plight of the innocent men who surrounded me; trapped in this siege, unable to leave as with myself, but also ever fearful of an attack which could be their deathblow. For the majority, whose livelihood lies in farming and trade, the siege may *already* have effectively ruined them. Harvests had been delayed, lifelong contacts had been slain and despair had swept through the settlement like a plague. Few are as blessed as I, to be old and bereft of ties or investment. None but I are so fortunate to know that their safety is more assured than it outwardly appears.

After hours of such grim contemplation, my limbs and back had stiffened and I felt that I had to move in order to avert total paralysis. To that end, I opened my chamber door and stalked my way to the hearth. It was there, I confess, that my day was much improved; for Alton and his adopted son were sat beside each other, and they were playing a game on a checkered board and being thoroughly amused by it. I was intrigued (having never seen this particular variation before), and the two of them invited me to watch as their carefully planned strategies unfolded.

The game is known as 'Fidchell' and is apparently popular only in Stilneshire. It was originally of Caillic origins, many holding that the Falken family, owing some bygone heritage to that region, were responsible for its importation (a theory Ewin himself denies). Whether true or not, Stilneshire has always enjoyed quite benign relations with Caill due to their proximity (especially Trēodæl Hundred, the inhabitants of which demonstrate a decidedly hybridised culture) and the former's peaceability; the rules may have been diffused by traders and other friendly interactions. These trivialities aside, Bayldon informed me that a stranger might make the acquaintance of one from the Caill by playing them at Fidchell, jesting that the knowledge 'may save your life someday' - so, obviously, I dared not forsake the chance to learn such a priceless skill.

The rules themselves seemed simple enough. Each player took a turn to move one of their own wooden playing pieces along one axis. In this case, Bayldon's objective was to smuggle one particular, differentiated piece (the 'King') to the edge of the board, while Alton's goal was to capture said piece. It is a highly tactical game of scheming and forethought, and the two of them competed more than admirably.

When their match was over and Alton was declared the victor, the two shook hands and invited me to pit myself against one of them. Not one to shirk a challenge, I accepted; first against Bayldon and controlling the king, then against Alton and trying to capture his. I was defeated soundly on both occasions. Clearly the two of them are wasted as civilians in an agricultural hinterland, and should instead be ealdormen in Ricbert's court!

After proving myself the least capable strategist by a significant margin, Alton excused himself to go take stock of his goods (the reeve had ordered such for every person who stored substantial amounts of vital goods, to prevent unequal distribution) and allowed Bayldon and I an opportunity to continue his Arcāna studies. The young man seemed eager to learn more of wider Pænvicta, as he had done yesterday, but I instructed him that he was to grasp some of the basics of the Arx's language first, allowing him to at least bluff an understanding of what I was intended to teach him. He agreed to these terms, so I retrieved the materials from my room and tutored him openly before the freshly stoked hearth.

Whether it was his impatience to proceed to other subjects or a genuine, untapped academic streak, Bayldon memorised the vocabulary with an impressive degree of retention. Within the hour he was able to recite and understand simple sentences. Nothing that would enable him to talk his way past an Arx Turrium blockade, but a good foundation of the language upon which more could be built. My expectations exceeded, I truly had no option but to forfeit some of the forbidden knowledge for which he was so desperate.

This necessitated a place of relative privacy, so Bayldon offered his assistance in returning the books to my chamber. Once there, I realised that I had left *Zich Suthina* on my desk; conveniently, its contents became the topic of the evening's education.

"*VEL-THUR*," vocalised Bayldon, testing the syllables in his mouth. "Given his other names, I'd say he was an unpopular fellow, right?"

The 'Baron of the Damned' had a posthumous talent for being largely enigmatic to most circles of society: his exploits are known in full by a rare few cults in Iliban; known in part by the upper classes of Sūþeard, mostly as a cautionary term of phrase for a problem which will escalate to unmanageable severity if left unchecked; and not known at all to those in society's lower rungs. The population of Caill, in my experience, are either entirely unaware of him, or purposefully silent at his mention. For now, it behoved me to carefully select the aspects that I would reveal to Bayldon, so as to avoid drawing an unfavourable and presumptuous comparison between Velthur and I.

"As you say. He was known for having slain a great many people with the powers as his disposal."

"What 'powers'?"

"A question for another time, when I can answer it more comprehensively."

"Alright," shrugged Bayldon tersely. "Who were his enemies, then? Dad always said you can judge a man by who his enemies are."

"It would be easier, dear boy, to provide a list of those who he would *not* count among his enemies. As it was, nigh every civilisation that caught wind of his doings responded to them with condemnation."

"How long ago was all this?" Bayldon asked.

"Nearly four-hundred years, or something close to that mark."

"Honestly?" he queried in disbelief and amazement. "So some poor sods, thirteen or so generations back, had to lock horns with the scoundrel?"

"Correct. Your ancestors may well have been in their numbers."

"In the Kingdom of Sunþrardiz, right?"

"Yes, very good."

"But you said *every* civilisation. There were others, different from today?"

"Of course. Sunþrardiz is thought to be the youngest domain of those with which it coexisted. I could describe them to you, if you would like."

Bayldon nodded fervently, so I began to narrate the history of Pænvicta as far as it is known by those who record it. The Kingdom of Sunþrardiz reached as far as what is called Sūþeard today, the name for Cemparīce and Sċeldlond before their division. Caill, too, was much as it now is and how it has always been. Its occasional title of 'The Evergreen Kingdom' is not solely a reference to its trees through the seasons, but through the ages. I attempted to portray Ancient Zeritmia, the enlightened temple-city once situated atop Pænvicta's central mountain range, before its regression into the tyranny of Arx Turrium.

North-east of there, Iliban had yet to be established by those displaced from Zeritmia's societal changes and seeking asylum from the lawlessness in the wake of the south's sundering. Prior to this, the area's inhabitants were limited to a collection of secluded (but powerful) nomadic plains-tribes who, after enriching themselves with the extortionate levies they charged for the rent of their lands, became the foundations of the aristocratic class of Iliban. Thus is theirs the primary language of that territory today, and it is from that same language that the name of the city-state itself originates.

Long before the time of Velthur, before the seas were closed off by the Sjórvǫrðr, Pænvicta appeared very differently to how it is now known. The propagators of Sunþrardiz were simply a number of settlers from an island whose very name and location have faded into mythology (which I was promptly ordered to tell Bayldon of at another lesson). Zeritmia began as a colony of men from Cyclopeon, thought to have been expelled from the island by the legendary Cyclopes themselves. No chronicle exists regarding how the Caillic peoples, nor the proto-Ilibanese tribes, came to be. It is possible that they were Pænvicta's native inhabitants, though it is impossible to predicate how long the great eastern ravine, known as 'The Fetters', has been impassable. The primordial, unexplored land beyond it has been subject to endless speculation, but the hypothesis that Pænvicta's earliest immigrants were from there is not a popular theory, not least because the aeons are difficult for most to fathom.

Certainly, the effort proved too strenuous for Bayldon's already beleaguered mind. I could see him crease his brow in the attempt to visualise the lengths, breadths and depths of the world unlimited for the first time. For a majority of those who dwell on this continent, Pænvicta *is* the extent of the world. For those who rarely travel, their country is their entire world. For a still considerable sum, they will never set their eyes further than the bounds of the village in which they were born. Bayldon was currently being thrust from one such category into another; and yes, he *was* proving his potential beautifully, but every man must have limits. I did not wish to push him further beyond his comfort than was absolutely necessary.

Bayldon did not require a significant amount of persuasion. He bade me goodnight gratefully (if slightly dazedly) and made for his own chambers, leaving me to meditate on my own thoughts and tomorrow's objectives. Watching the young man's perspectives shift and grow has motivated a change of my priorities, I think. I am optimistic of what I might impress upon him. Perhaps I should analyse the last of the tomes from the archives to sate my own remaining curiosities before endeavouring to sate more of someone else's...

...

The man slips through the door and closes it behind him. The interior of the building is a bleak shade of grey and, other than the multitude of candles fixed to every wall and stood on every surface, the rooms are largely featureless. The man wears a long, black coat, gloves, and a hat with a veil; funeral attire, or something that passes for it, considering how indistinct and changeable Ilibanese fashion is.

He walks over to a table in the middle of the next darkened room. On it has been placed a laminated wooden coffin, a finely crafted object in its own right, but half of it has been left open. In Iliban this practice is called a 'wake', a ritual of the aristocracy now fading into unorthodoxy. The coffin's occupant has been immaculately prepared and placed within for others to view and mourn. A plaque on the casket's flank reads simply: 'SICOUNIN'.

As the man leans over to inspect the deceased, he is astounded by the artisanry of the embalmer's efforts. The young woman, with her raven hair, restored natural skin tones, and tranquil demeanour, appears almost as if she is simply sleeping. Even in this state she is breathtakingly beautiful. Her family had evidently spared no expense to remind Pænvicta of the fact following her tragic demise.

The visitor did not know the details of Sicounin's murder. She had been strangled, that much was public knowledge. The embalmer had been especially attentive in hiding the disfiguring contusions about her neck, now all but invisible. Rumour speculates that the man responsible was a disfavoured, envious suitor, and that he has been either devoured by Iliban's justice system or disposed of by some machination of the aggrieved family. Whichever is the truth, the brute has disappeared and would not be missed.

The man withdraws the veil over the crown of his hat, revealing his face. He himself is young, of a similar age to her; some might suggest reasonably handsome. However, he appears somewhat pasty and sickly. He looks longingly at the cadaver before him, then reaches out to touch her soft, rosy cheek, tracing his fingertips to her brow, which he gently pulls with his thumb to open an eyelid. The faded orb beneath stares upwards. He lifts his digit, allowing the lid to close again.

Could I truly bring myself to do this? *he contemplates.* Have I honestly sunk so low?

His hand traces across her countenance once more, traversing over her sleek, pointed nose and towards her chin. On this occasion, he tentatively opens her mouth just enough to show some of the teeth behind the lips. A healthy set, all intact. Probably still sharp.

She would not bite unless you commanded her to, *he reminds himself.* Nor would she do anything else... unless you wished it of her, that is.

Reluctantly, he begins to focus the manna within him, readying himself for the reanimation spell. His hand drifts over her collarbone, probing experimentally, until it slides under her corset and takes hold of one of the voluptuous but icy-cold breasts beneath. He squeezes firmly, but gains no satisfaction from the deed. On the verge of discontinuation, he attempts one last sordid, depraved act; he bends down and kisses Sicounin's dead, scarlet lips.

Immediately, a disgusting concoction of tastes fills his mouth; formaldehyde, strong perfume, and fetid meat. The effect is instantaneous. The man stumbles backwards, retching heavily. His throat fills with bile, and only through sheer willpower does he prevent himself from vomiting. Filled with contrition and abashment for his intentions, the young man resets his veil, utters an embarrassed apology and leaves, vowing never to reattempt an endeavour of this shameful sort.

Sōlrest-Þridda-XXIV

I count four days without genuine sleep, yet still I can find no associated afflictions beyond the sensation of detachment. The strangeness persists.

I felt no motivation to visit the mausoleum today. Folly or no, even with my inexplicably elevated abilities, it all seemed so... *unimportant*. The failed ritual had stymied my enthusiasm to the point of a mental deadlock. Going there again would make me question my purpose, and sharing a space with the Hinthial Sceptre was an egregious prospect.

Instead, I decided to look over that miniscule grimoire brought back from the deep archives. *Favin*. As I looked at its relatively featureless sleeve, I sensed the same promise that I had when I first gazed upon it. There was something auspicious about it, as if it whispered of answers to questions I had yet to ask. I threw it upon the desk, slapped down the Zeritmian primer beside it and began the interrogation.

The opening text, as I had remembered it, seemed prosaic enough. The unnamed author wrote of forbidden 'findings' and 'teachings' in an... *interesting* quality. In truth, the style was pretentious and tested my patience. It demanded willpower to even persevere through its eccentric transitions and swings. It was, in short, not fantastically *readable*. Here is a translated excerpt:

'...and so he was taught that the people up above bow to those down below without knowing that they bow or knowing to whom they do not know that they bow and so they bow without the knowledge of bowing until they cease to bow without the knowledge of ceasing to bow a bow they never knew they ever bowed at all.'

I could feel the seams of my mind loosening like so much badly stitched cloth, but I was certain that meaning would be concealed among the nonsense and determined not to be defeated by such insincere chicanery. Even so, the efforts were undeniably exhausting. Some of these mindless digressions continued for leaf after leaf, sometimes relegated to marginalia so they could extend after the main text had moved along. The tome itself was diminutive, so such voluminous bodies of script written so close to each other created an *unbelievably* cluttered format. Yet the hand was elegant, meticulous even.

Turning another leaf, I found that a side was taken up entirely by four vertical lines equidistantly spaced. They were, overall, perfectly straight, marred only by erratic, tiny 'trembles' as if the illustrator had been jostled lightly at unpredictable intervals. This I could not decipher, if indeed it was not simply the beginnings of an unfinished index. Whatever the intended meaning of these markers was, they served as a boundary segregating the inane riddles from the invaluable discoveries that were to come.

The ramblings were still present after the divider, but they became more focussed and pointed. I received the first sure indication that the text was masking the maddened thoughts of a necromancer:

'He dug out the slaves and gave them armour and lined them up and armed them well so they could march and dig out more and give them armour and line them up...'

And so on, and so forth. In its own long form, it seemed to describe the subject of the narration was building for himself a mighty army of un-dead. In itself it was not especially informative, but it assured me that I was on a potentially fruitful path. There was even a section which I can only assume alluded to the making of a Construct:

'He built the beast from bones and spells to bind the bones to build the beast, a beast of bones from many men to break the bones of any men who sought to break his bones. Then he built a second beast from bones and spells...'

In this way the circular cant told of making an impressive amount of these 'beasts of bones' (though I did skip ahead, I estimated the number at around twenty). The items of *real* interest appeared soon after this. My mind raced as I read over my translation:

'The ones to whom they bow then told him how to moult his shell to shed the flesh to shed the weight and shed the flaw and pupate himself to make more slaves and build more beasts but never did they tell him why but never did he ever ask while making slaves and building beasts that march and kill and march and kill and...'

What else could this mean other than the transformation into an Arch-Lich? I pressed onwards, excited by the hope of finding answers in the madness. I interpreted the Zeritmian faster than I had ever thought possible, my quill forming the right words almost as soon as the ancient letters entered my eyes. I looked over the still-wet ink on my parchment in awe:

'It is done and his cocoon will last for fourteen days and fourteen nights and after that the darkest day will make him anew in one half-cycle and it is long but he can wait because the ones they bow to told him so that it will be long but he can wait for such a prize to make them cheer with many mouths and clap with many hands and watch with many eyes.'

One half-cycle. A fortnight for the ritual to be realised, his metamorphosis to be complete. I had believed that the process would be instantaneous. How blind, how presumptuous I had been! Just as new life must be brought to term in the womb, so too must my spirit ready itself before tearing free of its anchorage! I was overcome with a whirlwind of emotions. If I was correct, my life as I knew it would end in a mere *six days*. I, meanwhile, had been preparing for precisely the opposite outcome.

Other things arose that provided supplementary information:

'Eight days left and he sees his tether which tethers him onto his shell and keeps him here against his will and makes him weep and makes him rage and makes the others keep away for though he beckoned and they came he does not beckon and may not beckon again for he wants for nothing but to be left alone and so he does not beckon...'

I felt pity for the wretched writer of this small account. As I began my translation I had suspected the record to be of Velthur's doing, the disintegration of his coherence being a sign of his deepening insanity, but there was no meaningful comparison to be made between *Favin* and *Zich Suthina*. Both were handwritten, but the cursive was utterly different. Velthur's manner was eloquent but his calligraphy coarse, while the author of *Favin* wrote endless, disjointed ravings with utmost care and daintiness. I would come to surmise that the lesser tome before me represented the secret journal of a hapless mortal servant, whose mind was broken and his conscience suppressed. *Favin* may have been the person's name, or a pseudonym, or simply a title bestowed by the author. Regardless, it appeared that events were to transpire poorly for them:

'His needs are nothing so he needs me for nothing and will make me into nothing so I can say nothing because the things that whisper tell him so; that I will whisper to tell the men that want to make him into nothing before he breaks from his cocoon and sends his slaves and beasts to march and kill and he will send me marching too so I cannot whisper but only kill and march and march and kill...'

It seemed that, like myself, Velthur began to cast off his mortal needs. He openly questioned the usefulness of his sentient thralls, prompting *Favin*'s descent into a stream of abject paranoia. I had learned so much of value from the lunatic's loquacious commentaries that I felt I owed their memory a completed rendition of their tale, and so I translated what little remained of the tome. As their fear consumed what was left of their sundered wits, their final, commendable act of defiance was one of subversion; the delivery of *Favin* to Velthur's enemies. Their final written words read:

'He will surely make me into nothing soon but he will soon be nothing too if his hourglass is smashed into nothing so I send this book to you with my own servant to lead you back to smash his hourglass into nothing to make him into NOTHING.'

Thus concluded *Favin*, the last section of the diary consisting only of blank pages. Its author, who maintained anonymity throughout the entire text, was likely killed soon after sending it to somewhere it could be found by the Blood-Marked. Unnamed though they may be, they could conceivably be credited in part for their master's downfall. They were surely the informant whose warning escalated the organisation's searches and showed them the one weakness of the hated Arch-Lich. I find it gratifying to reflect that, even though *Favin*'s author likely aided Velthur in committing at least *some* of his atrocities, they were able to find a sort of redemption in death; even if it *was* principally inspired by a desire for vengeance.

As I sat and contemplated the ramifications of my ritual being ultimately successful, I was startled by a rapping on my door.

"Are you in there, mate?" called Bayldon's voice through a thin aperture. "Are you alright? You've got us worried!"

"Yes, Bayldon. On both accounts, I think you will find. Do come in."

"Glad to hear it," he smiled, opening the door and wiping his brow dramatically. "We didn't know if you'd wandered off early or not, and with the 'bandits' on the prowl, we were fearing the worst!"

"Did I not urge the two of you not to worry? The sum of both your years *together* would not equal the number I have survived without you."

"Alright! Have mercy!" he cried, quailing from me mockingly. "Who pissed in *your* bed this morning? Or afternoon, for that matter?"

"I have been awake for... since dawn," I caught myself, not wishing to concern the young man. "Why? What hour is it now?"

"Dark. And we've only had a bowl of soup today, and you've had nothing. Aren't you hungry?"

"No. Again, do not worry; I have the means to sustain myself."

"Glad someone does. Honestly. I wouldn't wish this on anyone," Bayldon sighed, clutching his midriff with both hands.

"Take this," I said without thinking, tossing him my satchel of victuals, "you will make more use of them than I."

"I can't do that, mate. You're an old man...!"

"Take them!" I insisted. "Share them with Alton if you wish. Just partake of them sparingly. They are mostly depleted already."

"But it's your last food... why...?"

"You have both treated me with more kindness than I deserve, and I cannot predict how long I have to express my gratitude."

There was something of a stunned silence in the room. The words had left my throat automatically, a factual, self-evident statement. Bayldon, I think, overestimated the intended sentimentality, and did not quite know how to respond. But respond he did, after a long, uncomfortable pause.

"Look, I know you're old, mate - you won't stop going on about it - but you're smart, and wise, and don't ask me why, but I have a gut feeling we're all going to need *your* help to get out of this mess. Don't give up on us."

"It is people like Alton, Reeve Ewin and yourself that will save Gerefwīċ, Bayldon. Not I."

"Are you planning on leaving, then? Will you *not* help us?"

"Please! You misunderstand me. I still have business here. Things I shall speak of to you soon. I shall not abandon you or the others."

"Thank you," said Bayldon softly, calming himself.

"I shall do what I can, when I can do it," I pledged, "but I do not yet know what that will entail. It cannot be relied on."

"What *are* you, mate?" he asked not with suspicion, but boundless curiosity. "What's your 'business' in Stilneshire? Are you one of King Ricbert's spies? A wizard? What?"

"Tomorrow. Provide me with the time to consider how I can make you understand. Be patient, and I shall ensure that all of your queries are sated tomorrow evening."

"Alright," he replied bluntly.

I was aware of the doubt in his tone, but he was mindful that I had confessed to previously lying to him. From his perspective, neither would I have trusted me. It will be all the more shocking to him, then, when I *do* inform him of my illicit and unsavoury practices tomorrow, as promised. I had made my decision in that moment and shall not be swayed from it.

Nonetheless, Bayldon's enthusiasm was clearly dampened by his perceptions. I offered to continue his lessons in Arcāna, and he accepted; but after an hour or so of tutoring, his attention waned. I could sense the more burning questions for which he was desperate to acquire answers, and the restrictions against his asking were irritating him. We eventually conceded defeat and wished each other well before he departed. It was not ill will he bore for me, but the distraction of more tantalising mysteries being held just out of his reach.

How am I to introduce the young man to necromancy without inspiring immediate revulsion in him? He was surprisingly untroubled when learning of the revenants; not completely at ease with the concept of their existence, obviously, but certainly more accepting than could be reasonably expected. Perhaps the aspect of them being under the control of a living man would prove a comfort to him...

... Or an intolerable evil...

... In either case, I have committed to myself not to countermand this pact, and must now see it to its fulfilment. If Bayldon's reaction is not too negative, he may be pliable enough to test his willingness to engage with necromancy himself. Another forbearing individual to share conversations and aspirations with would make an immortal existence much less... lonely. If he can no longer abide my presence, then I shall leave; for it would please me more to permit him to hate me based on the truth, than for him to grant me affection based on deceit.

There was no one to be seen when I left my chambers to experience the night outside. The sky was clear and the air frigid, though I could not feel it in my lungs nor see the mist escape my lips. I realised that I am now unsure as to whether or not I still breathe. The moon's thin, bright crescent glinted, and I envisioned its diminished shape as an indication of its submission; it would mock me with its glare no longer.

...

The wind whistles and howls through the ravine as the young man approaches the edge. He wears the lightweight and tightly fitted gear of a mountaineer, dark brown in colour and loaded with an array of implements. Above, it is reasonably warm and pleasant. The sky is free of clouds and the grass on the slopes is verdant in the sun's glow.

It was a long walk to get here, and the wait for perfect conditions had been longer still. Now the opportunity has finally presented itself, the man pursues his intrepid exploration with an unparalleled eagerness. The incline steepens before him and he pauses, taking a solitary section of parchment from his pocket, which he unfolds and examines, occasionally glancing upwards to compare with his surroundings.

His eyes come to rest on a particularly distinctive tree about ten yards away. It is a healthy oak, still clothed in its leaves, but it protrudes from an outcrop which juts from the ravine's edge. The adventurer would proceed no further without securing himself first. Thus he unslings a coil of rope from his shoulder, tying one end to a closer, less precarious tree, and the other about his waist. Then he treads on towards his landmark, tentative with each step.

The map tucked back into his pocket was given to him freely; almost unbelievable for something of such potential value. His anonymous contact is apparently sympathetic to his reticent interest in forbidden texts, but is either too busy or too decrepit to pursue the lead himself. Whatever the motivation, the young man found the prospect too exciting to resist.

He is almost at the strangely angled tree now, and the ground feels friable beneath his feet. Very likely the oak's roots are holding much of the soil together, but his harness is secure and his courage undaunted. Nevertheless, he moves gradually, extending his arm to meet the closest branch. He wraps his fingers around it, using it to steady himself as he nears the edge of the ravine, then he peers over the precipice and beyond.

'The Fetters'. That is the name of this unfathomably vast natural chasm. Though the fact cannot be perceived from one fixed point, it is this geographical feature which separates Pænvicta from the larger continent and ensures that the latter remains entirely inaccessible by land. North and to his left, one would eventually reach Glæsćiella; following south and to his right, one would, after many, many miles, find Magasæ. Across the estimated five-hundred yard division, another, different country stretches far beyond the horizon. It lies lower than Pænvicta and is covered in a boundless rainforest, densely wooded and obscured by an ubiquitous mist; The Savage Green, it is called. There are no signs or hints of civilisation, and no pioneer has ever found a means to venture into that primordial region.

His eyes drift downwards at the sheer rockface on the opposing side. It is as it was described to him years ago, and of an incredible clarity; horizontal lines of colour in the rock denote layers of deposition going back aeons, now made discernible after the continuous erosive activity of the ravine's churning waters. This is the other perilous aspect of The Fetters; at the base of the cliffs, tidal swells from the two connected seas, along with the inlets of several rivers which pour into the channel as waterfalls, make for violent, linear rapids. Even in steady weather such as this, the current shifts constantly from one direction to the other at the whims of the tides. They are unnavigable waters, fickle and hungry, and are surely one of the traits for which The Fetters are so named.

The sight, as the young man absorbs it, is both enchanting and daunting. The scale of it all is so grand as to be incalculable. The plunge would be considerably further than the mighty walls of the Arx are tall, and certainly just as deadly. Shivering, he tests the rope harness one more time, turns his back towards the bank and adds more slack, inchmeal, to his tether. Creeping backwards he comes to the edge, resists the urge to glance behind him, and lowers himself down.

The rockface beneath Pænvicta is of a similar composition to that of the other continent, but is significantly loftier; however, his objective and purpose for being here is already visible. A short tunnel has been mined into the rock, subtle but recognisable, in the precise location suggested by the improvised map... if a little further down than expected. The young man continues to backpedal while suspended by the rope. The opening must be ten yards below him and the effort is strenuous, but he increases his pace in the hope of carrying his weight for fewer agonising moments. His knuckles are white and his palms are red before his left foot treads into a void; initially he panics, believing that he has made a ruinous error, but his alarm quickly turns to elation as he realises his success.

In a last, painful exertion, he allows his feet to dangle freely while his arms bear his weight. A narrow ledge provides a merciful foothold, allowing him to relieve some of his burden and push himself onto the safer ground of the tunnel. The man collapses, exhausted, and his supine form rises and falls as he recovers from his ordeal. Then he sits up, waiting for his eyes to adjust to the new darkness.

The tunnel is a respectable size, with a diameter of about four yards and a length of ten or so. The walls have been smoothed and some rudimentary furniture items, including a number of wooden shelves, a desk, a chair and a bedroll, are placed haphazardly around the room. It is a makeshift living space, cramped yet cosy, but long since abandoned: one of the shelves has split and never been repaired; thick dust and cobwebs covered every open surface; and the small firepit in the centre has only old ashes in its base.

Many would see that chamber and find that, other than the fascination that such extraordinary measures had been taken simply to create a hidden alcove, it was otherwise a mess of worthless debris. To the young man whose bright eyes now scan the scene with a deep satisfaction, priceless treasures are scattered about the floor. Manuals, books, tomes, grimoires; an impressive repository of knowledge covertly stored, and for good reason. He hops to the side of the largest of the piles and crouches, collecting each work with utmost care and stacking them into a neat tower. He reads the titles as he gathers them; some of them prompt a nod of approval, others are in scripts he cannot decipher.

A temporary inconvenience. One that can be amended in time, *he thinks to himself as he withdraws and unfolds a burlap sack from his pack.*

The word 'inconvenience' unexpectedly provokes an uneasy sensation within his subconscious. He scratches his head, looking around himself for the unknown, important article that requires his attention.

"Ah," he sighs. "An inconvenience."

At the mouth of the tunnel he regards the length of rope, up which it will be necessary to transport every piece of this invaluable literature as well as himself. Spellbooks, as he would soon unequivocally understand, are quite heavy.

I shall, one day, take Bayldon to The Fetters. It has a way of altering one's perspective of Pænvicta, and the larger world around it.

Sōlrest-Þridda-XXV

Has ever a man who sought immortality been as undeserving as I? Has ever one rued their efforts so? A foul concoction of basal instinct and pure cowardice prevents me from taking my own life, but the thought of eternal persistence beneath this guilt is appalling to contemplate.

I must consolidate myself if I am to obtain clarity of mind once again.

The night's visions dissolved away like droplets of ink in a basin of clear water. I shall not call it 'sleep', for it is in no way restful; rather, it is an enervating experience, more akin to a trance. I find it now less concerning than previously, having taken it to be some side-effect of the Arch-Lich binding that my spirit is undertaking, but the lack of mortal needs is still disconcerting. Altering one's diet or schedule can manifest anxiety for some. Abandoning both entirely is slightly maddening.

On this occasion, however, I discovered something more sharply dismaying. Upon removing my gown to change it for my warmer, more durable cloak, I noticed a discolouration on my bare torso. Predicting it to be merely a trick of the darkness, I struck a fire with my flintsteel to light the lantern on my bedside. When the extent of the phenomenon was revealed to me, I was forced to stifle a shout; for the flesh upon my chest had so shrunk back and blackened that my sternum and its frontmost adjoined ribs stood exposed at my fore. They were intact enough, but that beneath them appeared necrotic and inert. The angle made for an awkward inspection, but I saw no evidence of billowing lungs or a beating heart. By definition I had, myself, become un-dead.

Realising the implications of such a transformation, I threw my cloak over myself and fled from the tavern at pace. Had my face been similarly afflicted? I could not say, and so I kept my cowl drawn low as I scanned the roads for the watchmen. The weather was wretched, the rainfall tumultuous, but I could make out that none were close. Taking sanctuary in the mausoleum seemed a practicable, if temporary, solution. Escaping the hundred would come later when I could prepare myself better. Smuggling my phylactery would be necessary to ensure a clean flight, and I could be guarded while I arranged the hasty departure.

Thus I sprinted to the graveyard as quickly as possible and, scrambling up the hill that had already become so slick from the precipitation, allowed myself into the mausoleum. The safer depths of the catacombs beckoned enticingly, and I leapt over the puddling water to answer their call. After rounding several corners more rapidly than I thought feasible, I met with my congregated servants, only then slowing to evaluate my circumstance. I paced back and forth with indecision as I debated myself internally.

If I should continue to deteriorate, I shall soon be incapable of concealing it. Then I shall find myself either outcast or executed, I considered. *Perhaps the sooner my escape could be realised, the less opportunity there is for mishap.*

But what of the others? Do you propose to desert them in their hour of need? asked another voice from within me.

I shall have to watch over them from afar. They will not so readily accept protectorship from such an aberrant form.

Craven! berated my conscience. But there was no argument to be had; immediate retreat was the only logically sound option. The un-dead about me tensed, standing straighter and facing forwards, ready to receive their directions.

I was primed to leave when a glint caught my attention. I turned reluctantly to see the unwelcome sheen of the Hinthial Sceptre. I walked over to it, all the way eyeing it with suspicion but inexorably reaching my hand out towards it nonetheless...

It was at this point that the worst, most calamitous injustice that I have ever witnessed came to despoil all that I had come to value.

"Who-" someone began to announce from the opposite end of the corridor, but the speaker was briskly silenced before their intent could be determined; Rēdawulf had reactively raised his powerful bow, nocked an arrow and loosed it in a heartbeat, and his aim was frightfully true. The reports of the projectile striking bone and the body falling to the ground met my ears almost before the echoes of their shout had faded.

Initially I exalted, pleased with Rēd's expert and prompt elimination of the intruder. But as I cautiously approached the twitching corpse, a growing sense of unease swept over me. The source of my apprehension was exposed as I came close enough to identify the open-mouthed face in the gloom. There, lying prone with the shaft of an arrow jutting from his left eye socket, was Bayldon, lifeless, his frozen features conveying an expression of innocent confusion.

I remained there for a few moments, stood in shock and disbelief as the body's convulsions gradually weakened. Then I panicked, rushing to his side while frantically searching for a way to reverse my grievous error. A last, desperate hope overtook me; I sent Haþuwīgą to retrieve the Hinthial Sceptre and, once she was at my side and looking over the casualty, I bade her make use of the eldritch artefact to mend the dire injury. But she would not. She simply stared at me, then at her task, then at me again. Even driven by my very willpower, the un-dead priestess (and thus I, too, if subconsciously) knew that the young man was beyond rescue, and that any attempt to do so now would result not in life but un-death. Still I could not accept it, but I had barely noticed the pooling blood until it began to soak through my clothes and wet my knees. Only then did I investigate its source, whereupon I tenderly lifted his head from the gore. There I saw, protruding from a jagged rupture in the hind part of Bayldon's skull, the arrowhead; the wound was terrible, and from it poured a seemingly endless flood of vital fluids. The perforation of his brain had been lethal, near instantly so, and could not now be undone.

And I wept. I wept for my lost friend, for the promising future I had stolen from him. I wept for his doting father, who had so selflessly adopted and raised him and now would see him nevermore. And I wept in sorrow for my despicable part in his pointless, untimely end.

I could scarcely bear to touch his limp body, but in trying to find the reason for his presence I happened upon a familiar object still clutched tightly in his offhand; a simple wooden stick. My walking stick, which I had forgotten in my race to flee. The deduction was a simple one and the answer intensified my shame. I felt revulsion then, towards myself and all else. I cursed and raged, hurling pieces of stone debris splashing into the spreading puddles and ineffectually beating upon the walls with my bare fists. My frenzied state was finally quelled when I snatched the Hinthial Sceptre from Haþuwīgą's skeletal digits and struck her a thunderous blow with it; the other-wordly thing reverberated as it swung through the air, accelerating preternaturally and smiting the hapless minion with a strident *thrum*. Though I hardly discerned the impact myself, poor Haþu's bones were scattered wildly throughout the chamber. I dropped the weapon in astonishment, shaken by the harsh noise and raw, unbound energy. So was I tempered, for the moment. I collapsed from my exertions and continued to lament a while longer.

I know not exactly how long I agonised there. It was strange for me to reflect that, though I have in my own lifetime destroyed the lives of many others and been present for the demise of many more, Bayldon was the first for whom I truly mourned. For most of my existence I have been disconnected, withdrawn from the plight of my fellow men. I was never entirely indifferent (certainly not *resentful*; I am not Velthur in that regard, at least) to the sanctity of men's lives, but rather ignorant of their individual complexity and importance. Now one so close to me had perished, I underwent the bitter sting of that loss for the first time.

My tears flowed until I could shed no more. The un-dead around me swayed and watched on unsympathetically. This persisted until I could not abide looking upon Bayldon's stationary decedent any longer, and I had the servants that remained intact carry him in procession and place him, shamefully, into one of the empty sarcophagi. I hesitated, the waves of self-loathing washing through me as I contemplated the sickening abhorrence of interring my friend in the same fashion as I had an inconsequential graverobber. I stood over him, shut the lid of his intact eye and placed a hand on his shoulder, my own eyes moistening again.

"Please forgive me, my cherished friend. I shall provide a more deserving funeral as soon as I can arrange for it. I am so sorry."

The skeletons lowered him into the sarcophagus, and I turned away as they sealed him in. I looked over at my phylactery, and I fully believe that I would have pulverised it, slaying myself then and there, if I had no commitments to Bayldon's people or his memory. I deliberated inwardly on the next course of action, eventually arriving at a difficult conclusion; I would inform Alton of what had transpired here, and of everything that I had hidden from him since we became acquainted. I had no further right to deny him.

Whether due to concern or a need for procrastination, I decided that there were chores that required my attention before I could leave the mausoleum. In particular, I adjusted the passive orders of the Blood-Marked so as to urge them to pursue less harmful means of defending the space before resorting to their deadly weaponry. In addition, I bolstered the intake of the sapping circles to augment their effect of inspiring dread. It was my ambition that such measures would deter another tragic incursion. The spells I had previously inscribed were still unbroken and ready to catalytically release should Gerefwīċ be threatened. My phylactery was aptly concealed, and the Hinthial Sceptre... was shut away, as out of sight and mind as I could manage.

By the time I could find no more excuses for delay, the rainwater's onslaught had become positively torrential, collecting into rivulets which disappeared into the crevices of the stone floor like a delta. Bayldon's blood was all but rinsed away by the streams. I waded through the meres, unheedful of the icy bath rising, in places, as high as my knees. The catacombs were drowning in a way I had never seen before. But I was past caring, pushing onwards to mete out the punishment I had allotted for myself. The gate was, of course, wide open when I reached it; in my struggle to take refuge in the recesses of my lair, I had forgotten to secure the lock behind me, allowing Bayldon to follow me directly. It is likely that he was in awe of my speed without my walking stick, but considered that I might yet need it and chased me unimpeded. Another blame that could be laid at my sodden feet.

The storm outside hammered down relentlessly, punctuated by frequent, dazzling, ear-splitting lashes of forked lightning. The air was charged and the environment felt dangerous even for my altered physique, so I stumbled through it (nearly sliding on the steep, muddy incline) and staggered, drenched and miserable, into The Old Boar.

"Thank the powers that be! You're alright!" cried Alton. "I don't know what gods are on your side, but I hope they'll show us all some of that favour!"

"Alton, I have news..."

"I'm sure it can wait a moment while you dry off!" he laughed, wiping a nervous sweat from his forehead.

"Please, Alton. You must listen!"

"Will you let me get that cloak off you, at least? You're going to catch your death before you get the words out, you look like you could drop in a heartbeat!"

Alton was already bustling over to me, reaching out to help me to remove the dripping outer layer, but I recoiled from his hands. He, in turn, flinched backwards, his brow creased with worry.

"What's wrong, mate? I think you're worse off than I thought. Where's Bayldon? Has he gone to fetch someone already?"

"Bayldon is gone, Alton."

"Gone where? Did he say? He said he'd come right back once he'd passed you your stick." He paused, the perturbation in his eyes deepening. "You don't have it. Didn't he get to you? Where's he gone, the stupid git!"

I was presented with the perfect opportunity to craft an easy, mitigative falsehood. Indeed it was, disgracefully, my first thought, but I suppressed my compulsion. I could not needlessly prolong his suffering.

"Bayldon *did* find me. He will not be returning."

"Why?" asked Alton, the ghost of a grin appearing on his lips. Evidently, he was beginning to believe himself a victim of an elaborate farce.

"Because he is dead, Alton. I am sorry."

My sincerity was absolute. I came close to breaking down on the floor of his establishment, but restrained myself. I knew that my coherency was of utmost importance in those brief, awful moments.

"That's not funny," uttered Alton dourly.

"Death seldom is."

"What do you mean, he's dead? How do you know?" he questioned, despair creeping into his tone.

"Because I killed him. I am sorry," I repeated. The statement seemed so hollow and meaningless. It could never portray the weight of my regret.

"You're talking shit," spat Alton, red-faced and visibly upset. "How could *you* have killed him? You're out of your right mind."

"It was an accident, I swear it! I had not anticipated him following me into the crypt, I would never-"

"What were you doing in the crypt? No one goes near that place any more, it's damned haunted or I'm a gelding!"

"It *is* haunted, Alton; I am the one who haunts it."

"Who... *what* are you? A ghoul? A body snatcher? What?" he demanded, the expectant disgust bubbling in his throat.

"I am a necromancer. I intended to tell you sooner-"

"A dead-raiser! Under my own roof!" the innkeeper exclaimed, horrified. "What did you do to my little boy, monster?"

"An arrow struck him, loosed from the bow of one of my minions. The wound was fatal. There was nothing I could do."

"What did you do that for?" the man wailed. "Because he saw what you were? Gods, did you turn him into one of your-"

"No! I would *never* have done that to him. The creature reacted to Bayldon as an intruder before I was aware of his presence."

"So that's it, then? He's dead, and that's it? Can't you bring him back? Nothing? *Anything*?" Alton begged desperately.

"If I tried to resurrect him, he would not be *himself*. He would be nobody. A shade. A soulless instrument. I wish it were otherwise, Alton. I would gladly give my life for his, if I could. But it cannot be changed."

Alton ceased conversing, seeming suddenly older. He hobbled unsteadily away from me and towards the counter, slumping heavily onto one of the seats. Wordlessly, he stretched an arm over the bar, took up an empty tankard and filled it from the solitary keg on the worktop, then he filled a second.

"I thought I'd take what I'm about to say to the grave. My *own* grave, that is," he added dolefully. "I don't suppose it matters much, now. Sit down."

"Alton, I..."

"*Sit.*"

He did not raise his voice, but the command was irrefutable regardless. I hesitantly joined him and sat in the next chair along. He grunted and placed the other tankard of ale on the surface in front of me, then he spoke at length in a resigned, unemotional monotone.

"We're both liars, you know. I've lied to Bayldon almost his whole life. I never told him or anyone else in Stilneshire what I did before I got here. It took a long, long time for folk here to trust me because of that. Some of the older ones still don't. It didn't matter, though. I was here for him, not me.

"The thing is, Bayldon wasn't family by any measure. Warin was rightly my brother's name, but he had no wife, or sons, or daughters, and he didn't die of a fever either. Actually, he was in the same risky business as I was, because things were tough through the Sūþeard split *and* on the other side of it. Hard for two men to make a living with no trade and most of the fields burnt down. So there were a lot of hungry folk about, especially the soldiers from Sċeldlond who deserted the army and carried right on looting after the war had stopped. Then, there were a few of us who made a good bit of coin collecting the rewards on those robbers' heads."

"You were a *bounty hunter*?" I affirmed, partially incredulous with surprise.

"I was. Me and my brother, we *both* were, and we worked together in a party. Since our old dad died, we couldn't be pried apart by beast nor man. We led it as an equal pair, watching each other's backs and keeping the rest in line. Two captains. And we were *damned good too*, by the end of it.

"So we went up and down eastern Cempaříce and western Sceldlond plying our trade with a writ from the king, offering the locals our *services* if they'd tell us about where our bounties' hideouts were and how many men they had. Then we'd take on a few more helpers if we thought we'd need them; after all, some of those deserters amassed quite a following themselves, and we weren't exactly running short of ex-soldiers with a grudge to settle ourselves. Funny, really. Sometimes the ones we hired would tell us how they remembered fighting at the side of the bloke we were going to kill. All in a day's work for them, I suppose, as it was for us.

"Anyway, what would *tend* to happen is, we'd sneak up on their camp - sometimes they were old mines, or caves, or shelters hidden in the woods - and try to get the drop on them, cut through as many as you can as quick as you can so they didn't have the numbers by the time they figured out what was happening. A bloody business, it was. Even to the last man, they barely ever surrendered; every deserter knows they're headed to the gallows if they're caught, and most would rather die with their sword in their hand than a rope around their neck.

"The last ones, they were always the most dangerous. We must have rid Sūþeard of about sixscore of their hideouts, each one with between about a dozen and ten dozen men. And of every single one of those men, the *most* dangerous one was Beadurof by a long way. That one had a *really* swanky place for himself and his mates. They'd managed to set themselves up in an old fort from the war; high, spiked stake walls, watchtowers, the lot. All built on a big hill, manned at all hours and well-armed. A real bastard to sneak up on, that was."

Alton chuckled to himself, staring at a fixed point as he reminisced. He took a lengthy drink from his tankard before resuming his narration.

I took a sip of my own ale, but otherwise remained silent and listened, the howling wind and the drumming of the rain pelting the surrounding structure providing an oppressive backdrop for his tale.

"Of course, Beadurof had a good head on his shoulders and played things close to his chest. No one knew for sure how many soldiers he had in there. It was the start of Sōlcyme, so we didn't want to freeze to death trying to wait him out in a siege. But Warin and I, we come up with a plan to climb over the part of the wall furthest from any of the towers, just as the others make like they're trying to break through the gates. Then we'd cut the head off the beast, start a few fires and get them all flustered. Disorganised men are that much easier to fight.

"It was a risky plan, but that didn't mean we took chances we didn't have to. Myself and Warin, we didn't go as just the two of us. We brought some of our best, thinking he'd probably have a bodyguard of his. It all went pretty well, at first. We waited until dark so we could climb the hill without getting spotted. Then we put the ladder up against the wall, still no problems. Inside it was like a tiny village, lots of wooden houses all different shapes and sizes. Didn't take us long to see Beadurof's place, mind. It was twice the size of the others, like a barracks all on its own. Getting to that was dicey, given he had patrols damn near everywhere, but it was the sort of thing we'd had a lot of practice in. All that we had to do then was give the signal for the main group, a long, loud whistle, then break our way into his command post and kill him dead, along with anyone who gets between us.

"Easy job, right?" Alton asked rhetorically. I offered no response and said nothing. He sniffed and continued the story.

"It would have gone perfectly, too, with any other deserter leading that band. Not with Beadurof. We should've listened to the stories. It's funny, so many of them try to get these myths spread about themselves, to make people think they're stronger, or smarter, or scarier than they actually are. Before long, you kind of figure out that it's all just gossip and hearsay. So when the locals told us that his spear was as fast and as deadly as a volley of crossbow bolts, how were we to know that it wasn't just another gloat? He played to his strengths, too. He made sure to fight us in the main hallway; a big, wide room with a lot of posts and things about. Barely enough space to swing a sword, but plenty of gaps to stab a spear through...

"Now I'm not saying he was *unnatural* or anything like that, but he knew his business better than anyone I'd ever seen. I'd always reckoned that a spear was a weapon best used in a line, working together so you couldn't get near, but I'll tell you; taking on Beadurof was like trying to take on a schiltron. His mates were average at best, but I'll be damned if he didn't move like lightning and put down six of our best men before we really knew what we were up against and stopped trying to rush him. Quicker than you could blink, he put holes in heads, necks, hearts, guts... I'd never seen a sharper or faster speartip, and I'd wager that I'll never see one again.

"Anyway, so there we were, trying to figure out our next move, him keeping us at a distance with that nasty polearm of his, when we hear a scream. A woman's scream, from one of the side-rooms. Warin runs off to see if they're a prisoner that needs freeing and Beadurof, who before was as cool-headed as you can be when you're fending off a group of armed men, mind, *howls* at him to stay and fight, like nothing I'd ever heard. And Warin comes back holding this lady with his blade at her throat, and she has a bundle in her arms too. Beadurof, he starts screaming at him to let her be, not to touch her and all that. That's when we realise we've got the bastard's *lover, and* his newborn kid, too!

"So now we're holding them ransom and telling him to lay down his spear, she's screaming at him not to because we'll kill him anyway, and he's telling her that it's all going to be fine, all while the baby's crying its little heart out. It's a right mess, but it all goes to shit when she uses the confusion to pull out a dagger and shove it in my brother's windpipe. He cuts the bitch ear-to-ear before letting her go, she falls to the side cradling her baby, and Beadurof goes *wild*. The last three men we brought with us were on the floor before you could say 'Back!' and then he was coming for me. I don't even know how I did it - must have been some sort of miracle - but I managed to get a hold of his spear's shaft as he stabbed at me, pulled myself close and shoved my sword through his chest.

"And you know what? I'll never forget the last three things he did. First, he got out a scramseax and cut me across the belly with it. Can't forget that one, really. I see it damn near every day. Second, he looks down, and I think it's the first time he realises that he's done for. Third, he looks back up at me, face to face, and tries to say something, but no sound comes out. So he nods in the direction of his baby and just looks at me with the most pleading eyes I've ever seen. And that's what's on his face as he dies, still held up by my sword. His legs give out and he gets heavy and slides off.

"Everything seemed so quiet after that. All I could hear was the fighting outside on the other side of the fort, Beadurof's baby crying its eyes out, and my brother choking his last. I kneel by him just in time to hold his hand and wish him well on his travels. Then, I go over to the woman who killed him. She's dead, probably since just after she hit the boards, so all that's left is what to do with this baby. The king's orders say that deserters' spawn has to be put down, to make the deserters think twice about starting families to carry on their tricks. I pick up the helpless little thing - a baby boy, as it happens - and see a name stitched onto his blanket."

"Bayldon," I surmised.

"That's right!" proclaimed Alton proudly. "Fact of the matter is, the moment I looked at him, I knew I couldn't hurt him. So I took him, and I left. I don't even know how the rest of the battle went. I didn't care. I just knew that I had to save that innocent life, take him away to something better.

"It wasn't easy, though. I had to work like a dog and scrape together the coin I had for wetnurses. Truth is, I put aside a lot of my own life for his sake, but it was all worthwhile when he grew up to be a grand young lad: polite; strong; a fast learner. I didn't even *want* children of my own, because I wanted to give him all the attention I could. Not many wives would be content with that, so that idea was done away with..."

Alton drained the last of his ale and stared into the bottom of his empty tankard.

"The only thing that scared me was him turning into his father," he confessed, " so I never told him about his dear old dad. I made up that story when folk first started asking, and I've stuck to it since. And I moved him as far away from war as I could. Somewhere quiet, with some opportunity for him to grow as a person. Of course, you could say that didn't work. Those Arx bastards brought strife to every corner of Sūþeard once they saw their chance. Still, it's a calmer place than most, here. Until very recently, that is."

"He was a fine young man," I agreed sullenly. What else could I say, when confronted with such?

"The best. I poured everything into making that boy into what he was, through thick and thin. You could even say that I lost my brother for him, in a way. Maybe, deep down, I just wanted to make something good from a place where so many people lost so much. Including me. I wonder if he knew just how much I loved him when he walked out of that door for the last time."

"He was an intelligent, perceptive individual. He knew, Alton."

"That he was. Until you took all that away, of course."

The innkeeper's hands clenched, his knuckles whitening, and his face twisted into one of scalding hatred. "I'll tell you, that lad was keener than me by all measures, but I can count one thing where I was right and he was wrong. The Scucca *is* real, and he sits right here beside me!"

We both stood from our stools, our tankards clattering to the floor. In all my years, even among those who sought my destruction after discovering my nature, I had never seen such a visage of pure detestation.

"And what's a man to do, if he sets his eyes on the Scucca, and he's worth anything at all?" growled Alton, drawing a seax from the sheath at his waist and advancing. I backed away with my hands raised, not in submission but as a gesture of placation.

"*Stop*, Alton. I am sorry about Bayldon, but this will *not* bring him back to you."

"Maybe not, but I can save others! How many sons have you stolen away from the world? How many daughters? Husbands? Wives? Good folk?" he seethed through gritted teeth.

"You have slain men too, Alton. You said so yourself."

"I killed *killers*! I never took an honest life, and may the gods strike me down if I have! *You*," he spat, "*you're* a *murderer*. Worse, a *monster*. You can't even look folk in the eyes when you kill them, you need dead men to do it *for* you!"

Alton swung his iron edge in a wide arc. I weaved, moving more swiftly than he evidently expected and causing him to throw himself off-balance. His fury was stoked further by the feat, however, and he was soon pacing after me again.

"I do not wish to harm you, Alton!" I cautioned.

"Why not? Why not finish what you started, and kill me too? Maybe afterwards, you can send my carcass to cut up the reeve, or anyone else who might get in your way!" he bellowed, swinging the blade again. This time the seax fell vertically, the tip burying itself in the timber flooring as it missed me by inches. He was nearly able to catch me with his other hand, but narrowly missed a second time. He roared in frustration and pried his weapon free, striding towards me once again.

"Why don't you just bring your army of corpses down here and kill us all? What's stopping you? Do you *really* enjoy making good folk suffer *that much*?"

"As I told Bayldon, and as I am certain he told you, they are not *my* army. I have been looking for a means to banish them! I have done many foul things, Alton, for which I surely deserve reprisal, but this is not a thing of *my* doing!"

"Then whose is it, dead-raiser? One of your mates playing games?" he patronised.

"I do not know from whence these un-dead come, but I shall defend you from them with all that I can muster, with my *own* life if that is what must be done!"

"Give me one reason why I should trust you, you cruel bastard."

"Because I am Gerefwīċ's best chance for survival," I reasoned. He was not sated.

"Bullshit, you're a liar and I'll kill you! Bayldon deserved better!"

Alton followed closely now, swinging his seax in ferocious, whirling flurries. He had positioned himself between the exit and I, ready to intercept me if I attempted to escape by passing him at either side.

"Do not force my hand, Alton. Bayldon deserved better, yes. Doubtless *I* deserve death for his fate. But I shall not allow you to doom Gerefwīċ's people in exacting your vengeance. Afterwards, when they are safe. Not before."

Alton had become deaf to my words. He flew at me in a blind rage, ready, I am certain, to hack me limb from limb and flesh from bone until nothing remained. I had no choice but to react, but I did so with restraint, or so I thought. I sapped a degree of energy from his arms and legs, whereupon he released his weapon from his weakened grasp and fell to his knees with an agonised pule. I waited warily, expecting a resurgence, but none came. After I steadied myself, I finally understood the subtle, barely audible noise that I was trying vainly to distinguish against that of the turbulent weather; Alton was *sobbing*. I maintained my distance, resisting the urge to approach and comfort him. Then he spoke in a murmur which I strained to hear:

"It's not fair. Please... go away. Leave me be, and never come back here. I wish I'd never met you. Please just go..."

Whether there was more to his plea, I cannot say. I conceded to his appeal, taking my leave of The Old Boar and its kindly proprietor, and swept into the deluge outside. My vision was blurred and my senses overwhelmed, but I found myself climbing my way up to the mausoleum. Once I was inside and the gate was sealed, I limped down: down into the catacombs, wading through the floodwater and into the embrace of the darkness; down to the scene which represented the culmination of a heinous existence, the location of my greatest achievement and my most solemn regret; down to the only company appropriate for a man such as I. And here I linger, pondering whether to curtail the eternity for which I have sacrificed so many innocent souls.

ACT III

"Deep into that darkness peering, long I stood there wondering, fearing,
Doubting, dreaming dreams no mortal ever dared to dream before..."

- Edgar Allan Poe, *The Raven*

Sōlrest-Þridda-XXVI

...

It is a day that could almost be described as picturesque. The sounds of a softly running river and birdsong make for a tranquil symphony, and the sunbeams break through the canopy of great oaks, lighting streams of soft mist like ethereal veils draped over a divine garden. Only one thing shatters the perfection of the illusion; a middle-aged man lies dead on the edge of the riverbank.

He wears the trappings of a rural inhabitant of Iliban; a stitched linen shirt and trousers, though his felt sunhat has fallen from his head. But he also wears waders, and a creel lies by his side. The man himself is quite rotund, and was likely somewhat puce in colour even before his untimely end a few hours ago. Evidently he lived well, possibly too well. That may have contributed to his fate, his comfortable life having been struck short by a weakness of the heart. It happens.

The staccato crack of a snapping twig interrupts the peaceful melody and some of the birds take wing. It announces the appearance of a figure on the edge of the meadow; a man with his head low, sneaking, wearing a drab brown cloak. Most of the face, including the eyes, is hidden under the shadow of the hood, but there is enough of the smooth jawline and narrowing chin visible to tell that he is young, only just an adult by the local standards. He takes a few steps at a time, then stops to look and listen, ever cautious. Most of the birds return to the branches behind him and resume their chorus.

It is a few minutes of creeping before the cloaked man is confident that no one else is in the meadow. He then strides quickly over to the older man's corpse, wishing not to waste any more time.

Such an opportunity is rare, *he considers, and decides to take the chance. As one last precaution, the hooded man places his fingers on the old one's neck and confirms that he is most certainly dead. Satisfied, the body is dragged away from the river's edge and the young man raises his hands high, as if about to give a grand speech.*

The vast sleeves of the robe slide down to the elbows and are moved gently by an almost imperceptible breeze. For a few moments, it is the only noticeable movement. Then, a shimmer in the air around the cloaked man's hands coalesces into a stream of shifting colours. Apart from the flowing of the river, silence now descends on the meadow as the living creatures watch this new strangeness with trepidation.

Just as the ritual seems to reach a crescendo, the man casts his hands down at the body. The flow of colour is redirected to gently drape itself over the cadaver, which jerks about before returning to lifelessness. The one in the robe curses loudly and redoubles his efforts. This time, the energy flows with less vigour and more control. Despite the fine weather, the air in his immediate vicinity grows colder, misted now by his breath and the hotter surroundings. The grass around the event begins to fade and die.

Suddenly the spell draws to a close. The localised oddities resolve themselves much quicker than they began, and the cloaked figure stands silently over the dead man in the meadow. A sharp intake of breath echoes around the trees, piercing the thick quietude; but it comes from the dead, not the living. A grin spreads underneath the hood. As the portly remains lift themselves to their feet, it is not lost on the cloaked man that he has met a milestone today. Though this walking corpse is ungainly on its feet and makes a chilling rasp with each unnecessary breath, it looks alive and seems to respond to commands. The fine-tuning could come later.

The body stumbles in its shambling and starts to totter, so the cloaked man rushes to catch it. He has no wish to attempt to retrieve this thing from the river if it falls. No, his practice has been successful and he has no need or desire to bring it with him. He will have the thing dig itself a grave to lay in, then he himself will bury it; a small token of respect to stand against the foulness of his desecration.

He begins to half-command, half-drag the thing away from the river when he is startled by a shrill shriek. He cannot see its origin, and he is in two minds whether or not to drop the body and dash for the trees. Ultimately, panic and indecision has him stand still until he can hear the rapid but soft footfalls of someone sprinting towards him.

"Sigilo! Oh Sigilo, what has happened! Who is this man?" comes a woman's voice.

Shit, thinks the hooded man. He turns so that he can look at the newcomer, and finds her to be a buxom woman, much older than him but not unattractive. She wears a simple linen dress and a face full of anxiety, and she now turns to address him.

"He'd best not be drunk again, or he'll be flat on his arse before he knows it!"

"I am afraid, madam, that he is not well at all. I was just walking along the riverside when I saw him collapse, and I was trying to get him to help," he lies effortlessly. He is clearly a well-practiced liar. She seems suspicious at first, but her worry pushes that aside.

"Oh, bless you, stranger! Here, I'll take him..." she says as she takes one of the body's arms across her shoulders from the opposite side. Her face betrays her dawning certainty that Sigilo's condition is serious. His body twitches with paroxysms of rigidity. His face is expressionless and of an unnatural pallor, and his mouth moves only to produce the mindless sounds of a disproportionate newborn.

"I shall go fetch help. I believe I saw a gamekeeper not too far from here," assures the hooded man.

"Please! Go! I'll... I... I don't know what I'd do without him," she stammers. "Come, Sigilo, I'm sure you'll be back with us in no time at all... Come back..." The corpse shuffles its feet strenuously, its weight slumped awkwardly on the lady.

Under the hood, the man grimaces at her compassion. Sigilo would not be returning. Outwardly, he nods his head to her and breaks into a run, heading downstream of the river. The moment he is out of sight, he darts into the shadows of the treeline.

A few moments later, a woman's anguished wailing carries far over the canopy as the forces barely animating Sigilo are severed, but the young, cloaked man disappearing into the forest never looks back.

...

Exile.

The concept rolls unceasingly around my mind. To be a necromancer is to impose it upon oneself, in a sense; but a self-imposed exile, a rejection of companionship in favour of privacy, possesses a measure of control. Choice. A hermitage can be abandoned at the behest of the hermit, but how can a man cast out for such a betrayal ever hope to make amends? What recompense can there be for an injury so dire?

I find myself staring constantly at the repurposed sarcophagus in which my once friend has been so unceremoniously shut away. Alton would be right to exact any vengeance he so chooses, but no punishment could match that of my eternal guilt. He cannot comprehend that his adopted son's murderer, an abomination in his eyes, could feel such remorse; but in that, he is blameless. If Bayldon had died by another's hands, I would have personally redefined their perception of suffering. Now, with only myself to condemn, my penance is to languish here among the dead, lest we become useful to the living once again.

My phylactery stands before me, inexorably coiling my soul into itself. I have frequently contemplated its destruction, to reverse the contract I created during the ritual. On the fourth night from now, that spell will reach its culmination. I have no precedent for what that event entails beyond the manner to which it is referred; 'the darkest day'. A literal description, I wonder, or has it a more metaphorical meaning? Velthur based the timing of his ascension on an incremental pattern of specific, extremely isolated dates he thought to have unique magical properties. I calculated the opportunity for my own attempt based on those same increments and this incidence, coincidentally, was the last to fall within my lifetime. Why the phenomenon occurs only on those days is unclear; Velthur records their importance but provides no explanation, nor does he name the source of his information. In retrospect, said knowledge may have been a gift from *them*, whispered to him in their chittering voices, or perhaps scratched into the tablets so wisely unmade by the Blood-Marked. *Zich Suthina* escaped them and survived, and so these periods of unknown significance were accidentally preserved. I shall experience it firsthand, I suppose, if I can tolerate the wretched existence I have wrought for myself.

And wretched I am, for the semblance of life is now truly forfeiting my mortal remains. The decay which began at my very heart has spread, and I can feel the desiccation overtaking my neck and jawline, exposing bone and enervating flesh. The remnants of my hair may serve to hide some effects of the transformation for the moment, but at its current rate of affliction, it will be a vain effort before long. My arms have already withered to the elbows; soon, only my extremities will be spared. Travelling unnoticed will become impossible. I am trapped in this mausoleum, a gaol of my own devising. Depending on one's perspective, it is 'fortunate' that I have been freed from such trivialities as hunger and thirst, allowing me to persist in this strict seclusion. Without these cravings I am given ample time for reflection; a torment in itself.

I hope only for fate to offer a means of redemption. It may be futile, but there is little value in this pitiful existence otherwise, much less in extending it needlessly.

The rain has ceased and the waters are draining away. Maybe it is a portent... but that is a frivolous notion; every storm passes eventually, and not at the whim or benefit of man.

Sōlrest-Þridda-XXVII

...

The inside of the house is dilapidated, and an awful smell lingers in the air. A young adolescent holds a lantern in his right hand, using it to inspect closely the various objects on the shelves. His other hand holds a cloth rag over his nose and mouth. It accomplishes little.

Biurtan should owe me overtime for this, *he thinks to himself. In fairness, his master always pays him an exceptionally good share of their profits, on top of handling the complex administrative procedures and footing the relevant costs there. There is an understanding between them that Biurtan enjoys the business; he just hates getting dirty.*

Bluntly, the youth suspects there is a corpse somewhere in the house. It has happened previously on a number of separate occasions, and this is a model example; an elderly man has deprived the landlord of their rent for some time, despite years of proven reliability. At such an age as this one's (eight decades at least, so said the landlord), chances are not exactly favourable that they have absconded. Yet, the landlords need their rent, and they are unwilling to deal with the unpleasantness in person. So they have a man like Biurtan to reclaim their money in Śalirk or in kind, in exchange for a cut. Their loss is his gain.

On this particular assignment, however, recovering the landlord's rent may prove difficult. The tenant seems to have owned nothing. *Nothing of any value, at least. The random things on the shelves are just that;* things. *Worthless. Old cups, dead spiders and an excess of dust. The bookcases are full of empty glass vessels and stacks of blank parchment. The pantries are empty. The reclaimer can scarcely believe that the place is habitable, let alone recently inhabited.*

The other aspect which begins to concern him is that he has not yet found a body. It is surely here - he is, from experience, well acquainted with the fetid scent of decomposition - but he has now checked every room to no avail. Where could it be?

In his lantern, the candle's light wanes. Frustrated, he swings its tiny door open to light a new wick; but in doing so, he notices something unusual. As the flame is removed from its shelter, it is drawn, if only slightly, in a quite illogical direction. It is not fluttering with the breeze from the entrance or in line with the corridor, but towards one of the vacant bookcases. The youth peers closer, holding the freshly lit candle to the shelves. At first, all it illuminates is more clutter, but then he sees it; there, behind this bookcase, is a void. A hidden stash, perhaps! He immediately attempts to find the way to move the furniture, but it appears to be fixed in place quite securely. The shelves, on the other hand, come free with only a gentle pull. To his surprise, many of the articles upon them are actually attached by their bases using adhesive.

Soon he stands beside a pile of loose slats and, in front of him, the wall opens. It looks as if it has been crudely excavated: the bricks first pulled away; then the insulation removed; and then, unbelievably, a tunnel dug out - through the foundations. The concept that this was undertaken by an elderly man alone is nothing less than absurd. He must have hired henchmen.

The way is more than a little intimidating (and he is now, by its relative intensity, fairly certain of where the fetid scent originates from), but curiosity overcomes apprehension and he climbs through the narrow hole. It angles downwards in a dextral spiral, steep but not perilously so, and a set of rough steps is hewn into the makeshift floor's incline. The descent is uncomfortable, but only because the surrounding surfaces are so featureless; it purveys the sensation of walking into an endless, bottomless abyss. In reality the entire tunnel is only ten yards or so (still an impressive undertaking), but the darkness is stifling and absolute.

The stairs level out into a diminutive antechamber which he is forced to crouch through, but the room behind it is staggering. More than that, it is terrifying. The bones of at least six men lie strewn about the stone floor. At their centre is the tenant, quite dead and still decomposing. A cursory glance suggests that his heart had failed him, as opposed to any misdeed having befallen him.

A strange old man with some apparently strange hobbies, the youth ponders. Other things of importance feature in the chamber, also. All the means for one to spend a great deal of uninterrupted time here. There is a bedroll in the corner, as well as a storage cupboard stocked with preserved food; dried fish, salted pork and the like. A chamber *pot, mercifully empty. Nothing valuable. Certainly nothing they would be able to sell.*

There is also a desk, upon which were things of far greater interest. A collection, a small library, *one could say, of mysterious tomes. Could they be...? Yes! Grimoires! The youth slaps the table in triumph. Spellbooks are, more often than not, worth more than their weight in gold, and these seemed to be rare volumes indeed. Biurtan would be positively* ecstatic. *The Baron seldom did much reading that was not* directly *business related, so it would be the adolescent's responsibility to learn the nature of what the text contained and to locate a buyer. A quick summary usually suffices, but as he scrutinises these ones, something seems...* different *about them. Their covers often lack titles. Their contents pertain to weird and forbidden activities such as the surreptitious acquisition of cadavers and (though he could be misinterpreting in his hasty translations) the* reanimation *of them.*

In most of its forms, magic held no attraction for the youth. This one, though... this one he had never heard of. He looked over at the tenant's corpse with novel wonderment. Such incredible lengths had they taken to avoid detection, and for what? To die in solitude? No; there is some allure to this practice. Its promises of power over life and death, the power to enact change upon the world, were undeniably enticing. Enticing enough to demand further research, at any rate. The youth stuffs his collection sack full of the grimoires, including several written in scripts he has never seen. Conveniently, as he searches for more, he happens upon a miniature lockbox. Emboldened by the excitement of his discovery, he rifles through the tenant's pockets to find the key. He meets with success and opens the box to find that it is filled to the brim with jewellery. Rings, pendants, torcs and gemstones glitter back at him as he swings the lid back.

Probably taken from defiled graves, *he presumes.* Still, more than enough to keep the Baron happy. He can take the majority share, this time. He need not know about the grimoires. After all, that which he does not know, cannot hurt him.

The youth slings the heavy sack over his shoulder, takes the lockbox and commences his reascent. He would inform the landlord of their tenant's vandalism and graverobbery. Their more 'eccentric' tendencies - and the grimoires - would remain his own harmless, little secret.

O, how different my fate could have been! And how different that of Pænvicta!

...

Seasons change; the birds migrate; the tide turns; and I? I have found the road.

Day became night and became day again, and scarcely did I stir from my bitter meditation. The stones in the walls and the indifferent faces of my minions provided no solace, and so I shut my eyes and appealed to my innermost thoughts for guidance. There I found comfort, of a sort, in my imaginings; I conjured visions of alternative paths. Some of these hypothetical fates were more favourable than my current reality, some were less so. But in the same manner as deep sleep helps to reorganise one's mind, so did my perception grow sharper. Order was gleaned from the chaos, and in it I rediscovered direction.

I opened my eyes with the instant realisation of an unexpected curiosity. Haþuwīgą was standing beside me, almost as if prepared to assure me of the veracity of my newfound determinations. Haþuwīgą, whom I had two days prior violently disassembled with the inordinate power of the Hinthial Sceptre.

How? I pondered with fascination.

It was a strange thing indeed, almost inconsequential in a sense, but its implications were more pivotal. My body, though it continues on its course of decay, has freed my consciousness to more finely attune itself to my surroundings, like the lifting of an encompassing veil from one's face. Despite the shadows, I could *see*. Better than I could in youth, better than with the enhancements of a lens, or if everything were bathed in flawless sunlight. My vision is more than sight; it is *understanding*. The energies of Pænvicta were laid bare to me, and in that moment a great many mysteries gave way to vivid clarity.

I could see perfectly the manna which bound me to the phylactery. It wound in a circular motion, each rotation depositing more of my being into its inanimate form before returning, lessened, to its source. But this system was not entirely contained, nor absolutely efficient. Dense swathes of magical energy were feeding into me from the siphons, and errant sparks dispersed sporadically into the environment like those from a roaring bonfire. In this way the system regulated itself, preventing both the premature death of my body and the destabilisation of the phylactery, either of which would result in the binding's failure. However, this tether, this... ethereal umbilical cord, remains attached and present at all times. It is infinitely flexible, but its minor inefficiencies affect the area between my phylactery and I; these currents were powerful enough to imbue Haþuwīgą's scattered remains with un-death once again, reassembling and reawakening her without my strict intention.

This was not necessarily a negative side effect in itself, but it brought with it much darker implications. In travelling with poor Bayldon to the River Leafbrym, I had unknowingly (still in the assumption that the ritual had failed) stretched this stream of manna over a considerable distance. And what has resulted from this possible spread of necromantic contamination? Could the things I had believed to be revenants in fact be wights of my own accidental creation? Could the erratic behaviour of this menace, arisen from the barrows of Stilneshire, be blamed on their lack of proper ownership? Could their actions truly be drawn from my subconscious fears? The 'Manna Glutton', too, developed only after my excursion, perhaps as a result of the energy's demands being overstretched by the immoderate span. A part of me knew it - *all of it* - to be true.

I expected my guilt to be amplified, to be repetitiously crippled by the fresh affronts to my morality. I attempted to fathom how many wasted lives could be added to my rueful tally. Scores, at least. Conceivably hundreds. But my emotions were as blank as unspoiled parchment. I contemplated the suffering wrought upon Gerefwīċ Hundred by the siege and was unperturbed. I came to realise that, far from lacking care for those to whom I had brought harm and misery, I had finally transgressed and surpassed that which was reasonably within the boundaries of any redemption. I had become an undeniable blight on the world, a Velthur in the making, and there was nothing for me then but to sever the links which invigorated my unsolicited, hateworthy army and to usher a similar end to my own existence.

It was as I reached these conclusions that I heard a voice, one I had never imagined to hear again. Alton was shouting from the entrance, his furious words echoing through the corridors of my sepulchral lair and overlapping in such a way that there seemed to be many of him clamouring as a crowd. The effect was auditorily confusing, and it took a few moments for me to extrapolate his meaning from the competing layers of distant noise.

"I know you're in there, coward! Come out here and speak to me like a man!" boomed the innkeeper in a number of variations. His words were punctuated with resonating clangs from his attempts to heave the gate open, or strike it with hard objects.

I hesitated in my surprise. What possible reason could Alton have to speak with me? Perhaps he had brought a mob and wished to see my executed. Regardless, I could claim no right to refuse him of all people, so I righted myself and obliged him. If his plan was to slay me, he would have to be shown the proper means, after all.

As I climbed the last stairs to the surface, I could see Alton's shape against a clear sky, blindingly bright after my internment. He was silent as I came into view, evidently astonished that I had chosen to reveal myself. It was not until I was facing him from the gate's other side that he spoke again, and he did so with a quivering, horrified tone.

"Gods! What's happened to *you*?" he asked, his features twisted with revulsion.

I was prompted to touch my fingers to my face in order to probe the progression of my deterioration. Though the sense of touch in my fingertips themselves seemed dulled, I found that my nose had begun to sink into the recess beneath and my cheeks were similarly hollowed. I surely appeared abominably ghoulish to his eyes. I looked at him vacantly, unsure of what answer to give him; but apparently, that was response enough.

"I'd say your outsides were starting to show us your insides. Look! Even the grass can't stand you. Black-hearted bastard," he spat.

Peering through the bars of the gate, I saw the phenomenon to which Alton referred. The decomposition of the greenery had indeed accelerated, leaving a colourless, barren earth reaching almost to the willows. Its growing desiccation was a mirror of my own, and it was little wonder why the flooding had been especially thorough during the storm. The desolate soil extracted no moisture from the rain, leaving it to pour indiscriminately into the crypt.

"Why do you call after me, Alton?" I queried gently, banishing the distractions.

"Because..." he began, disgusted, only going on after visibly swallowing his pride, "We need your help. And if there's even a single shred of real decency in the man I thought I knew, he'll help us."

"If it is the 'raiders', I have already found a solution."

"No. Worse, would you believe it," Alton shook his head grimly.

"Then who...?" I was initially intrigued, but as my thoughts drifted, I knew the answer before it was given.

"*Arx Turrium*," he confirmed. "They're coming, alright."

"Those in the temple have attacked another? Where are they?" I inquired with urgency, unlocking the gate.

"No. Not them."

"Urbānus' retinue has returned?"

"He's one of them, more than likely," Alton nodded. "There *are* a couple hundred of them, and I don't reckon he'd pass up a chance to see us all burn. What was it they said... 'may you all die warm'?"

"What! Where are they?" I exclaimed.

"Come on. I'll show you."

"I must not be seen, Alton."

"You won't be. Besides, I think Gerefwīċ has seen so much madness recently, you'll probably fit right in," he jested gloomily.

I departed the relative safety of the mausoleum and followed Alton as he scaled the edge of the basin behind it. The man was remarkably nimble and utterly tireless, and I noticed for the first time that he was wearing the armour he had lent to Bayldon for our expedition. It was a somewhat tighter fit, yet he bore its weight like a second skin and moved as if completely unburdened. I would certainly not have been capable of matching his pace if I were the same elderly man that walked upon the paved road of the Garfeldas. Neither was he the timid, doddering proprietor of ale that I first met in The Old Boar; adversity and loss had reverted him to his younger, more dangerous self.

"I do not intend to portray a threat to you, Alton, but most people are distrustful or fearful of necromancers. Are you not afraid?" I questioned during the difficult ascent.

"I suppose I should be," he mused, "but honestly; what more can you take from me? You could turn me to dust, or rip out my soul, or have a gang of your un-dead friends butcher me like a prize hog. If anything, those all sound like easy escapes to me!"

Alton laughed mirthlessly, and I, in my intense shame, could confer no appropriate rebuttal.

Once we had reached the peak of the basin's rim, our journey became much easier. Alton insisted we walk along the circumference until we were on its easternmost pinnacle. This stretch was fairly brief and uneventful, though there was a minor noteworthy incident; on one occasion, Alton pointed to something in the pastures to the south-east. On tracing the path of his finger, I saw a small scouting party of the revenants, a charioteer and two horsemen and, as I distinguished their distant shapes, they came to a sudden stop. Then they rode in circles, then in lemniscates, then away towards the woodland.

"You see that? The bastards are taunting us," Alton grumbled.

Truthfully, their unusual path was of my own devising to confirm that they were, indeed, under my command. I thought it best not to correct Alton on the allegience of the supposed 'Raider Revenants'. I was planning to destroy them, but in the light of the threat I was soon to comprehend, they may instead prove indispensable.

I needed no assistance in seeing what Alton had brought me to see. Initially I squinted, trying to attain a measure of its magnitude, but the extent was indisputably revealed when we were stood at the highest point of the eastern summit. A staggeringly vast column of thick smoke arose on the horizon, continuing to expand with each passing breath.

"How far do you suppose that is?" I asked, dumbfounded.

"I reckon about fifty, sixty miles?" Alton guessed with a sigh. "Maybe four days' travel if they've a baggage train."

"Three days, maximum. Possibly two," I countered. "The Arx will require no siegeworks to raze Gerefwīċ Hundred. They will be mounted, all of them, and will subsist on personal rations and what they can pillage."

"Maybe torching each village they cross will slow them down."

"I suspect not. They will do so only if convenient; and they surely now possess all necessary supplies for them to march relatively uninterrupted."

"*Shit...*" Alton exhaled voicelessly in a lengthy, drawn-out suspiration.

We sat quietly for a while, then, much akin to how Bayldon and I did on our adventure's first reprieve. The memory, though the sky in it was beautiful and the company good, had become sorrowful. I could tolerate my uninhibited ruminations no longer.

"It is definitely the Arx, I suppose?"

"A messenger got here from Bēagshire early this morning. Must have galloped non-stop to get past the 'brigands' safe. Anyway, he had a letter with Ealdorman Heorot's seal, warning us that his spies had tipped him off about the Arx sending an army to Stilneshire."

"And Heorot himself?" I cued hopefully.

"Not a word," Alton shrugged.

"Damn them!" I cursed, consumed by a precipitous but impotent rage. "I shall show them their need of humility. I swear it."

"Is it a lost cause, then? Are we all done for?"

"Potentially. Nevertheless, I shall not entertain the concept of surrender, least of all to Sōlis Mūnus. You know men better than I, Alton; the people of Gerefwīċ... would they prefer slavery, or to fight and risk being slaughtered in battle?"

"Not much of a choice," he huffed, "but it's not like they'd get far running. They'd be tracked and rode down like harts. Not that I think they'd want to leave, come to think of it."

"They would fight, then?"

"See, there's the problem, or part of it. With this siege and the priests holed up after their poisoning, they're itching to see some folk get their comeuppance, so to speak. Thing is, there's a lot of angry farmhands here. Not many soldiers."

"More than you would think, perhaps," I hinted, gesturing towards the line of willow trees which masked the graveyard. "More than Urbānus will have predicted."

"You think you and your pets can swing the balance in our favour then?"

"Not unaided."

"What do the un-dead need but more un-dead? You're not suggesting-"

"*No*," I interjected. "Alton, I shall preserve every life I can, you have my word."

"Well I'd be lying if I said your 'word' was worth much to me these days; but then, it's about all I've got now isn't it?" he replied sardonically.

The night was beginning to encroach, the sunset had been hastened by a gathering of leaden clouds, and the smoke of the Arx's most recent conquest faded against the darkening sky only to be replaced by the faint glow of faraway flames. Though I am numbed to the cold as of late, I could see from Alton's misted breath and the onset of his trembling that the temperature had fallen dramatically.

"We should retire and strategise," I proposed. "A plan must be devised, and it must be acted upon tomorrow. Time is not ours to waste."

"To the tavern?"

"No. We cannot be seen alongside each other. I know a secret way into the catacombs; we can have our discussion there."

"With those murderous corpses breathing down our necks?" he spluttered. "You're taking the piss."

"Soon, Alton, *all of Gerefwīċ* may have to acquaint themselves with the ambulatory deceased. If you yourself are unable to stomach their presence, how do you plan to convince the former to fight at the latter's side?"

"So it's *my* job to make sure they get along, is it? You really are a bastard," he chuckled.

"As much as I would be sure to present myself as a fine, trustworthy ambassador, I may not be particularly well received due to my developing... *appearance issues*."

"Fair reasoning. But you're still a bastard."

We then traced a route back to the graveyard in the failing light. I was, at first, concerned about Alton's ability to find good footing on the descent. Such worries soon proved baseless, however; before me was the same man who had spent years organising and participating in night-time ambushes against veteran opponents. Even with my enhanced awareness, his footing was undoubtedly surer than mine, and both of us avoided painful (or embarrassing) falls on the way down.

Stealth being our objective, I led Alton not to the crypt's front gate, but to the hole at the hill's rear. It was subtle, only practically visible by the solitary, protruding stone which I had used to seal it. Once found, I approached and tasked Audaward with shifting it so we could enter. Alton, however, seemed to have become ill. His face became pasty and he was wide-eyed with anxiety. It took a while - *too* long - for me to realise the cause.

"Sorry, my friend. I am not accustomed to company," I apologised as I exempted him from the sapping circle's influence. Piecemeal, his vigour returned.

"Damn. It really *was* you haunting this place!" he whispered in the murk.

My servants had managed to make a fire as I had silently commanded them, so the hole was lit by the soft luminescence of torchlight. I lowered myself in first, then beckoned my companion to follow.

"Are you prepared, Alton?"

"No. How am I meant to do that, exactly?"

"Fair reasoning," I reiterated him.

Alton sighed with unwillingness and exasperation, then dropped himself into the catacombs. Initially he said nothing, but then I noticed that he had shut his eyes tightly.

"You are safe. Safer than anywhere else in Gerefwīċ, I expect. Look upon your protectors," I assured him.

"I... can't. What if they take offence?"

"You are misunderstanding them. They do not think, nor do they feel. Consider them as machines."

"Machines that could kill me," Alton quipped.

"Could not a catapult, or a crossbow? Such things *can* be deadly, yes; but only to those whom their operators choose as targets."

"And you're the 'operator'? I feel better already!"

"Alton..."

"Alright, I know..."

With that, the innkeeper opened his eyes gradually. Ermunahild stood before him as he did so, still as a statue and hands at her sides. Alton winced, then tried again. His breathing was shallow, but he was able to steady himself enough to study her properly.

"It's... not so bad," he commented with uncertainty. "He's... *cleaner* than I thought he'd be."

"*She*, if her sex mattered, that is," I corrected Alton. "These are the ancient dead. Nought but bones and what did not perish in their sarcophagi."

"I see! Sorry, miss," he excused himself sincerely.

I stifled a cackle and could not resist prompting Ermuna to bow her head in acknowledgement of him. To my surprise, Alton seemed rather bemused by this exchange.

"Brace yourself. The others are behind you, to your left," I cautioned.

The man turned to see the others gathered there. Clearly, he was afraid; but he was also enraptured by their novelty. He looked over the equipment of each minion, even asking if it was safe to touch them, which I affirmed. He then scrutinised their armour and weaponry, tapping them for the sound and testing the sharpness of their edges. I could see in him a captain dutifully inspecting his soldiers. Eventually he met Audaward toe-to-toe, leaning back to peer upwards at his enclosed helmet.

"Gods, the *size* of this one!" he laughed, genuinely amused. "How'd they fit him into one of these boxes?"

"It *was* a particularly spacious tomb. Heavy, too!"

"Wouldn't want to be on the wrong end of that ax, mind..." he noted, pulling it closer by the haft. The blade was enormous, conceivably capable of cleaving a man from his scalp to his crotch. Alton relinquished it with a shiver, obviously imagining a similar scene. Then he paused in thought.

"Where's my boy?" he asked pointedly.

"Not here. I have kept his body secure... it may seem a meaningless gesture, but I had hoped to give him a worthy funeral when Gerefwīč's situation improved."

Alton nodded with mute, morose approval.

"Which one of them did it to him?" he demanded.

Rēdawulf stepped forwards at my behest.

"I want to fight him. Make him draw his weapon."

"I must stress to you, Alton, that what befell Bayldon was no fault of his. It was mine, wholly," I explained.

"I *know* that. I want to know just how well these things fight, and who knows? It might even make me feel less like slicing *you* up."

"I see," I agreed reluctantly, "but you must call out if you wish it to cease its assault."

"Fat chance," Alton murmured.

And so the two ex-warriors, one living and one dead, readied their weapons and began to circle each other. Alton wielded the arms that he had lent to Bayldon; the keen sword in his right hand, the sturdy roundshield in his left. Rēdawulf set down his bow and unsheathed his seax, already probing his wary opponent with feints and uncommitted slashes, which were defended with ease.

"You're holding him back," Alton seethed. "I said I wanted to *fight him*, damn you!"

Deflecting another blow on his shield, the innkeeper moved into the space and struck the skeleton with his pommel. The un-dead archer stumbled backwards, then righted himself. Rēdawulf's next attacks were more aggressive and unrestrained, and on several occasions I was positive that Alton would be wounded; but the man's shield was like a moveable wall, and always his vulnerabilities - and his sword - were well hidden behind it. When *his* attack came, it was explosive and merciless. The shield turned the minion's seax aside, exposing its arm to a strong downwards swing which dislodged the limb from its socket. Bereft of its weapon, it was defenceless against the crushing follow-up; a horizontal strike against the cervical spine with the shield's reinforced rim. The receiving vertebrae separated and the thing's skull toppled off its shoulders, bouncing upon the stone floor with an agonising crunch.

"They aren't bad," Alton gasped, slumping against an unshelved sarcophagus and breathing heavily, "but they'll have a hard time with those Arx folks. And there'll have to be a lot more than this, I reckon."

"Your opponent is not yet defeated, my friend."

Alton glanced upwards to see Rēdawulf, having retrieved his seax from his disembodied hand, holding the blade's tip at the innkeeper's chest.

"They will fight to their utter destruction and, though there will be variations in quality, there are as many potential reserves as there are corpses in this graveyard."

"That's starting to sound a bit more promising," he remarked, prudently cheerful as the skeleton withdrew and reassembled itself.

"Of course, a banner of Coercitōrēs will make short work of the weaker forms of un-dead, and even with every measure available to me, the chances of victory are narrow indeed."

"Will the living folk be any help at all? Is there any point in having them fight too?"

"The living farmers may be marginally more capable than the buried farmers," I indicated, "although we might tentatively count the numbers of the former group twice."

"Once alive, then again if they get offed..."

"Precisely."

"Now that *is* a desperate business!" Alton cried.

"Are we not desperate?"

"I know, I know..." he conceded. "It's just... I can't shake the feeling of how *wrong* this all is."

"Regarding *those* concerns, my friend, I can state categorically that I am not the correct man with whom to debate them. For the sake of our survival - *Gerefwīċ's* survival, even - we must temporarily put aside such moral quandaries. I shall hold myself responsible for my desecrations when the people are safe, but I can see no purpose in doing so before then."

"Fair reasoning," he repeated for the last time.

Alton was more pliable from that point and, under the empty sockets of the Blood-Marked, we began our strategising proper. Freed from the perplexities of 'right' and 'wrong', the innkeeper's thoughts became cold and cutting as steel. I realised, before long, that he had finally embraced the principal, compulsory tenet of the necromancer: self-preservation above all and without contrition; the manner of selfishness exhibited only in the eternally hunted.

In the proceedings, we recognised three imperative actions which could be undertaken tomorrow:

Firstly, that Reeve Ewin himself be informed that a necromancer wishes to provide succour for Gerefwīċ. The identity of the necromancer need not be mentioned. It must be presented as a fact that requires his acceptance and cooperation, and essential if we are to contest our doom.

Secondly, that outriders be sent to the other hundreds of Stilneshire in order to gather support. It is a reasonable assumption that they will be subsequently targeted, so it is within their interests to halt the Arx here. Like Gerefwīċ itself, each one should, by Cempariċe law, be capable of contributing one-hundred men in a call-to-arms. In ideal (unlikely) circumstances, this would equal five-hundred additional fighters; a respectable throng, even if assembled primarily from untrained local militias. A potential of one-*thousand* combatants when accounting for necromancy.

Thirdly, and most controversially to Alton, those organising the defence of Gerefwīċ, presumably the reeve, *must* be convinced to lead it at the graveyard. There is too much tactical advantage to be exploited here to be overlooked, and the other plausible locations - the guard barracks and the town hall - are much too small to contain the necessary numbers of people. Outside the walls would become a massacre, and the structures would be too vulnerable to even basic siegeworks. Fire, for example. In contrast, the graveyard's hill could be fortified relatively simply and with locally available resources, as well as being centred about the focal point of my influence. Alton seemed uneasy about this aspect, but I reminded him that I could immunise allies against the draining effect just as I had with him, and that the Arx would be pushing into territory where they would suffer the sensations he had earlier (albeit with greater severity). This decisively swayed his opinion, and he agreed to endorse the proposition and attempt to convince Reeve Ewin of its virtues.

Alton departed then, reassured that the 'raiders' would not trouble him. I implored him, as a favour, if he would bring my remaining articles from The Old Boar when he returns with his report. I shall await word on the success or failure of our designs; best I was not revealed to the people of Gerefwīċ, especially without forewarning.

Sōlrest-Þridda-XXVIII

...

A huge brick structure looms over a paved courtyard, twenty windows on its front face. It is a bland, soulless sort of place; one of slim hope and distant dreams. Above its doorway a corroded sign reads, in Ilibanese, 'Stena's Orphanage'.

A boy, barely a decade old by his size and looks, stands in a line among several others. His demeanour is decidedly downtrodden, but he is trying his hardest to wear a convincing mask of pride. An older gentleman paces up and down the series of candidates, Mistress Stena watching on.

The proprietor of the orphanage is an old woman, once sprightly, now in the final years of her mobility. The business she runs is, ultimately, a charitable one; but to help with subsidising costs, the orphans can be adopted - or put to work - at a fixed fee. The latter is generally the more probable outcome. This suits many of the children just fine: at worst, one is put to hard labour and guaranteed to receive food; at best, one essentially gains an apprenticeship under an artisan. The young boy always had the deepest pity for the girls. Mistress Stena asks very few questions of her clients (a degree of concern she cannot afford to indulge), and young women often leave in the hands of gentlemen of an unscrupulous-looking sort. They do tend to be wealthy, at least. The boy only prays that, wherever they end up, they are well looked after. And happy, if such a thing is at all possible.

On this particular occasion, the middle-aged gentleman with the waistcoat, spectacles, and cane had already specified his preference for a male child. Just as they had done countless times before, the boys raise their hands high if they fit the requested criteria, and lower them if they cease to do so when the specifications are refined.

"Yes, yes, a boy! With a good, strong back!" calls the buyer with a pompous, energetic affectation, his thickly haired upper lip bristling with enthusiasm. Manual labour, then. The boy's heart sinks not because he is unwilling or unable, but because he is of a small stature in comparison to the other boys, especially those from Sūþeard. It was a fact they reminded him of cruelly and all too often. His hand remains raised regardless.

277

"Yes, yes. Yes! And he must also be able to read and write..." the man begins to add.

Many of the hands drop, but not all of them. The boy of ten tries his best to make himself taller. During his time at Stena's Orphanage, he had been an avid reader of what little literature was made available to them, making every effort he could to acquaint himself with the various scripts of Pænvicta.

" Sūþrūna!"

A few are eliminated.

"And Ilibanese!"

A mere three boys are left. They glance at each other pensively. If their physicality is the deciding factor, the ten-year-old is, predictably, the weakest competitor. His arm begins to fold in preparation for his rejection.

"Well, well! I'm afraid I can only take one! Let's see, let's see... I don't suppose, young men, that any of you are fluent in Arcāna?"

"Possum, domine!" the boy blurts. He feels immediately embarrassed; it is improper to speak to clients unless directly spoken to. It is unsurprising that his is now the only hand raised. Arcāna is rare to even hear outside Arx Turrium, and is, as a rule, taught to no outsiders. Even Sōlis Mūnus converts are left in ignorance of the script.

"Marvellous! Splendid! Praeclārus!" the man claps and walks over to him, placing a friendly, gloved hand on his shoulder to lead him away. "Say, lad, how does a boy your age come to learn Arcāna? O never mind, it doesn't matter now - no! There'll be plenty of time for all that!"

As they leave, the boy looks behind him at the other orphans, who glare at him with bitter faces. Yet he is too elated to suffer guilt from his victory. His attention returns to his saviour.

"May I ask your name, Sir? And what work you do?" the boy inquires tentatively.

"Straight to business! I like it, lad - we'll get along famously. Yes! Do pardon me; I am the Baron Biurtan, at your service - or, rather, you will be at mine, I suppose!" he laughs uproariously and pats the boy on the back. "And my profession? Well, lad, have you ever heard of a 'reclaimer'?"

"No, Sir."

"Well, it's good work, says I! Hard, sometimes; but profitable too. Yes, very lucrative. And I daresay even a clever one such as yourself will learn something new each and every day!"

...

Events, predictably, have not transpired in an ideal manner. The current prospects of Gerefwīċ Hundred are bleak indeed. Short of an unexpected windfall, or a miracle, I foresee no deliverance for this hapless, beleaguered community.

Most of my morning was spent calculating and designing tactics for the inevitable battle. Assuming at least *some* men agree to fight, they can be well supported; un-dead chaff can hold the flanks to prevent mortal combatants from being caught in the pincer, while the more elite warriors from the sarcophagi will form a robust core. Integrating the un-dead forces with the living will be a significant challenge in itself, and some measures must be taken so that order and morale can be maintained. How can one reconcile with simple countrymen that their dying companions' bodies will continue to fight the invaders until dismemberment? And that a necromancer can be trusted any further than can the Arx? All of these articles I set aside to be reviewed with Alton, who was to be instrumental in imparting my strategies upon Reeve Ewin indirectly.

While I was cerebrating these quandaries, Alton had encountered a share of his own. Upon his arrival, he practically *fell* through the ceiling's aperture, panting and sweating. The sight might have been comical, if not for the distraught expression beneath the sweat, and the dire message portrayed between the panting.

"We've got problems, mate. Big ones," he gasped.

"Breathe, Alton. Then speak."

"Shit! I never thought..." he cursed impulsively before heeding my advice. After spending a few moments composing himself, he spoke again, more cohesively. "All the horses are dead. So is the reeve. Gods, we're fucked!"

"What!" I ejaculated. "How did this happen? Who killed him?"

"He killed his own damned self before I even got to talk to him!"

"But why?"

"He reckoned we were done for. Here you go, he'll tell you himself!"

Alton drew a crumpled parchment from his pocket and handed it to me. On it was written a hastily scrawled note. It read as follows:

'People of Gerefwīċ Hundred,

As your reeve, I served you as best I could; but I have failed, and I don't deserve to live when so many of you surely won't. My life's work is undone. I was foolish to hold the Arx to our laws, and now, in striving for justice on Wurt's behalf, I have as good as sharpened the swords and lit the torches myself.

Whatever road you choose now, I am unfit to lead you on it. Farewell.'

"Is this the reeve's mark?" I questioned, referring to the vaguely bird-like sigil etched below the valediction.

"It's his alright," Alton nodded soberly. "No signs of a struggle, either. Just him and his own blade in his guts."

"An indisputable suicide, then, is your conclusion?"

"For what it's worth, *yes*," he confirmed bitterly, "but to be honest, what difference does it make? He was the only man that had clout with the whole county, and he's saved Arx Turrium the trouble of cutting off the army's head before it's even been mustered."

"There are no other candidates for leadership?"

"The ealdorman, if he was here. I haven't told anyone yet, but the captain of the watch might step up once the news gets out. *Captain* Betlic. Or 'Bootlick', if you prefer. Cocky enough, but he's a bloody useless prick if there ever was one."

"Ewin's suicide is not yet public knowledge, then?"

"He'd locked himself in his office after ordering his guards away, 'to write a missive of supplication', so he told them. I only got in by using the spare key he gave to Bayldon. Locked it up again after finding what I found, too. No use in panicking folk before..." Alton began, but paused as his brow furrowed in cogitation. He looked up at my with a glint of genius - or madness, I could not say - in his eyes. "How lifelike can you make these pets of yours, Necromancer?"

"Surely you cannot be suggesting-"

"Don't give me that tripe, tell me straight; could you fool someone at a yard? Five yards? Ten?" he interrogated frantically. "Can they speak, if their lungs are alright? Sign their mark? Write letters?"

"It is a complex and intricate thing for which you ask, Alton. It may be possible," I advocated with unmistakeable ambivalence, "theoretically. I cannot be sure, as I have never attempted a deception of such arrant enormity."

"What would it take?" he pressed exigently.

"Either you must bring the reeve's body to *me*, or you must take me to *it*. Then, we shall have to clean any blood and conceal the wound, and redress him. O Alton, it is folly! A fool's errand! We shall almost certainly be caught," I groaned.

"We don't have a choice, mate. We've got to try. Without the reeve, we're stuck like a beast in a trap, muzzle-bound. No authority to send for help, no authority over the folk that're here already. We'll be pissing in the wind."

"Then we shall make an attempt, at your importuning; but I shall not hesitate to name you as my accomplice if we are discovered," I jested.

"Fair enough. If that happens, we're probably sunk anyway. Maybe we could both hang before the Arx shows up!"

I commenced preparations to leave, but remembered a point of information that had not yet been accounted for.

"Horses! What has happened to the horses?"

"Yes, that's our other problem. Seems those Sōlis priests caught wind that their nasty kin were on their way too, so they snuck out of their temple in the early hours, killed a pair of guards and went on to the stables. I just about heard the racket from the tavern, but I didn't dare check it out by myself. Turns out they were slaughtering all the mounts that weren't their own. Then they sped off east to join their fellows. Bastards."

"Felicia..." I sighed sadly.

"Pardon me, mate, but forget your bloody nag. What are the messengers going to ride out on? All that're left now are draught horses, and they won't run nearly quick or far enough to get to the other hundreds in time."

"There is a pragmatic solution," I informed him, "but your riders may wish to draw lots."

Alton, in his haste to report his ill tidings, had not stopped to gather my belongings. I forgave him for his forgetfulness due to the criticality of the situation; it could be retrieved later. The innkeeper himself, if only through the importance of our cooperation, had become a whit more amicable in his attitude towards me. The remote possibility of somehow restoring our previous friendship provided me a not insignificant measure of inspiration.

The weather's clarity had persisted, making for a reasonably pleasant day. I pulled my hood over as far as I could, nervous that my visage would be all too visible in the sunlight, and wore my thickest furs; thankfully, as I did not experience the cold, neither did I risk overheating under the excessive layers. In this way I was able to hide as much of my person as conceivably possible, and though my vision was almost entirely obscured, I could sense my heading to a practicable degree. Nevertheless, I walked with my stick and allowed Alton to lead me by the arm in order to complete the disguise. My companion, having already persuaded the watchmen once, was trusted enough to do so again; all but one of the guards allowed us both to pass unaccosted, and a brief exchange in which I was described as a friend of Ewin's was sufficient to remove the man's opposition. We were soon alone and locked inside the reeve's chamber. Alton drew my hood back with short warning, forcibly exposing me to the scene we had stepped into.

And there was Reeve Ewin Falken, lying crumpled in his terminal posture. He had, rather thoroughly, impaled himself on his sword. The right side of his face was resting in the gore which had thickened on the stone slabs and saturated the nearest rug. He had transfixed himself just beneath the sternum and directed the point upwards so as to split his heart, then stumbled momentarily before collapsing and expiring, evidenced by the streak of clotted blood dashed diagonally across one of the county maps on the far wall. It must have taken an incredible feat of willpower to avoid crying out during the ordeal (however fleeting), for the guards were never alerted to any such calamity, but untold agony was written upon his pale lineaments. It was a tremendously sorrowful spectacle, worsened by my exhaustive respect for the man he was.

"Last of his line, so I've heard," Alton remarked, shaking his head with earnest reproach. "I reckon that's why he took on Bayldon the way he did, because he never had his own son to raise. Almost like a second father to that boy, he was."

"He must have been devastated by the boy's disappearance, then," I commented plaintively.

"He was. But then, there were plenty folk that were," he added as he shot me with a resentful glance. "Rumour has it that he went out to parley with the bandit's leader and met his end there. Brave, honest, but gullible. I can live with that."

Alton turned away from me and sniffed, and I thought him to be weeping. I could summon no consolatory words, and so remained silent. The bereaved foster father need not know of the local gossip's coincidental accuracy; the revelation of the warband's true identity need not occur until the final hour.

I busied myself instead with the evaluation of our task, but the undertaking seemed an impossibility. How could such a ghastly carcass be given even the illusion of vitality? There would be no option but to remove him to another location before curiosity or worry got the better of the guards; an appreciably easier labour if the cadaver was ambulatory.

"Has the reeve a cloak? We shall have to relocate him. There would be pretence for us to bring him to The Old Boar," I posited.

"The watch might have something to say if they see us lugging a body out of here, even if it *is* under a cloak," observed Alton, obviously bemused.

"I can arrange for the reeve to carry *himself*, but we must first find a way to cover his injuries."

Utilising a vessel of water from his desk and one of the scattered blank parchments, I was able to cleanse a majority of his face of blood. His hair would require a more extensive treatment. Alton, meanwhile, happened upon the reeve's cloak hung upon a stand beside the door. It was a sizeable thing, only slightly more luxurious and exotic than one might see on the backs of any other man in Stilneshire; an umber, shaggy mass of hirsute pelt, possibly from one of Caill's great bears. Most crucially, it featured a hood of considerable depth. An heirloom, or a gift, perhaps, from a Caillic relative? Regardless, it was placed on the desk and ready for use. All that remained was to animate the reeve's body. Alton stood at my side with a blend of anticipation and revulsion.

"Are you certain that you wish to see this?" I asked him.

"Not one bit," he replied, snickering grimly, "but I'll have to get used to it anyway."

I nodded and turned towards the reeve's remains, raising my hands as I had done countless times before. The manna flowed through me freely, coursing like a river in a rainstorm. The raising could have been rathe and expeditious, but in this instance, the level of control was to be *unparalleled*. Ewin Falken would have to move, speak and *breathe* analogously to how he did in life. Any less and the ruse would falter. So, I proceeded with as much circumspection as I dared, meticulously spreading the manna to each muscle and fingertip, an operation both magical and anatomical. A half-hour later, announced by a harsh intake of air, Reeve Ewin finally stumbled to his feet and turned to stare at us expectantly. I had not previously noticed Alton's reaction to the reanimation of his once-friend due to my stipulation of unstymied concentration, but I then beheld him to appear quite unwell. He had grown nearly as pale as the exsanguinated reeve himself, and seemed to be having difficulty with finding the words to express his emotions.

"*Alton! How are you, old friend?*" rasped the reeve at my behest. The voice was guttural and gurgling, and bore little reminiscence of his cheerful demeanour in life.

"That's not funny!" Alton complained as he shoved my shoulder, nearly toppling me.

"It is not my intention to amuse you. I must *convince* you," I explained.

"He's not very convincing yet," sighed the innkeeper, running his hands over his face and squeezing the bridge of his nose in calculative thought. "He's probably got some lumps of dried blood in his throat. I reckon we can flush it through with some strong drink back at the tavern."

Alton walked to the desk to retrieve the cloak, but the reeve waved him away and strode over to procure it himself. Then he deftly enravelled himself in its warming folds and erected his hood, almost disappearing into its recesses.

"He moves pretty smoothly. Not like that jittery archer I smashed to bits," noted Alton with a hint of facetious mockery as he prepared himself to leave.

"You criticise as if you could do better," I quipped, doing the same and snatching the seal matrix from the desk.

"Well, you made it look so bloody easy, maybe I will someday!"

We shared a chuckle as the three of us departed the reeve's office, locking the door behind us. Immediately after we had left the building, however, we were hindered by a guard whose voice I recognised; it was the very same man who had challenged us before.

"Reeve! We were starting to think you'd snuck out! Do you have any orders for the watch, Sir?"

"*Post them...*" Ewin began, but his windpipe was still obstructed and he could scarcely croak. He grunted, attempting in vain to shift the blockage but producing only a sickening, hacking cough. The guard's face twisted with distaste.

"Reeve Ewin's picked up a bit of a sore throat. We're taking him back to The Old Boar to get him some medicine," Alton interrupted.

"Sick with worry? Can't say I blame you, Sir. Would you like us to come along?"

"Actually, Betlic, we were going to ask if you could keep folk *away* from the tavern for a while. We don't know if the Sōlis have left any *spies* among us," Alton tapped the side of his nose and winked for emphasis, "and we don't want our plans overheard."

"Does he have that right, Reeve?" asked Captain Betlic.

Ewin coughed again and nodded.

"Understood, Sir. Get well soon, won't you? We'll all need to be strong as aurochs if we're to be useful slaves!"

I saw anger flash in Alton's eyes, but he held his tongue and smiled dimly. Betlic, discouraged by the icy reception to his objectionable joke, lowered his head and ambled away. The three of us continued on to the tavern.

"*He* is the man you would entrust to maintain the secrecy of our activities?" I questioned in disbelief.

"Well, you see, I wouldn't trust Captain Betlic to find a leaf in Caill or a brick in Iliban," Alton explained with a waggish grin, "but he does have a knack for keeping people away, you might say."

No further elaboration was needed.

Once inside The Old Boar, Alton set to work on lighting the candles dotted about the establishment. With every additional meagre glow, I could see more of the ruin which had overtaken Alton's home, the neglect symptomatic of his grief in the past few days. The furniture was strewn about (the apparent aftermath of some violent outburst) and all efforts of housekeeping had been forgotten. The Old Boar had never been a hub of festivities, but now it has become to the tavern as a gravestone is to a man; a memorial to something that was once cherished and now is missed dearly.

Nonetheless, this depressing space was to become our grisly workshop. My animation of the reeve was, thankfully, precise enough for him to undress and wash himself, for the most part. One unpleasant task assigned to Alton was to perform a suture on Ewin's wound. His sword, which we had sheathed and brought on his belt, was not so finely crafted as Heorot's Mēċe; but it had certainly been keen enough to sink through the flesh until its path was obstructed by bone.

"It's going to look an ugly scar, even if no one'll see it. But at least his heart and liver won't roll out if someone pats him on the back too hard," assured Alton.

Next was the removal of obstructions from the throat. For this, we heated a measure of ale over the fire in the hanging pan, then had the reeve kneel, tilting back his head and opening his mouth.

"Sorry, mate," the innkeeper whispered, grimacing as he poured the liquid directly into Ewin's oesophagus.

The makeshift agent hissed softly as it met the cold flesh, but the un-dead reeve barely acknowledged it. He kept perfect stillness as the pot's whole contents were emptied, enough to make his midsection perceptibly swell.

"Alton; you may prefer to distract yourself for a moment," I warned him, taking a pail from the bar.

On this occasion, he accepted my advice and went elsewhere to find some suitable clothing for Ewin. Once out of eyeshot (but possibly not earshot), I prompted the un-dead to disgorge the contents of its stomach and lungs into the bucket. The sound was utterly abominable; the stench was little better. The receptacle was filled with the materials dislodged from the reeve's innards. I shall not describe it, but only note here that it was among the vilest of concoctions that I have ever had the displeasure of experiencing. I could hear Alton's retching from one of the side-rooms mere moments later.

"Dump that shit out back!" Alton called between heaves.

There was no disagreement but, being unwilling to risk the spilling of any of the foul substance, I had the reeve carry the pail instead. Once at the tavern's rear entrance, the mixture was discarded onto the grassy incline - vessel and all. When that was done, he returned to the communal area, and we waited for Alton to join us with a set of clothes on his arm.

"I think Ewin gave these to Bayldon as a gift. Lad never really wore them, kept saying he didn't want to get them marked up," he said. "Might as well see if they still fit."

The apparel was placed beside the reeve, and he proved capable of redressing himself. The clothes were loose-fitting and seemed suitable enough.

"This is a temporary solution. Would I be correct to assume that the reeve possessed a raiment of armour?" I enquired.

"That's right. It's kept in the barracks, if I remember rightly."

"Then the chicanery will be tested soon."

"We'd better practice. He looks... *almost* normal," Alton admitted uneasily.

"Good to see you, Alton. How are you?" said the reeve. His voice was clear and coherent, but flat.

"Too... *lifeless*. Somehow, he seems deader than when he was dead."

"Do you realise how difficult this is, Alton?" I suspired.

"I realise that either this works or we're all done for. Try it again, mate. I know you can do it."

"We shall not surrender to the Arx," the reeve told us, a hint of aggression in his otherwise neutral tone.

"Again. Like he has a life still worth losing!" Alton demanded.

"We'll *never* surrender to those arrogant *bastards*!" the mimic bellowed with righteous fury.

"That's more like it!" shouted Alton. He seemed unrestrainedly inspired, as if a divine flame had awoken in his chest. "By the skies above, I've wanted to hear Reeve Ewin Falken speak those words since the day they took Wurt. We might have let those priests get away, and we might not see the other side of the battle, but you and I, and the rest of Stilneshire; we'll give them a fight they won't soon forget!"

"Let us hope that the others are of a similar disposition," I interposed. Though I tried to remain balanced and pragmatic, Alton's enthusiasm was inescapably infectious and I could not help but yield to a tinge of elation.

"They will. Trust me. But first, we need to get *him* dressed *properly* and the messengers on the move, if it isn't too late already. Both of those can be done at the barracks, so we can hit two birds with one stone with that one. That being said, how're we going to get them going with no horses?"

"Show me to them, Alton. Let us inspect the damage."

Once I was adequately covered, the innkeeper unlocked the door and the three of us moved to the stables. A few patrolling men of the watch stood at attention as the reeve passed them, the latter nodding his head in return. The stables, when we reached them, were entirely still. The floor was bedaubed with bloodstained straw, and the large forms of a dozen or so dead horses lay on the bedding, Felicia and Feran among their number. Each animal's throat had been cut, evidently by use of an extremely sharp blade.

"It's like a knacker's shed. Poor beasts," Alton sulked.

"They may yet serve their purpose. Make sure we are not interrupted."

"Wait. How're you going to explain this to their riders? Everyone knows what happened to the stables."

I shrugged, completely bereft of suggestions. How could they be convinced that an un-dead mount was safe to travel on? Could their existence be explained without divulging the presence of a necromancer? It seemed doubtful. The shelter of our procrastination was quickly dissolving.

"Perhaps we can selectively inform the messengers..." I suggested finally.

"And what do we say to anyone who were to see five men ride off on dead horses?" grumbled Alton, understandably incredulous.

"We have truly no option," I agreed reluctantly. "They must be told. Perhaps it is for the best; should others come, the news of my involvement can be diffused among them by the people themselves. That perspective could prove easier to accept."

"It might!" Alton chuckled. "There's only one sure way to find out, though!"

"Shall I call a town meeting?" asked the reeve suddenly.

"I think that's for the best, mate. I..." Alton stopped himself, turning to address me with uncharacteristic sincerity. "Gods, that's a queer feeling. I reckon they might actually buy *him*. I'm just praying the 'reeve' can bring them around to *you*."

"How much do they trust the reeve?"

"Absolutely," answered Alton without hesitation.

"Then we must not delay. The messengers should have departed hours ago. If we eschew it much longer, it will be for nought that they are sent at all."

And so we left the stables and made our way to the courtyard. As we walked, Captain Betlic approached us and spoke.

"Reeve, Sir, the watch want their orders. They want to know what we're going to do, Sir."

"Bootlick! I was just about to summon you!" replied the reeve with believable glee, "I need you to send out the guard and inform everyone in Gerefwīċ Hundred of a town meeting, here and now."

"It's Betlic, Sir," corrected the captain, embarrassed and scarlet-faced. "I'll see to it."

As Betlic scuttled ahead to the barracks, Alton was wheezing behind me, trying and failing to suppress laughter.

"Is Ewin acting incorrectly?" I whispered.

"Not at all, mate, you're right on the mark. It's just... we never called him 'Bootlick' to his *face*!"

"Well," I reasoned, "we may not be graced with another opportunity. Why not make the most of it?"

"Right you are, mate!" agreed Alton, beaming like a jester.

Reeve Ewin followed Betlic and ordered a separate guard to have his armour brought out to him. One entered the stone tower and returned with two others in tow, each of the three carrying a piece of his wargear. The first handed him a lengthy mail hauberk, which covered his arms and touched his knees, tightly secured with a leather belt. The next man placed a helmet atop his head, a visored steel cap with the reeve's own bird-like mark impressed onto the brow. The last thing handed to him was his shield, broad and round, striped with green and white.

Thus was the reeve readied to address his people; Alton and I awaited their convergence, our nerves on edge for the potential consequences of our simulacrum. When the crowds had assembled before a hastily constructed wooden podium, there was a pervasive murmuring among them. There were men there, but also women and children, and the elderly. There must have been less than three-hundred in total. All had come to know the fate of their settlement, to separate fact from hearsay in the fading light of the early evening. Here, to the best of my memory, is a full account of the speech given by the un-dead reeve:

"Fine folk of Gerefwīċ; some of you may have heard rumours of a terrible reckoning on its way to your homes. I have gathered you here to tell you that those rumours are true. Arx Turrium is sending an army to raze Stilneshire, and of its people - of you - they will surely make slaves or corpses."

There came a great wailing from the throngs. Shouts of rage from the men, their children weeping. The reeve sued for quiet and went on.

"I'm telling you this, as your reeve, because you deserve nothing short of the honest truth. We have our Ealdorman Heorot's support. He's doing what he can from Bēagshire, but that is all we can expect. We must expect no help but that which is plainly offered to us."

"Nobody's going to help us!" heckled a man from the crowd.

"Not true!" retorted the reeve. "We'll be sending messages to the other hundreds with a call to arms. Now, hear!" shouted the reeve as utterances of dead horses and foregone doom arose from the masses. "We've been offered the help of an ally who asks for nothing but our own efforts! Who can provide four tireless steeds and more than a thousand warriors to fight at our sides!"

There was a confused silence. Few individuals could, alone, field armies of such size. Susurrated conversations theorised on which of the ealdormen from one of the larger counties could march swiftly enough to arrive in time, and which ones might be willing to oppose the Arx and, by association, King Ricbert. The reeve allowed the discussions for a while as his puppeteer carefully considered his next, crucial words.

"The one who offers his hand in our hour of need is no lord of men, but a lord of the dead. Good folk of Gerefwīċ, I must tell you that he is a *necromancer*."

The audience, it would seem, were stunned into quietude. What were they to make of this revelation? Had the reeve lost his mind?

"You heard me rightly, good people. These are grave times for all of us, but the necromancer has offered us his services unconditionally, and he may be our only chance!"

"You can't trust a dead-raiser!" yelled one man, his comment accompanied by jeers of almost unanimous accordance. Spurred on, he added; "What's his price? To have us all join his army!"

"The necromancer is oathsworn to save as many of you as he can!" Ewin attempted to recover desperately.

"What honour can a corpse-snatcher swear by?" asked another man rhetorically.

"I know this man, and he *is* trustworthy!" The reeve raised his voice over the increasing clamour. "I would not have let him live otherwise. But, good folk of Gerefwīċ, if you won't trust in his care for *you*, trust him in his *hatred* for the *Arx*!"

Some of the more doubtful noises were muted, to be replaced by thoughtful mutterings. Emboldened, the elected official persisted.

"Some of you know this man already. He wishes only to protect you, and to punish the Arx for their trespasses. He will risk himself just as you will. Afterwards you might judge him, but first allow him to prove his worth to you!"

"Who's the necromancer?" called a woman, to universal agreement. "Show him to us!"

Alton nudged me with his elbow, and I looked at him with disbelief. He gestured to the stage, to which I shook my head. Finally, he grasped my wrist firmly and pulled me to it himself. Gasps of astonishment erupted from the crowd. Presented to the public by Alton, I could think of no appropriate action... but to bow low in subservience. My reception was less than kind, and I was frightened for what they might do.

"The man before you has lived a life of debasement and regret," the reeve elucidated over the rabble, "but now he seeks to make amends for his crimes-"

"How?" interjected Captain Betlic, who stood at the side of the podium with a look of horror on his face.

"I shall resurrect those in the mausoleum to combat the invaders," I announced, "as well as the rest of those buried in the graveyard-"

"You would defile our ancestors!" screeched an older woman.

"Yes. But, ladies and gentlemen, if in death you could return to save the lives of your children, your grandchildren, or even your long descendants, would you not consent? Would you not wish your ancestors to make that same bargain for your own lives? But they cannot fight such formidable enemies alone. You must fight alongside them for your freedom, and for that of your families; and by my oath as a free man, you will fight harder, and you will fight after you have fallen, for the sake of your loved ones."

The soundlessness of the audience was stifling. The expressions of those on the nearest rows were unreadable, and I believed initially that I had exercised a drastic error in judgement. I was frozen with incertitude. Alton drummed his fingers on the hilt of his seax. The acuteness of the atmosphere seemed all but insurmountable, when I saw a young man raised up on his father's shoulders. He waved to garner the attention of myself and those around him, and I realised then that I recognised him as the young man from whom I had purchased Rēdawulf's bow. Putting his hands to his mouth, he cried triumphantly:

"If the dead can fight, then so can I!"

To my lasting amazement, a wave of approval swept through the crowd. Its intensity escalated, and the general din was soon punctuated by the shouts of those voicing their agreement.

"So can I!" I saw the remnants of Bayldon's friends contribute to the growing acclamation.

"My friends," the reeve addressed the crowd once again, "*this* is the spirit which will drive the tyrants from Stilneshire, from Cemparīċe! I need capable riders to take missives to Westfæsten, Trēodæl, Ġeolwæt, Sceoppaton and Beorgweġ, and to return with every able-bodied man that would not bow to slavery!"

Nine hands were raised. Their owners were beckoned forth by the guards and grouped together behind the podium.

"The necromancer and I have formulated a strategy which we believe will give us our best chances. All men of fighting age should

292

collect their arms and meet here. The rest we shall place out of harm's way before the battle begins. Meet back here in one hour. Go well!"

The reeve's address was concluded and the crowd began to disperse, chattering energetically among themselves. There was definite uncertainty within the multitude, but there was also a degree of compliance. Some were surely discontented with the arrangement, but more still were sceptical of the necromancer's very existence. They had, after all, been given no proof of my abilities. I suspected that, for some, facing the reality of an un-dead warband may blunt their enthusiasm; nonetheless, I decided then that it had become necessary to demonstrate candour. The living and the dead would have to be introduced to one another.

To that end, I identified an opportunity for such an undertaking. I passed Reeve Ewin his seal matrix as he had his guards sent for ink and parchment. Then, I approached those who had volunteered themselves as messengers. In their faces I saw a spectrum of curiosity, apprehension and fear, all of which I attempted to allay simultaneously.

"Gentlemen," I began, motioning for them to follow as I led us to the stables, "I must thank you all for your exemplary valour, but allow me to assure you; the steeds I shall provide for you will be both swifter and safer than they ever were in life."

When I saw that they were unconvinced, I realised that these men would need more than the words of an old man hiding beneath a huge cowl and a white beard. They would need to see *practical application*. I said no more until we were all inside the stables, hurriedly joined by Alton, who had just about managed to escape a deluge of questions. He had usefully acquired a lit torch, something I had quite forgotten owing to my extraordinary vision. When the men were settled (as much as could be expected), I announced my intentions.

"Here you will be the first men to see my art, which I shall show you openly."

The men shuffled with unease. Spreading my arms wide, I commenced my channelling of the magical energies. In the shadows of the stables, the manna swirled and blossomed, even to their eyes, and many of them were awestruck. The others stepped backwards and were cowed by the spectacle that followed. As unnatural ardour seeped into the splayed equine bodies, they twitched and shuddered.

Expletives, curses and warding invocations all were shouted out behind me, and two of the men fled the stables. Those remaining saw the spell's climax as the horses struggled onto their hooves. They snorted noisily with exertion, then were silent as they sauntered to our fore with perfect obedience. Those men that had not retreated already now kept their distance from the un-dead beasts. Among them were the mounts that once belonged to Bayldon and I, their empty eyes eliciting a momentary but keen sadness.

"By the gods... its Wyne!" cried a burly farmhand.

"Excuse me...?" I stammered, taken aback.

The man boldly approached one of the horses - chestnut in coat - and, to my surprise, ran his hands through its mane and patted it on its muscular neck. As he turned towards the flickering light, I realised that I knew this man's face also; it belonged to Galan, a friend of Bayldon's.

"I hate them for killing Wyne. Looked after her since she was a filly, I did. Now it looks like I'll get to ride on her one more time, at least!" he told us excitedly.

"It is not truly your steed, Galan."

"What do you mean? Whose is it, then? Seems only fair I get to ride my own horse," he complained, holding onto the un-dead animal's head selfishly.

"You misunderstand me, my friend. The animal will obey you, yes, but it is not the same as the one that died here in any sense except appearance. Consider it now as you would a hoe or a scythe; a useful tool, nothing more."

"Then... she'll feel different?"

"In some ways she will, indeed, be similar. She may well move and vocalise as she did, but she will exude no bodily warmth, nor will she ever suffer fatigue."

"I get you. I... I still want to take her, though. Even if it's not *really* her."

"Of course," I agreed, smiling fondly at him. "I should have known to expect such uncompromising loyalty from one of Bayldon's friends. He was evidently most discerning in his choices!"

Galan grinned tearfully and retrieved Wyne's tack, equipping her gear with practiced efficiency. The other riders were less discriminating in their selections, still unsure but encouraged enough, at least, to work with them. Felicia, however, was kept separate from the other horses; a purely sentimental decision, and not one which I deigned to explain to my peers.

As the messengers were preparing for their journey, the reeve pushed into the stables and distributed five sealed letters, thanking each receiver in turn. Accounting for the two deserters, two men remained with un-dead horses bereft of destinations, yet they were not without use; they kindly agreed to act as relays for urgent orders within the hundred, and to showcase their supernatural mounts to the population in the process. My hope was that some worriers might be somewhat acclimatised to the concept of un-death *before* they are exposed to a more *closely related* variety.

The evening's dark had set in as the messengers rode from the stables on their nightmarish steeds. Those that were tramping their way to the meeting stopped and pointed, their eyes wide and their mouths agape. Never had they seen such a thing; a part of me eagerly anticipated their reaction to necromancy of a greater magnitude.

The horsemen flaunted as I had asked them to, performing admirably, though they stopped beside me to ask one final question.

"How're we to travel when we can barely see?" one petitioned on behalf of the rest.

"Your mounts' sights will be flawless. You will scarcely need to guide them, but they will ensure your safety."

With that, I bade them good fortune on their quests and wished for their safe return on the morrow. Alton came to me with questions, but for the first time in many days, I felt exhausted. Not from any enterprise of necromancy, but from the stress of pressure. The un-dead require precious little responsibility, and I am not accustomed to the threat of *casualties*. Not casualties of any meaningful consequence, that is. Now, with every potential fatality a loss unto itself, the faith I had in my own competence is waning. The reeve's suicide and the incident at the stables has multiplied my burden immeasurably and necessitated an untimely acceleration of my plans.

I did not have the heart to extinguish Alton's heroic vigour, so I did not confide in him my true estimation of our chances. If Arx Turrium's forces arrive tomorrow, we shall be caught inadequately prepared and susceptible to being routed. Alton and Ewin accompanied me to The Old Boar to collect my things while Captain Betlic was summoned. Once inside, I informed Alton of my strategy for tomorrow, and that *he* would be the one to announce it to the militia. He protested at first, but I assured him that he would be heeded, adding that I needed time to configure the pertinent spells, and he conceded. Betlic was already waiting for us outside when we departed the building.

"You called, Sir?" he asked, addressing the reeve despite his cynical eyes never shifting from myself.

"Yes. I'm going to go with the necromancer to discuss the plan's finer details. You are to announce to Gerefwīċ's men that Alton will be instructing them on my behalf shortly," said Ewin curtly.

"As you wish, Sir. Remember to watch your back around that... *thing*. We don't know what it's up to," Betlic sneered.

"*Saving your skin*, Bootlick," Alton laughed mockingly, "though you don't half make me wonder why he's bothering!"

Betlic pulled an offended face, but acquiesced to the reeve's authority and led Alton away, who himself gave me a despairing sideways look. The un-dead governor walked by my side as we disappeared through the willows and into the mausoleum, into the comforting solitude within. Here we shall sit until disturbed, awaiting word of development or disaster.

Sōlrest-Þridda-XXIX

...

A woman in a heavy cloak carries a bundle of soiled rags. She hurries, but does not run; she cannot afford to draw attention to herself. Strands of flaxen hair protrude from the deep hood, hanging down far enough to rest upon the face of the small boy concealed in the linens.

The child looks up in wonderment, scrunching his nose occasionally as the fine locks tickle him. He has, in truth, no idea what is happening; being barely three years old, his bright eyes simply take in the passing surroundings. He does, however, remain perfectly quiet, just as he has been told to. An aspect of the silly game they are playing, he assumes.

From the boy's mobile nest he sees aspects of where he has lived his whole life. They are travelling with the citadel wall on their right, as far as he can tell. From this vertical angle, it seems even more impossibly high than they normally do. His father always explained that it was to keep the scary heretics out; his mother, when her husband was absent with the Ultōrēs, insisted that it was also to keep the faithful in. He never really understood what she meant when she said this, but the words stayed with him anyway.

Perhaps they are going to see the East Gateway. Mother took him there sometimes, to see the trees. There are no trees inside the citadel, and people who are not guards (especially children) are not allowed on the walls. So when the gate opens, that is the only time you can see them. And how strange they appeared to him! So gnarled, and topped with big, leafy heads. They were certainly unusual compared to the smooth, grand architecture in which he had grown up. The West Gateway has trees too, different ones, his mother said. But they have never been to see those; she thought it would make her too sad.

The boy risks turning his head slightly in order to get a better view. His mother does not notice. Overhead, the mighty, looming spires which give Arx Turrium its title point skywards, and intricate stained glass images decorate the exterior of the towers. Inside those buildings, the windows produce an explosion of fantastical colours, depicting the Vīvus Sānctus and scenes of expeditions carried out in his - and Sōl's -

name. It is one of the very few things the boy thinks fondly of the temples.

It has been an upsetting few days, actually. It all started when, in one of his group's learning sessions, the tutor had dutifully informed them that Sōl had need of their most favoured possessions, and that they must present them forthwith. The other boys handed over toy daggers, clay figurines of Arx soldiers, pendants and the like, without hesitation; but when the tutor wished to requisition the wooden wolf pup that his mother had so painstakingly whittled for him, he had refused and thrown a violent tantrum instead.

Of course the intended moral of the exercise had been that, in service of Sōl and the Arx, all else was secondary. It was something the other children knew instinctively; yet he, the son of an Episcopus no less, had clearly and demonstrably failed to absorb this message. He was sent home, but a report of his conduct preceded him. The finger of blame was swiftly pointed indeed. His father was furious, threatening to strike the boy, until his mother struck her husband first. The broom snapped on the man's head, but that just made him angrier; he hit her with his metal fists so hard and so many times that she was bruised all over. She could not even rise to prepare his food, so he went hungry that night. She did, however, whisper something curious to him as she lay there, through her bloodied, swollen lips:

"We must take you away from here. Your father will make you into monster."

Again, the boy did not truly comprehend her meaning. But it made him cry to see her so hurt and upset, and his father so angry at her for their son's misdemeanour.

And now this. He contemplates that he might finally be going on a mission with the Ultōrēs and his father, as the latter had often promised would happen someday. They always sound like such an adventure, and the Episcopus is always well celebrated and congratulated by everyone when he returns. Everyone except the man's reticent wife, that is. The boy begins to doubt that his father knows where his mother is taking him at all, but still he stays silent.

Eventually, they stop. Where are they? The boy's mother looks down at him and speaks frantically with tears in her eyes.

"My child; be free now. This man will take you far away. Take this," she slides a roll of parchment into his tunic and pats it down on

his heart, "read it only when safe. It explain all, and what do next. Remember; never, ever use your name. Your new one is written. I love you, sweet one! Go well!"

With one last, choking sob, the boy's mother passes him down to other hands.

"Greetings, little one," says the unknown man. "Come with me, you will be safe outside."

The voice is friendly and, though it is deeper than his mother's, the boy notices in it the same musical quality. But he grows nervous as he is lowered, because it appears that he is falling slowly into darkness. Panicking, he cannot help but let loose a high-pitched scream. The man and his mother shout something at each other in Caillic - too fast for him to understand - and his new bearer bolts into the gloom, the sound of rushing water in front and a clamour of men barking their Arcāna behind.

The boy, now, is gripped entirely by terror: he realises that he is in the sewer, *a place in which he has been told unequivocally that he must not play; and in a stranger's hands, perhaps one of the animalistic heretics his father had warned him against. He can think of nothing to do but cry out, yet his mouth has been covered.*

His kidnapper turns corners this way and that at a dizzying pace, and then... sunlight! Its intensity waxes until it becomes blinding. Then something sharp grazes the boy's back, and they are freefalling, and then...

The two of them land with a deafening splash. The air is knocked from the boy's lungs, but he manages to roll free of his captor to stand in the shallow pool. He turns to face him, expecting pursuit, but he just lies there, badly injured. A pilum has impaled his lung from the back, doubtless hurled by one of the Arx 'rescuers', and the impact from the fall had splintered the shaft and likely broken his spine. The boy had never seen the scraggly, bearded, ruined man at his feet, yet the stranger's penultimate act had been to shield him against the projectile and to cushion him against an otherwise deadly drop.

Before he expires, the stranger looks at him and mouths breathlessly:

"Run! The trees!"

And so the boy does. He turns his back to the drainage outlet and runs as fast as his tiny legs can carry him, east, into the treeline. And he continues to run, among the unfamiliar arboreal columns, further and further, until he can do so no more. Then he collapses against one and weeps. Suddenly he remembers the letter from his mother; he reaches for it and unrolls it, but the wetness from the sewerage has caused the writing upon it to run and become illegible. The blotched parchment stares back at him, useless.

Why has my mother done this to me? *he sulks.* My father will be very angry with her. And with me...

Every direction seems identical, except when he considers the canopy. Through it, he can just barely see the sun. East; in the morning, the sun arrives from the east. His father had always told him that if he were ever lost in the wilderness and no one knew where he was, that his best chance would be to follow a single heading until he reaches a road or a known landmark. His father said that he got lost in a Caillic forest once upon a time, and that he got back just like that. The boy hoped that he would not be forced to kill lots of Caillic barbarians like his father was.

So the boy began to walk, chasing the sun with every step. It was easily the longest distance his feet had ever taken him. He walked until every part of him ached, and after many hours and what must have been many miles, he discovered a dirt road which cut across his path left to right - north to south. Utterly exhausted and beyond constructive thought, he picked the north way at random. That way he went until he could ambulate no longer, and there he fell at the roadside in a paralysed slumber.

He is awoken by torchlight, a gentle, warming glow in the cold night. The woman holding it speaks something in a foreign dialect. Her tone is kindly and comforting, but he shrugs to show his ignorance. She says more indecipherable words, pausing briefly between each one as if recounting a list. Then, there is one he recognises.

"Arcāna?"

Noticing the boy's ears prick, she repeats the word. The boy exclaims loudly in response.

"Arcāna! Yes, I speak that! Can you?"

She shakes her head and his heart sinks. However, she takes a loaf of bread and a waterskin from her basket and gives them to him. He consumes both greedily as she kneels by him, wrapping him in a blanket.

"Come. Safe," she asks when he is done, offering her hand. The fire reveals the wrinkled, genial features of an old lady. Her smile is full of genuine care and, being unable to bear the thought of traversing the endless road alone again, the boy takes the hand she offers to him. He is hoisted with surprising strength onto a cart with a pair of hardy horses at its fore.

The old woman whistles and, together, they are pulled northwards into the night.

A vision from long ago. Long before I can recall. Whether the details are accurate or not, I cannot say; but perhaps I would prefer the memory to have remained in the distant past, buried and forgotten. Perhaps.

...

The Arx have not come today. In addition, help has arrived from some unlikely places. These attributes have permitted me the daring to hope. Perhaps they can be saved, these unfortunate people. Perhaps a necromancer can lead them to an improbable victory. With an organised defence, high spirits and an apt employment of inventive and unpredictable stratagems, a capable general might turn the tides of what would otherwise be a losing war. Every shortcoming must be accounted for, every advantage exploited to its fullest. Success may be credibly within our grasp. There is but one salient factor on which I am undecided whether to discuss with Alton; that of my metamorphosis.

There are a multitude of variables in place regarding this issue. I know not how rapidly the final transition occurs, nor the manner in which it happens, nor whether my mastery of the new form's abilities will be instinctive and instantaneous. How can one integrate such a collection of unknowables into a plan? And yet, if I am to become an Arch-Lich on the next day, and if it is as powerful as the records and legends tell, then it will surely secure our victory. Until that time, however potent I may be, I am not yet invulnerable. I would estimate the Arx's arrival to be tomorrow, the last day of Sōlrest's third phase; a narrow frame which could determine triumph or ruin. What else can be done but prepare for the worst possible outcome? It would be a foolish thing to rely on the uncertain, or to tempt others to do so. Their desperacy will be the fulcrum of their steadfastness; best they do not come to depend on such an indefinite salvation.

These are the things with which I was occupied when the first interruption came in the moonlit early hours; a visitor, though it was not Alton but a familiar stranger. Her sweet voice rang cheerily through the corridors as she descended through the hole with neither concern nor dubiety, her majestic dress of verdant leaves gently rustling as she found her footing.

"Only one lonely soul could inhabit this sad grotto!" sang the priestess, startling me out of my meditation.

"You are in *my* dwelling now, witch," I threatened, readying my servants to apprehend her. "Among *my* people."

"Neither is this dwelling yours, nor are the Blōþisōdaz your people," she retorted scornfully, her emerald eyes glowing brightly. The un-dead halted their advance unbidden, almost as if *fearful*.

"If you come to dispute my conduct, return at a time of greater convenience! I have no patience for idle meddling."

"Such ingratitude towards a bestower of gifts and a dispenser of wisdom!" she bemoaned, seemingly hurt.

"A vendor of pretty trinkets and riddles! You spy from the trees and offer your tit-bits, but to what end? Why should they be trusted?"

"You would not trust a gift from Caill, but make use of one from *them*?" she cried, gesturing towards the Hinthial Sceptre propped against the wall behind me.

"What do *you* know of *them*?" I demanded.

"Not enough, but too much."

"Beware, witch. I would have answers from you. The boy is not with me now, and I am not as disinclined to bloodshed as I was then."

"The boy did not sate your bloodlust, then?" she said spitefully.

My response to her was not delivered in words. Instead, the un-dead previously kept at bay lunged forwards with a resurgence of vigour. Audaward was upon her first, closing the long, bony fingers of one hand about her throat and lifting her from her feet. Rēdawulf occupied the space to her left, an arrow nocked on his bowstring and ready to draw, while Helparīks held a spear to her right side.

"Killing me will not restore the life you have stolen!" the priestess choked.

"Nor will taunting me serve to prolong yours. However, I am still yet capable of reason; I have no discrete quarrel with you, but you possess information which I do not. It is of vital importance that I know all that I can, and be assured, I shall extract that knowledge with whatever methods prove effective."

The moss and vines that were crawling through the hole and flowering in her presence shrunk back and shrivelled, overcome by the pervasion of deathly energies. The leaves on her flowing dress lost their viridescence. The druidess herself was visibly suffering, her resistance to the aura's influence weakening gradually.

"Why have you not left this place?" she pleaded. "Why do you stay after your banishment?"

"I believe you misunderstand your circumstance. Provide answers and I may consider doing likewise, if I can be persuaded into confidence."

She nodded as best she could, struggling to breathe in Audaward's vice-like grip, so I had him lower her to the ground and pin her against the wall instead. Rēd and Helparīks adjusted their stances accordingly, and the others gathered around, closing her into a circle of leering skulls atop armed skeletons.

"What is your name, druidess?" I began, adopting a tone of relative equitability.

"Just as yourself; there is not one of any meaning that I could give."

"I shall believe you, for now. As you are hunted by the Arx, I appreciate that we have a common enemy, and the value of anonymity against such a foe. Do you seek to act against them together?"

"It is not in my nature to act *against* anyone. I wish only to help *you*."

"Speak plainly; what succour can you provide?"

"A warning! A call to escape!" the priestess insisted as Audaward tightened his hand. "The men of the spired citadel are coming here with sword and steed, and they will raze this place to its foundations!"

"And you would have me flee? Save myself from sharing its fate?"

"Will you not?"

"No," I stated bluntly. "And if to urge me to do so was to be the sole intent of your visit, you have risked yourself needlessly. Why is it of your concern what befalls a necromancer? Speak!"

"I cannot say now, but you will know soon. Please!" she begged as Helparik's speartip pressed increasingly into her abdomen. "Anything else I shall answer, but not this! Not yet!"

Her words reminded me too much of those I had used with Bayldon, and my heart was marginally softened by the memory. The spear was loosened again, but remained at the ready.

"The amber mask. What is its origin? Its purpose?" I inquired.

"You do not know? *It* is a sacred relic of Caill, the *Mask of Marwos*," she described with reverence. "For generations, our most hallowed priestesses sacrificed a portion of their own ichor to Caill's greatest tree, Fuildair. It is from this mighty oak that the resin was gathered before being cast into its final shape."

"Then why bestow so auspicious an artefact upon a necromancer?"

"Marwos is our death-god, for whom the relic is named. Through its eyes, it grants the wearer the ability to see *Gelach-manna*, which is required of one who seeks to become an Avatar of Marwos as you do."

"'Gelach-manna'? I have not encountered this terminology."

"That is what the Caillic call the magical energy from the moon, an embodiment of the *Cáe Anman*, the Way of Souls. Not even the attuned can see it unaided."

"Indeed they cannot," I conceded. "An invaluable device, if it functions as promised. But you have still to answer: *why aid me*?"

The priestess hesitated, glancing in turn at me, then the waiting undead, then lastly allowing her gaze to linger on the Hinthial Sceptre. It appeared to give her a profound, severe discomfort to even look upon. Transfixed by anticipation, I said nothing; but eventually, she imparted her secrets.

"We know only that when the Baron of the Dead made *his* ascension, he could do so only with the direction of those who also created his staff; but in receiving their guidance, he subjected himself to their influence, destroying his mind and causing him to become their tool. We had hoped to turn you from his path, that you might yet be saved from their evil whisperings on your own way to immortality. If we are too late, Necromancer, I would have you slay me, for I would rather perish than see the horror you might wreak upon the world..."

I had Audaward release her from his grasp and the other un-dead back away. Then, I sat upon one of the sarcophagi and gestured to one opposite for her to do the same. She relaxed a little, smiling - or grimacing, perhaps - as she rubbed her marked neck, but listened with utmost sincerity to my reply.

"I have followed in Velthur's footsteps, druidess, but I am not him; nor have I had any dealings with the creatures of which you speak. Although, I believe I have encountered them once, when I was much younger. What are they?"

"To us, they are the *Cenainmm*, but they surely have many other names among the inhabitants of Pænvicta, for they are ageless and boundless. They see with many eyes and listen with many ears, and when they speak, though they seldom do so with mortals, it is with many chittering mouths, and they are infinitely compelling."

"How fortunate I was to so narrowly escape their dreadful clutches..." I reflected, stricken by a primal sense of perturbation. "In what manner do they regard man? And why their patronage of Velthur?"

"Who can guess what occupies such unworldly, alien minds? We cannot say. They keep to their deep, dark places and watch, seemingly with small interest in man's affairs. And yet, they weaponised Velthur and granted him the power to cleanse from life all that he could reach."

"There was something else. Zeritmia..."

"Please, Necromancer. We consider speaking of the Cenainmm to be invocative, an ill omen," she uttered desperately. "Let us not discuss that which is beyond our understanding, but matters of urgency."

"I concur. Let us instead contemplate how to win Gerefwīċ's freedom," I suggested.

"It cannot be done!" laughed the druidess mirthlessly. "We of Caill are all too familiar with the conquests of the citadel. The villagers are doomed to death or slavery, with or without your assistance."

"That may be so, but I shall not abandon them. I am indebted to them for their kindnesses, for which I have proven myself thoroughly unworthy."

The priestess was silent, but shook her head disapprovingly. I found myself enraged by her attitude which so closely mirrored my own before my recent epiphanies. With disgust spurred on by guilt, my hatred was thus projected undeservedly onto her.

"Mayhap I shall simply enlist your services *against* your will. You might save lives, even if you do so only under duress," I spat.

"You must not... you cannot!"

"Is that so? Verily, you may find yourself as astonished as *I* was, *witch*."

Hildirīks stepped forth and cut downwards, expertly glancing her cheek to inflict a bloody incision. The druidess shrieked in pain and shock, then flinched as the skeletal form of Haþuwīgą next approached her only to run its digits along the wound. To her surprise and disbelief, the injury was mended.

"*Marwos...*" muttered the druidess, staring at me with awe and wonderment.

"Leave! Cower among the trees like the frightened animals you are, craven Caillic filth. I shall have no pity when the Arx makes firewood of your precious groves. Go, before I decide on your behalf and remake you in *her* image!" I commanded, indicating her un-dead counterpart.

She took to her heels, then, swiftly climbing to the hole in the ceiling. Just before she slipped out of sight, she made her parting remark:

"The Cenainmm will soon come to entreat with you, I think. I beg you; refuse them, and trust in the mask. For all our sakes."

And with that last pertinacious caveat, the druidess was gone and I was alone again, contemplating the veracity of her words. If she spoke truthfully, the 'Mask of Marwos', as she had designated it, could be tested tonight. However, as I replayed the confrontation in my mind, I could not help but question the rashness of my reactions; and yet in years past, would I have allowed her to depart freely? My suspicion, and even her containment, were reasonable, but why did I exhibit such wanton cruelty towards her? Perhaps our magical antithesis, and the deepening intrinsicality of my necromantic form, awakened some elemental animosity within me. I quite regret driving her away so; but if she will enact no direct, personal intervention, it is probably for the better. I have, at least, been spared the necessity of justifying a Caillic priestesses' presence to Alton, whom I suspect is nearing or exceeding his tolerance of spellcasters.

Upon his arrival much later, the innkeeper introduced himself somewhat more gracefully than he had yesterday, preferring the front gate over the 'side entrance'. He seemed fatigued and anxious. and I would guess that he had slept little or not at all.

"They're here, mate. They're none too happy about it, but they're here."

"Any word from the other territories?"

"None yet. It's still early, mind."

"Every hour they are delayed could be the hour of Arx Turrium's invasion," I lamented. "May they not be too late!"

"Either way, mate, you're going to have to speak with the folk that're already here. They're wondering why they're to guard a graveyard, more than anything else. I don't reckon most of them are really sure what a necromancer *is*."

"It may be time to demonstrate my talents to them."

Lacking other options, Alton agreed. However, he was clearly dismayed when, as we made to leave, my skeletal retinue fell in behind us. I can only assume that he quickly came to understand my intent, considering the absence of any criticism from him.

The entrance greeted us with a bright, pale day, and there was a commotion outside. A dewy morning mist blanketed the hill and obscured the forms of a vast multitude of labouring men and women. As they had been instructed, they were gathering whatever useful timber could be found within the basin's limits, including that which had been used in the construction of their homes. Better it be repurposed into something useful than to be set alight by the Arx to provide a demoralising backdrop for their assault.

As soon as I was visible, those people of Gerefwīċ within sight turned to face me. As the Blōþisōdaz formed up at either side of me, though, their demeanour shifted from disdain to vigilant fascination. Many climbed the hill and gathered around to look closer, some children even being gently restrained to prevent them from advancing further.

"You need not fear them," I called out openly. "They will not harm you. You may come closer, if you wish."

Few initially accepted my invitation, but a small contingent of intrepid individuals did emerge from the crowds. They were all of them youthful and inquisitive, sizing up the un-dead carefully before moving along to others. The skeletons remained still for the moment, and more people were encouraged to approach and inspect their baleful allies. To my surprise, some began to tentatively approach *me* with their questions. I obliged them as best I could.

"How can you be sure they won't turn on us?" asked one nervous youth.

"Allow me to assure you that they are thoroughly under my control, as puppets whose concealed strings lead to my fingertips. Observe."

I flourished my right hand in an exaggerated gesture, the un-dead (exempting the reeve) uniformly raising their matching arms in response. I repeated the movement with my left one, and they again mimicked respectively. The people flinched and stepped backwards, alarmed by the briskness and perfection of the un-dead's performance. I believe they were impressed, but far from comfortable, and there were murmurs in the crowd. Some, however, braved their anxieties and returned to their scrutinising. Soon I was attacked with a plethora of new inquiries from various persons.

"My father's buried here. Will he be one of those... brought back? Can I speak to him?"

"In a sense, yes, but only his body will be animated. You may speak to him if you wish to, but he will not listen or answer. The un-dead do not live as they once did. I am sorry."

"What will happen to us if we're killed?"

"Your body will continue to fight on until it can do so no longer. Over your soul, I have no jurisdiction or business."

"What about when Arx-men are killed?"

"They will become your allies and turn on their prior associates."

Many such clarifications were given to those who were confident enough to present themselves to me directly. None showed much interest in the reeve, who was stood by my side. I had apparently been accepted as the new figure of authority. Useful, but it was a sensation I took no pleasure in; I felt as if I had been imposed on them, occupying their county and placing myself as a local tyrant. My motives of selfless protection seemed hollow indeed while I hid behind their numbers and utilised them as a wall. Doubtless my intentions were a topic of many a hushed debate, but there was one who brought their accusations to me personally.

"What happens if *you* are slain in the fighting, Dear Necromancer?" hissed a man hidden beneath a wide-brimmed hat.

"The un-dead will fall with me. You would have to fight on alone, though your odds would be drastically worsened."

"How *convenient*!" he remarked derisively. "So what's your stake in all this, O Kindly Wayfarer? When the Arx are gone, what happens to us?"

"You will all be saved from a life of slavery-"

"To be your slaves in death! *I see*!" he announced loudly in feigned realisation. "The beginnings of a brand new army! Where first, O Gracious Master? Bēagshire? Arx Turrium? War's a horrible thing, but then, we won't know anything about it, so you tell us, so I suppose we should be grateful!"

Confronted by such imputations, I found that I was frustrated; how can one answer them believably? It is surely a matter of trust, of which the people owe me none. Dissent is inevitable and expected even among the greatest of leaders, but those who repay it with violence are seldom much loved. Such is the very absolutism we now strive against. But the man's sentiment did prompt me to consider how many others he shared it with. A crowd had drawn in closer to spectate the recounter.

"You are free to surrender yourself to the Arx if you desire. You will not be hindered from doing so," I informed him, "though I believe it to be folly to sue them for mercy. It is not a currency they are wont to understand. Wurt's family would attest to that in his absence, I think."

My reasoning garnered some agreement. Many of the spectators' heads were nodding to the recognition of that memory. The man's opposition became more biting as his support dwindled.

"I'll leave, Necromancer, and any sane folk left in this forsaken shithole will come with me. But before we go, I have one more question for our most benevolent lordship; what do you look like, under that covering?"

I froze. In truth, I had no idea how my affliction of decay had progressed, what hideous visage was enshrouded from the people of Gerefwīċ; I dared not show them. None had asked such a question thus far, perhaps preferring not to know. I was saved the difficulty of providing an answer, however. Unbeknownst to me, Alton had crept up behind the man with a retort of his own.

"I'd rather see the face under *this* one!" he barked as he flipped the hat from the man's head. There, revealed, stood Captain Betlic, who wore a wolfish grin.

"What's it matter who I am, *thrall*?" Betlic snapped venomously. "You've no right to silence me. I reckon your *necromancer* here is none other than that old invalid who was staying at your pissy tavern. Come far have you, on your *pilgrimage*?" he addressed to me. "Stop at any lodges on the northern roads?"

"Get to the point, Betlic. You're making me sleepy," taunted Alton.

"The point is, he's a *killer*. Seven men dead, slain by dead men, no survivors? You're a slippery one, aren't you?"

"That is not what transpired that night. Deserters had seized the lodge and were using it to murder travellers for their possessions. I put an end to their antics," I explained.

"So in saving yourself, you saved *no one else*!" Betlic announced triumphantly. "Maybe you'll do better this time. Me? I doubt it. I doubt *you*. You've no reason to care for the living. Sōlis Mūnus is right; necromancers bring death to all they touch, and to trust them is to invite a plague into your homes. I'll take my chances with the Arx thank you very much, and if anyone *else* among *you* chooses life," he called out to the crowd, "follow on!"

With that, Betlic unsheathed his sword, raised it high to mark himself out, and began to walk through the crowd. Some individuals filtered from the main body to accompany him; but as he disappeared into the sea of mist beyond the willows, it was difficult to estimate precisely how many had joined his exodus.

"I am deceiving myself. I cannot lead living people to victory. Necromancers are not best known for their charisma," I confided to Alton.

"Don't give *him* the time of day, mate. If there's anyone less popular than you around here, it's Bootlick. He won't take many with him."

"Not exactly encouraging, Alton," I chuckled, "but thank you anyway."

"You know I'll tell you things straight. Nothing more, nothing less. As far as the hundred's concerned, you're their saviour. But that doesn't mean they're happy with the arrangement."

"It will have to do," I sighed. "So long as they loathe Arx Turrium slightly more than they loathe me, I suppose I should ask no more of them."

There was scarce consolation that Alton could offer honestly, so he instead gave a sympathetic look and patted me on the shoulder before departing to organise the militia. I myself waited on the hill's peak, sulking, sat at the mouth of the mausoleum. Watching the families work was tranquilising and served to calm my nerves. The people of Gerefwīċ, in their cooperation, were commendably industrious; fellers had begun their labourious task of removing the willows and other trees from the graveyard's circumference, while carpenters and their assistants fashioned the fresh and recycled timber into stakes. Others were put to work excavating a series of post-holes and an encompassing concentric ditch. A few of the outer structures, including the stables, had been deconstructed to expand the available space. Soon, far from being an area segregated from the rest of the settlement as it was previously, the cemetery had obtained a commanding perspective over the landscape. It is also, as I had envisioned, highly defensible. At the hindside of the mausoleum, the basin's edge is steep; far too treacherous to advance a force of armoured men down. Its more vulnerable sides have been fortified as effectively as any could hope for, given the urgency; a palisade wall surrounded by a collection of jutting spikes, and an ankle-breaking trench surrounding them, should stifle the momentum of attackers. Being a trained military the Arx soldiers will, eventually, breach the stockade, but it should stall their assault. A bridge remains to provide clear access to allies, but this will be withdrawn when the time comes. Overall, Alton had instructed the people with exception, demonstrating well what he had learned during his tenure as a bounty-hunter.

I was not entirely idle as I perched, however. As well as the people themselves, I paid close attention to the movements of the manna over the hillside. After carefully ensuring that they were not encumbered by the draining effects of the sapping circles beneath them, I worked to weave them into its empowering aura. It was a partially experimental effort; they seemed perceptibly heartened and energetic, but I cannot be certain as to whom that credit is owed, be it my machinations or their own strong spirits, or both.

Certainly an event which proved beneficial to their morale was the arrival of reinforcements - of the *living* variety. One of the messengers had returned, bringing with him a contribution of one-hundred men from Westfæsten. The locals were especially exhilarated to receive them, for they are known to be from one of the most war-ready hundreds within the whole of Cemparīċe. The constant threat of

Sjórvǫrðr incursion has hardened them against the menace of invasion. They are well armed and disciplined to an extent that far exceeds that of Stilneshire's other militias. If any men might hold the line against the Arx, it is the ones from Westfæsten, veterans already of numerous battles and skirmishes.

I saw Alton approach their number and discuss something with them. Something which visibly shook them. Then, one individual broke away from the party to approach me. I attempted to compose myself and brought the reeve closer, ready to speak through him. But, as he neared the summit and eyed the two of us, and my retinue especially, with suspicion, this is what he said:

"Necromancer. I don't pretend to know why you've come to the aid of these poor folk, but I wish to thank you all the same. Understand, my companions will follow my orders, but they don't fully trust you. Please... don't make me regret my decision to do so."

Before I was able to formulate a reply, Irwin (the Westfæsten leader's name, as I learned only later) gave a quick bow and turned to rejoin his company. Awestruck by his forthrightness, I could do nought but watch as he and his men immediately set to assisting the locals with the shoring of their defences.

More of Stilneshire's subsidiaries came to answer the call to arms. The next to arrive was a group from Beorgweġ Hundred, to the south. Their showing was less auspicious, falling short of their target by almost half and bringing only fifty-eight men, blaming a disappointing harvest and an unwillingness to fight the Arx for their low attendance. They appeared almost ready to flee as Alton informed them of recent happenings, but they stayed themselves and settled in, starting fires to cook their meals over. They sent no delegate to speak with me.

The men from Trēodæl to the north and Ġeolwæt to the north-east arrived somewhat later, past midday. The former, with their faces painted in patterns of blue woad as a nod to their Caillic neighbours, brought eighty-four reasonably armed men, while the latter, plainer hundred brought another seventy-six. Of these two groups, only the leader of the Trēodæl party came to talk with me.

"Leafbrym bade us trust your words and deeds, Death-Lord," he said cryptically. "She foretold that you are to become Marwos' Avatar."

Being hardly a firm believer in oracles and prophecy, I simply nodded at him with approval and expressed gratitude for their support. Even among the rest of Stilneshire's people, those from Trēodæl are considered to be 'strange folk'. Not untrustworthy, but perhaps more akin to their Caillic cousins than they are to their Sūþeardic ones. Alton later informed me that it was not typical behaviour for them to don the warpaint when answering a summons.

The evening dragged on and night began to fall, and there was growing concern for the absence of any word from Sceoppaton. The people feared the worst had befallen that hundred, and those fears were soon confirmed by the returning messenger, Galan. He reported to me directly, portraying that the Arx had arrived there shortly before he had. He described the destruction as complete and unsparing, and that there would be nothing at all to bring back. Though he spoke of his experience only to me, the others were easily able to deduce the sum of what had come to pass.

The grand total of Gerefwīc's living defenders, then, could be counted at two-hundred and ninety-seven (for Betlic had taken twenty men during his departure). The shortfall was noticeable even as the mists had dissipated in the sunlit hours, the inadequacy of their numbers fully realised, and their already fragile morale was further impugned. Our thin army will doubtlessly continue to shrink as militiamen and their families slip away in the night, seeking to escape an unwinnable battle. I was fearful that the defence would break before it could be tested, even. If the Arx had razed Sceoppaton today, then their forces would come here tomorrow. Stilneshire's collective spirits were balanced on a knife's edge, and inspirational words for them I had none.

Thankfully, fortune did not utterly abandon us. A blasting horn announced the arrival of allies from further afield and, as they marched into the basin from the southern road, many began to cry out in joy at the coming of Ealdorman Heorot. His forces were small; only himself and a bodyguard of fifty men, but all were unmatched in the quality of their armour, their skill, and their strength of arms. Alton reconvened with Ewin and I, preparing to meet the ealdorman and explain the current arrangement. Several people, including the leaders of the hundreds' forces, approached him to personally pledge their fealty to him; and when he did eventually climb the hill, he did so with his bodyguard and a consternative disposition.

"Reeve Ewin. Alton. What is the meaning of this?" he interrogated them, glancing behind us at the row of skeletal warriors, and at me. "Is it as the townsfolk say? Have you truly aligned yourself with this... *necromancer?*"

"It is true, Ealdorman," said the un-dead reeve. "He offered us aid in our time of need. He is a friend. *And, Heorot,*" he whispered, "*you know him.*"

"*Impossible,*" the ealdorman hissed, though he sounded uncertain. "I have known no necromancers."

"O but you have, Ealdorman Heorot," I corrected him. "At least one, I can assure you. And it would be this one's honour to lend his abilities to the hero who stood against the Arx so valiantly for the sake of a single, innocent man."

I bowed low to him, the realisation of my identity dawning on his face in the unsteady torchlight.

"I *do* know you, friend of Ewin, and I once judged you to be an honourable man. But now, revealed to me as a necromancer, I know not what to think!"

"I have had a... *regrettable* past, Ealdorman. I wish only to make what amends I can to those that matter, and to deny those that would enact injustices upon them."

Heorot came close to me then, speaking almost directly into my ear, his susurrations barely audible through the fabric of my hood.

"It is because of my prior familiarity with you, Necromancer, that I do not slay you now. But your presence here, be it noble, may be our only way to transmute victory from martyrdom. Know that if I see treachery on your part, I shall see to it that you fall, *personally.*"

"We have an accord, Ealdorman Heorot, and you have my highest respect. I swear, you will find no such action necessary."

I bowed low once again. He backed away slightly, recomposed himself and returned to his usual demeanour of confidence and conviction.

"Where is that promising young boy; Bayldon. Is he present?" he called out cheerfully.

"Bayldon was killed, Ealdorman, Sir," Alton answered sadly. "Quite a bit's happened while you've been gone. The Arx aren't the

314

only ones that've been nipping at our heels, so to speak. Come on, I'll fill you in on it, and the plan, and we'll leave Reeve Ewin and the necromancer to talk things over."

Heorot nodded, and Alton led him away to narrate some of the previous fortnight's events to him. The innkeeper had successfully read my sense of unease and rescued me from further awkwardness. I must remember to thank him. Controlling the reeve so minutely demanded impeccable concentration, and I was not accustomed to such public exposure. In fact, such a thing is completely unprecedented, for a necromancer to be acting openly in defence of a settlement.

No good will come of it, probably, I laughed to myself.

I decided to perform one more experiment before I retired into the mausoleum and awaited news. From my belongings I retrieved the amber device, the 'Mask of Marwos' as the witch had called it. After confirming my solitude, I uncovered my head and held the thing to my face, looking up at the bright moon currently nearing its apex position. The mask did indeed reveal a unique phenomenon to me; the so-called 'Gelach-manna' leapt from the astral body in caressing tendrils of shimmering particles, like gold dust panned from a riverbed and flowing downstream towards Pænvicta. It was somehow comforting to see the invisible energies that were long theorised to exist by wizards, mages and philosophers alike, yet I could not, and still cannot, understand their specific relevance to myself. Perhaps the mysteries will be solved in tomorrow's moonlight. That is, if we can only survive what the day before it brings.

Sōlrest-Þridda-XXX

...

A woman, flaxen-haired and fair-skinned, lies in a bloodstained bed. She is pale and exhausted from her ordeal. Yet on her face is a look of unshakeable contentment, for she has emerged victorious, and now holds in her arms the fruit of her labours; a newborn, still covered in the fluids of birth. It is only a few moments since he was screaming, but he has finally settled into the warm comfort of its mother's breast. The attending midwife, after cursively assuring the health of both parent and child, leaves them in peace. Just as their eyelids begin to droop, a voice echoes down the corridor.

"My wife! Is she here? Do I have a son?" *calls a man in fluent (if frantic) Arcāna. Evidently pointed in the correct direction, the rattle of layered steel precedes his arrival.*

The man walks into the nursery with a broad grin. He is young and handsome, with sleek, black hair, neatly cropped but dishevelled from sweat. His shining plate harness is defaced with nicks and dents, and both gauntlets are coated with gore, the left one still clutching a crested helmet. The baby cries immediately at the sight of him.

"Go take off armour! You scare him!" *scolds the mother. Her Arcāna is imperfect and heavily accented with Caillic intonations.*

"Why? If he is to be my son, he should come to know the smell of heretic blood!" *he laughs.*

"I think he does already, no?" *she derides him.*

"Silence! You submitted to Sōlis Mūnus when you submitted to me, remember? You owe my your life. And your obedience."

"Yes..." *the mother concedes, defeated and dejected.*

"Good! Now, let me hold my beautiful son!" *demands the father eagerly.*

The man scoops up the baby in his free hand, supporting its neck carefully in the angle of his elbow. As it calms, its eyes open to reveal corneas of emerald green, like its mother's. Not an Arx trait, but it pleases the Ultor regardless; it was those eyes that first drew him to her, and now they could serve as a mark of conquest, of the superiority of Arx Turrium.

"He is flawless," observes the father, bursting with pride. "I have a name for him; Ultiō. That is what we shall call him!"

The mother looks visibly upset. The name is a word with which she is familiar, one commonly recurring in Arcāna speech, especially in the sermons she is forced to attend. Vengeance. *Inwardly, she finds it hateful; a name which predestines a continuation of his father's violence. Yet she is powerless to protest, and unwilling to be reminded again, in no uncertain terms, that his wishes are absolute.*

"Then Ultiō he will be, my love!" she agrees, her manner sweet, her smile adoring. A practiced illusion.

I have heard reports from Ilibanese physicians of individuals who, approaching death, recount their life piecemeal as it flashes before them. What is one's soul shedding their body if not death? Thus am I here, at the convergence of my beginning and, likely, my end. At when and to where will be my next, and last, step?

...

So have we come to the day of Stilneshire's reckoning. For posterity I shall record today's events as thoroughly as I am able, though I may have to do so incrementally, for obvious reasons.

It is not yet dawn. Needless to say, I have neither ascended, nor has Arx Turrium set foot in the basin thus far. Everything is in place; the non-combatants have been safely harboured in a secure location, the more mundane defences have been erected, and the necromantic ones are readied and hidden, kept as traps to be sprung on our unsuspecting foes. I can only hope that the cowardly Captain Betlic has not acted the spy and cheated us of our element of surprise. A part of me regrets his survival. Perhaps I should have had the barrow-riders run them down outside the hundred's limits, but I would not risk them being spotted; they will be of greater potential use if widely considered to be absent.

In fact, there are a plethora of special measures which, enabled by my supernaturally tireless body, I have laboured through the night to emplace.

Firstly, the Blood-Marked have now been raised in their totality. I do not know precisely how many now line the catacombs' passages and await their orders but, including those who were already ambulatory, there must be close to one-hundred.

Secondly, the soil of the graveyard is primed, the corpses beneath ready to burst forth at a whim. Being not the strongest combatants (possessing little in the ways of armour, effective weaponry or skill, and matching themselves against soldiers solidly rounded in all three of those fields) their utilisation will be threefold: some will erupt directly under the sabatons of the Arx to create a quagmire of grasping hands, snagging and tripping the interlopers; others will be raised to envelop the opposition on every exposed flank, surrounding and pressing them, hindering any efforts to fall back and regroup. A few un-dead, of course, may be used to bolster the numbers of the defenders, but for this the skeletons of the mausoleum are better suited, being superior warriors and considerably less... *distracting*... for the militiamen to fight beside.

Thirdly, as briefly mentioned, those from the barrows of Stilneshire's countryside will come to sow death and disorder among the enemies of their distant descendants. Even *I* am unsure of their exact count, but their lancers and scythed chariots will surely inflict untold mayhem upon the enemies' ranks whatever their quantity. Their charge will come when the Arx are fully entrenched, the immaculate organisation of the servile un-dead allowing for the fodder to part with impeccable timing. No momentum, then, will be wasted, and the invaders will feel the full impact of a Sunþrardic mounted assault.

Lastly, with the headstones having been moved as I had instructed, the effectiveness of my secret armament has been significantly increased. Within the charnel pit there-

I have just heard a cornu's call. The Arx have announced themselves. I must go.

...

At the first light of dawn, the Arx column marched on horseback from the east road and into Gerefwīċ's basin. Like a shining steel beast of many legs, their ranks coiled and cornered down the path this way and that, fierce drums keeping their white stallions in step, before eventually stopping to establish a camp some distance away.

There were gasps and prayers uttered among the defenders as the knights filed over the basin's rim, for it was not three, but *five-hundred*. *Five-hundred* men they have brought, all bearing the rank of 'Ultor' or greater. These are the Coercitōrēs' seniors, transcending their title of *enforcer* and reaching that of *avenger*. The 'Arx Ultōrēs' seldom leave the citadel, but do so for the sake of waging war on the unfaithful. In comparison to the Coercitōrēs, the Ultōrēs are better equipped, better trained, and yet more fervent in their fanaticism.

From this fearsome warband came forth a rider alone; a herald, seeking to parley with the garrison's leader. His segmented armour glinted like fire as it reflected the light of the rising sun, and he did indeed seem glorious in his appearance. After being granted entrance, he addressed the gathering openly, his loud, clear voice carrying well, but his message was not a welcome one.

"Men of Stilneshire! By the holy order of Sōlis Mūnus, and in the name of Sōl itself, you are to lay down your arms. Surrender yourselves to us and you may be forgiven for your transgressions. Do not, and you redouble your sins. Choose carefully; your toils tomorrow may save your lives today."

"A life of toil under the whips of Arx Turrium is no life at all, says I!" called out Ealdorman Heorot in reply. "I would choose death first!"

A wave of murmurs swept through the crowd, an even mixture of doubt and consensus. It had been noted that Captain Betlic and his companions in flight were conspicuously absent, and unspoken questions of their fates lurked in peoples' minds. Had they been given their freedom? Had they been slain or enslaved? The herald's offer was tempting, but none could forget the temple's truly vitriolic and deceptive nature.

"This dog of a man does not speak for all of you. Come forth, repentant ones, and save yourselves and your families from a dire and pointless end."

This time, his phrasing elicited a more unified response. Jeers and profanities began as grumbles before growing into a veritable din of defiant taunting. More than one stone was hurled at the messenger, their impacts marked by a noisy clattering as his armour deflected them harmlessly. Evidently seeing no need to pursue the hollow appeal any longer, he spun his animal about, trotting back to their camp to confirm his entreaty's predictable results.

At present, the Arx's attack force is loitering outside the reach of our missiles, the most prominent of their number assembled, likely to conduct their strategy. We await only their next move.

...

The skies are cloudless and of a vivid aquamarine tint; bright and clear, far from the prophesied 'darkest day' whose arrival was to mark my rebirth. Perhaps it is a mere metaphor. What choice do I have but to wait and hope?

The Ultōrēs have decided to fight on foot. A logical conclusion for them to reach. Our palisade and the shield wall behind it would make a cavalry charge, even an Arx one, a precarious undertaking. A line of spears is seldom best met head-on, especially by horses, so they have dismounted and advanced in formation; just as we had predicted.

During their close-order march to the entrance, they were pelted with a variety of projectiles. Slingstones, arrows and javelins fell upon them like a hailstorm, but proved only as devastating as a shower of light rain. They carry no shields as their armour is all but impervious to such flimsy, impersonal weaponry, and they themselves scorn such tactics. They must have thought us demoralised as we quickly yielded the entryway, allowing them to lay their own bridges across the trench and dismantle a portion of the fence with ease.

Against a more numerous force, they might have assumed, *the correct strategy would be to hold the narrow space. In surrendering it, the smaller party leaves itself open to the full strength of the larger one's numbers.*

In ordinary circumstances, this would be good reasoning. They were soon to realise, however, that their situation was not as they had first thought. They engaged with the militia immediately, certain that their foe's mistake had guaranteed them an easy victory.

Unlike the rabble of Stilneshire, the Ultōrēs indulge in no battle-chants or war-cries, but those not actively fighting instead sing a continuous, droning Arcāna chorus of litanies and protective prayers. It is both maddening and intimidating to hear; but on this day we have managed to break their stride. The ground trembled as masses of un-dead excavated themselves from their resting places. From my peak I saw several Ultōrēs dragged to the ground and restrained. One of their officers, mounted so as to provide them a better perspective of the battlefield, was pulled from his saddle by the newly arisen flankers which multiplied about their formations in expanding rings. There was confusion, then; turmoil within their ranks as they came to understand the character of their enemy's reinforcements.

"*Necromantor! Necromantorem habent!*" came a shocked cry in Arcāna. For the first time since they had arrived, the Arx Ultōrēs were shaken.

The defenders gave some ground, allowing the skeletons who now poured from the mausoleum beside me to filter through the dense throng and meet the front line. Some were kept by my side as a precautionary measure - Rēdawulf, Ermunahild, Haþuwīgą and Audaward - but the others joined the fray imbued with a lust for carnage. In the carefully manufactured chaos of the fighting, I saw then a few of the Ultōrēs die, their plate harnesses defeated by lucky blows from farming implements or skilful ones from spears, swords and axes. Those of the Westfæsten and Trēodæl Hundreds are performing remarkably, but the most effective warriors are Heorot's men and the Blood-Marked. The others, being inexperienced in combat, are faring poorly. The rate of their losses is hard to estimate, but the un-dead within their number is proliferating rapidly.

"How's it going? Well?" asked Alton nervously, panting from his uphill sprint.

"I was contemplating whether to pose the same question to you, my friend," I answered to his dismay.

Spying a mounted Arx officer deep within their formation, I noticed that his visor was lifted as he shouted encouragement to his men. His emboldening words were brought to a sudden, abrupt end when he was struck in the face by a long-shafted arrow, loosed expertly from the bow of Rēdawulf. Alton cheered the man's demise, and I chuckled to myself as the others of his commission promptly lowered their visors.

Despite Haþuwīgą's desperate attempts at healing the wounded, the ever-increasing multitude of un-dead to animate was beginning to drain me. I stumbled as another surge of manna ebbed from my body, but was caught by Alton before I collapsed entirely.

"You can't give up now. Come on mate, these folk need you!" he pleaded, his voice trembling with panic.

"I must recover. The un-dead will fight on, but I must refocus myself."

"What do you need?"

"Take me into the crypt. There is a nexus there; you will recognise it when you set eyes on it. Place me within its circle."

"I got you. Come on! Here we go!" he said as he put my arm over his shoulder, carrying me into the mausoleum's depths.

Ermuna held a torch to light the way for him, but it proved barely necessary beyond the second corner. The manna nexus, which had formed organically about the dominant sapping circle, was blindingly bright to the extent that Alton was compelled to avert his gaze in its vicinity. It was only with trepidation that I allowed him to place me into its core, for I was convinced that I would be destroyed by the torrents of energy within; but I was unscathed, granted resilience by my partial transformation. Crackling bolts of errant manna flashed about me, but my invigoration was instantaneous and powerful. The phenomenon was too frightening for Alton to tolerate, and he did not delay his departure when I assured him that I could be safely left alone.

From here I am interconnected with the happenings above through a network of energy. Akin to a spider on its web, I can detect the changes like subtle pulses in the manna's flow...

There. An anomaly. An alteration of impetus. My presence is required.

...

Thus charged by the vortex beneath the graveyard, I emerged from the mausoleum with fresh potency. However, it was instantly clear that the situation had deteriorated. The Ultōrēs had surmised that the only way to stem the un-dead tide was to slay its master; their objectives had been amended, then, from the total annihilation of the resistance, to a targeted push towards the necromancer in their midst. To this end they had allowed their formation to narrow into a tight circle, and so meticulously were they drilled that they could advance in the mausoleum's direction and still maintain the shape's coherency. They were variously armed, but organised in such a way that those with shorter weapons (like bastard swords, maces and warhammers) bordered those with longer ones (including pollaxes, halberds and greatswords), providing mutual protection. This strategy was proving terrifically effective, and many were cut down, skewered and trampled on their steady but inexorable path. Only the repositioning of the defence's most capable fighters from the flanks to the fore had slowed them, but our casualties were surely massing.

I had to act decisively if I was to stall or reverse the battle's outcome. Fortunately, the enemies' close order had left them vulnerable to my covert siege device. I strode to the charnel pit and poured forth all the manna I could muster. The ground heaved as the deposition of countless disarticulated bones reconnected into weird and novel forms, combining and refining themselves in the soil until the machine of my intention was perfected. What finally burst from the pit when the process culminated was nothing if not *art*.

Standing thirty feet tall and anchored firmly in the hole from whence it came, this masterpiece of a Construct takes the shape of a monstrous *arm* (topped with an array of writhing, tentacular digits), built exclusively from the remains of the charnel pit. Longbones, ribcages, vertebrae and grinning skulls all contributed to its horrifying structure. It moves with astounding fluidity and speed, and with its enormous size would be capable of brutalising anything within its reach. But that is not its primary function; instead, it uses its vast strength and leverage to propel massive objects - the collected headstones, to be exact - at long distance and high velocity. An un-dead trebuchet, for which the Arx Ultōrēs were ill-prepared.

The first headstone's collision was delivered with a sickening report. The crunch of steel plates and limbs alike being smashed apart, the agonised wailing of the third and only surviving victim. It is not common practice to assign a *name* to such a Construct, but I overheard a mocking chant sung by the remaining men of Trēodæl Hundred to the traumatised Ultōrēs. Its lyrics went something like this:

"Know death's name! Know death's name! The Hand of Marwos beckons you!"

Each syllable was accompanied by a unified striking of their own shield bosses, and for once the Arx-men seemed dispirited. The concept of a foreign god manifesting itself against them seemed to erode their usually unshakeable confidence. I could not resist the adoption of the Trēodæl militia's byname for my skeletal amalgamation, so it henceforth came to be known among the defenders as 'The Hand of Marwos'. Its following two throws were of a similar violence to the first; those afterwards were mitigated somewhat by a loosening of the Ultōrēs' formation. But this, too, was an aspect of my plan.

As the un-dead siege engine did its work, the Sunþrardic barrow-men trickled into the basin, clearing their camp of any Sōlis adherents who had been left there to guard it. Then they formed up into a wedge, readied themselves, and stampeded towards the rear of the Ultōrēs. Perplexity overtook the caudal invaders as the un-dead they were engaged with suddenly scrambled to either side, parting like a pair of gigantic double doors; but that was quickly replaced by startled realisation as the skeletal cavalry thundered through the opening towards them. The wedge reached the line, a long-dead chieftain driving an ornate, scythe-wheeled chariot as its point, and swept into the spaces between the infantry. As they went, those with swords cut this way and that, their pace adding weight to their blows. Those with lances shattered them on the heads and chests of their foes, sending many a man crashing limply to the ground. More still fell victim to the spinning, bladed wheels of the chariots, which broke and sliced through legs to leave a trail of crippled men in its wake. The un-dead horses themselves behaved with a supernatural aggression; kicking, biting and trampling any that had not been slain by their riders.

Deep into the enemy lines they sank, but that is not to say they did so unopposed. Upon losing some of their momentum, they became susceptible to the Ultōrēs' pole-arms especially, and those that were not brought down by collaborative efforts were driven back. This was to be expected. I withdrew them and shall repeat the exercise, beating them over and over like a blacksmith's hammer striking an anvil. Perhaps, this way, I can break the back of their army.

"Nice move. I can't believe these bastards are still fighting," said Alton. In my state of concentration, his approach went quite unnoticed and I was jolted back to my immediate surroundings.

"Of whom do you speak? The men from Arx Turrium, or from Stilneshire?"

"Both, if I'm honest!" he affirmed. "But those Arx-men... what's it take to rattle *them*? What do they *teach* them at that *damned citadel*?"

"That to be defeated is to be excommunicated; to them, a fate worse than death," I shrugged. "Sōl supposedly devours the souls of heathens, and of those who fall from his graces. To show cowardice before a heathen is to share their fate."

"I see," remarked Alton contemplatively. "Gods, if there's one man on this field I'd love to show some fear, it's *him*."

As he spoke, he pointed to the front of the attackers' formation. There, resplendent in his familiar decorated wargear, was Episcopus Urbānus, his sword matched against Ealdorman Heorot's; but the encounter seemed to be transpiring unfavourably for the latter party. Heorot's Mēċe was ill-suited against Urbānus' steel harness. As I watched, transfixed by their expert swordplay, I saw a mortal blunder committed by the ealdorman. Urbānus had grasped his opponent's blade in one gauntlet, the other raising his longsword to aim a lethal thrust.

"*No!*" cried Alton.

My intervention was reflexive, direct, and in essence, simple. I channelled the raging seas of manna which flowed over the battlefield, every stream and strand I could gather in that split second, and injected it into the Episcopus' body. Urbānus was demonstrably capable in the crafts of war, but in magic he was uninitiated; and to all who were within his sight, I exhibited the perils of manna oversaturation.

The effect was instantaneous. Urbānus' scream was mortifying as he released his grip on both swords, tearing the sallet from his head and trying frantically to unlace the armour as it began to glow with heat. Allies and enemies alike backed away from him and stopped to observe the gruesome spectacle. Steam billowed from his skin and the seams of his metal shell. Boiling blood poured from his eyes, nose, mouth and ears, and his shrieks died with him as his armour began to deform and fold, sealing to his body. Urbānus burst into flames even as he fell; a pile of molten steel and charred flesh. The Ultōrēs previously at his side shrunk away, indecisive of how to respond to their leader's hideous and unanticipated passing. Heorot turned his head to us, raising his sword-arm in acknowledgement and, possibly, gratitude.

"Well, that was hard to watch!" commented Alton, who then appeared rather sickly. "Can't say there wasn't a part of me that enjoyed it, mind."

"It was taxing. See the un-dead; they are becoming sluggish! I must replenish myself," I bemoaned, burdened with guilt for my repetitious absence.

"We can't afford for those things to slow down, they're all that's keeping us from getting trounced. Go do what you need to; I'm going down there to see if I can't squeeze a few more drops of fight out of Ġeolwǣt, or what's left of them, anyway!"

With that, Alton left me to my own devices. To execute someone in that way is *drastically* inefficient. The Hand of Marwos had stalled, exhausted of its driving energies and heaving at the stones ineffectually. I staggered, faint and unsteady, down the stairs of my lair. Here I shall recuperate as best I can, but I dare not overstay lest the battle conclude without me.

...

Hunters! I know now the method with which Sōlis Mūnus disposes of troublesome spellcasters!

As I knelt within the manna's convergence, my eyes closed to better perceive the vicissitudes above, I felt... *something*... close to me. Immunised to the temperatures though I was, a ghastly cold - a pervasive *emptiness*, a *void* - emanated from the presence and drilled to my core. I reacted instinctively, swatting at the air with my bare hand. Had I not been at that time a conduit for incalculable energies, it would have been a frail and insufficient response. As it was, however, the dark being was flung back with unfathomable destructive force, shaking the catacomb's very foundations as it met the terminal wall. My body shook and my ears rang from the reverberations, and a vile scent drifted from the pulverised remains of the creature. It was as if a butcher had tossed a bucket of festering offal against a wall, but the parts within the stinking vestiges were quite unrecognisable. Shining ebony plates, like outsized beetle-shells, lay in fragmented shards among the viscous yellow substance which now dripped from every surface. Having walked over to inspect the strange thing, I was almost too late to notice the *other*; it was man-shaped, and I initially took it to be one of the heavily armoured Ultōrēs, albeit coated with slick, black oil so as to be nearly invisible in the gloom. Having already mutely dispatched Ewin's remains with a flurry of exacting punctures (likely interpreting him as a living adversary), it then scrutinised my phylactery, reaching its gauntlets towards it, somehow yet undetected by my servants. In a fit of dread and rage I set my un-dead to slaying it, and as they leapt forwards, the torchlight allowed me to see the creature properly for the first time.

An Arx knight it was, or some abhorrent facsimile of one. A segmented carapace mimicked the plates of a steel harness, but the organic joints allowed it to move in relative silence. It replaced the phylactery, hopping nimbly away from its aggressors and towards the Hinthial Sceptre. As it did so, a second set of spindle-like arms unfolded from its back and pivoted about its elbows, sweeping upwards to be clasped in the hands of its larger primary arms. These limbs terminated in vicious points like a pair of chitinous rapiers, incomprehensibly sharp and wielded with all the speed and precision of a predatory insect.

The skeletons rushed to their quarry, empowered with the needful agility to intercept the creature before it could reach the dangerous artefact. Ermunahild raised her shield in time defend against an impaling stab, but it was of little use; the deadly limb penetrated the wooden barrier with ease, piercing through the back of her skull before coming to a halt. Fortunately, such an injury is scarcely debilitating to the un-dead, and the ancient shield-maiden retaliated by sweeping her sword through the offending implement's joint, severing it and the arm which held it. Hemolymph drooled from the wound as the section below its elbow dropped away. I stared in fascinated horror as that which I had taken as a bevor bisected itself, revealing a collection of palpitating mouthparts beneath as the thing chittered in pain - or fury. With one sinuous leg it kicked, the clawed foot springing out like a loosed crossbow and bludgeoning Ermuna's midsection with terrible might. It was enough to send her remains hurtling into every corner of the corridor. The creature was wholly unaffected by my sapping circle's aura, but I redoubled the investments into the other three un-dead, pressuring them to match the abomination's own feats. Rēdawulf dashed forth and bodily tackled it, closing his arms around it in an attempt to restraint the thing. Its strength was matchless and it broke free, detaching both of the archer's arms; but the misdirection had held it long enough for Audaward to swing his hefty ax sideways and into its thorax. The blow split the monster through the middle, separating its legs from its torso. The former thrashed and flailed wildly as they fell, but the rest of the creature dragged itself along the ground, trying again to reach the Hinthial Sceptre. Audaward, like a headsman, raised his ax high and brought it down on its neck, dividing it. The monster's head rolled free, its mandibles opened in a soundless scream, and it was, at last, finished.

Reeling from the surreality of the attack, I had Haþuwīgą lift the disembodied head from the ground to inspect it closer, only to be horrified at the many-faceted obsidian eyes set behind the visor. The complex mouthparts now hung loosely as if half-disgorged.

What a thought, that such aberrations should share Pænvicta with us! I considered. Were they in league with Arx Turrium? Their timing certainly suggested that they were working in tandem, and their forms were deliberately reminiscent. But such a thing would never be accepted within the wider society of Sōlis Mūnus; the very visage of them would be detested, and they would be dismissed as demons or magicians' pets. And yet, what would be more efficient a killer of mages, those most hated heretics, than one so concealed to the spellcasters' attuned senses? Only fortunate circumstance had saved me, one singular moment from a swift death. Perhaps they are something employed in secret by the upper echelons of the Cursus Fideī, the Arx hierarchy... it is a matter that will have to be investigated, provided I am ever to receive an opportunity to do so.

Thoroughly disturbed by the implications of its existence, I could look no longer at my would-be killer; Haþu hurled the vile face as far as she could, and I had Audaward shift the other pieces out of sight. I hid the reeve's perforated body in one of the many empty sarcophagi, lest a prying militiaman discover it and make a regrettable and incorrect assumption. As I turned to rejoin the battle and tell Alton of my experience, however, I noticed something amiss where the first menace had been disintegrated. The sheer force of the collision had dented the wall and caused a few of the stones to tumble into a pile at its base. Behind them was not the compacted, sodden earth I had expected, but another chamber!

The cleverly disguised false wall had evidently been erected in order to conceal this final interment. I freed a few more of the stones and stepped through the hole, accompanied by my remaining bodyguard. This new chamber was nothing less than the tomb of a most auspicious individual, decorated as it was with banners, ornaments of gold and silver and hanging incense burners of a variety of different shapes; all surrounding the most beautiful and valuable artefact of all, the magnificent, mummified remains of Krumpą, whose true identity I now understand.

With the head, wings and talons of an immense bird of prey and the elongated tail of a great serpent, Krumpą was of an extinct type of legendary creatures known as the *Grȳphī*. Its carved likenesses, which I had once thought to be exaggerated, I then knew to fall short of justice; though its once vibrant plumage has greyed and its musculature had become thin and desiccated, it remained an impressive beast, posed as it was in its threatening stance. What could any self-respecting necromancer do but attempt to raise the majestic animal as his own?

Knowing that the undertaking would be drastic and that time was of the essence, I took up the Hinthial Sceptre without hesitation, confident in my ability to control its exponential manna flow. Within minutes, Krumpą's taxidermied corpse was twitching with the throes of un-death; a few minutes more, and the Grȳphus reared back, letting loose a deafening screech from its razor-honed beak. My skeletal servants and I stood aside as it roared past us to join the battle above. I followed behind, ultimately unable to keep pace with the ferocious beast... but most excited to see what violence it could visit upon our enemies.

My enthusiasm waned as I set foot on the surface, however. The Arx have reorganised themselves and pushed the defenders to the base of the hill, leaving the scattered pieces of their victims behind them. They have taken to dissecting their opponents as they fall to prevent any further danger from them, and they are now advancing with systematic ruthlessness. The un-dead at their back are all but depleted, and between the Ultōrēs and I were precious few; the number of those whose hearts still beat, I cannot say. Their numbers are rivalled, now, by the Blood-Marked in their ranks. I could see no sign of Alton.

The direction of my powers had to be refocused. The drain on the Ultōrēs must be intensified, and our men must be as gods in their toughness and indefatigability. The Hand of Marwos has emptied its surroundings of headstones and waits for its enemies to trespass into its radius, wherein it can protect the mausoleum. Haþuwīgą has been commanded to ride upon Krumpą just as she once had, mending our injured while her airborne mount plucks Arx-men from the ground, tearing them apart with its iron beak or releasing them from fatal heights. I pray it is enough, for there is now little I can do but weave my necromantic spells at the nexus and hope against the odds.

...

I must make this record hastily, as it may be my last. Alton flew down the stairs to retrieve me, panting heavily, an expression of abject terror on his face.

"Is this your doing? Is it?" he shouted to me.

"This is not the time for vagueness! Of what do you speak?"

"Come outside here and see, you idle prick!"

There was an urgency in his voice quite unlike any I had heard from him before, so I said no more and elected to accompany him immediately, pausing only to retrieve the Hinthial Sceptre and my phylactery (lest more of *them* come to destroy it). Around the corners and up the stairs we ran, and it was not until we arrived at the entrance that I perceived the unparalleled *darkness*. But it is not yet evening. Indeed, it is barely beyond midday! The sky, though still clear and now infinitely sable, is *utterly bereft* of stars. All that occupies it now is a thin, flawlessly circular ring of gleaming argent light. I realised, then, that *this* was the 'darkest day'; the moon's total eclipse of the sun, stealing the already scarce daylight of late Sōlrest.

My mind raced. I was distantly aware of Alton's railing, but I ignored him and took the Mask of Marwos from the recesses of my robes, placing it over my face. This I saw; as the sun's rays crept around the moon's circumference, they acquired new colours, new mannerisms, new diffractions... and there, distilling from these unique energies, the ethereal form of an Arch-Lich - *my* form - is materialising.

But how am I to transfer my consciousness? I was shaken from my stupor by Alton, who was indicating frantically that the Arx Ultōrēs were moments away from breaking through the line.

"I hope you've got another trick or two up those sleeves, mate, because they're coming!"

"I may have one more, Alton. Have the others fall back to the hilltop; then Marwos' Hand will help them," I demanded. "Afterwards, join me in the mausoleum. Go!"

Alton sprinted down to the fighting to convey my message. I, meanwhile, have situated myself and my phylactery behind the crypt's gate. The clamour of the fighting comes ever closer. The indistinct shape of the Arch-Lich beside me is visible, now, to the naked eye; it grows in volume and definition like a sculpture of arcane mist.

But how to make it mine! Am I simply to wait until the transfer is complete? Am I missing some final, elusive ritual? How can one's soul be stripped from one's body...?

Of course... *of course*! I shall meet the Arx yet, and it is through me that they will come to know death's true name. Vengeance! Vengeance! Vengeance!

EPILOGUE

"The Grave the last sleep?-no; it is the last and final awakening."

- Sir Walter Scott

The King's Hall at Bēagshire is, without competition, the finest architectural accomplishment of Sūþeard. Though it would pale in comparison to the magnificence of the great temples of Arx Turrium, it has no equal outside the citadel; its main chamber stretches back one-hundred feet and forty across. The floor is paved in slabs, covered with the most luxuriously patterned carpets of scarlet and flaxen yellow, and the ashlar walls exhibit a series of intricate tapestries depicting the old heroes of Cemparīċe, and gods whose names have long faded into obscurity. Central to the chamber is an enormous brazier of etched and polished bronze, at present containing a roaring flame. A gift from Arx Turrium named the 'Sōlis Crucibulum', it is an undeniably beautiful ornament, bringing light and warmth to the King's Hall; though these are secondary functions. Its true purpose is to remind onlookers of the Arx's divine radiance - and, by extension, the darkness that would ensue without them.

The royal guard are lined either side of the hall, clad in polished helmets and coats of shining mail, their shields bearing the king's colours and hawk-head insignia. At the end of the chamber, a raised platform stands overlooking the rest of the room. Upon it is a company of archers, bows in hand. All are present to protect, at current, three men, who sit silently in tiered seats.

The foremost man on the simple folding stool is the King's Champion. His name is Tilian, though most know better his epithet 'The Dreadnought'. He is a veritable beast of a man, tall and broad, a hoary bearskin draped across his shoulders. His black-bearded face is a lattice of battle-scars, and his brow is frozen into a permanent glower. Serving as the king's personal guardian, spymaster and prize warrior all, few men would dare his wrath by issuing threat or insult to the king; for though he appears in every part the brute, Tilian is, in fact, both remarkably intelligent and fiercely loyal to his liege.

Sitting in an ornate golden throne is, of course, King Ricbert. Though his vivid, silken attire boasts his immense wealth and (supposed) power, the image is betrayed by the demeanour of the man himself. The inscribed ceremonial half-helm and neatly trimmed silver kemp do little to hide the wrinkled, worry-ridden face beneath. He alternately hunches and slumps in obvious discomfort, drumming his fingers on the throne's armrest.

Behind him, in a chair of carved marble, sits the elderly Volesus. He is both the Royal Advisor to the King and holds the Sōlis Mūnus office of *Sinister Sānctī*, the so-called left hand of the Living Saint (*Vīvus Sānctus*) Apollo. His grand robe is of the purest white, and a matching wide-brimmed hat sits above his cleanly shaved head and face. His velvet-gloved hands rest atop a lengthy aureate cane, a symbol of his high position. The stance adopted by Sinister Sānctī Volesus is everything the king's is not: quietly confident; self-assured; arrogant.

The trine were awaiting the arrival of an emissary for whom they were to hold an audience. Except they were late. *Very* late. And to keep the King of Cempariće waiting is generally considered to be unwise.

"Perhaps they are not coming, my lord," Volesus mutters in Ricbert's ear. "Perhaps we should retire. It is quite dark. Could they not come tomorrow?"

"Who is this untimely bunch, anyway? They'd better be worth the trouble," grumbles Tilian.

"And must I inform you both of every visitor who plans to grace my hall? If you *must* know, among them is one of my own ealdormen, Heorot of Stilneshire, bringing honoured guests and important news from his county," scolds Ricbert irately. "And from what I understand, they've come far and fast - so I am *certain*, gentlemen, that you can find patience enough for them to *compose* themselves. In case you have *quite* forgotten, you enjoy the warm shelter of my Hall while a storm rages! So stay your spiteful tongues, or I shall have you *both* stood outside as greeters!"

The Dreadnought grunts with bemusement. He knows Ricbert well enough to call his bluff. To annoy the king is something of an exclusive pastime; Tilian knows from experience how far he can push the monarch before he makes good on his threats. The fact is that Ricbert, at heart, is a kindly, soft man. To a fault, many would maintain.

Volesus, by contrast, raises his bald brow imperceptibly. He seems uncharacteristically concerned, and has done so since Stilneshire was mentioned. Nevertheless, the Sinister Sānctī says nothing.

A few awkward minutes later, a pair of guards push open the large oak doors, allowing the entrance of three men. The leading figure is so heavily cloaked that not his face, nor even an inch of skin, is visible. The man to his left wears a bloodied mail hauberk and a fine but warworn helmet. To his right is a stern-looking middle-aged man in a simple woolen tunic and trousers.

"Heorot! Good to see you, old friend!" King Ricbert smiles genuinely, standing to address his guests. "What news of your county? How goes the Sōlrest harvest?"

"The crop is lost, my liege. All of it, and much more besides," answers the ealdorman solemnly. "Your advisor, I expect, knows why."

"Is this true?" Ricbert turns, preparing to interrogate Volesus.

"I know not of what he speaks, King, but most probably he refers to the lies he is sure to conjure."

"So speaks the highest authority on lies," remarks the cloaked man. His voice bears an unpleasant, rasping quality, as if he is suffering some grave illness. This, in conjunction with his assiduous wrappings, leads some to postulate that he is a leper. "Come, Arx-man," he goes on, "conjure a lie for us."

With that, he pulls a small woven sack from within his clothes and tosses it to Volesus, who catches it reflexively. With curiosity, he unties the string which keeps it bound and glances inside. Wholly unperturbed, he looks back to the guests with sharpened sincerity.

"*Heretics.* You insult me with the presence of this vile counterfeit? I shall have you *all* destroyed."

"I think you tried that one already. At least, your mates did, anyway. Didn't go so well for them, and there were a fair few of them, too," taunts the commoner.

"What is he talking about, Heorot? What has happened?" Ricbert demands, growing increasingly exasperated.

"It is as he suggested, my liege. Arx Turrium has led an attack with the intent of razing Stilneshire," reiterates the ealdorman. "Many lives were lost, and the county has been occupied. The invaders, you may be pleased to learn, were, all of them, slain."

"Impossible. Impossible!" spits Volesus. "Your paltry peasant village would be scattered as shadows in the sunlight before the glory of Holy Arx Turrium!"

"You mean to tell me that your armies marched in my lands without my consent?" King Ricbert shouts with precipitous anger.

"This one marches still, Good King. Albeit, it now does so under another banner," comments the cloaked one.

"Did you not say that they were slain, Heorot?" pleads Ricbert, his anxiety and confusion continuing to escalate.

"I did. This is my trusted friend: Alton of Gerefwīċ. He can explain the events better than I," the ealdorman gestures to the commoner.

"Yes, spin us one of your 'tall tales', *peasant*," mocks Volesus. Tilian fixes the advisor with a vicious glare, which the latter repays with only a contemptuous smirk. The attention of chamber does, eventually, transition to Alton, whereupon he begins his narrative.

"Now I'm no bard, Good King, nor a messenger, so I'll make a long story short. The Arx reckon they're above our laws - *your* laws, your majesty - and pillaged their way across Cemparīċe to tell us as much. We were done for alright; even after the other hundreds, and Ealdorman Heorot's lot, came to help us, we had no chance. And we were desperate. So we... *I*, I mean. I guess I'm to blame for my part. Anyway, *I* reached out to a newcomer in Gerefwīċ, and begged him to save our skins. An old man he was, but as luck - good or bad luck, you might say - would have it, that man also happened to be a *necromancer*."

"Then I trust the Ultōrēs to have slayed it, just as they always have when dealing with such filth," yawned Volesus dismissively, "*and* those vermin who would associate with it."

King Ricbert does not heed the Sinister Sānctī, but is paralysed in rapt horror. His eyes move between Alton and the cloaked one, fearing the implications of what words might pass the commoner's lips next.

"Those Arx bastards *did* cut their way through us," Alton persists. "The best men of Stilnshire were all put down, Good King; most of their families are moving to greener pastures, so to speak. It's a dead county now."

"I see..." reflects Ricbert grimly, nervously running a bejewelled finger along the bridge of his nose. "And the necromancer...?" he asks with clear reluctance.

"I have a *name*, gentlemen," complains the shrouded individual in his hoarse, unsettling whisper.

There is a subtle shift in the chamber as the statement is heard and interpreted, though most find the conclusion difficult to accept. Was this a chancy attempt at humour? Was this walking pile of rags a danger to them? Volesus wastes no time in exploiting the confusion to make his wishes known.

"The necromancer is in our midst! Archers, let loose upon him before he murders all of us!"

"Wait, *stop*! Please! You do not understand...!" cries Ealdorman Heorot with unhinged despair.

None have ever seen the ealdorman, who has always been the very embodiment of courage, react so pusillanimously. Yet the royal guards are already apprehensive, and so they obey the order as it is given without pausing to question its origin; a hail of arrows is in the air even before the king can regain control of his men and cancel their volley. Heorot and Alton dive bodily in opposite directions to escape the deadly shower. The central figure, by contrast, makes no attempt to alter his fate; the archers chosen to defend the king are among the best, and a majority of the shafts find their mark.

The man falls backwards from the cumulative impact of the projectiles and, as his weight strikes the carpeted ground, the cowl drops from his shoulders to reveal the twisted face of an unknown, middle-aged man. However, it can be seen even from the distance of the throne that the person has been dead for some time. The flesh is swollen and discoloured a sickly, pale green, and the eyes are marred by black stains. The fresh punctures release a putrid miasma of rot into the hall, prompting spectators to cover their mouths and noses in surprise and disgust.

Alton, meanwhile, has disregarded the stench altogether, opting instead to cup his hands over his ears and shut his eyes tightly, remaining prone.

"Gods!" he laments, tearful with dread. "I really wish you hadn't gone and done that!"

Heorot rises to his feet but turns away, his head bowed low as if unwilling to see what is to come. Ricbert and Tilian look sideways at each other with incertitude. Volesus retains his usual conceited grin.

All are made to tremble, however, when a new voice echoes throughout the King's Hall. It is piercingly shrill in a manner unlike any thing which lives; more akin to the howling tempests of frostbitten mountains given speech. It carries with it a terrible chill, and no man who hears its words can help but cower. Yet it speaks not with outright malice, but only the raw energy of an immortal, godlike being, frightening for mortal ears to fathom.

You have, regrettably, elected to make this conversation more unpleasant for yourselves, the voice informs them. *Your recklessness will earn you no pity.*

As the weird presence orates, a shape coalesces in the air before them; a dense graveyard mist in a swirling, ephemeral form, the vaguest, transient suggestions of a skeletal visage and limbs endlessly waxing and waning. But one feature demonstrates permanence; twin eyes blaze perpetually, bright flares of manna glinting from the ethereal haze like lit torches in a field of fog.

Some of the guards flee the hall; others quail at the sight of the apparition. All shiver from the sudden cold, their breath emanating from their lips and noses as vapour, but only a select few know from the forbidden histories what manner of thing suspends itself thus.

"Velthur? Returned?" gasps King Ricbert, pointing at the apparition with panic and disbelief.

No, hisses the wind, *Velthur's nature I share, but not his name.*

"Tell me, unworldly thing, before we parley; is my kingdom doomed?"

Every kingdom is doomed, Good King. Time sees the end of all lineages. But the cessation of yours will not be my doing. I have another business to discuss.

"Such an abomination cannot be reasoned with!" harangues Sinister Sānctī Volesus, rising from his seat with indignation.

This transaction does not involve you, charlatan. Begone.

With a facile wave of the Arch-Lich's shimmering talon, the Royal Advisor is flung backwards by an invisible but potent force. He collides with his own marble chair painfully, shattering it and falling instantly unconscious. The ghostly being turns back to Ricbert purposefully.

I offer a trade, Good King. A military alliance, in exchange for a token offering. And your tolerance.

"But Cemparīče is not at war," interjects the king.

That is to be negotiated.

"Please, Necromancer-Lord! Do not draw this beleaguered kingdom into a war it cannot survive!" begs the king, his composure fracturing.

"My liege," calls the reeve, finally finding the mettle to turn and watch the debate, "Stilneshire County has paid a dire toll to teach us this lesson; Cemparīċe as we know it cannot survive *without* a war. Given time, the Arx-men will bleed your kingdom dry, if not figuratively, then literally."

Listen to your ealdorman, Good King. Cast off the yoke that is the Arx's dominion, for the welfare of your subjects. It will be no mean feat, but I shall help you, provided I have your cooperation.

"Dare I ask... at what cost can be purchased the allegiance of one so... *ascended*?" inquires the king. "What price must be paid?"

Firstly, the war effort will necessitate the creation of a thousand times a thousand soldiers. You will make these available to me with immediate effect.

"You are insane, Necromancer!" accuses Ricbert, incredulous. "The Kingdom of Sūþeard *before* its sundering could field no such army, and even the Cemparīċe territories themselves are but a shadow of what they once were. Are you truly so cruel as to have me send every man, woman and child to die under your banner?"

The Arch-Lich takes on a darker aspect then, its body broiling and its eyes burning furiously. The monarch shrinks into his throne.

No, mortal king. I shall not waste the lives of your men so carelessly as you have. Gerefwīċ is your own failing; under your rulership it has become a dwelling of death, and so I have annexed it for my own domain. To recognise this is my second condition. I trust there will be no dispute, the Arch-Lich stipulates, its voice that of a ferocious blizzard. Ricbert and Tilian are utterly awestruck and motionless; but the Arch-Lich takes a moment to temper itself, its intonations settling back to a frigid draught. *As for the first, Sūþeard does indeed possess such an army, its numbers swelling with every generation's passing and every battle fought on its soil. An army I alone can command.*

"Raise the dead from under the feet of their very descendants? If I agreed to those terms - if my assent became public knowledge - there would surely be an outcry. Uprisings, even-"

You are surrounded by sycophants, Good King, likely at the behest of your advisor. But the people are unkind and unforgiving, and you are not held in high esteem. In any case, I can see to it that you are well warded against treason and regicide.

"As shall I," adds the Dreadnought, "from *any* source, my liege."

"What is *your* opinion on all of this, Tilian?" the king rotates in his throne as if noticing him anew. "Have you dealt with things of this kind before? Can it be trusted?"

"I've *fought* a necromancer before, my liege. Can't say it was much fun, neither. We weren't exactly on speaking terms, so I can't really tell you if he was 'trustworthy' or not. What I *will* say is that necromancers are practiced deceivers. They have to be, or they'd be dead. That said," Tilian appends hesitantly, "the one I fought, the ones you hear about, are themselves flesh and bone. Not... *this*," he indicates the lurid shape of the Arch-Lich.

"You suppose it will behave differently?" queries the king.

"Well, maybe he thinks himself strong enough that he doesn't need to hide anymore. Then again, something tells me he must've been a bloody good liar to get where he is now..."

"Gentlemen!" Alton interrupts loudly. "Let me tell you; I knew the man when he still had a heartbeat. Maybe I could clear a few things up for you."

"By all means, tell us what you know," Ricbert encourages him. The commoner obliges his king, but what he says provides the monarch no solace.

"Right: first of all, yes, he *is* a liar. And he's an utter bastard, and a murderer too. But, so far as I can tell, he's trying to do right by us. He could have left us in the shit at Gerefwīċ, but he didn't. That's got to mean *something*. Secondly, it's hard for me to say, but I'll say it; you'd best just take the easy option and accept what he's offering. Believe it or not, he's doing it to be nice. Throwing you a bone, you could say. But if you don't give it to him, he'll take it. You're not able to stop him. No one is.

"So there's your choice. Every corpse in Cemparīċe is rising up against the Arx. It'll be the biggest revolt Pænvicta has ever seen. Will you stand aside... or stand in their way?"

The king and the Dreadnought sit, paralysed by the sobering revelation that their choice is merely illusory. The former mourns inwardly; yet another tyrant has come to stake their claim on his fragile kingdom. The latter, though none would know from looking, is making a mockery of his own byname. Both, in turn, attempt to read the emotions of the semimorphous entity which so torments them. But there is nothing there to be analysed; not face, nor expression, nor allusion of any sort. Only the occasional disturbing flash of a stripped, spectral skull within the mist, its bared teeth elongated into icicle-like fangs. Its soulless stare is mesmerising and resolute. There would be - *could be* - no recalcitrance.

"I yield, Necromancer," concedes Ricbert. "The kingdom yields. Its dead are yours to harness. I only ask that you and your followers have mercy on my subjects; that you do not make my failure complete."

Worry not, Good King. You have acted with wisdom this evening. Goodnight; you may await our messengers.

"Hold, Necromancer!" calls out Tilian as the Arch-Lich and its companions turn to leave.

Can I be of service to you, Dreadnought? the gale answers.

"What did you want us to do with *this one*?" asks the spymaster, approaching the crumpled heap of the Sinister Sānctī and nudging it with his boot. The latter produces a weak groan and stirs unresponsively.

What finer symbolic action could there be than that for which every ingredient has been provided?

A sadistic, wolfish grin spreads across Tilian's face. "I was hoping you'd say something like that," he growls, hefting the man onto his shoulder. Carrying him in this way, he strides between the Arch-Lich and the bewildered ealdorman, towards the Sōlis Crucibulum. Heorot and Alton realise what is transpiring and shield their eyes, but the Arch-Lich watches on intently as Tilian slings Volesus from his back and holds his face to the flames. The heat of it rouses him and he begins to scream, struggling ineffectually against the Dreadnought's iron grip. Soon, however, his breath is stolen by the fire as his skin peels away.

"Don't forget to let Sōl know who sent you to him, Arx-dog!" bellows Tilian as he hurls Volesus, flailing, into the pyre.

Satisfied, the Arch-Lich drifts over the smouldering, writhing form of the Sinister Sānctī and sails leisurely in the doors' direction, its two mortal followers circling the brazier on opposite sides to join it. Behind them, Tilian rejoins his king on the platform and sits beside him, both speechless - or holding their tongues while the visitors are in earshot.

"You really are a bastard, you know that?" Alton whispers to the Arch-Lich. "A right, proper bastard."

I hope, at least, that my allies think better of me than my enemies, if they cannot be made to see that I am acting in their interests, susurrates the nebulous manifestation. *Speaking of which, I have a crucial task for you, Alton. One I would assign only to a most trusted friend...*

Printed in Great Britain
by Amazon

28834656R00195